Jus:
Patic Lap
sisterhood of the
Crazy is my Super power
Matt Farmer

WILDFLOWER

THE DRAMATIC LIFE OF BARBETTE—ROUND ROCK'S

FIRST AND GREATEST DRAG QUEEN

KYLE TAYLOR

FIRST EDITION

Cover Art designed by Kyle Taylor and utilizes the 1926 cabaret poster of Barbette by Charles Gesmar.

ISBN-13: 978-1494839598

ISBN-10: 1494839598

This is a work of fiction. All of the characters, organizations and events portrayed in this novel are either products of the author's imagination or are used fictionally.

For more about Kyle Taylor novels: www.billiondollardreamer.com

This book is dedicated to the LGBT community in
Round Rock, Texas.

KYLE TAYLOR

"All the souls in distress, sick, desperate, worn out by the forces that plague us in and outside of death, find rest in the silhouette. After some years of Americanism, the wave where the Capital of the United States hypnotized us like a revolver, le numéro Barbette finally shows me the real New York with the ostrich plumes of its sea and its factories, its buildings in tulle, its precision, its siren's voice, its finery, its electric aigrettes."

—Jean Cocteau

KYLE TAYLOR

PREFACE

In 2005, Sarah Roberts, proprietor of the Round Rock coffee house, Saradora's, hosted what was touted as Round Rock's first drag show. Over one hundred fifty customers packed the cafe located in the heart of the town's Main Street. Other citizens called the city to protest the show. Nyle Maxwell, a car dealer and mayor of Round Rock at the time, was quoted as saying, "The constituents we've heard from are concerned about the immorality of it, that it's promoting homosexuality." The town's fire marshal and city manager looked into the gathering for code violations. (None were issued.) Roberts publicly responded to the imbroglio asking, "What's the big deal? This is . . . a talent performance. These guys were impersonating famous performers, and one of them was an acrobat." She noted Saradora's had overflow crowds before for a variety of events, none causing the investigation of the mayor, city manager, and fire marshal.

The tenor of the protests was clear, Round Rock was a family town. The performance at Saradora's went against the very sort of community some residents sought to maintain. The irony of moment, however, wasn't lost on everyone. Long before Rue Paul slipped on his first pair of sequined six inch stilettos or Boy George donned his whimsical multi-colored caftan, another drag queen's aerial performance caused a sensation in the swankest night clubs and theaters of the world—and he happened to have grown up in Round Rock in the early 1900's. Born with the name, Vander Clyde Broadway, his star shined brightest as Barbette, a drag queen aerialist whose talents mesmerized audiences for almost twenty years.

Barbette was a calculated, stylized female persona born out of excruciating training and effort. Vander Clyde Broadway wasn't merely an acrobat who donned a dress and a wig for salacious effect. Barbette's complex performance challenged the audience to contemplate what truly made a woman a woman and a man a man. Barbette was an erotic, angelic fantasy come to life. Like the rituals of a Japanese geisha, each female gesture Barbette enacted was honed to elegant perfection, making his transformation back into a hyper-masculinized man at the end of the routine all the more shocking.

Barbette influenced many artists of the time. He was Alfred Hitchcock's muse for his 1930 film, *Murder!*, featuring a diabolical transvestite trapeze artist as a villain. The story of Barbette is also believed to be the impetus for the 1933 German film, *Viktor und Viktoria*, which became the template for Blake Edwards and Julie Andrews's smash hit, *Victor Victoria*.

Attempts have been made to sanitize Barbette's drag and his homosexuality, saying he merely dressed as a woman because it was the only way he could get a gig at the circus, but this is not true. One could say Vander Clyde Broadway was forced into drag out of necessity at the start of his career. However, he chose to create Barbette, in all her ostrich-plumed glory, when he could have instead become another male aerialist in the circus.

Vander Clyde Broadway was homosexual. Barbette, as he wanted to be called even off stage, befriended and had affairs with some of the most noted members of gay French society including Jean Cocteau. He joked about his homosexuality to friends and was even banned from Great Britain in the 1920's because he was discovered having sex with another man backstage.

Today, in an era when drag is widely accepted, the persona of Barbette still intrigues. How did a 1914 graduate of tiny Round Rock High School become one of the most successful and celebrated stage performers of his era? The experience of Barbette, even to this day, whether it is his story, or the fabled images taken of his male to female transformation by surrealist photographer, Man Ray, still cause us to have a reaction. Barbette demands we respond to him.

In that vein, this book is my own response to Barbette. While based on solid research and ensconced in many historical facts, the work is a fiction—a fantasia of how I perceived his life. There are aspects of his story that most personally moved me; these are themes I wished to explore.

At the end of the work, I added research commentary to help the reader better understand fact vs. fiction. Like all of my books, I encourage the reader to look up people and places mentioned in the work as they go along. My web page, www.billiondollardreamer.com, has links to various sources for further exploration.

Barbette was an extraordinary entertainer of the 20th Century. My hunch is that if he was alive to see Saradora's show, he would have found the whole uproar at once amusing and yet distastefully unfortunate. I sincerely hope you enjoy this presentation of his life story. — *Kyle Taylor*

PROLOGUE

NEW YORK, 1938
WINTER

Barbette stretched on the floor backstage at the Loew's State Theatre, in the heart of Broadway in New York City. As he did so, he felt an uncommon chill. February in Manhattan was a sloshy mess of dirty snow and frigid, overcast days. He moved his body about, jumping up and down, trying to warm his muscles. Ivory makeup covered all of his body's aging flaws—the cracked skin, his blackened hands, the bruising his torso took at points where it met the trapeze. He stretched out again, trying to loosen the muscles of his legs. Then, he felt another draft of icy air swirl into the backstage area.

That was enough! He didn't give a crap he was in full drag, including his elaborate ostrich-feathered headdress and silvery, luminous gown. He was going to find where the draft was coming from. As he moved through the curtains and down darkened hallways, he saw it—the loading dock door wide open! Two beefy men were loading in trunks of equipment even as it neared eight in the evening.

Barbette was livid. He turned to the two workers.

"We've got a fucking show going on! Close the door!" he hissed.

"We need get this stuff in!" one of the stage hands protested.

"Do it some other time!"

"Fuck you, princess. We do it now!"

"You stop now, or I don't go on!"

"Oh, all right! Don't get your fancy girdle in a knot!" the worker said as he motioned to his buddy to stop unloading.

"Close the damn door!" Barbette demanded again. He stood there in his costume, plumes still billowing from the biting air pouring into the space.

"Fucking fairy," the stagehand muttered.

Barbette heard the comment. He was furious.

"What the fuck did you say?" he asked as he approached the man. "You wanna say that to my face, because I'll rip your fucking throat out!"

"Hey—what's the shouting?" the stage manager asked as he approached the three.

Barbette turned to him is disgust. "I can't go on if they're going to work with this door wide open. It's too cold!"

"Fellas, wrap it up for now. We'll do the rest tomorrow," the stage manager said as he looked seriously at the men.

"Okay, boss…That's what we're doing."

"*Thank you,*" Barbette said sarcastically to the stage manager as he marched backstage to where he would attempt again to warm his body.

From his vantage at one of the wings leading to the stage, Barbette could see the contorted image of Dorothy Lamour on the massive silver screen. The film was *Tropic Holiday*. Dorothy Lamour smoldered sensuality in the heat of a Mexican night as she sang the film's signature song:

So lovely is the moon on a tropic night

11

No heart can be immune on a tropic night
As a lonely guitar plays a serenade

It was still too cold for him! Barbette's muscles were tight and tense. He felt every bit as old as his thirty-nine years while he stretched and jumped about. His body felt especially weak this evening. There were extra aches in his joints, but after the film ended and he heard his theme music begin, he felt everything right itself. Like he did thousands of times before, he would give the audience a wonderful performance!

Everything was going well. Barbette looked stunning, making an entrance down a deco-styled silver staircase—a statuesque woman, so feminine and yet seductively playful. Once she removed her headdress and abundant ostrich-plumed cape, she climbed, panther-like to her lofty perch on one end of her slackline wire. She moved about it on pointed toes with great speed and delicacy, the orchestra rising with dramatic flourishes, embellishing her daring moves. Next, it was on to the rings where it took all her strength to hold poses designed to look as if they took no exertion at all. Finally, she swept over the audience with fearless abandon on her trapeze. The crowd gasped as she released her legs only hanging from the backs of her ankles. It all took great concentration and physicality—especially her trapeze.

"Hey, let's go," one of the stage hands who tussled with Barbette gestured to his buddy. The frustrated stage hands saw Barbette was up doing the act and started their loading once again. "The old cow can't bitch now."

The two never saw it, when they opened the loading dock door. Barbette was near the end of her routine. She was about to release into a daring angel's fall onto the stage. Suddenly, an extremely strong gust of frigid air billowed the stage curtain behind her. It caught her attention at the exact worst time! The release was all wrong! There was no net below!

Barbette came crashing down onto the stage with a tremendous force! Some in the audience shrieked—others fainted.

The stage manager saw what happened from the wings. Panicked, he ordered the curtain dropped immediately.

CHAPTER ONE

ROUND ROCK, TEXAS, 1912

"Vander, do you think winter's fixin' to come early?" Rose asked. She looked up at Vander Clyde Broadway with big hazel eyes framed by thick, brown lashes. Vander was twelve to her seven. They lived next door in the flats of Round Rock, a windswept piece of Texas prairie just north of the city of Austin.

"Feels like it," Vander replied. He was small for his age with a large forehead and ears that stuck out a bit from his light brown hair—not so much they were embarrassing, but enough for his teacher to grab a hold of if he was acting up.

"Momma says a cold winter's good for the earth, Vander, helps the cotton," Rose said. She wore her only jumper besides the one she had for church on Sundays. It was dark blue, printed with small, white flowers. Beneath it was a faded lavender long-sleeved blouse with a simple Peter Pan collar secured by a tattered lavender ribbon carefully tied about her neck—the same ribbon pinned to one side of her bobbed, brown hair.

Rose liked walking with Vander after school, the way he took her by the hand. Maybe it was because he was gentler than the other boys or maybe it was his short stature, but she thought Vander was the sweetest boy in the whole neighborhood.

Just then, a gust of northern wind snapped at their faces, kicking up dust from the dirt road as they walked down the town's primitive Main Street. There wasn't much traffic this day. All the farmers by now picked their last bushels of cotton and brought them to the gin. The earth was dry. It had been some time since the last rain.

Fighting the dust sweeping around her, Rose shielded her eyes with her free hand as the two crossed the street to the busiest part of the new town, just two rows of mostly wood framed one story buildings with deep overhanging awnings and horse tie ups out front. The businesses along the street were the sort of things you'd expect to find in a small Texas town in 1912—hardware store, a general store, bank, post office, and a tavern. The rutted up dirt road ran right through the middle of the two rows of buildings—a main drag through town connecting it to other towns nearby, which were not much different than Round Rock itself.

Vander looked past the primitive power lines strung down the street and overhead up to the sky. It was grey and overcast, but it didn't look much like it was going to rain. The sky painted everything in a dullness that day, the earth matching the faded paint washes of the clapboard buildings.

"Honk, Honk!" They heard the obnoxious sound of an automobile horn. It was the postmaster making way down the street in his dirt-covered, black Model T. Vander didn't much like the postmaster or his flashy new automobile. On many an occasion, he witnessed the postmaster blast his horn no matter what, even if there wasn't another cart or carriage in sight. He did it just so people would see him sitting ram straight upright, proud as a peacock in his new automobile.

Rose and Vander watched the postmaster from across the street pull up front of the white-washed post office. A rail thin man, he was dressed in a worn but tidy navy blue suit with gold brass buttons and jaunty cap. When he opened the door to step out, another biting northern wind whipped across the street. A handful of flyers of yellow and orange paper blew out of the cab of the vehicle and scattered across Main Street.

Instinctively, the two children rushed into action, grabbing all the flyers they could before another wind whipped down the simple boulevard.

"Oh dear!" the postmaster exclaimed as he rushed to pick up some of the flyers himself. "Oh my!"

"Don't worry, Mister Johnson, we've got most of them!" Rose called out. She loved the chaos of the moment, racing around trying to get every last loose sheet of paper. Vander was in such a rush to pick up the flyers, he didn't give them a second look until he had a fistful in his grasp. That's when he saw what was printed on them—an announcement— framed by elaborately adorned elephants standing on their hind legs. The scrolling words of the flyer proclaimed the circus was coming to Austin! A rush of excitement filled Vander's senses!

"Is it true, sir? Is it true?" he asked anxiously to the postmaster.

"Sure is. The train'll roll through Taylor 'round midnight tonight. They're expecting to have a big parade in Austin tomorrow. They'll be in town a whole week."

Vander couldn't believe what he was hearing! He looked excitedly at Rose and then back at the postmaster. Then he glanced at the flyer and saw the general admission price was twenty-five cents. His spirits sank. It was too much. There was no way his mother could afford such an extravagance on what she earned from making her fancy hats and stitching her lace. Vander and Rose dutifully handed the disheveled flyers back to the postmaster.

"Bet you two would like to go, wouldn't you?" Mr. Johnson asked as he put the flyers back in his leather satchel.

Vander nodded earnestly. The postmaster dug into his shiny blue wool trousers and produced a fifty cent piece and put it in Vander's hand. "Why don't you two go? I appreciate your help!"

Vander looked at the shiny silver coin in his hand. It was like pirate's treasure! Something he shouldn't be holding, yet he felt thrilled to take possession of it.

"Thank you, sir! Thank you!" His eyes glowed in reverence.

"Thank you, Mister Johnson," Rose replied.

"Can we take one?" Vander gestured to the postmaster's satchel. "I need to show my momma the notice."

"Why, of course!" the postmaster replied. "It'll save me the trip." He handed a flyer to Vander. "Be sure to hold it real tight—or this wind'll get it!"

"Yes sir!" Vander said, knowing if a band of bank robbers came through town and demanded the notice at gunpoint, they wouldn't be able to pry it out of his fingers.

Vander shoved the coin deep into the well-stitched pocket of his coveralls and took Rose by the hand. Their grimy boots made way up the street. At the end of the block, they turned down another dusty road and headed home.

"Vander, what are we gonna do?" Rose asked seriously. "We have enough for two tickets, but no more."

Vander stopped in his tracks. She was right! There was no way his mother could afford another twenty-five cents for one more ticket to go to the circus. And what about train fair into the city? Vander knew he had two dimes in his pillowcase, but that was all. It wasn't enough.

Rose looked at the crestfallen expression on Vander's face. She took a deep breath. "Vander, there's no way my daddy's going to let us go. He'll say it's too much for me and momma and him, no matter the twenty-five cents." Rose bit her lip and then said, "Suppose you take it all. You can go. That means all your momma needs to come up with is train fair. But you gotta to promise me that you'll tell me all about it. Will you do that, Vander? Tell me about the circus? I don't much mind if you make things up even. I always like your stories."

Vander looked long and hard at Rose. He couldn't believe what she was saying, but could see the earnestness in her eyes. "It's a deal!" he smiled. "An' I won't make anything up! I'll tell you all I see exactly as it happens!"

Rose smiled. It made her feel good to make Vander so happy! The two raced home to tell their families the good news.

. . .

"What are you doing, Vander?" Rose asked as she walked back to the small yard framed by a fading white-washed picket fence behind Vander's simple, hand-chipped limestone house. There wasn't much to the residence, just a one room limestone cabin with an ample porch out front and a pitched cedar shingled roof overhead. In the back, a few paces from the family outhouse, Vander's mother set up her laundering business. She had deep basins and a fire pit to heat her water, tubs for soaking and washboards for scrubbing. Several clothes lines spanned the back yard. Vander was engrossed working with one of them. Rose sat on hunk of tree stump and watched Vander sweat, even in the cool, fall Sunday afternoon.

"You sure you're supposed to be doing that on the Sabbath?" Rose asked with a quizzical expression on her face. "My daddy says no one's supposed to work on Sundays, not even the colored folks. Besides, Vander, you went to the circus yesterday and you haven't told me a word about it!" Rose folded her hands across her chest. She was dressed in her Sunday dress, a dark navy blue jumper with a white blouse

18

and fresh white ribbons in her bobbed hair. Her usually tattered boots were polished clean, even the laces were freshly washed by her mother the night before.

Vander was her special friend for sure. There was nobody as sweet as Vander and Rose knew she couldn't be mad at him too long. All she wanted was for Vander to give her time, tell her about the circus in those words and gestures, only Vander Clyde could do.

Vander stopped his working on one of the clotheslines and wiped his brow. He too was dressed in his Sunday best, a clean set of dark brown woolen knickers with a starched white shirt—only it was now smudged with dirt and dust. Vander looked at Rose with excited, almost wild eyes. "It was magical Rose! That's the only word for it! Magical!"

Rose clapped her small hands in delight as Vander sat on another stump next to hers.

"We got there barely in the nick of time for the matinee. We had to sit far up in the stands, but it didn't seem to matter. It was the biggest circus I've yet seen! Three rings all set up. In the middle there was a cage that was all closed in with bars. And a man came out, dressed all dandy with a big whip in his hands. And he went in the cage—and that's when the biggest, most ferocious tigers you ever did set your eyes upon were released inside that cage."

Rose's eyes were riveted on Vander.

He pushed the hair off his broad forehead and continued, "I don't know where they got them from, but these tigers looked real hungry, starving really, and they looked like they had an in for that man. It was all that man could do taking his whip and a stool in his hand…" Vander got up to act out the drama. "Those cats were ornery too! But he got those tigers up on risers and up on their hind legs all pawing at the air looking at him—it was like Miss Janek with her choir at the Sunday service—all standing at attention! I never seen anything like it!"

Rose laughed with delight. "Tell me more Vander! Tell me more!"

Vander looked up at the sky, clenching his fists and then back down at Rose. "I just don't know where to begin!" He eagerly sat down again and leaned into Rose, "But let me tell you about the angel—high up in the big top, she must have been a hundred feet in the air..." Vander impulsively loosened the laces on his tired Sunday shoes and kicked them off so he was only in his stockinged feet on the pounded dirt of the back yard. "On a wire strung between the two poles holding up the tent—it looked no thicker than the thread from a spider's web...and there she was...."

Vander stood up on his tippy toes, holding his chin upright and his arms delicately out to his sides. "It was as if Jehovah blew down a kiss from heaven above!"

Rose looked at Vander enthralled by every word. "She looked like some kind of angel, in pink, delicately placing her feet on the tiniest rope—and never staring down at the little specks of people below—only ahead—so gracefully." Vander demonstrated for Rose, his chin held high while walking forward on his tippy toes. "And when she got to the middle, you could have heard a pin drop in that whole place, no one dared even clear their throat! Because when she got to the middle, like a little fairy sprinkled with pixie dust—she danced a jig!" Vander daintily held his hands out as he imitated her actions with deep knee bends and little steps and leaps.

Rose applauded again, thrilled by Vander's tale.

Vander watched Rose clap and then said seriously, "I wanted to clap! I wanted to get up and shout—we all did! But we were all too afraid to say a peep. And just as soon as she appeared, she was gone! Up in the sky, somewhere, like she must've hopped onto a passing cloud."

Rose's mouth was agape.

"Where did she go, Vander? Where did the angel go?"

"All I can say it was in the blink of an eye, when we all stood up to applaud, there she was, standing next to the ringmaster taking a bow." Vander placed one leg in front of another and with studied elegance, his face beaming, he allowed his hands to float down as he bent his torso in a regal bow.

"That was beautiful! Just beautiful!" little Rose enthused. "Tell me more! Please, Vander, tell me more!"

"Sorry, I can't. If I'm gonna be one of them, I need to start now." Vander strode over to where he was working, admiring the galvanized steel wire. "You see, this rope's plenty strong. But the poles need to be secured. I got these boards down at the scrap pile behind the lumber yard..." With an old, rusted hammer, Vander began cross bracing one of the poles holding up the sturdiest of his mother's clothing lines, nailing more wood in place.

Rose looked at Vander shocked. "You wanna run away and join the circus?" she asked a lump forming in her throat as she stood up and walked over to where Vander was working.

"More than anything!" Vander smiled broadly.

Usually her heart swelled when she saw Vander this excited. But it was too real. She could see it in his eyes. "You can't leave me, Vander..." she murmured as her bright hazel eyes filled with tears. She felt lost at the notion of Vander ever leaving her.

Vander looked at his little friend and her quivering lower lip. "I won't ever leave you! Not for a long time, anyway!" He knelt down and gave Rose a hug. Rose wrapped her arms around Vander, trying to hold back her tears, but it was impossible. She had to admit, she loved her very best friend.

CHAPTER TWO

"Vander Clyde Broadway!" Vander's mother, Hattie shouted. "What are you doing?" She stood on the wood planked back porch of their hand-chipped limestone house. Hattie was a thin woman of medium height and build with long brown hair she gathered into a modest bun. Her arms were lean and muscular from hours of scrubbing dirt from the clothing of her wealthy Round Rock customers. She had welcoming brown eyes with friendly air about her, but her face was drawn and bore the stress of having to make her way and raise a child on her own. That is not to say she was unkempt. Having washed and repaired the very finest clothing in the community, as well as creating her own line of stylish hats, gave Hattie a keen eye for fashion. Living amongst the brown people of Texas for most of her life, she learned from the abuelitas how to sew and even embroider with great skill. White folks who were too afraid to deal with the brownies came to her for all their millinery and embroidery. She managed to make enough to keep a roof over her head and provide for her son. She was even able to save some pennies and buy lovely fabric down at the general merchandise store so she could work up a smart Sunday dress and hat just for herself.

Teetering six feet off the ground, Vander walked his mother's clothesline he worked so hard the weekend before strengthening and tightening. His arms fluttered and swung about, startled by his mother's shouting. Vander strained with all his might to keep his feet on the clothesline, but he lost his balance, falling with a thud onto the dry earth below him. He quickly brushed himself off, realizing he soiled his Sunday knickers and white shirt yet again.

"I did it momma! Did you see? I did it! I walked on that line!" Vander smiled at Hattie whose furrowed brow was proof enough she was not amused. Hattie stayed on at church that day, while Vander quickly headed to their back yard after services to practice walking on his newly fashioned tight rope. It was the middle of the afternoon by the time his mother returned home. A strong southern wind made the day unseasonably warm. Vander was too excited trying to elicit approval from his mother's weary eyes to notice the man who came onto the back porch and stood behind his mother.

"Vander, come over here," Hattie said. Vander stepped up onto the porch and made way to his mother. He now saw the man, tall, with broad shoulders dressed in a too small black wool Sunday suit standing alongside of his mother.

"I want you to meet somebody," his mother said. "This is Mister Loving. Mister Samuel Loving. He's a war hero. A veteran from the Spanish American War—why he rode with Teddy Roosevelt's Rough Riders."

Vander wiped the dirt from his hands in his knickers and held his hand out to shake the stranger's, just like his mother taught him.

The tall Mister Loving looked at Vander intently and shook his hand, squeezing it hard, which made Vander's small hand hurt.

"Sir," Vander said reverently with his head bowed slightly.

After releasing his hand, Mister Loving frowned.

"Not much of a boy, if you ask me," he said to Vander's mother. Vander squinted at the man—his overly bushy salt and pepper brows matched his full walrus-like mustache and the small thatches of nose hair pushing forth from his nostrils.

"I did my best," Hattie said apologetically.

"Some folks say when a boy is raised only by his momma, he's a sissy. You a sissy, boy?" Loving scowled.

Vander's eyes squinted. "Some people say old men chasing after young lady-folk are dirty codgers."

"Vander!" his mother admonished. "I'm sorry, Mister Loving, I don't know what has come over my son. Ever since we went to the circus, he's got it into his head that's what he wants to do. I think it has made him forget his manners."

"No mind," Loving said as he tugged at the lapels of his dusty Sunday suit. He then turned to Vander with dark eyes. "Nothin' a good whoopin' won't help fix. That's what the boy needs is a good whoopin' so he'll show respect to his elders and his momma."

"Vander, you need to apologize to Mister Loving."

Vander looked intently at his mother's eyes. He could see she meant business. He didn't like Loving. From the moment he set eyes on him, he didn't like him one bit. But he knew to obey his mother when she gave him that look.

"Sir, I'm sorry for my forward manner." Vander bowed his head again.

Loving smiled a half smile. "Well, at least you taught the runt some manners."

"Vander, we're going inside for some cake and coffee. Why don't you wash up and join us? We have something we need to tell you."

...

"How's 'bout it boy? You ready to have a daddy?" Loving asked Vander as the three sat in the tidy one room house. Vander now understood why he and his mother were down on their hands yesterday, stripping and waxing the floor. He now knew why his mother made extra sure he took a hot bath and his boot laces were boiled and scrubbed fresh. Why hadn't his mother told him about this man? Why didn't she say anything? He looked at Loving—searching for anything likable in the man. But in the light of the simple one room home he shared with his mother, all he saw was a smug, pompous veteran who thought too highly of himself. Vander looked at the fabric and cut of the man's coat, noting it was old and a size too small. He took in the way the man heavily waxed his mustache—trying to darken the grey under his lip in order to appear younger. The creases and folds about his eyes and cheeks told a different story—this was a man who had been through some hard times.

Vander witnessed his mother and how she assented to Loving's forward manner. He could tell his mother's mind was made up. He was incredulous at the thought of his mother marrying Samuel Loving.

"We get on just fine, sir," Vander said.

"You got a chip on your shoulder, boy, that's for sure," Loving said putting down the china coffee cup onto the saucer resting on his black, woolen leg. His face darkened again, "If you don't start showing more manners, you best get yourself ready for a whoopin' the likes of which you've never seen."

That was enough for Vander. He got up and ran out of the house.

"Vander!" Hattie shouted. "Come back!"

"That's the last time that boy will disrespect his elders, the very last time!" Loving scowled.

...

Vander hated to cry. He even hated when he got mildly upset. He knew his mother was going to marry that filthy man, and their lives would be ruined forever. By now the fall sun was setting on the western Texas horizon. He'd been walking through a growth of woods along the train tracks leading eastward out of town to Hutto and Taylor. The crickets of Brushy Creek—which ran alongside the tracks—began their symphony. Vander didn't know where he was going. He just knew he needed to walk. He felt the warmth of the setting sun on his back as his mind turned again to the magnificent spectacle of the circus and the beautiful creature up on that high wire—so gentle, the way she balanced herself.

Vander decided to walk the rail of the train track. He wanted to be just like the high wire angel. Putting his hands out to his sides exactly like the angel did in that elegant way, he carefully placed one foot in front of the other. Vander pivoted on his feet, turning on the rail, so now his whole face and body were illuminated by the sun.

In his mind—feeling the warmth of the sun's final rays bathe his face—he imagined he was illuminated by the arc light of the big top, shining on him, making his body dazzling and radiant. Vander told himself not to look down, but hold his head upright, just like the angel did, not looking at his feet. He felt himself grow in the light, more confident with every step, and then he imagined he was at the center of the wire. With dainty hands and supple knees, he danced his little jig, the way the angel did, gliding over the rail of the train track. His spirit felt free, like a dove released from a cage, as he moved about the rail, his whole body illuminated in the golden light of the setting sun.

That's when he heard the word, shouted out, coming from a dark patch of forest to his right—"Sissy!"

Then, he felt the large rock hit him in his back and then another slammed into his shoulder. He could pay no attention to the searing pain they caused. His eyes were too blinded by the sun to make out how many there were. So he leaped from the rail and ran. He ran as fast as he could into the light of the sun as it started to dip below the horizon. Vander's chest heaved as he raced with all his might to get away, but he heard the footsteps coming up faster and faster behind him. Vander prayed to the angel to lift him up and deliver him, but to no avail—soon they were upon him! Boys from school! Vander felt the fury of their punches crushing into the side of his head. He fell to the ground and tried to curl up and protect himself from the kicks to his ribs and skull. "Sissy!" he heard them call. "Stupid fairy girl!" another shouted. In a flash it was all white and then it went black.

...

"Vander! Wake up! Please, Vander, wake up!"

Vander Clyde tried to shake off the dullness in his head. As he did so, he became more aware of the crushing pain he felt throughout his small frame. Illuminated only by the soft glow of the new fall moon, Rose cradled his head in her lap. Vander's mother, Hattie, had been by Rose's house earlier looking for him. Rose managed to slip away, knowing where Vander went when he was feeling blue—down by the train tracks running along the creek. She knew if she didn't get back soon, her momma and daddy would be looking for her too. Even in the light of the rising moon, she could tell Vander had been beat up real bad.

The pain was unbearable, causing Vander to cry. This upset Rose. Her big hazel eyes welled with tears. "You've got to get up Vander! We need to get home before we both get a switchin'!" The tears on his face stung the cuts on his cheeks. Slowly, with Rose's help, Vander tried to stand up. He felt searing pain in his ribs, but managed to stand upright.

"That's it," Rose said as she held onto her beloved friend. "Just take little steps, Vander. If that's all you can do. Take little ones." Rose knew not to ask who did this. She knew in her mind who it was. All she could do was get Vander home so he was safe.

CHAPTER THREE

Vander Clyde slept for a long time after that. About a year before, his mother made a special cot for him across from her own bed in the single room of the limestone house. But now, he rested in Hattie's bed. Christmas would soon be here and his mother was working sun up to sun down providing the laundering and millinery needs of her wealthy clients, all the while tending to her battered child.

The draft from the opening and closing of their front door kept the room cold no matter how much wood his mother stoked in the potbellied stove. Vander watched her do her hat work by the stove, keeping her hands warm so she could manipulate the fabric and dried flowers of her creations. When she was able, she took care of Vander. His ribs were cracked, and the doctor, who she used every last penny to pay, said Vander needed rest. Vander heard Mister Loving pontificate in his presence this was what Vander needed in order to become a man. Hattie begged Vander to tell her who did this to him, but Vander refused. As he lay in his mother's bed, all he could think about was getting better so he could get out of Round Rock as fast as possible. He was going to be a circus performer if it took his dying breath.

He opened his mouth to take spoonfuls of soup Hattie fed him amidst the busyness of her day. Vander looked at his mother. They had been through so much together. He admired her toughness and discipline, because those were the things that got her though the day. Finally, Vander was feeling better.

"I'm going away, momma. I'm joining a circus. It's what I want to do."

Vander's mother put the bowl of soup down on a small table next to the bed. She brushed the hair out of her son's eyes and off his broad forehead.

"You love the circus, don't you Vander?" she said gently.

"Yes, momma. With all my heart. I would leave tomorrow if you let me."

Vander's mother knew he was different from the other boys. She saw he had that spark of creativity she felt came from her. She understood the power of the circus and its magical allure. All she wanted was for her boy to be safe and somehow she knew it wasn't going to be with her in Round Rock.

"I won't let you leave until you finish your school," she said earnestly. "Vander, if you're going to the circus, you need to know about the things of the world."

Vander tried to sit up more in the bed. He winced at the pain in his torso as he did so.

"That's three years from now!" he protested.

"Double up, Vander. You're the smartest boy in that school—you always were. If you want something bad enough, you have to earn it. When you're done with your schooling, you have my word, you're free to go."

Vander felt his face flush and tears run down his cheeks.

"Don't cry Vander, please. Big boys don't cry."

CHAPTER FOUR

The warm air of springtime blew through the open windows of the humble wood-framed church. Pastor Merton was also his usual windy self. Every Sunday, when the pastor began his long discourse, summoning the power of the Spirit of the Lord and rebuking the sins of the damned, Vander's mind would wander. He would look at the painting inside of the church. All the decorative scrolling and details upon the whitewash walls—brilliant sky blues and rich greens. The heads of primitively painted angels of red and pink with yellow flowing hair framed with silver wings, grasped harps and floated high over the sanctuary. Other symbols too were painted onto the bead boarded ceiling. Vander's favorite was the all-seeing, all-knowing eye of God. Each week, he tried to guide his mother to a pew right below it, so he could stare up at the eye within a triangle. There was the eye of God looking straight at him, discerning his heart. Was he good or was he bad? Could his damned soul really be saved by that eye looking down on him? Preacher Merton said all were saved by the glory of God through their baptisms. Vander was never quite so sure.

Today, Vander Clyde wasn't sitting in a pew below the eye. After the regular Sunday service, he stood alongside his mother, up on the raised step into the sanctuary. She was dressed in a modest tan dress and matching hat she fashioned just for the occasion. In her gloved hands was a simple bouquet of bluebonnets and daffodils she and Vander picked just that morning on their way to church. To the other side of his mother was Samuel Loving. Vander had to admit, he looked better this day. His mother worked up a new suit just for him, one of good black wool cloth and cut to fit his frame. Just as his mother reconciled herself to his ambitions, so too, Vander tried to reconcile himself to hers.

Vander listened to the vows the two spoke to one another. He thought of Samuel Loving and he thought of the vows the man was professing before God. Vander didn't believe the words coming out of Loving's mouth, and he wondered if God Himself felt the same.

Life would be different, from here on out. When they walked out the doors to leave the church on the way home, their life would be different for sure. Samuel Loving was now joined to his mother and because of this holy alliance, Loving was joined to Vander himself. He felt nauseous at the thought.

"I pronounce you husband and wife," Pastor Merton finally proclaimed. His mother smiled warmly as Loving kissed her cheek.

CHAPTER FIVE

The scorching summer heat beat down upon the vast expanse of cotton before them. Everyone in the whole town of Round Rock, if they were able, was out in the fields in July and August picking cotton. A good cotton crop meant prosperity for the small towns around the county. It was the reason why the railroad laid tracks through Round Rock—to haul tons of cotton into the mills in Austin.

Vander and his mother moved quickly through the fields. Like all the rest of the pickers, they wore long sleeves and deep brimmed hats to protect themselves from the punishing sun. In the dawn of each new day, they were out in the fields, moving from one row of cotton to the next.

At the start of the season, some of the women folk would gossip a bit between themselves as they picked. The Mexicans who lived in the area, stayed mostly in their own groups with their own families. Sometimes, Vander's mother would speak to them, knowing Spanish. The Negroes also worked the fields farther off in the distance, not wanting much contact with the whites; sometimes they would sing a song about Jesus to keep their spirits up. Vander could hear them. When the wind blew just right, their voices rolled across the hills like little waves until their songs washed over him. By the end of the July, when Texas became an ungodly furnace, and the work began to take a toll, all talking ceased. Each picker carried empty burlap sacks into the fields, the larger, and the better. At the end of the day, their sacks would be weighed, earning them pennies on the pound.

Vander picked close to Rose and her family. An old, oversized bonnet covered Rose's head, but her fair cheeks were blush red and burned. Her hands were raw from picking and pulling, but she knew she dare not complain. No one did. She went barefoot through the fields, amassing thirty-five pounds of picked cotton a day.

Vander's mother could pick a hundred twenty-five pounds sun up to sun down. She had to lug her stuffed cotton sack over her aching back to bring it in from the field. The summer, 1913, was the first year Vander out-picked his mother. His short stature and increasing strength allowed him to move quickly up and down the rows of cotton. He also had an inspiration. Hattie said he could keep some of his money this year—save it so he could use it when he graduated from school to get him where he wanted to go. Out of the corner of his eye, he watched Loving. Vander had to admit he was a good picker too. He was orderly and dutiful in the way he cleaned out a plant. But Vander thought if he was really a good husband, he wouldn't have his wife out in the fields working herself to the bone. Vander watched the older boys move about the field too. Some of the boys were the very ones who whooped him down by the train tracks along Brushy Creek. They were too hot, too beat down to come after Vander in the summer.

On days out in the fields, Vander tried to let his imagination turn to the circus and its allures, but in the inferno of Texas, one month into the harvesting season, his mind was too overheated to think—all he could do was pick.

...

34

The Main Street of Round Rock bustled with activity during the fall of 1913. Horse drawn wagons loaded high with cotton pulled up to the gin down by the rail depot. On the weekdays, school was back in session. All the kids were glad. With sun-burned faces and leathery hands, they readily worked at their studies, none more than Vander Clyde Broadway. That year, all the students moved into the brand new Round Rock High School building. It was three stories tall and one of the only buildings in town faced solid with brick. All the grades went to classes there—even children Rose's age had handsome new classrooms with high ceilings and large, broad windows which were opened in the fall to let in the breeze of the Texas plains.

Vander spoke to his teacher, Miss Nelson, and asked her if he could accelerate his studies. He didn't tell her why, his secret dream, but knowing how smart he was, Miss Nelson could see no reason to not to try. Vander tore into the work. He was determined to get out of Round Rock, and leave the town the first chance he got.

This Saturday afternoon, Vander had more pressing demands...

"Ladies and gentlemen!" Rose bellowed just the way Vander rehearsed her. "You are about to witness the most amazing, the most awe-inspiring show on earth!"

She wore a bright red cape draped down to her waist which Vander himself personally sewed. Rose stood before the thirty or so spectators piled into Vander Clyde's little backyard. They were an assemblage of neighbors or clients of Hattie's. Some of the older folks sat on chairs up on the porch, while others stat on the stairs leading to the packed dirt ground of the back yard. During the week, Vander worked to move his mother's washing equipment to the side of the yard. He took down all his mother's clothes lines—save one—the galvanized steel line with the extra bolstering.

"Set your eyes upon the great Vander Clyde!" Rose gestured grandly toward the direction of the outhouse, trying to imitate Vander's explicit instructions to her. On cue, Vander grandly stepped from the far side of the outhouse into view and confidently strode over to where Rose was standing in front of the wire. The crowd of neighbors applauded. Vander's mother stood in the doorway of her one room house looking over the backs of the heads of the rows of neighbors sitting on her porch. Her son was wearing an old white sheet he remade into a draping long cape he tied about his neck.

Vander undid the cape, and the little girls and boys squealed at Vander's appearance. He was bare-chested. A yellow sash wrapped his waist and new blue knickers reached just above his calves where they met his bright, green stockings. Vander grandly handed his bed sheet cape to Rose, and she curtsied, just like they practiced.

"You look silly!" one of the younger boys shouted eliciting a roar of laughter from the crowd. Vander's mother winced, but Vander seemed unfazed.

He walked to one end of the tightly strung wire, which was some six feet above the ground. He stacked a number of apple crates together allowing him to step up to the top of one of the posts securing the line. Vander climbed the crates to the top. With serious eyes, he looked out at the crowd.

"Jump!" one of the boys shouted. "Shhh!" hissed another voice. Vander turned and slid one foot onto the line, testing its tautness. All of his focus was now on the wire. He exhaled deeply and then placed both feet onto the line. His arms shook about, fluttering to gain his balance. For a moment, it looked as if he would fall to the ground, but he quickly gained his footing. Vander gingerly walked across the line, carefully placing one foot in front of the other until he reached the far post supporting the wire. The crowd was noticeably impressed and gave him warm applause.

At the other end of the line, Vander had placed a slender, ten foot long pole he fashioned by taking two tall reeds from Brushy Creek and tying them together. He grabbed hold of the pole. Clasping it in his hands for balance, he slowly, with great determination, walked backwards on the line. Vander was counting the steps in his mind. When he reached the halfway point, using his pole for balance, he crouched and then lay down on the taught rope. The crowd applauded enthusiastically. Looking up at the blue sky above, Vander listened for the crowd to quiet for a moment, then he turned to them, "Oh, are you still her?"

The audience laughed and applauded. A moment later, Vander deftly swung back up on the rope and quickly walked backwards, counting each step until he reached his starting point. He stepped onto the stacked apple crates and tossed the pole to the ground. Beaming broadly, he triumphantly thrust up one of his hands into the air. The crowd cheered!

Rose walked out again from behind the outhouse in her little red cape. She shouted, "The great Vander Clyde!" Amidst the applause, Vander stepped down from the apple crates to one side of the line until he was back on the dirt of the yard. He took a bow, just like the angel in the circus, with one leg forward, his one hand held high, bending deeply at the waist.

After the show, with the crowd gone, Vander sat on the back porch stoop with Rose. The two were still dressed in their costumes and they had yet to return the back yard to its normal condition.

"It was thrilling Rose! That's all I can say!"

Rose smiled at Vander. She had never seen him this happy before. She looked at his dazzling eyes, how they seemed to be illuminated from within. And then she looked down at her dusty shoes, caught in a moment of grief. Vander noticed her expression change.

"What is it, Rose?"

"You were good Vander, really good. Like a real circus performer…" She tried not to cry. She didn't want to upset Vander, but she couldn't help it. Then she looked up into Vander's eyes.

"Will you take me with you, Vander? To the Circus? Will you take me with you?"

Vander hugged Rose tightly and then he let go.

"My little Rose, I don't think so. I have to go alone."

Rose didn't want to hear those words, not today, not after all she witnessed.

"Please Vander!"

"I'm sorry Rose. You're a little girl! I can't take you."

Just then, they both were startled out of their conversation.

"What the hell is this?" Loving asked. The sun hadn't even started setting, but the two could both tell by the way he got the words out and how his body teetered just a bit, that Samuel Loving, rough riding war hero, was dead drunk.

Vander and Rose were silent, looking up at Loving as he took in the setup in the back yard. Loving wiped his face as it darkened. What he saw he didn't like.

"Looks like Hattie raised a sissy, that's what it looks like," Loving scowled.

Rose could feel her blood boil. She stood up and faced the giant before her. "Vander had a show today and it was real good! And he ain't no sissy!"

Loving squinted his eyes, looking at the little girl before him, her hands on her hips, defiant. His sinister face broke into a toothless smile, revealing the deep caverns and creases of his leathery skin. He started to wheeze a deep laugh. This only made Rose more furious.

Finally, Loving gathered himself looking at Vander, who refused to make eye contact with the man he detested. "Looks like this girl's more of a man than you, sissy!" Loving let forth a self-satisfied guffaw. It was too much for Rose who rushed towards the big man.

"Rose, no!" Vander called out as he stood up. It was too late. With all her might, Rose kicked Loving in one of his shins with her thick, old boots. Loving let forth an earsplitting yelp.

"Get back here!" He reached down to grab her but she was too fast.

"Run Rose!" Vander called out.

Rose fled the back yard as fast as she could, leaving only Loving and Vander. Loving wiped his mouth again and then unfastened the buckle of his belt.

"Looks like someone's finally gonna get the whoopin' he deserves," Loving said as he moved towards Vander.

Vander looked at the man before him. He detested Loving with every ounce of his being. He knew there was no use running, sooner or later Loving would track him down.

With clenched fists, Vander attacked, hurling a flurry of punches into the man's gut. Loving wasn't expecting it. The punches landed with great force toppling the man to the dusty ground. Vander did not retreat. Instead, he pounced upon the man, all his anger and rage built up like a volcano exploding. He straddled the war hero and landed another flurry of punches to the man's face. Vander's eyes were wild. If this was the night for Loving to meet his maker, so be it! Vander could have cared less if he had to spend a thousand years in jail for what he was about to do. Blood flew from Loving's battered face as he poured his rage out on the man.

"Vander!" he heard his mother's shout. "What are you doing?!" She leapt onto her son's back and wrestled him off Loving. Then, she turned toward Loving, crouching down and holding Loving's bloody head in her arms leering at her son, she cried, "What have you done?"

"He had it coming!" Vander felt horrible, never having ever raised his voice at this mother like he was now doing. "He will never call me a sissy again! Do you hear me? So help me God, I will rip his throat out!"

"Get out, Vander Clyde! Get out!" Hattie shouted.

Vander stared at his mother astounded. He was breathing hard. He saw the rage in her eyes, the resentment she felt for him at that moment. It was too much for him to bear, unbelieving she would take Loving's side. He ran from the yard, into the oncoming night.

...

"Vander! Vander Clyde!" Rose called out in a loud whisper. Finally, she spotted him, sitting on a rock along the bank of Brushy Creek. Vander didn't look up. He was curled into a ball and shivering in the cold, autumn night.

"I heard what went on!" Rose said as she came up to him. She sat alongside of Vander on the rock. Just sitting next to him in the thicket of woods, she could sense his anxiety. "I snuck out again. I looked for you everywhere, down by the train tracks. Then I tried here."

Vander didn't say anything as he listened to the stream move through the woods, glints of moonlight occasionally reflecting off its unctuous surface.

"My momma an' daddy said you beat the tar out of old Loving. He had it coming, Vander. I know he did. I wish you could stay with us, but my folks, they wouldn't permit it."

Rose glanced at Vander's profile. He kept looking out onto the creek. She could tell a whole lot of thoughts were clouding his mind.

"Well, I guess they won't be calling you sissy no more! Those boys in school probably already heard what happened. The whole neighborhood is talking. Vander, they're gonna be afraid of you now."

Vander looked at Rose for a moment, his eyes were filled with sadness and defeat.

"Rose, did you ever think you were all bad, just evil to the core?"

Rose looked at Vander with her big, honest eyes.

"Vander! I've never had that thought and you shouldn't neither! You're *good* Vander! No doubt about it!"

"No, I'm not Rose."

"Listen here Vander Clyde, this world is a whole lot bigger than Round Rock, Texas. You're the nicest, sweetest boy I've ever known. I know you want to join the circus. Maybe we can do it together, just you and me."

Vander looked into Rose's earnest face. He smiled.

"You'd do just about anything for me, wouldn't you?"

"Yes, Vander I would. I would swear it on a hundred bibles, I would."

Vander hugged his little friend.

"Thanks, Rose," Vander said as he then stood up.

"Come on, let's go."

Vander extended his hand to Rose.

"Where're we going?" Rose asked as she grabbed hold of Vander's hand.

Vander sighed, "Home."

Rose looked at Vander surprised.

"I'll sleep out in the back yard. There's an old horse blanket out there. I'll talk to Mister Loving and momma tomorrow. Besides, we've gotta get you home! There's no way an eight year old girl needs to be out in the dark past her bedtime."

Rose smiled as she looked up at Vander. She liked when he took care of her and minded her. She was glad they were heading home.

...

"Vander Clyde, get up!" his mother admonished from the back doorway of their simple limestone house. Vander was at one end of the covered porch, curled up in a ball under the old horse blanket. "I know you're under there, Vander! I won't wait another minute, get into this house!"

Vander hadn't heard that tone coming from his mother, not at least for a long time, since he was a little boy. He did as his mother requested. He tried to smooth out his hair and neaten his appearance before he entered the simple home. Finally, he opened the door and went inside.

On the other side of the room, in his mother's bed, close to the potbellied stove, was Loving. He looked terrible sitting on the edge of the bed. His face was swollen and fleshy, his eyes blackened like a raccoon.

Hattie looked long and hard at her son. He could see the fury in her eyes.

"Vander, look at what you've done," she gestured to Loving who was still wearing a long night shirt.

Vander took a glance at Loving again and then lowered his head.

"Sorry momma."

"Sorry? Is that all you've got to say? Is it Vander? You almost killed a man last night!" Hattie tried to wipe her sweated palms in her apron.

Then Samuel Loving spoke up. "Now Hattie, let's not get over excited." He winced as he stood up from the pain in his ribs. He took a step over to Vander. When he did so,

Vander instinctively clenched his fists. Loving noticed it through his swollen eyes.

Loving's pulverized face cracked into a smile. "Atta boy. That's what I've been tryin' to teach you! How to be a man!" Loving started to laugh. "You know how to throw one hell of a punch, boy!"

A bewildered expression came across Vander's face.

"A man fights back. Don't you forget it, son."

Loving then extended his right hand. Vander quickly looked to his mother. She nodded. Vander extended his hand, still filled with fury. As he shook Loving's leathery hand with a firm grip, Loving didn't let go.

"Just watch yourself, boy." Loving started to squeeze Vander's hand with a great deal of force. "I may not be as fast as you, but I can still whoop you if I wanted."

Vander felt Loving pressing his hand with tremendous pressure, but Vander squeezed right back refusing to let Loving win his little game. He took a step closer to Loving and looked up at him, "You watch yourself old man, or I'll finish what I started." Then he let go.

Hattie looked at them both uneasily. "I will have no more fighting in this house! None of it, or I will throw you both out! Do you hear me?"

The two both nodded and then Vander left out the back door.

CHAPTER SIX

"Miss Nelson said I should be done by the end of this month!" Vander said cheerfully as he walked Rose home from their school. It was April, 1914. The big live oak trees overhead were flush with new, bright green leaves contrasting against the vast, blue sky.

Rose smiled lightly. She let the heat of the spring sun warm her cheeks.

"What are you gonna do then?" She knew all too well what it was, but asked anyway, just so she could see Vander grow more excited.

"Hop on the first train out of here."

"Where'll you go?" Rose asked quietly as they turned the corner and walked on the wooden planks making up the sidewalk between the row of small businesses and the dirt drag of Round Rock's Main Street which seemed to fill up with more automobiles every year.

"A circus, of course," Vander smiled. He felt contented and free. "Rose, it's like I can see light and I just have to walk towards it!"

Rose looked down at her feet. As much as she liked to encourage Vander's dreams, she knew too, one day, she would have to let him go.

She looked down at her boots for a moment while they walked.

"Look Vander!" Rose pointed to a lone, bluebonnet wildflower growing up between the planks of the sidewalk.

"How did that little thing get there?" Vander asked as they both crouched down to admire it.

Rose looked at the beautiful blue flower and then back up to Vander. "It's you, Vander! You're just like this wildflower. Nothing should have grown in this spot, but somehow that seed found enough water and light and came up through the cracks in the walk where nobody would expect it!"

Vander smiled. He reached over and picked the flower and handed it to Rose.

"You're my best friend, Rose, you know that."

"Of course Vander, I know."

Then, they both heard the voice call out, "Vander! Vander Clyde Loving!"

It was the postman, Mister Johnson. He strode up to them both with his lanky frame and shiny, worn, blue suit with the old, brass buttons. He nodded as he approached them.

When he made it to where they were standing, he reached into his leather satchel and produced a magazine and held it out to Vander.

"Here you go, son!"

Vander took the magazine and asked, "What is it? We didn't order anything."

"What you have in your hands, son, is Round Rock's only copy of *Billboard* magazine. Don't know why they sent it here. Must have been some mix up. There's no address on it, so there's no place to send it to...." Mister Johnson watched Vander look it over.

"What is it?" Vander asked.

"My wife says she's seen one of your shows. She says you're real good. Everyone's talkin' about you. It's *Billboard* magazine son. They list all the openings for vaudeville and the circus! You want a job in the circus, I recon this is the only place you're gonna find a listing! Have at it boy!"

Vander wiped his face in astonishment. Rose tried to look over Vander's arms at every page as Vander thumbed through the publication. His face beamed.

"Thank you Mister Johnson! Thanks! I'm gonna take it home right now!"

CHAPTER SEVEN

Hattie Loving could hear the sound of the train coming from Hutto. This Monday morning, she stood on the platform in front of the new Edwardian-styled depot in her immaculate Sunday dress. She listened to the chugging noise of the steam issuing forth, like a bull running out on the prairie in the winter cold. The train's whistle blew as it rounded the bend and came into view. Samuel Loving said he was too busy at the broom factory that day to see Vander off. It was all for the better because no one wanted him there, his wife included. Hattie felt anxious and clutched her handbag. She looked at her son as he stood next to her. In the early May morning, with the heat of an early summer already encroaching, as much as she wanted to think of her fifteen year old offspring as a man, he was still a boy. He was tough for sure, but smaller than the rest. The years and the memories raced through her mind. She remembered as if it was yesterday holding her infant son in her arms, kissing him, playing with his tiny hands and feet. She remembered his first smile, his first tentative steps, nursing him back to health when he was sick. It all came back to her on the train platform as she watched the black, iron machine approach the station.

Hattie wanted to tell her child how much she adored him, how proud she was of him, but at that moment, she couldn't find words.

"Vander!" came the voice. "Vander Clyde!" Rose called out breathlessly as she ran to the station. She came upon Vander and his mother. She was gasping for air. "I couldn't miss it! I couldn't! I know Miss Becker will punish me for leaving her class, but I had to come."

Vander Clyde smiled softly, as a lump formed in his throat.

The iron behemoth pulled into the station. It released a blast of steam when it stopped. The conductor, in black suit and hat, proudly stepped onto the platform, producing a shiny, gold watch from his vest pocket.

"All aboard for San Anton!" the conductor called out.

Rose started to cry. "I don't want you to leave Vander! I don't want it!" She handed him a fistful of wildflowers she picked for him. "They're the last of the season…for you…"

Vander took the small bouquet and hugged her. Trying not to cry himself, he turned to his mother. But when he saw tears on her cheeks, he could no longer keep it in. He wept as he hugged her goodbye.

"Don't cry," his mother admonished through her own tears, "big boys don't cry…"

"All aboard!" the conductor shouted again.

Hattie took in her son one last time.

"Bye, mamma," Vander said softly. Then, he turned from them both and hopped onto the stairs leading to the coach of the train and entered the doorway.

His mother watched the great thrust of movement beneath his feat even before he was seated. Through her cloud of tears, Hattie Loving watched her son look out from the train windows as Rose stood next to her waving goodbye. The train gathered speed, heading into the thicket of woods. Only its cloud of smoke could be seen above the tree line until it faded into the horizon.

. . .

Vander looked out the train window at the rolling hills and expansive Texas sky. The breeze blowing in through the cracked window grew warmer the farther south they travelled from Austin. Vander took in the aroma of the wildflowers Rose gave him. Longing filled his heart as the sweetness of the flowers' scent filled his senses. Putting the bouquet down on the open seat next to him, he rose up and opened the train window some more. A blast of heat rushed through his hair. He took hold of the bouquet one last time. Saying a small prayer, he tossed the flowers out the train window and watched them scatter in the air. The train gained speed as it raced to San Anton. Vander sat down again. He closed his eyes, letting the force of the breeze wash over his face.

CHAPTER EIGHT

"I'm looking for the Alfaretta Sisters," Vander Clyde said tentatively to the teenage dwarf standing before him.

Vander clutched his issue of *Billboard* magazine in one hand and a small satchel in the other. It only contained a change of clothing, the special shoes he made for walking wire, and extra food packed by his mother for the train ride.

Luckily for him, Vander spotted the red and white striped circus tent from the train when he pulled into the San Antonio station. The air in San Antonio was still and hot. Anxiously, he exited the mission style building and walked toward the big top. The sky was a brilliant blue that afternoon, making the weathered red and white canvas of the big top look fresh and immense.

As Vander drew closer to the tent, he could feel his heart beat in his chest. He walked between a row of exotic tigers and lions lazily asleep in their ornately painted circus carts. Vander's nose filled with the aroma of the manure and feed of the assemblage of exotic animals he passed. Immense elephants grazed on bales of hay next to brilliant white Arabian horses eyeing his movements. Some trainers nodded at him, looking Vander over, and returned to their chores when they realized they did not know him.

When he made it past the animals' pens, that's when the dwarf approached him. The little man, who didn't seem to be much older than Vander himself, pushed back the worn, pork pie hat perched atop his too large head, squinting to look at Vander's face which was shadowed from the sun at his back.

"What you want them for?"

"The magazine."

Vander Clyde held up the *Billboard* magazine in his hand. The magazine trembled slightly and Vander hoped the little man didn't notice.

"They put an advertisement in *Billboard*. I'm here for the job."

After the words came out of Vander's mouth, he was surprised how adult he sounded. In that quick instant, he realized he had no one to rely on—not his mother, not Samuel Loving or Rose—only himself.

"The big top," the dwarf gestured toward the tent. "She's inside."

The young dwarf walked off as quickly as he appeared. Vander took a deep breath and moved toward the opening in the tent. With only a couple of dollars in his pocket, he knew he needed the job.

Once Vander's eyes adjusted to the inside of the tent, he was immediately drawn to a woman swinging high overhead on a trapeze. First, she was seated on the bar, pushing herself higher and higher into the upper shadows of the big top, then in the blink of an eye, she swung below it, catching the bar on the back sides of her bent legs. Swinging freely, her legs gave way and she slipped further down so only her ankles and feet wrapped around the ropes at either end of the trapeze bar. As she swung, she made elegant, presentational gestures with her arms. Vander was transfixed by her movements so much he didn't see the stout, bald man with the sweaty face stand alongside him.

"Beautiful, ain't she?" the fat man proudly asked Vander in a southern accent as thick as September honey.

The man produced a cigar from his moist, shirt pocket and lit it, taking a grand puff. "That's my girl. Can you believe it? Married a sorry sack like me. Name's Bobby Fuller." Fuller extended his hand to Vander's.

"Vander Clyde, Vander Clyde Broadway Loving," he said extending his hand to shake Bobby Fuller's perspiring palm.

"That's one hell of a name!" Bobby exclaimed. "Accent sounds like you're from the Confederate states. That true boy?"

"Yes, sir. I'm a Texan. Born and bred just north of Austin."

"That so?" Fuller asked. His high clear tenor voice, didn't match the girth of his frame. He was probably in his late forties, stout, five foot six, maybe, with a round face and strands sweated, dark colored hair swirled atop his head—whipped around like a tornado had at it. "You an acrobat or something? Not much to ya."

Vander looked at Fuller blankly. He was so overwhelmed, he didn't know what to say.

"I'm here for the job, with the Alfaretta Sisters."

Bobby Fuller looked at Vander Clyde more seriously, taking a handkerchief from his pocket to wipe his fleshy face.

"I'm afraid there's only one Alfaretta sister, boy, Audrey, an' that's her up there. Lydia passed three weeks ago in Galveston. Audrey's still broke up about it."

"What happened?" Vander asked with a curious eye.

"She fell of course—net gave way. No one saw it comin'. Broke her back."

Vander swallowed hard and looked down at the ground.

"You do trapeze work? You look pretty young, son."

"Some," Vander lied, knowing the only thing close to trapeze work he did was swinging out on a rope tied onto a thick branch overhanging the Brushy Creek swimming hole, "but rope walking is my specialty."

Fuller puffed on his cigar.

"We need someone on the trapeze an' rings too. The circus says there's no act with one girl. She needs a partner."

"Well, it's your lucky day, because that's what I'm here for, sir."

Vander wasn't sure what possessed him to say it the way he did, but he knew he had to get the job and he would do just about anything to secure it.

"Great to hear, boy!" Fuller slapped Vander's back. "Now have at it and get up there. Let's see what you can do!"

"Now?" Vander's eyes bulged.

"What you waitin' for?" Fuller looked up at his wife. "Audrey!" he called out. Audrey was now standing on a small platform affixed to one of the massive poles holding up the tent. She wore pink tights under a lavender leotard. Her light brown hair was pulled back into a bun. She was a robust, meaty woman with strong, thick arms and legs.

"This here's….Loving…"

"Vander Clyde," Vander tried correcting Fuller.

"Vander Clyde Loving…He wants to try out."

Audrey nodded in their direction as she caught her breath.

"Sure thing Bobby. Send him on up," she called back in an accent sounding just as back woods as Mister Fuller's.

There are few moments in one's life where one just has to get on with it and Vander knew this was one of those moments. He dropped the magazine and his bag. He took off his white Sunday shirt which he wore for train ride—his trousers, boots and stockings as well. He was standing there in nothing but his white undershirt and shorts.

Fuller looked at Vander's skinny frame and frowned.

Vander saw his expression.

"I may look like a slight, sir, but I can assure you I'm as strong as a bull!"

"Well, get up there," Fuller chomped on the stogie not all that convinced.

As Vander climbed the tiny ladder higher and higher into the big top to get to the small platform where Audrey awaited him, his mind raced. He felt anxious and frightened, but told himself not to show it. Sure, he swung from that old tree branch over Brushy Creek, but he never did this before! Vander thought about what he just witnessed Audrey do on the trapeze. He tried to recall her movements. If he could just do what she did, maybe they would see promise.

When Vander reached the platform, Audrey was waiting for him. Vander looked down for a split second— Fuller was tiny and unimposing from the height. Standing so closely to Audrey made Vander feel even more uncomfortable. In their own ways, each sized the other up. Vander thought Audrey Fuller must have been in her early twenties. She was a handsome woman with light, almost translucent skin, a round face dotted with red apple cheeks. Her eyes were we a shade of pale, silvery blue. They were both about the same height, but with her bosom and thick, muscular legs, Vander imagined she weighed more than he did.

"Name's Audrey, Audrey Fuller, from Alpharetta, Georgia," she smiled. "Though we spell it differently, for the act. Changed the 'ph' to 'f'."

"Vander," he said trying to sound confident, but he was terrified inside.

"The bar's slippery, you may want to chalk up." Audrey looked into Vander's eyes. "Hell, boy, you look as scared as a mouse starin' at a cat! You ain't never done this before have you?"

Vander didn't respond for a moment. Then he said, "I walk line mostly. But I'm a fast learner. Fastest you've ever seen."

Audrey smiled. "Hell, I remember the first time my daddy put me up here. I was scared to death! Must have been seven or so. But not no more. Listen, do you remember what I did?"

"Pretty much."

"Good. Why don't you try it and let's see how you do."

Audrey handed the trapeze to Vander. He felt the bar and looked down across the expanse below him. A net was secured, but it looked entirely too small. He took the bar and focused his thoughts. He would do exactly as he watched Audrey do moments before.

Vander sat on the trapeze and held onto the support ropes. Steeling himself, he felt his feet let go of the platform. He swung out in a deep lunge under the center of the big top. The feeling was exhilarating as the hot breeze of the upper air of the tent blew through his hair. He swung higher and higher, remembering to point his toes, and hold his back straight. Then, he released his arms and swung below the trapeze, catching the bar with the back of his legs where his knees bent. He imitated, with elegant perfection, the movements Audrey made with her arms. Two lavish swings later, just as he watched Audrey do, he straightened his legs and slid down further, catching the ends of the trapeze ropes with his ankles and feet. Vander couldn't believe the strength he needed to hold this position, but he again held in his pain, and gestured with his arms in a way that made it seem like his agility took no effort at all.

That's when he realized he had no idea how to return back to the top of the trapeze or get back on the platform with Audrey! A couple more passes in this position, and he knew he would fall, so he thought of doing one of his cannon ball flips, like he did when he swung on the rope over Brushy Creek. With all his might, Vander swung the trapeze as high into the air as he could tolerate, the muscles in his feet screaming out. As he reached the apex, he released his feet, tucked into a tight ball and did a backward somersault. In an instant, he was bouncing on the safety net, thrilled by what he had just done!

Bobby Fuller stuffed his cigar into his mouth and applauded loudly. Audrey too was impressed. From the platform, she did a swan dive, turning onto her back at the right instant for a soft landing on the safety net. She then walked over to where Bobby and Vander were standing.

"Now, son, I need you to be honest with me. You're new to this aren't you?" Bobby asked as he stared intently at Vander.

"I did shows in my back yard—on the wire. I'm good!" Vander said trying to sell himself. He wanted more than anything to get back up to the trapeze.

"You a run away?" Audrey asked with her hands on her hips.

"No. My momma sent me off today on the train, from Round Rock."

"He's got balance," Audrey said. "It'll take him time to train."

"I'm a fast learner! I even doubled up my studies and finished high school two years early!"

Bobby rubbed his chin. "We've only got a week, ten days tops, to get him trained. If we don't get this act back on track, they'll can us and then where'll we be?"

Audrey's pale blue eyes looked serious. "Did you see, how he moved his arms? He sure looks the part. He'll look sweet in a dress."

Vander's mouth dropped. "A dress?"

Bobby Fuller scowled, "The part's for a *female* trapeze artist. Didn't y'all read the advertisement?"

"We're the Alfaretta *Sisters*!" Audrey interjected. "World famous aerial queens."

Vander Clyde was trying to absorb what they were saying.

"He's got a good figure, not quite a man yet," Audrey said looking over Vander's body. "A little taking in here and letting out there and Lydia's costumes could fit."

"You ever put on a dress, boy?" Bobby asked. "It's no big deal. Wouldn't be the first time a boy in a trapeze act did it."

"You look better in a dress, up on a trapeze," Audrey encouraged. "More beautiful, the dress flows, you know."

Vander remembered Miss Nelson told him all the actors during Shakespeare's time were men or boys and they played the female parts as well.

"Like Shakespeare, you mean the way the boys played the girl's parts?" Vander asked.

Bobby and Audrey laughed.

"Yes, son, just like ol' Will Shakespeare!" Bobby chuckled. "You'll get five dollars a week—no pay until we get the act back up. Deal?" Bobby extended his hand.

Vander Clyde couldn't believe it was all happening so fast! He enthusiastically extended his hand. "Deal!"

CHAPTER NINE

"The art of the circus is illusion, son," Bobby Fuller said as he sat before the mirror that was set in a make-shift dressing room in a smaller tent next to the larger big top. He opened a leather-covered flask resting on the table. His eyes darted about to see if anyone else was in their screened off section before he took a deep swig. The booze felt good draining down the back of this throat. "PT Barnum struck it about right. He knew, people see what they wanna see. What we do is help make the dream come true."

Bobby unscrewed a ceramic jar of black, shoe polish-like makeup and dug his fingers into the container. He started smoothing the makeup onto his face. He worked quickly, in an assured manner, impressing Vander.

Vander sat next to the man on a bale of hay, only in his long johns, taking in the transformation before his eyes. The week before, he and Audrey worked sometimes twelve hours a day perfecting the new routine. Every inch of Vander's body ached from the physical exertion he put himself through during the past seven days. Audrey taught him the basics of her routine. He watched her intently, not only to learn the tricks, but to study how she moved, how she carried her body. In one week's time, even Audrey remarked Vander moved more like a woman than she did. Vander, for his part, loved the trapeze. He loved the new tricks. He also loved becoming a woman.

"We're all actors, Vander," Bobby continued philosophizing. "We're all are puttin' on a show one way or another. So you see—we circus folk—we're the real ones. The illusion is more real than reality itself—'cause everyone knows we're playin' a part. You ask me, the circus is the only honest place in this whole world."

With his face paint complete, Bobby Fuller stood up and went behind an old screen decorated with oriental motifs. A moment later, he came out from behind the screen in a bright, red tuxedo with tails, white gloves, and a sequin-studded, red top hat. His face was painted shiny black, his mouth lined white. His brown eyes now circled in white, stood out from his black-as-night face.

"Well, I'll be, praise the Lord!" Bobby said in his deep southern slave dialect. "I don't think we's met—Doc Holland—the Destroyer of Gloom!" Bobby smiled broadly revealing his tar-stained teeth as he shook Vander Clyde's hand with both his gloved mitts.

"Now we's gots to do somethin' 'bout y'all! Shhh! Don't say nothin' to Miss Audrey, 'cause she done tan my hide!—But you gots to be the most beautiful Alfaretta sis-tah of 'em all!"

Vander laughed as Doc Holland grinned and gestured for Vander to sit before the mirror. Holland produced more ceramic jars and bottles and a curly-haired brown wig.

Vander took one look at the wig and exclaimed, "I can't wear that!"

"Oh, my! Not a day in the circus yet an' look at y'all!" Doc Holland frowned.

"I mean, it's a mess!" Vander took the wig in his hands and started fussing with it.

"Oh, I do declare!" Holland said dramatically as he put the back of his white-gloved hand up to his forehead. "I do think a princess is born!" Doc Holland guffawed loudly.

"Before y'all be puttin' on dat hair piece, we gots to make you purty. Now, I don't wants no mo' complainin'. Open this here jar an' dig in—start puttin' this stuff all over yer purty face. Don't you be forgettin' yer your neck an' arms neither!"

Vander started doing as he was told.

"You don't have to speak like Doc Holland. You can be Mister Fuller."

Doc Holland looked at him seriously. "What you talkin' 'bout? Massa Fuller's done left. Doc Holland's wit you now Miss Alfaretta."

Vander grinned for a moment of understanding. He looked at himself in the mirror, at his features, as he applied more pale foundation to his face. In his mind, Vander could see a beautiful woman coming forth. He would do everything in his power to sustain the illusion. She would be lovely, an angel sent from above.

"Lip paint, Doc," Vander said looking at Holland in the mirror. "I need lip paint."

Doc Holland smiled. "Sho-thing! Gots it right here!..."

...

There was one more act before the ring master finally came to their introduction. Vander Clyde's heart was racing. He looked at himself one last time in the full length mirror perched against some bales of hay just outside the big top. If he squinted, he imagined he looked like a woman, but surely he thought, the crowd would laugh when they saw him, knowing he was not really a female. What if the wig came off during the performance? The dress he wore was still too ample. Even with the false padding he added into the breasts, it just wasn't quite right.

"Lydia!" Audrey called out. She was wearing an identical costume. Then she caught herself. "Vander! Come inside—we're almost on!"

Audrey and Vander stood in the wings awaiting their introduction. In a flash, Vander thought to run. He was literally shaking. Then Audrey, standing inches from him, looked him straight in the eye.

"Pull yourself together…" she said under her breath. "Do as we rehearsed or we don't eat."

The arc light shined on them as the ring master made their introduction, *The magnificent Alfaretta Sisters—world famous aerial queens!* Audrey's face radiated a luminous smile as she led the two out to the center ring. Vander's eye caught Doc Holland's nearby in the shadows. Doc gestured with his white-gloved fingers by his cheeks for Vander to smile. Just like that, something snapped in Vander's head. He was in his back yard, putting on a show. He was the angel he saw up in the big top circus in Austin, so many years ago. It took hold of him and flowed out of him. He was an elegant, young woman of impeccable aerial skills.

Audrey also noticed something different in Vander that night. He changed. It was as if it was no longer a costume he was wearing, but he became absorbed by the illusion and transformed into a true Alfaretta sister.

The two focused on their routine and preformed it with great skill. With the breeze of hot air blowing through his pinned-on wig, Vander didn't hear the crowd gasp in excitement as the duo worked through their stunts. It was all quiet in his head, all concentration. It wasn't until they completed their last move and wound up back on the same small platform, arms raised in triumph he realized the audience was enthusiastically applauding. Through his painted lips and powdered face, Vander Clyde Loving beamed!

...

"That's the way it's done, son! That's the way it's done!" Bobby tipped his chair and leaned back, taking a long swig out of his flask. The crowds had long gone, while the three were alone in the makeshift dressing room in a smaller tent next to the big top.

"You did a top notch job, tonight, Vander," Audrey said as she sat on a small stool in front of a vanity mirror lit by several kerosene lanterns. She worked removing her stage makeup from her face. Vander studied how she did it. He went up to the little table.

"Can you help me?"

"Sure thing," Audrey said. "But you've gotta get one thing straight, this is the last time we're gonna show ya. You've gotta start doing this on your own."

Vander eagerly nodded as Audrey went to work cleaning his face.

"You know, if I didn't know it, there were times tonight, when I would swear to the good Lord Lydia was up there with ya!" Bobby smiled. His face was pink and clean, already scrubbed clean of black makeup.

Audrey pursed her lips. Vander could see a deep sadness well up in her pale, blue eyes.

"Sorry, babe, I didn't mean to…It's just it was…"

She stopped wiping Vander's face with cold cream and stood up. She didn't look at Bobby and she didn't look at Vander. With stony deliberation, Audrey left the tent.

Vander turned to Bobby who fell forward on his tipped chair. Bobby wiped his sweaty forehead with a damp palm.

"I messed up boy. I messed up real good," Bobby said as he took another liberal swig from his flask.

Vander turned from him and looked at his half-cleaned and half-made up face in the mirror. He felt for Audrey and somehow he felt guilty for having replaced Lydia.

"Sorry, Mister Fuller."

"No mind boy, no mind," Bobby said as he held up his flask again to his fleshy lips only to realize his last liberal swig finished off all its contents. Vander watched the man's face wince with pain. "No mind..." Bobby mumbled to himself, caught up in his thoughts.

CHAPTER TEN

The whole caravan of the circus moved north on the railroad as the summer wore on. Vander was amazed by the sheer logistics of the army-sized brigade of entertainers, exotic animals, equipment, and surly circus hands—how they pulled into a town and streamed out of their lavishly painted railroad box cars, like ants from their mound, all moving about with a purpose to ready the show. Stakes were driven into the back earth to erect the red and white big top in towns scattered throughout the Midwest: Ames, Kansas City, Tulsa, and Saint Louis.

Vander had to participate in readying the show, pitching hay and feed for the livery of horses, camels, ostriches, and elephants. He climbed poles untethered, high up in the big top, running lines and rigging. The elder performers approached each stop with a ritualized nonchalance. They rode the circuit for many seasons and each town began to resemble the next, but not Vander. He was given a low bunk on one of the rail cars carrying the male entertainers. In the bunk, between the thin mat substituting for a mattress and the planks of siding for the box car, he kept a map. He found the map blowing across the grounds of the circus one day. Claiming it as his own, Vander charted each move the circus made. He noted where they were and where they were heading.

Once the big top was erected, the circus marched to the middle of the town in an elaborate parade. Vander took in the wonderment in the eyes of young and old alike as the townspeople marveled at the size of the massive grey elephants or the hysterics of the audacious clown routines as the circus parade made way down the street. Sometimes, Vander dressed as a lovely Alfaretta sister, in a shiny blue dress puffed full of crinolines, riding the back of an elephant, imitating the feminine wave Audrey taught him.

When they finished the parade, it was time to perfect and rehearse. All around him, he saw artists and craftspeople, striving to improve their routines. He and Audrey were no different. Audrey learned Vander was an extremely quick study and so she added more complex tricks to their act. Vander also helped create new costumes which would hide his more masculine attributes while emphasizing his feminine qualities.

No matter the town, while most of the entertainers managed to stay within a hundred yards of the big top, Vander set out on foot to explore the city when he had the time. He'd tour churches and courthouses and maybe even visit museums if the towns had one nearby the rail depot. He witnessed school children congregate around the circus posters displayed in the town—noting the excitement in their faces. It was strange to him, thinking just a summer ago, he would have been one of them. His chest swelled with pride as he listened to their comments. For the first time, Vander's life felt as if it had meaning and purpose. He was a circus entertainer!

At the end of each day, after the last performance, with the crowds gone, all that was left was the lingering aroma of roasted peanuts and salted popcorn. Vander was exhausted, but extremely contented. It was too hot now to go back to the boxcar bunk to sleep, and so he usually found some scraps of bundling canvas or even a soft pile of hay to lay his weary body on. At first, the sounds of the circus at nighttime were mysterious—pachyderms calling out under the moon intertwined with murmurs of hushed conversations and the lonely sound of the Hungarian equestrian rider playing an old tune on a tired accordion. Some nights he'd hear shouting or a fight break out. It all dissettled Vander at first and made him long for his comfortable bed in his mother's small, limestone cabin in Round Rock. But soon enough, the nocturnal sounds grew in familiarity to the point it was easy to sleep under the blanket of evening stars.

This particular sweltering night was no different. As Vander readied his nest of hay for sleep at the edge of their camp abutting an open field, he thought about the heat of the cotton fields of Round Rock in July. He wondered how his mother was faring with old Samuel Loving. He tried to block her out of his mind these past several months, but tonight he thought of his mother. Did she miss him, he wondered or was she too taken with Loving? He also thought of Rose, his one true friend. What would she think of him now—a big time circus performer? Yet, he chose not write them, not yet anyway. He was proud of his beautiful presentation under the big top, but not so sure either one would understand the ways of the world and his flowing, feminine portrayal.

There were times in the past months he constructed letters to them in his mind, telling them of all the people he met, the hard work he put in to perfect the act—yet it never seemed right. The Vander Clyde they knew was dead, somehow. He had to admit it. Now, he was so different than the boy from Round Rock. In the midst of his discovery and exploration, being honest with himself, he wasn't sure he even knew who he was or what exactly was ahead. He just knew he had to keep moving forward.

Laying down and looking up at the stars, Vander felt the heat of the warm, still night on his body, no wind or even gentle breeze, just a muggy stillness. That's when Timmy, the dwarf he encountered that fateful day in May, lay down beside him.

"I was looking for you," the little man said with a boyish half-smile. He was dressed only in a pair of tattered, white long johns.

"Hey Timmy," Vander said, still looking up at the stars and the brilliantly illuminated quarter moon in the clear night.

"What's on your mind?" Timmy asked.

He was resting a little too close to Vander for his comfort, but tonight, feeling a bit lonely, Vander enjoyed his new friend's company.

"Thinking about home, I guess."

Timmy put a little straw in his mouth and folded his hands behind his blocky head as he looked up at the starry night.

"Not me. I never think about it. No sir."

"You got a family?" Vander asked as he turned to look at Timmy with his button nose and China doll lips.

"Yeah, I've got a momma and daddy just like everyone else....I haven't seen them in a long time, though. When they saw I was gonna be a little runt, they took me to the circus. They brought me here on my eighth birthday. Hell, I thought they were giving me a present, seeing the circus and all. But it was planned. They left me here...all alone."

Vander looked seriously at Timmy. "I'm real sorry, Timmy," he said.

"It's okay. Probably the best thing they could do for me. Made me grow up real fast. Real fast. You work for the circus, you've gotta stand on your own two feet. Look at me, I'm seventeen and I've been earning my own paycheck since I was eight. But you've gotta watch out. Everyone'll take it. These circuses are run by Gypsies. They'll take it, in the nicest way. Heck, you might not even know when your pocket's getting picked, they're so nice."

Vander listened more intently to Timmy.

"Take you for example—bet you're being taken right now, but you're too green to even know." Timmy looked seriously at Vander, his face was shiny and moist with evening perspiration, illuminated by the glow of the quarter moon. "How much they paying you, Vander?"

"Five dollars a week. But Mister Fuller takes out some for expenses like costumes and face paint."

Timmy started laughing. "Hell, you've been had! There's no performer under this here big top who doesn't pull in at least ten a week! I make fifteen myself. If I was you, I'd get right up in that drunk's face and tell him you know what he's up to."

"The Fullers treat me fairly!"

"Sure thing, it's just you better watch yourself or..." Timmy stopped himself for a moment.

"Or what?"

"Well, let's just say after that net gave way, lots of folks were talking about the manner in which Lydia fell. I for one didn't witness it, but there's fellas here who claim old man Fuller, before the show, loosened that net..."

"That's impossible!"

Timmy kept looking up at the stars. "Not really. It can be done. There are ways..."

"But why?"

"Easy there, Vander, don't get yourself all worked up. Some say it was over money...Others say old man Fuller did it because Lydia was going to come clean about their affair..."

"This is all rubbish!"

"Easy there, Vander. I didn't mean to upset you. Now they've got you. Their own fresh little flower. It was like heaven sent you, if you ask me."

Vander's brow furrowed as he looked back up at the stars. Anxiety welled up in his stomach.

"I'm saying this because I like you, Vander. You remind me so much of myself when I first got here. From the day I saw you coming my way from the depot in San Anton, I said to myself that is a beautiful, young man. And when I see you up in that big top performing the way you do, I start to thinking maybe we have a little more in common than you know…These long, lonely nights wouldn't be so much so if you find a little companionship…You ask me, everyone needs someone…"

Vander felt Timmy's hand reach for his privates. Shocked, Vander immediately stood up. He was too overwhelmed to even say anything! He scowled at Timmy's surprised expression.

"Keep to yourself!" Vander seethed. He caught the volume of his voice and repeated his words again except lower. "You keep to yourself, you hear!"

"I'm sorry, Vander. I thought we had something in common, you know. Didn't mean nothing by it. It's okay Vander." Timmy stood up and brushed himself off. "I best be heading out then. Honest, Vander, I care for you." Timmy searched Vander's eyes for understanding, instead all he could see was surprise and shock. "I best be moving on…"

Vander was breathing hard as he watched Timmy depart into the night. He looked around to see if anyone heard their exchange. No one was in sight, at least what he could see. Vander's mind clouded over, filled with everything Timmy said and did.

…

"What the hell got into you, boy?" Fuller chomped on his sweaty cigar and pushed his fleshy index finger into Vander's corseted chest. "That was the most pitiful show I've ever seen! You know we've got one foot out the door of this circus—and then you put in a performance like that!"

Bobby Fuller turned away from Vander and began to pace. Dressed in a pair of worn trousers and a sweat-stained undershirt, Bobby angrily strode back and forth in the empty box car which was used to haul the canvas of the big, red and white tent. The space was engulfed in blackness, save for a kerosene lantern propped up on an old melon crate. Vander stood silent breathing hard—still wearing his flowing pink organza costume, his lips painted a deep crimson red and powdered cheeks blushed with rose rouge.

"How much are you taking in on account of me?" Vander mustered, a lump forming in his throat. He felt his hands tremble, but he told himself to push on.

Bobby stopped in his tracks, and intently looked at Vander's innocent eyes. He squinted as he took a long puff on his cigar. He wiped the sweat from his bald dome with his other hand, again moving closer to Vander. He cracked a half smile.

"So that's what this is about? So that's what this is about!" He nosed up to Vander sticking his fleshy finger into his rhinestoned sternum. "We give you the break of the century. We take you in. We feed you and train you. We clothe you. When you came to us you had nothin'! Nothin' at all!"

Vander clenched his fists. They were shaking so much. "I want my fair share!" he demanded.

"So you want more money?"

"Yes I do!"

Bobby stuffed his cigar butt into his mouth and dug deep into his worn, tweed trousers. He produced two crumbled dollar bills and held them up high in the air.

"This is all I've got, boy! This is all I've got! You want that too? Well, suits me fine! You can have it!" Bobby tossed the two bills into the air and stepped down off the boxcar.

Vander stood alone, his chest heaving as he tried to calm down. He looked at the two crumbled bills sitting on the wide, wood plank flooring of the boxcar and then down at himself, dimly illuminated, in his performance costume. He wanted to cry. He felt like crying, but he didn't. He quickly grabbed the moist dollars from the floor and put them in the palm of one of his hands.

"Hey Vander," he heard in the now familiar southern accent. Audrey entered the box car. Vander's face flushed and he turned away for a moment trying to collect himself and then he looked back at her.

"I earned this!" he protested. "I earned every cent and more!"

Audrey wore a drab, oatmeal-colored robe over her costume. She unpinned her light brown hair which fell to her shoulders. When her hair was down, with her ivory white skin and pale, blue eyes, she looked like one of those pretty women featured on Coca-Cola billboards Vander saw in bigger towns.

"We didn't get paid for a long time, Vander, after Lydia passed," Audrey said moving closer to him. "You don't go on, you don't get paid. An' we put a lot of money into you. Sure, you don't see it, but it was there."

"So you agree with him? All the while I've been working, you've paid me only half of my wages!"

"We'll get you more, Vander, I promise."

"Why do you stay with him?" Vander asked. After the words came out of his mouth, he wondered from where they came.

Audrey looked away from Vander and walked toward one of the boxcar's shed doors which was rolled open several feet. Past her, Vander could see the small fires still burning amongst the circus encampment. He heard the distant murmurings of conversations, many spoken in unintelligible foreign languages. Vander watched Audrey, lost in her thoughts as she turned her head up to the darkened sky which was cloudless and filled with stars.

"You're still a boy, Vander," Audrey said.

Vander stood next to Audrey as she looked out at the horizon. She had a lovely profile, Vander thought, handsome and noble, yet feminine.

He wanted to ask her, it was what was really on his mind—but he didn't quite know how.

"Did...." he stammered. "What happened to Lydia?"

Audrey turned to Vander Clyde. He saw her devastated expression, but then she grew more serious. "You must never speak of her, Vander, never."

"I've gotta know. I can't go on unless I know. Is it true what they're saying about her?"

Audrey took a deep breath. "No."

She turned from him and began to climb down the steps of the boxcar and made way through the nearby menagerie of exotic animals until she disappeared into the shadows.

Vander watched her and then he looked at the money in his hand. He felt the moist bills—Bobby Fuller's sweat now mixed with his. Then he clinched them tightly, promising to himself not to let them go.

"Vander! Vander Clyde!" the voice said urgently.

Vander squinted from his vantage in the opening of the box car to see where the voice came from. When his eyes adjusted, he saw Timmy breathlessly approaching the box car.

"Come down here! Vander, come down here right now!" Timmy insisted as he looked up to Vander standing in the opening of the freight car doorway. Vander grimaced at the sight of Timmy and his insistence, but he complied with the young dwarf's demand and hopped down from the rail car.

Timmy held forth a late edition of the Tulsa Tribune, revealing the front page headline for Vander to read: *Austria Has Chosen War*.

"It's war, Vander, in Europe! The whole camp's talking about it!"

Vander read the headline. He didn't much think of such things before. Samuel Loving enjoyed telling tales of his Rough Riders and some of the old timers in Round Rock used to tell stories of the beastly battles in what they called the War of Northern Aggression, the Civil War. For sure, he studied the conquests of Napoleon and Alexander the Great in Miss Nelson's class, but these conflicts all seemed to be things of the past and no interest to him.

Vander frowned at the headline and what he was reading. None of this could be good. Maybe it was God's way of retribution for the sins of the world, for the sins in his own heart. Pastor Merton, back in Round Rock, no doubt was working up a sermon this very minute expounding on this notion, Vander surmised.

Vander handed the paper back to Timmy.

"Thanks, Timmy," he said as he turned and started to walk away.

"Wait!" Timmy called out. "Don't you care?"

"Not really."

Timmy watched the young aerialist disappear into the midst of the uneasy night.

CHAPTER ELEVEN

In the shadows of an opening to the big top tent between two sets of bleachers where the acts made their entrances for the show, Vander squinted to see the action in the large cage. It stood empty, ready to be bathed in the bright rays of the circus spotlights. He was still wearing his pink rhinestone costume having just completed his performance with Audrey.

Since he was a young boy, Vander always loved big cat acts. He loved the way the trainers had command over the wild beasts, how any moment, with one wrong step, one mistake, and the saber-toothed predators would pounce. Their circus big cat trainer was unlike any Vander witnessed before. He was young, no more than twenty-three. It enthralled Vander to watch the confident, young man enter the cage with the huge, formidable cats. Jungle James was his circus name, but Vander knew it was really Anthony. He was exceedingly handsome, with dark, shiny hair and noble chin. When the arc light shined on his winning smile before he entered the cage, Vander secretly felt as if the smile was just for him. Vander so admired Anthony. The lion tamer performed only in tights and slippers, completely naked from the waist up. Anthony carried his muscled body with a cock-sure confidence before the big cats with their menacing roars. Vander must have seen the act over a hundred times, but he swore he would never tire of looking at Jungle James's mastery over the big cats.

"He's a god," little Timmy whispered as he stood next to Vander. Dressed in a flouncy purple and white striped costume, Timmy's face was painted white; the space around his china doll lips was styled red in a festive upturned grin. The two entertainers' faces softly glowed by the light emanating from the cage in the center ring.

Vander winced as he looked down at Timmy, who was standing too close to him.

"You know, his father was a trainer too. Toured all over Italy. That's where he's from," Timmy whispered loudly. The sound of the circus orchestra swelled as they played Jungle James's entrance music. "They say his father was torn up and killed by one the big cats. That's why Anthony had to move away. It was all too much for him. So he came to America to do the act here."

Vander said nothing as he looked back at Jungle James. He was upset Timmy disturbed his own private moment. He wondered if Timmy was full of outlandish stories of circus performers and if there was truth to any of his tales.

"You appreciate him—men, I mean," Timmy said looking up to Vander. "So do I."

Vander looked at Timmy. He didn't want to acknowledge it, but in the moment, so many things fell into place in his mind. Vander turned away from the dwarf. If he was being honest with himself, Vander knew in his heart he had to agree.

"If you ever wanna do something about it, just let me know."

Vander felt his face flush. He wanted to tell Timmy to shut up—that he didn't know what he was talking about, but he didn't. Instead Vander watched the young lion tamer in the ring, admiring Jungle James's powerful confidence, his chiseled dynamism.

CHAPTER TWELVE

"What?!"

Bobby Fuller looked at Vander Clyde with wide eyes. They stood alongside the gaudily painted box cars which had just disgorged all their contents. The red and white big top was pitched nearby in the Atlanta rail yard. The afternoon overcast chilled the mid-November day.

Vander Clyde glanced at the seven dollar bills in his hand and then back up at Bobby.

"You agreed I would get my full pay once we hit October."

"We'll be down in Florida soon, son. You'll have a nice holiday in Florida an' when we get back on the road in early spring, we can talk."

"That's horse crap and you know it!" Vander said shoving the bills into his trouser pocket. He looked seriously at Fuller. For over a month he practiced in his mind what he was going to say. Finally, this day, in Atlanta, he mustered the courage to do it. "Either you give me what is due me this very moment, or I walk."

Bobby pulled a cigar from his shirt pocket. He bit off one end and spit it to the ground. Then, he lit the stogie, taking several robust puffs.

"Calm down, boy. It's all gonna to be fine. Think for yourself. You leave us, where you gonna go? Who would take you? Think about it. You're an Alfaretta Sister. Without us, you ain't nothing."

Vander knew it may come to this. He prepared himself for it. Before he met up with Bobby, he gathered all his belongings: his change of clothes, body makeup he purchased, hand sewn leather high wire shoes, and his carefully folded map all stuffed into his worn satchel. Mustering his courage, he replied, "I get my ten or I walk, Bobby. This is it. You pay me now, or I walk."

The north wind lifted the few errant strands of Bobby Fuller's greasy hair off his bald dome. He looked Vander Clyde over. Vander had grown in the half year with the circus. Even with his petite frame, Vander's muscles had thickened, his shoulders were broader. He carried himself differently too. He was no longer the scared young boy who auditioned that sweaty day in May down in San Anton.

Bobby squinted and looked straight at Vander Clyde. He knew he was being challenged and he wanted to call Vander's bluff. "You wanna walk, you walk. That's fine with me."

Vander's heart was beating so strongly he felt it was about to explode from his chest. If he was going to be a man, he had to stand up for himself. He refused to back down. "Well then, this is goodbye," he said as he extended his right hand in Bobby's direction.

The fat man's hands held onto his suspenders, not flinching as he puffed on his cigar. Vander's hand retreated.

"Please give my regards to your wife," Vander Clyde said in a dignified air. Bobby's sour expression did not change as Vander turned, satchel strap over one shoulder, and started to walk towards the Atlanta train station. Vander kept walking, waiting to hear Bobby call out, but the only thing he heard was the north wind growing stronger, whistling through the tiny slats on the walls of the now empty rail cars he walked beside. Vander bit his lip and somewhere in his mind, he heard his mother's voice, *"Big boys don't cry."*

…

Standing in line at the ticket kiosk, Vander could see by the board hung high on the wall, the next train south to Florida was heading out in the morning. He would buy a ticket to Sarasota. All the decent performers wintered down there, even if they weren't in the biggest shows. There, they would rest a while and retool their acts for the early springtime. If he could get there early, maybe he could see if there was another troop who needed him.

A heaviness filled his heart. Vander thought about his childhood ambitions to be in the circus, to be an aerialist, high up in the big top, like an angel. It would all be so perfect and free. A hopelessness filled his heart. Would Rose think him a failure? What, dare he think it, would his mother say? He thought of Samuel Loving laughing at him with his disgusting teeth and creased face.

"Where to?" the gentleman behind the glass kiosk asked Vander through a hole cut in the glass.

The question snapped Vander Clyde from his darkened mood.

"Sarasota, Florida."

The man looked at Vander for a moment.

"The next train won't leave 'til morning."

"Yes, I know. That's fine."

"Six dollars."

Vander was so preoccupied, he hadn't checked the fares. He knew with the seven dollars Bobby gave him, plus the three he had saved, all he had to his name was ten measly dollars. He swallowed hard and dug into his trousers and counted out the money.

The teller handed Vander his ticket. He read the typed words on the blue rectangle: *Sarasota, Florida: ONE WAY*. Then, he shoved the ticket into his front trouser pocket, mindful of pick pockets and petty thieves.

Around him, in the late afternoon, men and women moved though the grand concourse. Some of the wealthier travelers hired Negro porters wearing spotless navy blue suits to haul their stacks of trunks and luggage on wooden dollies. Vander sat on one of the long, hand-carved, pew-like benches, just below an ornately styled, four-sided, wrought iron clock. It was five thirty.

The circus performers would be finishing their supper by now, taking care of their last personal chores before they started to prepare for the evening show. Vander pushed his satchel closer to him and folded his arms, slumping in the hard, wood bench. He wondered what the Fullers would do without him. They couldn't go on without him, not tonight anyway. Eventually, they would find some other chump, he supposed.

Vander felt hungry, but chose not to eat, wanting to save every last penny he could for his journey. Six months ago, he boarded the train out of Round Rock filled with dreams of the big top. He couldn't go home, not now, defeated and cast down. He wouldn't regret anything or let anyone get the best of him.

"Vander!" he heard the voice call out.

"Vander Clyde!"

He looked up from his darkened mood. It was Timmy.

Vander noticed all the eyes of the passersby turn to gape at the little man calling out.

Timmy hopped onto the pew next to Vander.

"Old man Fuller's really steamed!" Timmy reported as he caught his breath. Vander looked away. "You ask me it serves him right, taking advantage of you, yes sir! They pushed a little too far, tried to take too much of the pie and now look what they got."

Vander turned toward Timmy. "Did they send you here?"

"Can't say they did. Old man Fuller's too proud for that."

Both were quiet for a moment. The commotion of Timmy's entrance died down. Now people stared with guarded glances, turning their heads away when Timmy looked in their direction. Timmy finally caught his breath.

"So where you going?"

Vander sighed and looked up at the iron trusses supporting the roof of the Atlanta train station. Without looking at Timmy, he replied, "Sarasota. I'll find work down there."

Timmy pushed one of his diminutive hands into one of his trouser pockets and produced some wadded up magazine pages. "I snuck into bossman's caravan and ripped out these for ya—here, take a look at 'em."

Timmy handed the crumbled magazine pages to Vander who took them and opened them up. They were from this week's *Billboard* magazine. Vander hungrily began to read them over.

Timmy squinted at the copy on Vander's lap.

"I'm not much for reading. You ask me and it all looks Chinese. What's it say?"

Vander quickly appraised the want ads. Nothing matched his talents until his eye caught the last ad at the bottom of the page. "Female Aerialist Wanted—Erford's Whirling Sensation. Vaudeville Act. Auditions October 26 and 27. The Star Theater, Mohawk and Genesee, Buffalo, New York. Vander's mind began to race. Today was the 26th. He looked up at the clock before him and then at the large board to one side of the hall. That's when he spotted it—the last train of the day to depart for New York City was in ten minutes.

"I've got to go!" Vander leapt up from the pew and gathered his satchel of belongings. He turned to Timmy for a moment who was speechless.

"Thank you, Timmy!" Vander paused awkwardly, then in a flash, he raced to the kiosk to exchange his ticket.

Tomorrow was the 27th. The overnight from Atlanta to New York would hopefully arrive with enough time to make a connection to Buffalo. He had to make it in time!

Vander nimbly passed through the crowds until he disappeared amongst the last of the late day travelers. He didn't look back at the little man. He was too far gone to see the tears running down Timmy's china doll cheeks.

CHAPTER THIRTEEN

The bite of the frosty, fall air of Buffalo, New York, made Vander shiver as he set out on foot from the train station to Mohawk and Genesee. It was early morning, October 28th. Yesterday, he arrived into Grand Central terminal in New York City too late to catch the northbound train to Buffalo. Vander was beside himself with worry. Even though he would be a day late, he prayed fortune was on his side. He was determined to meet the Whirling Sensation in the hopes maybe they would still have an opening.

Taking large, forceful strides toward his destination, Vander smelled the aroma of breakfast bacon and fried eggs wafting onto the sidewalks as horse drawn carts and fancy new motorized trucks made way down the freshly paved Buffalo boulevards en route to their first day's deliveries. The aroma of food made the pangs in Vander's empty stomach all the more acute.

While in the Manhattan train station awaiting his departure for Buffalo, he spent the last of his change on lip paint and eye charcoal. If he was to try out as a female aerialist, he would somehow have to convince the troupe he could pass as a member of the opposite sex. The woman behind the notions counter at the station looked at Vander queerly as he carefully examined the cosmetics, until he spoke up and told her the purchase was a gift for his mother. Save for a kind soul on the train north, who offered Vander a delicious, red apple, Vander Clyde hadn't eaten since he departed Atlanta almost two days before.

Vander knew he was desperate. Without a dime to his name, he didn't want to think what if the position was already filled. God forbid, he would have to wire his mother back in Round Rock, begging for money. What would she say—or for that matter, what would Loving say, with his fowl, condescending grin? Vander would find work in Buffalo no matter what—if not the Whirling Sensation, he would wait on tables or sweep floors, anything to make a buck so he could save enough to head back down to Florida.

In no time, Vander was upon the Star Theater. He tried all the front doors, but they were locked. Taking a few deep breaths, he attempted to calm his feverish mind. Even with the morning sun filling the streets, he realized he was shivering from the brisk fall air, not having a top coat and only dressed in a shirt and trousers. Deciding to head around to the rear of the building, his cold cheeks cracked a slight smile when he saw the loading dock doors were open with the rear of a delivery truck abutting the back entrance. Two men were loading up the truck with wooden crates. Vander eagerly approached them.

"Good morning sirs! I'm looking for the Erford's Whirling Sensation." Vander searched the two worker's eyes for any hint of recognition.

"Who's looking for 'em?" the taller one said, stopping his work.

"Vander Clyde Broadway Loving, sir. I've come to see if they have work. I'm an aerialist by trade."

The man took in the funny sound of Vander's southern accent and smiled.

"Where you from, boy? Kentucky?" he laughed.

"The proud state of Texas, sir," Vander replied. "You ask me, y'all talk kind of funny yourselves!"

The two men laughed. The taller one started, "They were looking for a woman, not a Texan. Sorry bud, but I think you came this way for nothing."

Vander wouldn't accept the answer. He couldn't.

"If you would be so kind, I'd like to talk to them myself."

The other worker spoke up. "They're across the street on Mohawk, with the other acts, at the rooming house. Bernice and Bertha, real nice gals. Now leave us be so we can get back to work."

Vander smiled a bit and gratefully bowed his head in the workers' direction. "Good day, sirs," he replied and then quickly made his way back to Mohawk Avenue.

...

It must have been no more than seven thirty in the morning. Vander hastily tucked his shirt into his trousers, cleared his throat, and then knocked on the door. Already, guests on the third floor of the rooming house were stirring. The water closet down the hall had a short line of unusual looking characters sleepily awaiting their turn at the toilet. Before he even knocked on the worn door with chipped paint and soiled finger print stains, he could hear voices behind the wood. It wasn't English. He wondered if he could even communicate with these people. Then, his fist knocked on the door, almost as if on its own, more eager to get on with it than his own imagination. Vander heard the conversation stop and the loud voice of a woman got closer to the door. The sound of the latch dislodging met his years. The door cracked slightly open. A young woman with a round, full face and dark, bushy eyebrows, slightly shorter than he, stared at Vander seriously.

"Vat do you vant?"

"My name is Vander, Vander Clyde Broadway Loving. I saw the advertisement. I've come for the job."

The cherub-cheeked woman scowled. "No job for man. Need a vooman. Vat, you don't read?"

"But I'm from the circus!" Vander hastily added. "I, I can...."

"Listen, ve need a vooman! Not a man!"

The door slammed in Vander's face. If it was any consolation in his mind, it was that it sounded as if the position wasn't yet filled. Flustered, but refusing to be denied, he knocked again, shouting through the door, "But I can play a woman!"

"Go avay!!"

Vander stood in the dilapidated hallway of the third floor of the boarding house. He was breathing hard. He had to think fast. He looked again at the line to the water closet, only two guests—*Wait! Now, only one!*—waiting to get inside. He hustled to stand in line.

The young aerialist from Round Rock stood in line for what was fifteen minutes, but seemed like an eternity. When the guest before him finally departed the water closet, Vander stepped in and locked the door. The odor in the room was moist and foul, even with the filthy window half-opened. The water closet was equipped with a grimy toilet and a small, white, cast iron sink below a round mirror. A lone light bulb dangling from its exposed wires extended from the water-stained ceiling above the mirror.

Vander tried to calm his shaking hands as he fumbled through his satchel for his face powder. He settled himself and went to work. If the Erfords needed a 'vooman' a 'vooman' they would get!

Fifteen minutes later, Vander studied his finished appearance in the mirror. His face was powdered a soft, luminescent pink with dashes of gentle blush about the cheeks. Lips heart-shaped and painted a full, luscious red. Eye lashes charcoaled for a hint of sophistication. He took the large rag he used to remove his makeup and affixed it above his head in a turban style, which he watched Audrey Fuller do so often with a towel after their performances. He then grabbed the tails of his white shirt and tied them off in a knot mid chest, revealing his midsection which he thought was reminiscent of the costumes of the belly dancers wore who toured with the circus. Vander looked one last time into the mirror. *"We're all actors, son,"* the voice of Bobby Fuller reverberated in his mind, *"we're all putting on a show. People see what they want to see."* Vander giggled to himself staring at his visage. *Erfords, you are about to meet one pretty Alfaretta Sister!*

Vander Alfaretta unlocked the door. There was a line of a few men and women waiting to use the facilities. Their mouths were aghast at the sight of him.

"Good morning, Buffalo!" Vander called out as he flounced by them all, making way down the grimy hallway.

Again, Vander knocked on the door. He heard grumbling in the same foreign language coming from the room behind the door. He heard the door unlatch and saw it swung open.

This time, a tall man with a full mustache and head of blond hair opened the door.

Vander didn't miss a beat. He daintily extended his hand.

"Madame Alfaretta, from Texas," he said in a sweet southern lilt. "I don't believe we've had the pleasure."

The tall man with the bushy mustache burst out laughing! A loud boisterous guffaw!

"Bertha! Bernice! Come! Come here!" the tall man called back into the room.

The two women squeezed next to the big man. Vander could see they were identical, almost indistinguishable twins. The two young women with cherubic faces burst out laughing.

"Vunderful!" one called out with tears in her eyes.

"Dis, ve must have!" the other one said placing her hand on her heaving chest.

"Please," the tall man with the mustache began, "you must come inside."

CHAPTER FOURTEEN

"Your advertisement said nothing about this being an 'iron jaw' act!" Vander protested angrily. He stared at the apparatus before him—a tall mast of metal some twenty feet high was quickly assembled by Johan and his twin sisters Bertha and Bernice on the stage of the empty Star Theater. *This was why no one had taken the job!*

The Erfords were recent German immigrants Vander learned from the eldest of the trio, Johan. He came to the United States from Germany before his sisters. Down on his luck and penniless, he got a job in a vaudeville house in Brooklyn sweeping the floors after the shows. Between cleanings, the young Bavarian watched the acts perform on stage. His favorite were the aerialists. Telling his sisters life was easy in the United States, he entreated the young twins, who were all of nineteen years old, to join him in the new country. Their parents refused to come, but no matter, Johan only needed his sisters for his scheme. With wide eyes, he explained his idea to his sisters. An aerial act like no other. At first his sisters protested, but with the thought of lives shoveling slop for swine back on a small farm, up to their ankles in manure, the girls eagerly attempted to learn as Johan tried to teach them.

Like so many other immigrants, Johan changed their Ehrfurt surname to one more manageable and elegant sounding to his ear, 'Erford'. With the population of the United States growing increasingly wary of Germans since the outbreak of the war in Europe, the simplified moniker also provided the benefit of sounding Anglo enough to pass as a name from the British Isles.

"Vat?" Bertha scowled. On the way from the boarding house back to the Star Theater, Vander learned it was Bertha, the more boisterous of the two twins, who first slammed the door in his face. "It's not so bad!"

From the upper region of the twenty foot tall main mast, three metal prongs, each about ten feet long, emanated from the center—like spokes from a bicycle wheel. They were held into place by connecting wire strung between the prongs. Wire was also affixed to the endpoint of the prongs and strung back above, onto the center mast.

"Ve need to see your mouth," Bernice said as she marched over to Vander and grabbed hold of his head with her very strong hands. "Open up!" she demanded.

Vander was getting exceedingly annoyed by the Erfords, but he complied with her request. Bernice pushed back his lips examining his teeth as if he were a horse.

"Not bad!" she called out to her siblings. "He's young, zees one!"

"Here, put zees in your mouth," Bertha said as she walked over to the two. Johan was adjusting cables hanging from the ends of the poles. Bertha held out a leather mouth piece that looked to be the size of a cow tongue. It was attached to a long wire.

"Wait a minute!" Vander protested. He had taken off his turbaned headpiece, but there was no time to remove his face powder and lip paint when they headed over to the theater from the boarding house. He felt his face flush with anger and anxiety beneath the powder on his cheeks.

"Dis not so bad!" Bertha added.

Vander was not pleased with her pushy demeanor.

"I'm not putting that in my mouth and hanging from that pole!"

Bertha and Bernice both scowled in identical fashion. Their faces were round and cherubic, but both displayed a stern seriousness.

"Ven was da vast time you got a goot supper?" Bertha asked, her brown eyes looking intently at Vander's. "Ve know vat it's like to struggle. I can see dis in your eyes too. You vant the job, dis is vat ve do."

Vander Clyde swallowed hard. He looked at Bertha and then Bernice. He felt the pangs of hunger in his stomach. Very few aerialists ever attempted the iron jaw. It was dangerous. It took tremendous strength—clenching one's teeth onto a leather strap attached from a rope—one's entire weight plus centrifugal force relying only on the jaw muscles, swinging about the stage, sometimes even over the audience.

"What happened to the other Erford in your act?" He wondered if he again was replacing another performer who met her untimely demise. "Did she fall?"

"Ya, ya! She fall!" Bernice answered as she started to laugh.

Vander was taken aback by the expression on her face.

"Relax!" Johan called out as he approached the three. "Olga, our cousin—she fell in love! She got married, and then the baby started to come…"

"She got fat!" Bertha said. "No one vants a fat, pregnant vooman hanging from dis!" She gestured to the now ready apparatus behind her.

"Olga lives in New York City now, mit her husband," Bernice added.

"Here, open up!" Bertha demanded. "Ve show you how to do it. Dis not so bad. Den we go get something to eat."

"I want twenty a week, starting today. Twenty a week."

"We have to train you first. Besides, we don't know if you're strong enough," Johan said stroking the ends of his thick mustache.

"I train quickly and I'm plenty strong. Twenty a week, starting today."

The two women stared at their older brother to see how he would respond.

"Fifteen. We are taking a great risk you can even do this."

"Twenty. If I'm unable to do it, I'll leave you today and that will be that." Vander knew if he wanted to be successful in this business, he would no longer be the kid from Round Rock. He would have to claim what he deserved.

Johan sighed, "Twenty, but you have to do your own costumes. I will not pay for them."

"Deal!" Vander said enthusiastically as he held forth his hand for Johan to shake. As the two did so, Vander felt the strength of the strapping Johan, stronger than even Samuel Loving's grasp, stronger than his own.

"Now, ve need you to put dis in your mouth," Bertha said seriously.

Vander took the leather tongue and put in his mouth.

"You must relax your body," Bernice added. "Relax your shoulders, your back. Dis is how you do it. Only use de muscles in your jaw—everything else must relax."

Bertha and Bernice walked back to the tall mast with the three spokes emanating from the top. They each grabbed a rope hanging from one of the spokes. They wrapped the rope about their arms and held it secure so they could counterbalance the weight Vander was about to put on the apparatus as he learned to hang from his own tether.

"I'm pulling the line up, so the slack will be tightened," Johan explained. "Keep clenching the strap. I shan't lift you yet off the ground, but I want you to feel your weight."

As Johan tightened the rope, Vander felt the force of his weight transfer from his feet up to his clenched teeth.

"Relax!" Bertha shouted out. "Your shoulders—dey are too tense!"

Vander told himself to calm down. He slowly released his shoulder muscles. In the moment, he surely thought his head was going to be ripped off his neck!

"Stay calm!" Bernice encouraged.

"I'm going to take you up just a bit. So the tips of your toes are on the ground. Lean back, relax your muscles," Johan said. "If you need me to release the line, tug on your shirt."

Vander felt more pressure in his mouth. Tipping his head back, he bit down hard. He could feel his body rise, so now, he was only on the tips of his toes, like a ballerina on point. In an instant, thoughts of his mother, Loving, and Rose filled his mind. More images came to him—Bobby Fuller's sweaty face, chomping on his cigar shaking his head, Audrey Fuller, the Alfaretta sister and her beautiful eyes studying his every move, even Timmy, lasciviously catching a stolen glance. Then, Vander thought of her—the woman high up in the big top, the one he witnessed with his mother so many years ago—the way she walked on wire doing her dainty little fairy dance, like she was a butterfly gently with fluttering wings on the stamen of a milkweed.

"Remember to tug on your shirt if you want me to stop," Johan called out. "I am now going to lift you six inches off the ground."

The pulling from the rope was excruciating in Vander's mouth, but he continued to clench this teeth. He felt the tips of his toes leave the stage floor. Now, all that kept him secure were the muscles of his jaw.

"Relax, Vander," Bernice coached.

"Goot," Bertha encouraged, "Very goot!"

"Now, gently, we are going to walk in a circle, one time around," Johan continued. "Grab your shirt if you need and I will release you. Whatever you do, do not let go with your mouth."

Vander closed his eyes and thought of the woman high up in the big top on the wire, delicate and light. He started to feel his body begin to move. He was flying! Tentative for sure, but the thrill was there. Vander felt a flush of freedom as he gently moved in a circle—one lap around the tall central mast hanging from a rope only by the sheer strength of the muscles in his jaw.

"Very good, Vander!" Johan called out. "I am going to start to lower you. That is good for now."

Vander felt the tips of his toes meet the ground. Gently he felt the weight of his body set onto the balls of his feet until all his weight rested on them and the rope affixed to the leather strap in his mouth was slack.

Vander took the piece from his mouth. He looked at the three Erfords and smiled, "Let's do it again!"

CHAPTER FIFTEEN

Vander stood nervously next to Bernice and Bertha from one of the stage wings at the Star Theater in Buffalo, New York. Johan was next to the tall-masted swinging apparatus preparing to roll it onto the stage. It had only been a few days since they all first met. Vander knew the Erfords had to get the show on the road lest they lose their spot in the vaudeville troupe. The act was simplified so Vander's mouth and jaw muscles could strengthen, but it was still something to see, he had to admit.

There was a full length mirror next to the trio and Vander gave his costume one last look. Each of the three, Bertha, Bernice, and Vander were sheathed in flamboyant costumes of shiny, flouncy silver lamé adorned with ropes of fake pearls about the waist and across their busts. All were made up identically. With their curly top platinum blond wigs, each festooned with a headband of more fake pearls, as well as their crimson painted, heart-shaped lips and powdered faces, the three could easily pass as triplets and that was the look Johan wanted them to have.

Pauline's Pugnacious Pooches were about to finish their routine and the Erford's Whirling Sensation readied to take the stage, when Johan hurriedly came up to Vander.

"We forgot a name! You must have a name! The announcer needs it!"

Vander thought of the two sisters, Bertha and Bernice. Something more exotic, more French sounding would be perfect.

"I am Barbette," Vander finally said.

Johan looked at Vander expressionless for a moment and then smiled.

"Perfect! I shall tell the announcer right away!"

Vander Clyde Broadway Loving, a.k.a. Barbette, went over the routine one more time in his imagination. Then, he cleared his mind, thinking of himself as a beautiful flowing creature of the air.

The announcer's voice filled the theater, "Would you welcome please, Bertha, Bernice, and Barbette—the magnificent—Erford's Whirling Sensation!

CHAPTER SIXTEEN

"Where's my face powder?" Vander demanded as he looked atop the cramped and cluttered vanity table. The summer air of 1918 was stifling in the dressing room of the Albany Majestic Theater. The two Erford twins and Vander encamped at one end of the room, fumbling over one another as they removed their butterfly costumes and makeup. After a solid week of playing the Majestic with one more week booked, Vander was happy to be in town for the duration.

No one answered him.

"You ladies are slobs!" he scowled at Bertha and Bernice. "If you had half the professionalism of a circus clown, we would be out of here in half the time!"

"Here it is," Bernice muttered. She handed the powder to Vander. Then, in one grand gesture, she dragged her hand across the table before her, scooping all of her cosmetics into an oversized needlepointed bag.

Vander grimaced. "Y'all! Could we have a modicum of civility back stage, or must we always act like a band of Gypsies?"

"Ve, *VE*, are doing just fine Vander! Dear me! You are such a czarina!" Bertha shook her head. She was slightly tidier than Bernice, but Vander watched her pack her makeup kit and sighed loudly.

"Vat?" Bertha looked at Vander as she quickly brushed her hair.

"You both would be so much lovelier with just one ounce of refinement, you know that? Once a pig farmer, always a pig farmer, I suppose."

"Get out!" Bertha scowled. "Vander you are making me insane!"

At that moment, Johan made way to where his sisters and Vander were packing up.

"Vander, this is yours." Johan handed Vander Clyde his weekly pay.

"Thank you, Johan," Vander said taking the money, quickly counted it and putting it into his tidy billfold. He turned to Bertha and Bernice.

"Did you notice ladies, when I accepted the wages for my services I made eye contact with the gentleman and thanked him? That, my dear ladies, is refinement!"

"Oh brother!" Bernice sighed.

"Get out!" Bertha demanded. "You are making me insane!"

Vander smiled and slightly bowed, "Good evening ladies!"

"Get out, czarina!" Bertha said tossing her platinum blond wig at him.

Vander chuckled and turned around.

He started to make way past the other performers in the cramped dressing room, carrying his custom-made makeup box in one hand and derby hat in the other.

"Vander—wait!" Johan called. Shirtless and wearing only his performance tights, he came up to Vander. He lowered his voice as he stood inches from the aerialist.

"You want to come? I know this place…the ladies…they know how to keep a man happy…"

Vander looked into Johan's twinkling blue eyes, so youthful, so strikingly German.

"Vat are you two talking about?" Bertha demanded as she called after the two.

"Mind your own business!" Johan shot back at his sister.

"How about it—see the sights of Albany?"

Vander looked down at the ground and got quiet for a moment.

"No, Johan, not tonight. I'm going for a very long walk. Enjoy yourself."

"Okay, but should you change your mind one day, let me know. You're a good looking man, Vander! Women find you attractive." Johan put his powerful arm around Vander's shoulder and turned his head and called back to his sisters. "Don't the ladies find Vander attractive?"

"Ya! If you fancy the Queen of Sheba!" Bertha shouted back.

They all laughed.

"Have a good night," Vander said as Johan lifted his arm from Vander's shoulder.

"You too, Vander Clyde."

. . .

Vander headed out the blackened, back alley and stopped at the corner. The rooming house they were staying in was down the street to the left. But tonight, he didn't want to go straight back. Vander wanted to take in the night air which was still warm despite a recent evening shower. He started to do what window shopping he could along Albany's busiest streets, strolling by shop windows only illuminated by street lamps. It was past midnight, most of Albany had turned in for the evening. An occasional automobile passed him by, the cars' wheels splashing into errant puddles along the boulevards, but otherwise, the streets were empty and still.

Then he heard it.

"Barbette!"

He turned to look behind him thinking it must be Johan, coming after him one last time, entreating him to come along on his nocturnal dalliance. However, when Vander turned, all he saw was a finely dressed man making his way up the street. Even from the distance, Vander could tell it was not Johan, because Johan did not own such custom-tailored attire as this man was wearing.

In a moment's hesitation, Vander contemplated running, but surely no street thug would be so well turned out as this young gent appeared to be.

As the man came forward, Vander could see he was dressed in an evening tuxedo and fine top hat, all exceedingly well cut. He was about five foot ten. His face was clean shaven and Vander could tell from the clip of the raven black hair around his ears, he recently received the services of a barber. The man smiled at him as he extended his hand. He was older than Vander, twenty-six perhaps. When he smiled, his well-proportioned face was rakishly handsome—straight teeth, clear, brown eyes, and a confident, but not too substantial nose.

"Please forgive the crudity of my calling about after you, but it was the only way. Monty is my name, Montgomery Pearson from New York."

Vander looked at the extended hand of the elegant young man.

"Vander, Vander Clyde Broadway Loving, from Round Rock, Texas, that is," Vander replied in his melodic, soft twang as he extended his hand to shake Monty's.

"Indeed. I hope you don't find me forward, but I would very much enjoy an evening stroll with you."

Vander considered his options of walking alone on the lonely streets of Albany or in the company of Monty Pearson. He chose the stroll with Monty.

The two set off together down the desolate Albany streets which were silent excepting for the occasional brawls of feral alley cats.

"How did you know I was Barbette?" Vander asked. He took great pride in the fact when he was made up, no one imagined he was a man. He was virtually indistinguishable from Bertha and Bernice. To think a customer discovered his was a man proved most dissettling to Vander.

"Let's just say I am a great student of the human form," Monty reported. "I saw your act Thursday night, and something piqued me about your performance. It was different from the other two women. You were more delicate. Please, take no offense at my suggestion, but the other two, their performance, well, let us just say it isn't quite so refined."

Vander smiled slightly. He felt vindicated his admonitions to the Erford sisters had some validity.

"And then of course, it is the Adam's apple," Monty said gesturing to his throat. "No woman has an Adam's apple. I noticed yours upon my returning Friday night to witness again your magnificent performance, which by then I realized was quite more startling than I had at first imagined."

"Are you put off that I'm not a woman?" Vander asked, curious this man surmised the lovely Erford sister, Barbette, who so engaged the audience, was in reality a gent such as he.

They continued their stroll down the empty streets illuminated by the glow of tall iron street lamps casting glassy reflections onto the still-wet sidewalks.

"To the contrary, I find it quite tantalizing. That is why I had to return once again, tonight, to see you, for a third time."

Vander smiled to himself.

"Forgive me if you think it too queer, but last night I watched all the performers depart back stage, from a distance, after the show. As I said, I am a student of the human form.

While I looked upon all the performers exiting the theater, I thought *you* were Barbette, but I wasn't quite sure enough. But tonight, I can see it plain as day."

"You can?" While it was all quite odd, Vander enjoyed this discussion, because he never heard before, from anyone, how his act was being perceived. Not to mention, there was a certain buoyant energy about Monty Pearson which Vander found captivating.

"Yes! Most definitively. It's not only your overall proportions, your Adam's apple, but also the line of your nose. It is quite elegant, really. Very distinguishable."

Vander reached to touch his nose. He smiled, pleasantly flattered by Montgomery Pearson's attentions.

"The fact is, you are an equally handsome young gent! It is really quite uncanny really…and if you will forgive my saying, quite beautiful."

Vander turned toward Monty Pearson and smiled.

"That's the most generous thing anyone has dared say to me. Thank you, sir. You're very much forgiven for such flattery."

The two walked together for a while, neither saying a word.

Monty cleared his throat.

"I hope I am not being too forward, but might I assume you may appreciate the human form as much as I?"

Vander felt his heart beating in his chest. He thought about how he wanted to respond.

"Why yes, Mister Pearson, I do appreciate the human form very much. Female and…and if you will forgive me…" Vander swallowed hard, "the male form as well."

Montgomery Pearson's expression lightened at Vander's reply.

"I am a man of great discretion," he said quietly so his voice would not carry down the street.

Vander turned his head to look into Monty's eyes. His voice lowered to just above a hush.

"As am I."

Montgomery Pearson searched the shiny, rain-slicked streets. Not a soul was stirring at this hour.

"I do believe I lost a glove. Yes, I had two and now I only have one. Of course! I recall I came from down the alley—a shortcut really. Might you be so kind, Mister Loving to accompany me so we might find my glove?"

Vander looked around the streets once more and up the sides of the facing buildings. The windows were all blackened. No one was awake.

"But of course!"

The two silently made way down the darkened alley, flanked by stone and brick five storey buildings. The pavers below their feet were older and more uneven than the ones on the streets in front of the edifices. Amidst the darkened shadows, the gentleman and the aerialist found an inlet revealing a small loading bay. In the blackness of the grimy alley, with a sweep of enticement, Vander felt Monty's lips upon his. Monty confidently held onto Vander's toned shoulders as their bodies joined. Vader took in the elegant aroma of this gentleman, growing in excitement as Monty sought more. He let Monty lustily ply him with affections, thrilled by every sensation he was experiencing. The exultation built in intensity, increasing ever more so. Then the release—Vander's body shuddered as he relinquished control. He was thrilled by the encounter.

That's when they both heard it. A nearby trash can falling over and crashing to the ground. Then, a man's voice called out.

"Hey, what's going on over there?"

Monty finished wiping his mouth with his kerchief. His frightened eyes met Vander's. And then he disappeared! Vander couldn't make out where Monty's figure went, only hearing his expensive shoes running the opposite direction from where the voice came.

Instinctively, Vander did the same, running as fast as he could. He was no longer a twenty year old man, but he was fourteen again, feeling the sting of rocks thrown at his head. He ran. He ran as fast as he could. This time, he would not be caught!

Vander raced down block after block, until, he finally stopped. His frightened eyes looked around him—yet the streets were completely empty. Vander caught his breath, knowing he escaped this time for sure! Then, when he came to his senses, he thought about Montgomery Pearson. One moment in his life—the next he was gone! The pleasure he felt was now clouded over in guilt. Still scanning the streets for Monty or any human soul, he decided to head back to the boarding house, alone.

CHAPTER SEVENTEEN

The passenger car of the train was nearly empty on the overnight from Dayton to Toledo. The Erfords and Vander boarded the train sometime after one in the morning. The other acts in their vaudeville troupe booked Pullman sleeper bunks for the journey, but the frugal Erfords always chose to ride coach. The only other soul in their darkened car was a plain-looking, young mother who sat at the opposite end of the car discretely nursing her infant. The seats of the car faced each other, so when the train passed through small towns with electric lights, Vander caught flashes of the woman's face as the lights of the town swiftly illuminated the interior of the coach. Vander could see the woman was young, maybe not even as old as he. What was her story, he wondered. There was a desperation, a sad desperation to her eyes which reminded him so much of his own mother's eyes.

Already it was 1919. Where had time gone? Vander Clyde Loving was almost twenty-one years old. Occasionally, he sent his mother some funds he managed to save while being on the road with the Erfords, but there always seemed to be expenses, so what he did manage to hold on to would only be in his pocket for a day or two. Vander never heard from his mother or Rose. He knew it would be virtually impossible to track him since he never disclosed where he was going or the nature of his act. He would only tell his mother that he was okay and she need not worry. Sometimes, he wondered if the funds he sent her ever really made it into her hands, or would Samuel Loving open the posts? Would Loving use the money for his degenerate behavior? In his mind, Vander would even imagine his mother finally having had enough and throwing Loving's sorry soul out the door.

And Rose? No doubt by now she met her first love. Would she think back on her girlish fancying of Vander with nostalgic amusement? What would she surmise of him now, if she saw him in one of his shows? Her wildflower was now a beautiful woman, whirling about, high over the stage, another lovely Erford sister. Would Rose think of him as degenerate? Would all the good feelings she had for him evaporate like dew on morning grass?

The railcar was warm that night. With many of the windows of the passenger car open, Vander could smell the earth about him. Cornfields and cattle pastures had certain sweet aromas in the summertime. He could make them out as the train rolled through the moonlit fields onto their Toledo destination. He looked behind him and could see Bertha and Bernice were already curled up together, resting their heads on each other's shoulders, gently swaying back and forth as the train rolled down the rails. Johan sat across the aisle from them, several rows back. His face was illuminated by the tip of his lit cigar. Their eyes met for a moment and then Vander turned his head forward. He took his satchel and pushed it up by his shoulder alongside the casement for the open window, trying to find a comfortable way to rest his head, but the breeze blowing into the car was too random to be peaceful—one moment barely a wisp of air entered the car and the next a great whoosh blasted in his face.

Johan moved to sit beside him. He pulled out another cigar and offered it to Vander. Vander shook him off, but sat upright.

"It's a lonely night," Johan said quietly. He was a handsome man, for sure, Vander always thought. Blonde hair, broad shoulders, mustache always well waxed. A true Bavarian specimen in Vander's eyes.

"Yes," Vander replied. He was not sure he even wanted to engage Johan—he was so totally comfortable in his own thoughts.

"We will be in Toledo by morning."

Johan worked hard at his pronunciation, trying to sound as American as possible, but there was still a slight, distinctly German inflection to his words.

"Yes."

"How is your mouth?" Johan asked as he turned his head and looked seriously at Vander.

"It's fine." He was lying. Vander spit out another tooth between shows in Dayton. He could feel his teeth shifting in his mouth, but he didn't want to complain. He didn't want anyone to know the pain he was in when he bit down onto the leather strap swinging from the rope.

"When we get to Toledo, we need to get you to a dentist."

"Dentists cost money, and we both know, neither one of us has any."

"It's not good, these mouth problems. It jeopardizes the act."

"Johan, I'm fine!" Vander looked up and could see the young mother's eyes down at the other end of the rail car meeting his.

"I worry about you," Johan sighed and he took another puff from his cigar. "I feel like an older brother to you, you know that? I feel like I have to protect you like my other sisters."

Johan caught himself and winced.

"Sorry, I didn't mean to call you that."

"It's okay."

"You don't care, do you, what people think?"

"Of course I care what people think. Everyone cares what other people think, even when they say they don't."

The two were silent for a moment.

"You never fancy my sisters. Not once. A lot of the other performers do. When I ask you to come with me on the town, you brush me off. You're a good looking gent, Vander. A handsome one at that. A lot of girls would come your way if you wanted. Even Bertha or Bernice…"

"Johan," Vander interrupted. He wanted to explain what was in his heart, but he didn't know how. He didn't know if he would be accepted or if Johan would kick him out. "Johan, you can think of me as one of your sisters. It's okay."

Johan's eyes met Vander's for a moment as the two studied each other. There was a flash of knowing in Johan's eyes.

"I will protect you. You are a good person, Vander Clyde. A good person indeed. I will protect you. You have my word."

Vander managed a small smile. It was all he needed to hear. He pushed his satchel up to the window railing and rested his head on the bag. It no longer mattered whether the wind blew hard or hardly at all, he slept well that night on the way to Toledo.

CHAPTER EIGHTEEN

Vander clenched hard onto the leather mouthpiece. The pain in his jaw was so excruciating, tears flowed down his powdered cheeks as the three Erford sisters hung from the tall mast center stage, whirling overhead at a great speed. It was the last show of the day, the last show of the week in Toledo. Tonight, they would head out again on the rails up to Columbus. Vander would finally have twenty-four hours to rest his mouth. But the force of the whirling was too much for him. He felt his blond wig, which he absentmindedly affixed to his head amidst coping with the throbbing pain in his mouth, start to feel as if it was going to give way. In the time he performed with the Erfords, he never signaled to Johan he was in distress. He never had problems with his costume or wig. He was too much of a professional. But tonight, he just couldn't bear it any longer! He pounded his fist on his chest. Johan immediately spotted it and slowed the spinning of the apparatus, easing the three back down onto the painted wooden floor of the stage.

Vander's platinum blonde wig with its interwoven pearl headband felt as if it was going to fly off when he finally landed. In retrospect, he's not sure why he did it. Was it delirium from the pain he was feeling? Frustration? He was never quite sure. But in the moment as the other two girls disengaged from the hanging apparatus, Vander stepped forward into the floodlights at the foot of the stage. There, alone, he looked at the crowd as they applauded. Then, he removed his wig! Gasps were heard throughout the vaudeville hall. A hush fell over the crowd. A worried Johan frowned and tried to hustle his sisters up to the floodlights so they all could take a bow and exit as quickly as possible.

But then, Johan heard the roar. The crowd spontaneously erupted in thunderous applause! Vander mugged for the audience, flexing his toned muscles, posing the way he had seen Sampson the Man of Iron do when he toured with the circus. Vander smiled broadly as the Erfords came to him for a bow amidst the warm approval of the audience. And just as quickly as he became a man, he transformed again, back into the demeanor of a woman—a sweet southern debutant! He beveled his body and gave the audience a coquettish glance and blew them a kiss. The crowd laughed and loved it! The Erfords and Vander all bowed to great applause. Vander skipped off the stage with Bertha and Bernice, only, just before he was to go behind the curtain, he changed his demeanor one last time, become a masculine man, with one last flexed muscle pose. The crowd roared again— and then Vander skipped off behind the curtain.

Bertha Erford was furious! Back stage, she hurled every German cuss word she could muster at Vander as she dragged him by the ear out the back door of the theatre and into the alley. Vander was delirious. He spit blood onto the paving stones as the smell of rotting food from a nearby trash can filled his nostrils. Bertha pushed Vander against the brick wall with all her might as she continued to curse at him in German, spit flying from her cherubic lips.

The back door to the theatre swung open again. This time Johan and Bernice came storming out. Johan was yelling bloody murder in German, only it wasn't at Vander—it was as his sister!

"Anhalten! Anhalten! Stop! Leave him alone!" Johan scolded Bertha.

Everyone was breathing hard. They were sweated and tired. Everyone turned to Johan to see what he would do next.

He cracked a smile—a big, toothsome Bavarian grin! "Vander, that was brilliant!"

Johan turned to his sisters, "Did you hear that? Never have we had such applause!"

"It vas an insult!" Bertha said stomping her foot. She was still fuming. "Ve vork so hard mit dis one! And he *ruins* our show!"

Johan protested, "He did not ruin the show, Bertha! Come on! It was theater! It was performance! We will keep it in the act every night! We will be closing the first half in a week's time!"

"I vill not! I vill not have it!" Bertha turned to her brother shouting. "If you permit it, I vill not go on!"

"Bertha! Calm down!" Johan admonished. He turned to his other sister, "Bernice—you saw it—the way the audience reacted. This is what we have been looking for! All the while I thought it was more stunts, but this—this is something new!"

Bertha turned to her twin sister, her thick brow in a furious scowl. "Bernice, you tell him! Ve vill not go on mit dis!"

Bernice looked at her two siblings not sure what to say. Then Vander spoke up.

"You don't have to answer, Bernice," he said. He spit more blood onto the cobbles of the back alley. "I can't go on. I can't do it anymore. My mouth. It's too much."

Johan slammed his palm against the brick exterior of the theatre.

"I told you we needed to get you to a doctor! I told you!"

"I'm sorry, Johan!" Vander said earnestly. He looked at Bernice and then back at Bertha.

"I didn't mean to upset you, Bertha! I don't know what came over me, really. Maybe it was the pain. But I know one thing, I can no longer be Barbette Erford."

Johan ran his hand through his thick, blond hair. "Vander, you don't know what you are saying! We are all tired..."

"I'm tired, for sure, but I know I can't go on."

"If you just see a doctor—he can fix your teeth! He can extract them—then everything will be fine!"

"No, it isn't just my teeth, Johan. Did you ever know inside you had more? You had more to offer—that this wasn't enough?"

Johan kicked the ground with his foot. The cool fall air blew down the alley.

"You are asking a man who is wearing stockings and a funny costume if he has more to offer? Vander, I didn't leave my country, leave a farm where I shoveled shit, to come to America for nothing! Sometimes I think you are so much in your head—you don't see good people around you who truly know who you are and care for you!"

Vander bit down hard on his lip. He looked straight at Johan.

"This is my last show."

"Vander!...I'm pleading!...Don't go!"

"It's for the best. Thank y'all for everything. Now I need to take off these things so the next girl can use them."

Vander went to the theatre door and opened it. He made way back to the dressing room and began to remove his costume.

"Do you vant us to stop him?" Bertha asked her elder brother.

"No, no..." Johan said distantly. "Let him go."

CHAPTER NINETEEN

JULY, 1919

"Mister Pearson, please, Mister Montgomery Pearson," Vander Clyde said while shoving his hands in a newly cut, black, wool suit so the bank teller he was speaking to would not see them tremble. Vander tried to puff himself up, to play the part and not be intimidated. But standing beneath the immense, ornate glass dome of the Greco-Roman lobby of the JP Morgan Bank at 23 Wall Street in lower Manhattan, attempting to pass himself as a member of the upper class, overwhelmed the young Texan from Round Rock.

Just several days ago, he was in Ohio, suffering on the tethered line, hanging by his teeth, pretending to be a delicate butterfly fluttering overhead on stage. Somehow that wasn't nearly as intimidating as what he was now attempting to do.

When he left the Erfords, gathering his humble belongings, he headed to the rail depot, alone, yet again. Vander contemplated heading south to Sarasota, where he could meet up in six months' time with other acrobats and aerialists who wintered there.

But then, he conceived another idea. It was a spectacular notion! He guessed it had been lurking back there behind his duties and obligations as a performer. Now he was free of the Erfords, the concept came out from the shadows and presented itself in the light of his thinking. He second-guessed himself. Was it desperation of an overly-tired mind in extreme pain? Vander had to admit to himself it quite possibly was. Yet, what did it really matter?

Vander contemplated the reality of his situation. How to get from here—sitting in a shabby rail depot with scant funds—to there, realizing the dream erupting within his imagination. That was when he remembered Monty Pearson. Monty said he was from New York. Vander decided to head to Manhattan. Monty was enthralled by his act. If Vander could just meet with Monty, secure some funding, then his vision could be realized!

On the train from Ohio to Manhattan, Vander's thoughts raced. How would he find Monty Pearson? Walking the fashionable streets of New York hoping for a chance encounter seemed ridiculous. His mind was still preoccupied by this dilemma when he departed his rail car in the bustling Grand Central Terminal in the heart of New York.

It was midday and the station was filled with well-dressed men in dark wool suits and derby hats moving purposefully by him. They were a sea of Monty Pearsons! Vander caught his sad reflection in the glazed window of an arcade shop along one wall of the terminal. With his worn trousers and tattered sleeve cuffs, not to mention barely stitched together shoes, he appeared no more impressive than an errand boy. If he met Monty again, he would have to look like one of these gents who passed him by. If he could just get some cloth, he knew he would be able to work up a very fine suit for himself.

In that instant, the goddess of fate reached down from the heavens and provided him with the clue he desired. Out of the corner of his eye—such a chance happening—something caught his attention in the nearby news stand, only a pace away. The name 'Pearson' in bold letters on the front page of a financial record. Vander moved to the rack of newsprint. He eagerly reached for the paper.

"Five cents," the man behind the counter said leering at him.

"I just need to see one item," Vander stammered.

"Yeah, I'm sure you do."

The man grabbed at the paper from behind the counter, but Vander was too fast. His eyes raced to read. "Standard Oil Inks Deal with JP Morgan: Montgomery Pearson Credited." The headline was all he needed!

"Five cents!" the man behind the counter demanded.

"You can take your lousy paper," Vander scowled as thrust the paper back at the man and started to walk away. "Learn some manners while you're at it!"

Vander had been to New York several times with the Erfords. He knew his way about the streets. He set himself up in a shabby boarding house he stayed at before. Then, without hesitation, he trudged down to the garment district to purchase some dark, wool fabric, white shirt cloth and black silk for a tie. Vander shopped there before, securing shiny silver lamé fabric for the costumes he worked up for the Erfords. He knew the material he was purchasing would take up almost all of the meager funds he saved.

The woman who Vander was boarding with had a pedal-pump, Singer sewing machine she lent him once before to stich the costumes. She would lend it to him again, he was sure. While working with her sewing equipment, Vander would take the woman's scissors and trim up his hair—a crisp cut about the ears, just like Monty's!

It only took him a couple of days to complete his tasks. When he finished, he set off for 23 Wall Street, JP Morgan's temple to banking in the heart of the Financial District. There, he would see if his plan would come off as he imagined.

As he set out on foot traversing the avenues of Manhattan, he caught glimpses of his newly turned out self in the reflections on storefront windows. There were flaws to his appearance for sure. He had no money for a proper hat. And his shoes. He could not possibly afford new leather shoes. He polished and restitched his own shoes the best he could, but they were still a dead giveaway to his ruse. Vander figured if he could move through the bank quickly enough, no one would notice.

He steadied himself as he stood across the corner from the bank on Wall Street, looking at its noble classical architecture, massively thick walls, and deep-set square windows. People who entered and exited the corner bronze entrance doors looked successful and prominent. Vander imagined Montgomery Pearson's refined, yet buoyant personality. He surmised if he only could somehow imitate that refinement, become just like Monty, as it were, his scheme would have a chance.

Vander permitted the crisply uniformed doorman to open the door for him as he entered the House of Morgan. He was aghast at the opulent elegance of the interior of the bank, how its coffered ceilings soared. He admired the fine plaster, rich woods, and the hushed seriousness of everyone within. As was his plan, he swiftly and confidently strode through the lobby until he arrived at the burled walnut counter where several tellers were stationed. He presented himself to one of the tellers who he thought possessed the kindest visage.

"Good afternoon," Vander began graciously.

"Good afternoon, sir," the teller said. The man was probably in his mid-thirties. His face was welcoming, yet wise.

"I was wondering if you could help me."

"I will do my best, sir."

Vander could tell the man was already assessing his intentions. He cleared his throat.

"I would like to speak with Mister Pearson, Mister Montgomery Pearson."

"Is he expecting you, sir?"

For whatever reason, Vander never rehearsed the answer to this question in his mind. Call it instinct, or gamble, but Vander answered without hesitation.

"Of course."

"Very good."

"Would you please tell him Mister Vander Barbette that is, Mister Vander Barbette of Erford Holdings is here to see him?"

"Of course sir," the man responded. He left his teller's counter and disappeared behind some partitions.

A few moments later, the teller returned, with Montgomery Pearson striding beside him, impeccably groomed.

"Mister Barbette," he said as he passed through the Corinthian-columned passage which flanked the tellers' counter. "So good to see you!" Montgomery Pearson eagerly shook Vander's sweaty palm.

"Please, won't you join me?" Pearson gestured for Vander to pass through the columned portal to the inner sanctum of the House of Morgan. Monty turned to the teller, "Please, we're not to be disturbed."

Montgomery Pearson silently led Vander past clerks at immaculate wooden desks busily thumping away on shiny black typewriters until the two reached the back wall. There, an elevator operator tipped the brim of his red cap and slid open the bronze relief door for the two men. Vander was thrilled to be in an elevator—the first chance he had to ride in such a thing! He tried not to show his wonderment as the two stood silently together, side by side in the confined space which was covered in tiger maple veneer and golden scrolled trim. Vander caught the elevator operator appraising him, including, his tired shoes, but it did not matter what the elevator man thought. Vander had his audience with Monty!

After they exited the elevator to the topmost floor to walk down a long hall, the two arrived at the door to Monty's private office.

"Please, after you," Pearson smiled.

Vander entered the office. It was like the quarters of a king's palace. Massive fireplace to one side, finely woven tapestries affixed to the walls and a hand-carved mahogany desk before them.

Once inside the room, Monty's demeanor changed. He did not offer a chair to Vander. Instead, Monty produced a golden cigarette case from his coat pocket and took out a smoke. He went to his beautiful hand-carved, wood desk and reached for a box containing matches and lit the fag. Then, Monty inhaled deeply. He exhaled.

"What is the meaning of this?" he asked as he turned to Vander, staring at him intently.

Vander was taken aback by the change in Monty's demeanor. He was speechless.

"If you came to extort me, I shall tell you now, I will ruin you. I shall have you thrown in jail so you will never see the light of day."

Monty took another drag from his cigarette.

"Oh, please no!" Vander pleaded. "Monty, you have it all wrong! I've come to do nothing of the sort!"

"You've entered into my place of business. I thought you were a man of discretion!"

"I am! I had no other way! It was a miracle to even find you! I merely came here to get your help." Vander didn't want the words to come out but they just did, "Monty, I'm desperate! If you could just listen to me, just for a moment…"

The banker turned from Vander Clyde and walked over to one of the massive windows and stared out onto the surging traffic below.

Vander did not hesitate.

"I need a loan."

"Is that what they are calling extortion these days?"

"Please! If you would just let me speak!"

Monty looked at Vander and took a long sigh.

"Very well," he responded. "Have a seat."

He gestured for Vander to sit in one of the barrel armchairs whose burgundy leather was lined with thick, brass tacks. As Vander sat, Monty moved to his own substantial leather arm chair behind the ornate, polished desk.

Vander felt insecure about what he was to say, but proceeded anyway.

"I left the Erfords to create my own act. It will be something different and unique. No one has quite seen it before. I want to make something beautiful, you see. I want to be like an angel that's come down from the heavens...."

Vander took a deep breath as he looked at Monty's blank expression. He knew he was sounding ludicrous. "It will be a performance like no one has witnessed before, part on the tight rope and a part on the trapeze. And maybe even the rings. So beautiful, like a vision, a dream. It will be a sensation!"

Then there was silence between them. Monty looked stoically at Vander who was aching for some sort of response from the gentleman banker. Monty then cast his eyes downward.

"I don't invest in Broadway and I would certainly never think to invest in vaudeville."

Vander could not be stopped.

"Oh, it isn't much money, not for the likes of a man like you. And it would be a loan. We could work out the terms. Only two hundred dollars. You see, I need money so I can make costumes. I need to create a wire and make a proper trapeze. You have no idea how foolish I feel coming to you to ask for it, but I couldn't return home. I haven't been able to save enough. I used the last ten dollars to my name to make this suit up to meet you. It was all I had."

Monty took one final drag from his cigarette and extinguished the butt in a crystal bowl on his desk. He leaned forward.

"Vander, I'm a husband and a father. My position at Morgan grows in importance every day. I can't have the likes of you sullying my reputation."

"I'm here to do no such thing!"

Monty waived him off.

"If it's funds you wish, I have a counter proposal. I will pay you two hundred, plus two hundred more if we reach a gentleman's agreement. The agreement is you are never to call on me again, never here nor at my home. If you see me in public, you are not to acknowledge me in any way, for if you do, I will come after you, Vander. I will. I have considerable resources at my disposal to destroy you and mark my words I will use them if necessary. That is my counter proposal."

Vander swallowed hard. He felt so completely insulted, like refuse to be swept away into a gutter, but as he watched Montgomery Pearson reach into a side drawer in his desk, open a black, lacquered box, count out four, crisp, one hundred dollar bills and place them on the massive desk before him, Vander made his choice.

"I agree to your terms, Mister Pearson," Vander said has he stood up, taking the money. He hastily put it into his pants pocket.

"Excellent, dear chap!" Monty smiled as he also stood up and came from behind his desk. He approached Vander quite closely and lustily reached for his head taking hold of the thick of Vander's brown hair.

"We must seek opportunity when it arises, don't you agree?" Monty Pearson said lustily, standing next to Vander. Vander could smell the tobacco on his breath and felt the power of Monty's hand on the back of his head.

"Not always," Vander said quietly and confidently as he broke away from Monty's grip. He strode over to the door they both entered.

"Good day, Mister Pearson," he replied as he departed Monty's office chamber. Vander rode the elevator down to the main lobby of the Morgan Bank. He graciously smiled to the teller as if they were long lost friends. The distinguished doorman held open the grand, bronze door for Vander as he passed. Once outside, Vander felt the bile forming in his throat. He gathered it in his mouth and spit it onto the sidewalk in front of the House of Morgan.

"Good day, Montgomery Pearson!" he muttered. Then, he strode off, having so much work to do.

CHAPTER TWENTY

"You're gonna look adorable!" Sadie Kozak said to Vander as she appraised his costume now taking shape on the alterations mannequin in the parlor of her apartment in her Manhattan boarding house. Vander said nothing. His mouth was full of pins while he studied his work from every direction. He designed the costume with open arms and a full gathering of petticoats about the waist. He wanted to be able to move freely, yet create a more feminine shape—a curve about the hips—to give him a womanly figure. His skirts rested just below the knee. This, Vander surmised, was the perfect length, providing him with enough freedom of movement for his legs and long enough to billow and flow while he performed his act.

After a couple of weeks' worth of toil, the costumes were coming to completion. He took the pins out of his mouth sticking them into a nearby cushion.

"You ask me, I still think you ought to perform as a man. You're a good looking man, Vander! Why go to all this fuss?" Sadie asked.

Sadie was in her late forties with silver hair swept into a tight bun. She had a strong, confident face with a prominent nose which was framed by a pair of deep canyon creases running from her nostrils to the tips of her thin-lipped mouth. Ralph, Sadie's husband, died several years back and she lost her only child in the war. Sadie took what money she and her husband saved and opened a boarding house on the lower East

Side. With no one to look after, she became a mother to all the vaudevillians who passed through the theatres of Manhattan. As long as you paid your rent and weren't up to any 'monkey business' as she called it, Sadie became a surrogate mother, nurse, and psychologist to all her boarders.

"A woman looks more beautiful on the high wire and the trapeze. The audience enjoys it more. It adds daring," Vander said seriously, lost in his appraisal of the costume.

Sadie shook her head.

"Nope, not me! I like my men to look like men and my women to look like women. Now, the men are all dressing like fairies! You take Mister Brewster down the hall, don't you think I seen him all dolled up like a goil prancing about in his room at night when he thinks no one's looking."

"Really?" Vander smiled, enjoying when Sadie gossiped about her clientele.

"You otta give him a lesson or two! He looks terrible! Now you, you look like a woman when you're all dolled up. You ask me, if you walked down the street and passed me dressed like a woman, I wouldn't think anything of it. But when I peeked at the cracked door of Mister Brewster prancing around in a dress even my mother would be ashamed to wear—oy! What's the man thinking?"

Vander laughed to himself.

"Men dressing like women and women dressing like men. What is this world coming to?" Sadie sat on one of her balloon-backed dining chairs with an embroidered floral cushion while she watched Vander piece together his costume. "So when's your big audition?"

"Two days. E.F Albee's having auditions at the Palace. Open call. I don't like to admit it, but I'm nervous, Sadie."

"Why? I've seen your act when you run through it out back my house. You're terrific."

"Albee controls all vaudeville. If it goes well and he likes me, I'll be set. He controls over seven hundred vaudeville houses on the East Coast. He *is* vaudeville."

"He's gonna love you. You'll see."

"And if he doesn't, I don't know what I'm going to do. The smaller vaudeville chains are even more prudish…and the circus, they don't pick up single person acts like mine."

Sadie stood up again and went over to Vander. She thumped her index finger into his chest. "Believe in yourself! You've got something here, and I'm not just saying that because you're paying your bills on time!"

Vander smiled slightly.

"Thanks Sadie," he replied trying accept her praise.

…

"Okay, listen up!" the stage manager barked out to the performers standing in a line extending from the lobby of the Palace Theater, out its doors and well down the block. "We're taking the next ten acts. You'll have ten minutes together to set up your acts and then we're running through them one by one. You'll have three minutes to impress Mister Albee—and no more than that! Okay, let's go, the next ten acts."

Vander felt the lump in his throat. He would be in this set of ten. It was late in the afternoon. Earlier that day, in the August heat, he arose before sun up and trudged on foot up to the Palace pushing a large wooden cart on bicycle wheels containing the apparatuses of his act. While standing in line awaiting his turn to audition, his nervousness grew. He already heard the stage manager calling out the instructions to the acts who were in groups before his.

While in line, Vander feverishly plotted which three minutes of his act he would reveal. His act consisted of slackline wire walking, stunts on the rings, and finally he moved to the trapeze. Once the act was completed, he would provide the audience with his gender bending surprise. He had it down to ten minutes. How on earth would he work such a routine into three? How could he set up his equipment in time? And then costuming and makeup? Vander's mind frantically spun.

As the group of ten acts was led to the passage to the backstage, Vander's legs felt loose and wobbly. How was he going to walk a slackline in this state?

"Okay, ten minutes!" the stage manager yelled as the menagerie of acts walked on the stage of the Palace. They could not see the audience of the hall because the massive burgundy curtain was closed. Vander's group of ten included a husband and wife juggling act, child tap dancers, comedy and dance duos, a ventriloquist act, even an animal trainer with a trick horse.

Immediately, Vander raced to construct his slackline. He had all the equipment fashioned so it was easy to assemble, but it all still took time. In seven minutes, he had the line ready. Then, he hustled over to the stage manager who was watching them all. In his hands, Vander had the rope lines and bar for his trapeze. Breathlessly, he asked the stage manager, "Can you string this up? I need it for my act."

The manager looked at him for a moment and then called somewhere up above. "Hey, you awake up there? We got a guy on the trapeze. Get it down here!" The stagehand turned to Vander. "We got you covered. Why don't you get in your costume? Settle yourself down too. Mister Albee's not gonna hire a shaky acrobat."

In all his time as an Alfaretta sister and then an Erford's Whirling Sensation, Vander never took less than an hour costuming and making himself up. But today, he knew he had less than half, counting the time the other acts were on stage before him. In the dressing room of the Palace, Vander forced himself to concentrate and accomplish what was needed. He calmed his tense body. Now, his hands were like a surgeons moving about his frame, affixing his corset one moment and applying his ivory leg cream the next. Then came his facial makeup and his blond wig with soft curls. Vander just finished tying a dramatic, silver lamé cape about his neck when the stage manager called out, "Next!" It was Vander's turn. He headed over to the stage manager. In his hands was sheet music for a Brahms romance piano concerto.

"Can you be a doll and tell the pianist to start here?" Vander asked still in a masculine Texas twang.

"Sweet Mary and Joseph!" the stage manager exclaimed looking Vander over. He took at the aerialist's sheet music. "What's the name of your act? I've gotta give Mister Albee a name."

"Barbette...It's French."

When Vander said the name, he felt a rush of excitement come over him. Barbette was here! She was alive!

The man walked out from one of the wings of the stage which now had its rich, red curtains drawn. He gave the sheet music to the pianist nearby and pointed to the place where Barbette wanted him to begin. Then, he called out broadly into the massive, nearly empty auditorium with its opulent baroque plasterwork and deep burgundy velvet seats, "From France, we present, Barbette!"

The first notes Opus Number 118 by Brahms sounded out across the floodlights of the stage as Barbette, with a delicate, almost floating walk, presented herself. She was subtly sensuous as she removed her dramatic cape and broad brimmed hat which was adorned with a lavish ostrich feather sprayed a shimmering silver. Barbette flirted innocently, revealing her feminine figure in her newly made costume. The spotlight upon the garment made the sequins Vander had laboriously sewn into it, sparkle.

With a matching parasol in hand, Barbette mounted the slackline rope. Rising upon pointed ballerina feet, she moved about the line with a feline agility demonstrating her deft skills. After a scant minute, she gracefully dismounted the line and made way over to the trapeze which was lowered for her sit upon. As she did so, Barbette gestured for the stage hands to raise the bar up higher. Barbette swung back and forth upon the apparatus with great speed, swinging out over the stage, above the first rows of seats. She performed in quick succession a series of stunts, all the while positioning her hands and legs in seductive postures. When her routine was complete, she left her grip of the bar, executing a somersault and then landing smartly on her feet, center stage. Barbette headed downstage so she was bathed in the floodlights at her feet.

The pianist ended the Brahms piece with a flourish while Barbette took a generous bow. There was silence in the auditorium. No applause, no cheers. In an instant, Barbette second-guessed and contemplated ending the act just like that, but then, she decided to go ahead as rehearsed. With a dramatic flourish, Barbette removed her wig revealing her manly head. From across the floodlights, about fifteen rows back, a woman gasped.

Vander smiled as he flexed and posed like a muscle man, then he quickly changed back again, pantomiming feminine surprise on his face, blowing a kiss out into the hall as he skipped off stage.

When he reached the wing, Vander could see the other acts who managed to stay behind and watch him were all taken aback. The stage manager just shook his head and then went out to the now empty stage to gage a reaction.

"Call him back here!" came the booming voice from the blackness of the Palace auditorium.

The stagehand gestured for Vander to come back out onto center stage.

"What's your name, son?" Vander heard in a voice that sounded serious and tough.

"Vander, Vander Barbette. But my stage name is just Barbette," he replied.

The male voice chuckled.

"That sure doesn't sound like a French accent to me!" he responded.

"Well, I'm from *southern* France, sir!"

There was more laughter from the empty auditorium.

"You sure had my secretary fooled!" the male voice laughed some more. "Didn't he Kate?"

Vander heard a female laugh as well.

"Listen, I'm not sure how they're gonna take you. They're either going to love you or rip you to pieces."

Vander then heard voices murmuring, but could not make out what they were saying.

"Listen here son. You got any prejudice against playing to mixed houses? I've got an idea of where I'm going to place you, but I've got to be sure you're not afraid to play in front of colored people—a whole lot of them."

"No sir, not at all," Vander replied. "I think the folks up in the balcony will enjoy my act just like anyone else."

"So do I son, so do I! Stan! Why don't you bring this boy down here so we can get him a contract? You'll be opening the first half at the Harlem Opera House in one week."

"Yes, sir!" Vander said excitedly as Stan the stage manager started to lead him down to the seats in the auditorium. Vander beamed with satisfaction at the news! *He did it!*

. . .

"Well kid, it looks like you hit a home run!" Sadie Kozak exclaimed as she paced her tidy front parlor of her boarding house. She was holding the September 4th edition of the *New York Dramatic Mirror* in her hands. Vander reclined on Sadie's blue velvet, camel-backed sofa—his head perched on one of its tufted arm rests.

"Listen to this," Sadie continued as she read aloud the overnight review of Barbette's Harlem debut, "*It is a real shock as no one would think for a moment that he is a man while the act is in progress.*"

"Really? Why would you think anything else?" Vander joked as he listened to Sadie present the review.

"Shush! It goes on: *She is not a bad looking girl at all.*"

"I think we could use the word *stunning*, actually."

"Shush, I say!" Sadie protested again. She held the paper up closer to her face. "*The first thing she does is a good slack wire walking routine. Then she performs on rings and lastly on a trapeze. She works hard and fast and her stunts are quite thrilling.*"

"Barbette aims to please!" Vander laughed.

Sadie rolled her eyes and continued, "*She is liked so well she is called out to make many bows. About the third bow, she pulls off her wig and 'she' surprises everyone by being a man.*"

"Praise the Lord!" Vander laughed.

"*Barbette was just the opening act, but it is clear that she will soon become the headliner.*"

Sadie put the paper down on one of her balloon-backed chairs. "You're a hit, Vander Clyde! A genuine, bona fide hit!"

Vander listened to her words as they sunk in. It had been five years since he left Round Rock. Five years of toil until this moment. Now he had his own act! He was a hit in his own right!

"I suppose you're celebrating on the town tonight," Sadie said as she looked at Vander laying on her sofa.

"Of course not," Vander said sitting up. "After the shows today, I'll start work on making the act better. It can always be better."

CHAPTER TWENTY-ONE

SEPTEMBER, 1923
FOUR YEARS LATER

"How much have you saved Vander, working for Albee?"

The middle aged man looked seriously at Vander Clyde as the two sat in a desolate, open-all-night diner in Poughkeepsie, New York. Autumn came early to New York that year. Merely the start of the month and already leaves began to change from rich greens to brilliant yellows. It was past one in the morning, when the two clandestinely chose to meet. If anyone saw Vander with the man, surely word would get back to Albee. Albee would blacklist him in an instant if he knew Vander was speaking to the rogue talent agent, William Morris.

"Not much," Vander replied quietly.

"You know, for a long time, I've watched your act develop. I've read the notices you've received, but I'm going to be frank with you, Vander," Morris began as he put down his cup of black coffee.

William Morris was a distinguished looking gentleman, with a well-groomed head of hair greying at the temples, matching the salt and peppered flecks in his mustache.

"At the end of the day, you're still a novelty act. What happens when the novelty wears off? What will you have? Albee will move you out. You've seen it, I'm sure. Acts were once headlining, falling back until they're dropped from contract. Not to mention, vaudeville won't go on forever. Albee can pretend all he wants that his kingdom will never end, but it will. Moving pictures are the new thing. So where does that leave you? No work. No prospects."

Vander stirred more cream into his dark brew. As much as he hated hearing the words coming from Morris's mouth, he knew the man was speaking the truth. For some time, William Morris sought a meeting with Vander Clyde. It wasn't until Vander felt secure they could meet without detection, outside of New York City, when he agreed to do so. Vander listened to the man who was revolutionizing the talent field representing the likes of Charlie Chaplin and the Marx Brothers. He felt flattered this important talent agent, who so bucked Albee's domination, travelled all the way up to Poughkeepsie just to meet with him.

The act had reached a refinement, and he was physically still young enough to mix agility with a young, feminine visage, but how long could it truly go on? He knew if he was going to make a move, he would have to risk everything and do it now.

"I'm listening," Vander said. He looked around the humble diner. The owner, who was part waiter, part cook, was the only soul in the place.

"Maybe you're making two hundred a week," Morris continued.

Vander's eyes widened because that was exactly his rate.

"An act like yours has expenses and investment. You need money for boarding and for travel as well. Vander, have you ever thought of taking your act to Europe?"

"The Marx Brothers did, and they were blacklisted by Albee."

Morris looked intently at Vander for a while. "True, but then they went to Broadway where they are now making considerably more. Albee doesn't respect his talent. I do. I want to see you developed to live up to your fullest potential as an artist. Vander, what I'm proposing is a tour of Europe—Paris, Berlin, London, Amsterdam—for one year. I can get you bookings, where if you're successful, you'll be earning at least ten times what you do today. Ten times more and only two shows a night. Less work for more pay. You can see the world, get out of the United States!"

"Are you willing to guarantee what you're proposing?"

"All I can guarantee is a slot on the bill at the Palladium, in London. Two weeks, two thousand. I will even pay for your transport. First class to Europe, my boy. If you're a hit, I can get more bookings. We'll move onto Paris, where they'll easily double or even triple this take!"

"If I'm a failure, where does this leave me? The Marx Brothers did just as you are proposing and when they returned, Albee made sure—they'll never again play any of his houses."

"Albee! Albee!" Morris winced. "See where you go with Albee? Vander, I'm taking a considerable risk in you, but I know your work ethic. I know your discipline. I believe my investment will pay off. We'll secure your passage on a steamer straight off. We can have you on stage in London in three weeks."

"And what's your take?"

"Fifteen percent, not a penny more. I mean what I say, Vander, and I say what I mean."

Vander Clyde took a deep breath. He knew he had to push on, no matter how afraid the risk made him.

"Mister Morris, we have an agreement," Vander said as he extended his hand across the diner table.

"Excellent! We shall make plans at once!"

CHAPTER TWENTY-TWO

The RMS Majestic crept out of New York Harbor. She was the largest ocean liner to brave the icy waters of the Atlantic so late in the season. Letting forth a blast from her powerful horns warning smaller craft to make way, she began to increase her speed. The tugs sailing astride the massive ship left her, while passengers onboard began to feel the rolling action of the great Atlantic.

Vander stood on the fantail stern of the ship, watching the blackened skyscrapers and smoke stacks of the Manhattan slip from view. The ship passed Lady Liberty on her noble perch. Her torch-bearing arm no longer raised in welcome, but rather, in a goodbye salute. A chilling breeze gusted up from the water and blew off his derby hat. Vander turned quickly to retrieve it before it blew overboard, when a gentleman who was several paces behind him picked it up. The two were alone on the stern of the ship, other first class passengers preferring the comforts of the enclosed promenade with attending stewards bearing blankets and hot toddies.

The man was taller than Vander, six feet perhaps, and seemed from the looks of his fresh face and thick blonde hair to be of a similar age, twenty-three or so. He was well turned out. His top coat was made of a very high quality material with the line smartly tailored to his broad shoulders.

Somehow, in the gusts of wind which were blowing about the ship with increasing force, the man's top hat managed to stay perfectly in place.

The man held Vander's derby hat in his leather-gloved hands and handed it to Vander.

"That will be five dollars, dear chap!" he smiled. His spoke in an elegant, refined, British accent.

"Will y'all take a check? That way I can add one more zero to it. A generous tip!"

The British gentleman smiled.

"Of course dear man, fifty it is. Why, I would even forsake my entire fee, if you would speak again. I find your accent quite captivating!" His eyes twinkled.

"As I do with yours, sir," Vander replied. "Please, my name is Vander Barbette, from Texas."

"Of course! A genuine cowboy! Please forgive me. The name's Winston. Winston Darby. As I am sure you can well judge, I am *not* a Texan!" he laughed.

Vander appreciated Winston's gaiety of spirit. There was a hint of mischief and daring in his dashing brown eyes which Vander found appealing.

"Well, Mister Barbette, I believe I have assessed every passenger in our class and I can fairly attest we are the only chaps onboard remotely attached by age. The other gents easily have a good ten years on us."

Vander nodded as he put his derby back atop his windswept, light brown hair.

"I suggest we make the best of it! Are you travelling alone?"

"I'm with Mister Morris."

"Ah yes, the talent agent. Do tell me, am I speaking with an entertainer? Your carriage would most certainly persuade me that I am." Winston Darby moved slightly closer to Vander.

"That is correct, sir," Vander replied. He didn't want to reveal the nature of his act to this man, feeling perhaps it may put him off. "Forgive me for asking, Mister Darby, but are you traveling alone as well?"

"Not exactly, dear chap. I am traveling with my sister. Separate quarters of course. We were in America to fish for a possible suitor for her, an Astor or a Vanderbilt perhaps, but I don't want to be a bore. Say, Gwyneth—that's my dear sister's name—Gwyneth adores the theater. And I would quite enjoy getting to know you more. Won't you join us for supper tonight? We can meet in the palm court, say seven? Oh, and do please invite Mister Morris. We want to hear all about you both!"

"I think we can manage that. I'll tell Mister Morris."

"Very well then, we shall see you at seven. Good day, Mister Barbette." Winston Darby tipped his hat and Vander did the same.

The mists of the ocean now made the city skyline of Manhattan all but disappear. Only the Woolworth building could be faintly made out. Lady Liberty was wrapped in a blanket of cold fog. Vander continued to stand alone on the deck. He thought about himself, the awkward boy, back in Round Rock who just wanted to perform—to be someone, do something! Now it appeared his dreams were being fulfilled, but he knew he could not rest. When he got to London, he would have to purchase more fabric and set about working at once. Barbette would have to be a sensation in London if he was going to propel himself on further. A sensation she would become!

Vander watched the black waters of the Atlantic churn below him, sloshing about from the enormous force of the four massive screws propelling the Majestic. He had never been in love. Not really. On the road, he spent many long, lonely nights living as if he were a monk. But when he set down to rest in single beds at one of the nondescript boarding houses he resided in while on tour, his mind would turn to his fantasies—fantasies not filled with women, but rather, men. His lusts overwhelmed him. He desired to be with a man. If Monty Pearson wasn't such an ass, maybe perhaps there could have been something there. But what? What exactly did he yearn for? He wasn't quite exactly sure. All he knew was he wanted to be ravished. Yes ravished!

The thought of being so desired by the likes of a handsome gent like Winston Darby was all at once overwhelming. Yet, Vander smiled to himself as he savored the idea of five days on the high seas with such an engaging, young man.

...

"You must tell us, Mister Barbette, are you in anyway related to the lovely Barbette—the trapeze artist who is gathering such attention?" Gwyneth Darby inquired across the elegantly set table as a white-gloved waiter poured her more champagne. She must have been nineteen or twenty years old. She wasn't exactly handsome. If one took off the veneer of wealth—the delicate diamond tiara adorning her head, her coiffed, soft brown hair, curled so fashionably, and her sumptuously cut light blue silk gown—she could easily be the girl behind a notions counter at a drug store.

As for Mister Barbette, he learned long ago if he was to be recognized in society he must be immaculately groomed. He wore a tuxedo of the finest cloth and exhibited impeccable manners. Being an excellent seamstress and possessing a keen eye of observation permitted him a comfortable entrée into his newfound world of wealth and luxury—even if it was being paid for by Mister Morris.

"Yes, Madame Darby, she is my sister," Vander smiled. He looked over to William Morris who was seated alongside Gwyneth Darby and gave him a telling smirk.

"Oh dear! If you don't mind my saying that is indeed wonderful!" Gwyneth said as she raised her champagne cocktail to her precisely painted lips.

The sumptuous dining room of the Majestic was ablaze in the soft glow of electric light. The room was immense, nearly three stories tall and circular in shape. Gold-painted Doric columns encircled diners while supporting an oval dome of cut glass above. Heard from the two hundred well-tended passengers now savoring meals, was a healthy chatter, a mix of jolly guffaws, and the merry tune of sterling silver flatware making contact with custom, insignia china from Royal Dalton.

"Mister Barbette," Winston Darby began as he turned to Vander who was seated next to him, "If you don't mind my inquiring, what is the nature of your talents?"

"An actor," Vander replied, not missing a beat.

Gwyneth leaned forward looking at Vander as if she wanted to disclose a secret.

"I have heard on good authority your sister—how shall I put this delicately—that your sister is really—I feel embarrassed to say it—she is really, your *brother*?"

Winston looked at his sister and then turned to Vander, "Please, Mister Barbette, you needn't answer such salacious questions from Gwyneth."

Vander laughed lightly.

"Oh my! How do these rumors get started? I can assure you she is all woman. Isn't that so, Mister Morris?"

Morris nodded and answered with a poker face, "Of course. We're joining her at the Palladium where she will be performing in several weeks. I'm sure I can speak for us both, would you be so kind to be our guests at the show?"

Gwyneth turned to Winston, "Mother would be scandalized! Me going to such a place!"

"She need not know!" Winston replied with a wicked smirk on his lips. "Besides, mumsy always taught us to never be impolite. I do believe turning down this tantalizing offer would be exactly that."

"Very well!" Morris replied. "I'll see when we arrive in London tickets will be sent to you straight off."

"Excellent!" Winston replied. Winston looked winningly at Vander. "It shall mean we will be London friends as well, not merely shipboard acquaintances. I think I shall quite enjoy that."

Vander smiled, "I couldn't agree more."

…

Their bodies heaved, pitching and rolling like the giant RMS Majestic mounting the waves of the belligerent Atlantic. Vander savored it all—Winston's lusty aroma, the feeling of his strength, the ferociousness of his approach. He felt overwhelmed by Winston's passions, yet urged him on. The two succumbed to their desires, perspired and spent.

It was well past midnight. After cognacs in the library where they settled by a roaring fire, more interests were revealed. Then, the two traversed back to Vander's cabin. They could no longer contain their desire for one another.

Now, exhausted from their intimate interlude, Vander rested beside Winston in the single bed. He liked the fact their two bodies were so close together. He savored the warmth of Winston's naked flesh next to his on the cold night.

Winston turned toward Vander, perching his head upon his arm. He lazily ran his free hand over Vander's torso. The gentleness of the touch aroused Vander yet again.

"I've never seen such a magnificent specimen," Winston marveled at Vander's toned, muscular body. "Dare I say it, you are more striking than anything carved from the hand of Michelangelo."

Vander smiled.

"Have you seen his statue of 'David'?"

"Of course. We have holidayed in Tuscany many times, since I was a boy, really. I shouldn't reveal it—it is too indiscrete—I favor Italian men, but then I never mounted a cowboy until tonight," Winston laughed. "So yes, I have been to Florence and marveled at the perfect form of Michelangelo's statue. Now I must correct myself, for David is not perfect—what I am touching now, is far more ideal."

Vander was silent. Since he set eyes on the sketched image of David in an art book Miss Nelson lent him while in high school in Round Rock, he marveled at Michelangelo's skill. One day, he would look upon the statue itself. How wonderful it would be to travel with Winston to see such a work of art! Vander wanted to reveal to Winston the nature of his stage act, but it all seemed too inappropriate to explain in the moment. Perhaps later in the week, when they neared Dover.

Vander felt Winston approach him again. The ocean liner continued to pitch and roll into the night.

...

"The Savoy," William Morris said to the attending taxi driver as a porter secured his trunks and Vander's on the rear of the taxi.

"But my equipment," Vander said in a rush of confusion. All around him passengers from the Majestic moved about, some heralding taxis, while others set out for the nearby train depot.

"Never mind, Vander. The White Star Line insisted they will personally deliver your trunks to the Palladium. Now we must depart, for I'd like to have a word with you."

Morris and Vander stepped into the back compartment of the taxi. The area for the driver was open-aired, but the compartment for customers was well-sealed, which in this moment, Morris was more than pleased for what he needed to say.

As the motor car left the port terminal, he didn't waste time.

"Did you disclose to Mister Winston Darby the nature of your act?" he asked.

"Not exactly," Vander replied.

"Then he doesn't know you portray a woman? That you are a transvestite."

Vander gazed over at Morris. He could see the concern in his eye.

"No."

"You two were inseparable on the crossing. Don't you think anyone with half a wit would know what you two were about?"

"Mister Morris!"

"Do not fain disgust with me, Vander! This is serious. I've been in the world of entertainers for a lifetime. You're not the first pretty boy I've represented." Morris stroked his mustache in a concerned manner. "Winston Darby is an earl, who will one day become a lord, perhaps even representing his countrymen in parliament. He is highly respected. He cannot be seen with the likes of an entertainer—and an entertainer who impersonates a woman."

"Of course not."

"I don't make judgments. I leave that up to the God, but if you wish to continue such activity, you must do so in secret. You must be discreet. Certainly more discreet than you were on the Majestic."

"I understand," Vander replied as he wiped the condensation from the inside of the taxi window with his gloved hand. The five days aboard Majestic were very clearly the most wonderful five days of his life. He didn't think it possible in such a small time, to so fully, so encompassingly adore another human being, but that was how Vander felt towards Winston. He was charming, lusty, beguiling at every turn. Vander barely slept, the two were so engrossed in their affections for one another. If this was not love, he didn't know what it was!

"I don't think you do. There are strict sodomy laws in Britain, Vander. If your proclivities are discovered, you will force the magistrate to serve you with a strict sentence. We're talking imprisonment. They did it to Oscar Wilde. They'll certainly do it to you!"

Vander swallowed hard, taking in William Morris's admonitions.

"For the sake of both our careers, until we see how you're received, at the very least, you must not be seen out in public cavorting with anyone—male or female."

"I'm not a celibate priest, Mister Morris!" Vander protested.

William Morris turned toward Vander and stared into his eyes. "Of this, I am abundantly sure!"

...

"Dear Lord, we aren't in Texas anymore!" Vander Barbette remarked as he took in the sweep of the suite William Morris booked for him at the Savoy in the heart of London.

Morris ran his hand across a gilded-gold accent chair.

"Why the Brits adore French furniture is a mystery to me," he said.

Vander looked at the parlor—tall with white walls and ceiling embellished with plaster filigree. Bands of gold paint accented the trim. Pale blue upholstered furniture complimented the dramatic blue, silk drapes which were pulled back to reveal comely wintertime vistas of London and the River Thames beyond.

"It's magnificent, but surely this will take up all my funds for the week, if not more." Vander said looking at Morris seriously as the agent took in the vastness of the suite.

"Consider it a gift from me. I thought you needed more space. You said you wanted to work up more costumes. Well, you can do it here. Your sleeping quarters are in the adjacent chamber. Besides, I want the French to see you are staying at the Savoy. It'll increase your rates. I've secured a wardrobe mistress for your stay as well. She will assist you in making additional costumes. If she is any good, you may want to take her along with you when we get bookings in Paris."

"*If* we get bookings in Paris," Vander corrected him.

Morris sighed, "Vander you must be magnificent when we open—a sensation. I know this will be a fact. But in order to fulfill this promise, you must put everything you have into it. The mistress's name is Mimi, I'm told. Use her to your best advantage. Now, I must go. I'm supping with some of my other clients." Morris turned and headed for the door.

"Wait!" Vander called after him. "Thank you, Mister Morris. From the depths of my heart, thank you."

Morris bowed slightly.

"Have at it, son! This is the chance of a lifetime."

CHAPTER TWENTY-THREE

"Well done, my boy! Well done indeed!" William Morris congratulated Vander Barbette who just walked to the wing of the stage after his umpteenth curtain call. Vander was in full makeup and costume. He was breathing hard and feeling exhilarated.

"They were so quiet at the start. I didn't know what to expect when I finished," he smiled.

Mimi, a middle aged woman with a thick frame, and grey hair pulled tight into a no-nonsense bun, was standing ready with a towel and a robe. Vander took the items from her.

"Thank you, Mimi. Please, get the head piece and my other things. I don't want the stage hands tampering with them."

"Of course me lord," she replied dryly.

Vander turned to Morris as they headed back stage. "I think she's more dedicated to her job than me!" He laughed. He and Morris headed back to his private dressing room.

"I don't believe the first half of the show has ever closed with such an act that was so well received!" Morris enthused.

"Do you think word will get out—that Barbette is really a man?" Vander asked as he wiped perspiration from his face with the towel.

"We've printed in all of the programs the audience must be bound to secrecy. But of course they will not! It'll only increase the curiosity of others who'll want to see your act and judge it for themselves."

Vander closed his dressing room door behind the two after they entered. It was not large, but at long-last, Vander was thrilled to have his own space and not have to share it with other performers. The room even had its own toilet and shower, which pleased Vander to no end. Mimi already tidied the room, making sure all Vander's makeup and supplies were in good order.

"Did you see him?" Vander asked blotting his face. He sat at his vanity table, starting to remove his performance slippers.

"Who?" Morris asked.

Vander stopped. "You know who! Winston and his sister, Gwyneth! Tonight, in my mind, I thought about him. In my mind—I was only performing only for him!"

William Morris grimaced. "I don't know if he was in attendance. I didn't see him. Vander, if he was here, you must promise me you will not be seen with him in public. Remember, you mustn't be seen by anyone at all. At least until you get to Paris. You must remain a mystery. It's vitally important!"

"Yes. I only was asking if you saw him. That's all."

Morris looked at his tuxedoed visage in the vanity mirror. He straightened his white bow tie and moistened a pinkie and then ran it through each eyebrow, smoothing them out. He addressed Vander's reflected image in the mirror.

"A motor car will be here in an hour to take you back to the hotel. Mimi will let you know it has arrived. Good night, Vander." He went for the door. "Good night indeed!" He smiled.

"Good night, Mister Morris."

Seated in front of his vanity, Vander started to remove his makeup. He hoped Winston was in the audience.

Vander expanded his act. He added a more dramatic beginning, a glamorous entrance down a flight of stairs in full Barbette regalia, ostrich plumes and golden lamé. Three weeks before, when he first took in the cavernous space of the Palladium—over two thousand seats—he knew everything would have to be grander if he was going to make an impression on the audience. The routine tonight was nearly perfect. Barbette got rather carried away at the ending, surprised when the silent crowd burst into such enthusiastic acceptance.

Lost in his appraisal, Vander did not hear the knocking, but then it burst through to his consciousness. There was distinctly a pounding on his door. *Winston was here!* Vander eagerly rose from his chair and flung open his door. He was beaming.

"Don't get yourself so worked up, me lord," Mimi replied as she pushed past Vander. "Looks like one of the ostrich feathers on the headdress is lose. I'll tend to it."

Vander sighed, deflated by her site.

"That'll be fine. A car is coming in an hour. We can take back what we need to fix when it arrives. Now, I must shower and remove my paint."

"Yes me lord," Mimi answered dutifully, already straightening things Vander used on the vanity.

"Well then," Vander began, standing nearly naked, consumed in his thoughts of Winston for an instant. "Off to the showers I'll go."

"Water's cold," Mimi replied as Vander entered the toilet.

"A cold shower. Well, that's exactly what I need."

CHAPTER TWENTY-FOUR

"You must make a decision," William Morris said to Vander as he paced the parlor of the elegant Savoy hotel suite. "The Alhambra in Paris is offering us two thousand a week. One month's booking. It's one of the largest music halls in Paris! The Palladium will only come up to one thousand five hundred and only one more week booked. We must leave London now. Leave them wanting more, Vander! We'll come back in half a year and demand three thousand!"

Vander looked sad and lost. "How could it be?" he muttered quietly.

Morris knew where Vander's heart resided. He had seen it before with his other entertainers.

"Consider it the fate of the gods! For all we know, Earl Winston Darby left a week ago to sail to South Africa. I hear his family has considerable interests there—or maybe he moved on."

Vander leered at Morris for a while, but he knew he had to let go. Where had his discipline gone? Where was his fortitude? If Winston Darby didn't wish to see him, then what they had together must not have been worth anything at all.

"Tonight'll be my last show at the Palladium. Let's take Paris, Mister Morris!"

William Morris smiled broadly, the ends of his eyes twinkling, "Outstanding!"

...

It was an uncommonly sunny, midmorning in London, as Vander departed the Savoy and headed to the train station. He dressed smartly in a fashionable Saville row custom suit and Burberry topcoat and hat. He had the garments worked up last week and they were delivered to the hotel the day before. He hoped putting on the new set of clothing would encourage his spirits and ease the great upheaval in his heart over Winston.

Vander took it upon himself to use his days in London touring the city. He visited elegant shops and historic churches. He traversed the London Bridge of his nursery rhyme memory and marveled at the royal jewels on display in the Tower of London. With one more day in the fabled city, Vander decided to set out to Stratford Upon Avon, to see for his very eyes the place of William Shakespeare's birth. *Wouldn't Miss Nelson be green with envy*, he thought.

Vander's imagination turned to Round Rock. He needed to write his mother and perhaps include a letter for Rose. What became of Rose, he wondered? She was now entering the age when she might be married. He thought about the paychecks he was beginning to receive. He was making more money in a week than what old Samuel Loving would earn in a year! He promised himself to send his mother funds. It was some sort of vindication for sure. As much as he wanted to never return to Texas, he vowed when more funds came in, he would buy up land there—if only to show the people in town his growing importance. It would be some sort of sweet revenge.

Although taken by his internal musings, Vander managed to glimpse out of the corner of his eye, a particular person entering a haberdasher's store. Could it be? Most certainly it was—Winston! Feeling fleet of foot, Vander quickly crossed the street and walked toward the shop window to have a look inside. Vander could clearly see, sure enough—it was Winston! Vander watched for a moment through the shop window as Winston spoke to the man behind the counter. Then the man took the derby from Winston's hands and walked over to a steamer. While the man's back was turned, Winston's eyes wandered—it was when he spotted Vander!

Vander saw the startled expression on Winston's face, the instant recognition. Without hesitation, Vander opened the store door, hearing bells jingle as he did so.

"Winston!" Vander said eagerly.

Winston nervously looked at the haberdasher who turned around from his work and watched Vander enter his store.

"Vander, are you in town?"

Vander was taken aback by his question. *Could he even not acknowledge the simple fact they sailed together on the Majestic from the United States? Did Winston need to lie even about this?*

"Why yes."

"How charming!" Winston replied. "We will have to get together some time."

Vander looked at Winston in an astounded way.

"Yes, we will," was all Vander could muster. "I have time now…It's early,"

The haberdasher handed Winston's derby back to him. Winston placed it on his handsome head, his deep brown eyes looking at himself in the oval mirror resting on the wood counter.

"Yes, that will do," Winston told the store owner. "Please, put it on our tab."

"Of course, sir," the man answered. "Have a good day."

Winston tipped his hat to the man.

"I'm so sorry good chap, but I am already running late for an appointment. Perhaps some other time?"

Vander looked deeply into Winston's eyes. He was furious and wanted Winston to see his anger.

"I head to Paris in the morning."

"Oh dear, I guess we shall miss each other. Well, it was delightful we had this chance. Good day, sir." Winston coldly tipped his hat to Vander and then headed out the door— the bells affixed above them ringing out his exit.

"Anything I can help you with, sir?" the haberdasher asked Vander.

"No, thank you very much. You have a lovely store."

The man smiled. "Why thank you sir!"

Vander tipped his hat, "Good day,"

"Good day, me lord."

Vander saw the direction Winston departed. It was the opposite direction from the train station, but he refused to tail after Winston like a timid puppy. If Winston didn't want to see him, so be it! Instead, he headed to the station and Stratford Upon Avon to have a rendezvous with someone far more reliable and satisfying.

CHAPTER TWENTY-FIVE

"What a sensation you've become!" William Morris gushed. "All of the revues of Paris are begging for Barbette!" He paced the suite of the Hotel Moderne near the Place de la République in the heart of Paris.

Vander reclined on settee nearest the large window which permitted a gentle, afternoon illumination upon his robed body. He smiled.

"I feel like I found my city," he said as he gazed out the window. "At the theater this past week, I could tell that the audiences appreciated all the little refinements I'd worked on so hard."

William Morris smiled, "Léon Volterra from the Casino de Paris is demanding to have you in his revue once you finish at the Alhambra. He's the highest bidder. Five hundred!"

Vander looked up at William Morris and asked, "Per week?"

"No, no, my boy! Per *show*! Six a week."

Vander felt overwhelmed. The number seemed unreal. He felt a wave of appreciation for his toil.

"So I take it you shall want me to contact Volterra and agree?"

Vander smiled, "Yes, of course."

"Consider it done!" Then Morris's expression changed. "I've been wanted to tell you this, Vander, for several days." He stopped pacing the room. "I must return to New York. I've booked a steamer that shall depart tomorrow. I'm concerned it is too soon for you, but as you can understand, I need to see to my family and tend to my other interests."

Vander took in the news. Usually he was the one departing, but now the tables turned. "I understand, sir." He stood up and looked William Morris straight in the eye.

"Do you remember that cold autumn night in Poughkeepsie? I was so afraid to sign with you—to give up all Albee promised. What a fool I was. I can't thank you enough!"

"You're very welcome, Vander! Very welcome indeed! But this is your creation, your fantasia, not mine."

Morris turned away for a moment to look out another of the expansive windows of Vander's hotel suite. He grew pensive.

"Vander, I worry about you...I...I have seen it before, with my other entertainers. I don't want you to succumb..."

Vander came up behind Morris and put his hand on his shoulder.

"I understand what you're suggesting, Mister Morris. You know my discipline. I won't lose it now."

Morris turned around and faced Vander again. "It's just sometimes a talent is like a comet—it shines bright, catches the eye streaking across the sky—and then it's gone, vanishing in the night. You must mind yourself, Vander. Save your earnings. Remain in good health. Do you understand? This city is full of many temptations."

"Of course, I will."

Morris grabbed hold of Vander's muscular shoulders. The edges of his brown eyes crinkled as he smiled. "Of course you will!"

CHAPTER TWENTY-SIX

"Arrêtez la voiture! Je crois que je vais vomir!!" Princess Violette Murat shouted in her high-pitched voice as the freezing-cold air of the Parisian night blasted through her short, bob cut hair. Her corpulent frame, ensconced in an ample, monkey fur coat was plunked down next to Vander Barbette's in the back seat of her brand new, bright yellow, Citroën automobile.

"Parler anglais! Parlez anglais vous gouine graisse!" Jean Cocteau shouted back at her from the front passenger seat of the car as it swerved and darted down the empty boulevard of the Champs-Élysées some time past three in the morning. "Speak English! You fat dyke!"

Raymond Radiguet laughed hysterically from his vantage behind the wheel. His foot put more force on the accelerator pedal. The car increased speed, careening toward the massive roundabout encircling the Arc de Triomphe. The car entered the roundabout and continued its ridiculous path.

"Stop or I will vomit!" the princess protested. The yellow automobile swerved up to the curb and Radiguet slammed on the brakes. Without a moment's hesitation, Violette Murat swung open the door to the automobile, stepped out past the running board and promptly upchucked into the gutter. Her ample body, sheathed in fur, silhouetted by the arc lights aimed at the massive, triumphal arch before them, made her look like a foraging bear in a forest clearing.

Cocteau and Radiguet burst out laughing. They exited the automobile, Cocteau taking with him a half-full flask of whiskey.

Vander Barbette hopped out of the back seat and went over to Violette who daintily wiped her lips with an embroidered kerchief.

"Are you okay?"

"Oui!" she said coming to her senses. She looked up at the Arc de Triomphe, in the cold, clear Parisian night. It looked down at her with its white marble reliefs, stoically silent. "I am sorry my great grandfather Napoleon, for such debasement!" she said. She brought her fingers to her lips. She kissed them and then raised her hand as if she was blessing the arch in a benediction.

"I am sure he well heard you!" Cocteau called back at them. He and Radiguet were huddled together, closer to the famous arch. "I love Paris!" Cocteau exclaimed.

They were alone in the circle at this hour. Not a single automobile or truck entered the expansive round about. In the distance, a searchlight, beaming from the top of the Eiffel Tower, swept over the city cutting through the blackness of the night like a sharp knife. Cocteau took Radiguet's head in his hands and kissed him passionately on the lips.

Vander's mouth was agape.

Violette Murat laughed as she and Vander approached them. She sighed, "Look at the two lovebirds! So pretty, so adoring!"

Vander couldn't take his eyes off the men.

"Have you found a man yet?" Violette asked Vander, her eyes innocent and interested.

Vander was taken aback by her presumption. No one ever asked him such a question so openly before. Without formulating a more explicatory response, he answered sincerely, "no."

Violette happily patted Vander on the back. "That is okay, you will!"

Vander's gaze remained on the two men kissing a few paces from them. He could not believe the two were so passionate out in public! It astounded him and excited him all at once. He felt a flash of emotion—he wanted to be a part of their display.

"They are cute, aren't they?" Violette laughed. "Our two little finches!"

It had only been a little over two hours since he first met the three. He was in his dressing room of the Casino de Paris sometime after midnight. Having showered and removed all his body and face makeup, Vander was chatting with Mimi about this and that when they heard a knocking at the door. Vander had grown accustomed to such happenings in the week since Barbette started performing at the casino. There was something to the allure of Barbette—it was as if people needed to personally come in contact with the enigma. Was she really a man? What sort of man? The French scandal tabloids were already spilling ink with their speculation.

Mimi looked at Vander to see what he wanted her to do. His eyes gestured for her to respond.

"Who is it?" she called out.

From beyond the door, Vander heard some whispers and then a very proper high-pitched female voice called out in impeccable English with a slight French accent, "It is the Princess Violette Bonaparte Murat and her consorts."

When Vander clearly heard the woman's voice properly call out the title, he was immediately intrigued. He stood up and walked over to a garment rack rolled to one side of the tidy dressing room. From it he took a rich red, silk robe and put it on, covering his nearly naked frame. He then slipped on some finely sewn leather slippers and signaled for Mimi to open the door.

The princess promptly entered the room—a stout woman in her mid-twenties, sheathed in diamonds and monkey fur. She chose to wear little makeup. In a second-natured sort of way, Vander assessed her movements, the way she carried herself, the way she gestured with her eyes and hands. She was completely over the top, preposterous, yet refined.

Vander bowed before her as she extended her bejeweled hand which he elegantly kissed. Fumbling into the room behind her were two other gentlemen who looked so alike and so remarkably French to Vander—young, clean-shaven with thick, luxurious heads of dark hair swept off their foreheads, prominent, intelligent noses, and dashing evening clothes.

"Might I present Raymond Radiguet and Jean Cocteau," Princess Violette announced. "They are the very finest writers in all of France!"

Raymond and Jean bowed deeply, in a somewhat tipsy fashion. As Jean Cocteau rose, he looked into Vander's eyes with a deep sense of admiration. Vander found his intense gaze almost worshipful.

"How delightful! I'm presently reading a translation of one of Monsieur Cocteau's books," Vander said. "Please, won't you be seated? I was just getting dressed. This is Mimi, my wardrobe mistress." The three guests nodded pleasantly in Mimi's direction as she pulled another chair forward for them.

"I'll be turning in, me lord," Mimi replied as she took her simple winter coat from a hanger on the rolling rack.

"Goodnight Mimi. Thank you for all of your hard work tonight," Vander said as she left the room, closing the door behind her.

"You see?" Jean Cocteau said turning to Raymond Radiguet. Radiguet found the chintz armchair and comfortably reclined in it while Cocteau perched upon one of its rolled arms. "He is not French! That accent is not French. Nor is he German or British."

"I'm a Texan," Vander said confidently as he laughed.

"And a handsome one at that!" Radiguet smiled.

"You'll forgive me for saying, but I appreciate y'all speaking English. I'm afraid I haven't been in Paris long enough to learn French."

"You need to take a French lover. It is how you will learn quickly," Princess Violette said instructively. Her voluminous frame rested on a simple wooden chair, similar to the one Vander sat at in front of his vanity. Her girth permitted her to only sit like a man, with her legs open, the heels of her shoes flatly on the floor.

"Yes, preferably one with a mustache!" Radiguet joked.

Vander's face colored.

"Ah, look he blushed!" Radiguet laughed robustly.

Jean Cocteau grew more serious as he looked intently at Vander.

"I must confess, I have seen your show many times in the past week. You are an angel, a flower, a bird."

"Oh dear!" Radiguet rolled his eyes.

"Please!" Cocteau turned to Radiguet his eyes darting a flash of anger. Radiguet slumped into the armchair, knowing when Jean Cocteau had a point he wanted to make he would not tolerate distractions.

"I have written a review. It shall be published tomorrow, but I wanted to come back here tonight, for what I have written in it, I can only say to you personally—tonight's performance was again confirmation of my earlier impressions."

Vander nodded toward Cocteau apprehensively as the Frenchman pulled from his coat a couple of sheets of scrawled manuscript. He started to read from them:

"The curtain goes up on a functional décor—a wire stretched between two supports, a trapeze, and hanging rings. In the back, a sofa covered with a white bearskin."

"I love the bearskin!" Radiguet smiled, but Cocteau immediately silenced him with his hand as he continued to read from his manuscript.

"*Barbette enters adorned in ostrich feathers and a flowing lamé evening gown. As he removes his evening gown, he begins to perform a scabrous little scene—a real masterpiece of pantomime, summing up in parody all the women he has ever studied, becoming himself* **the** *woman—so much so as to eclipse the prettiest girls who precede and follow him on the program. Bursting on the audience as a ravishing creature he throws his dust with such force that from then on he is free to concentrate on his wire work, in which his masculine movements will help him instead of giving him away. He is no mere acrobat in women's clothes, nor just a graceful daredevil but one of the most beautiful things in the theatre.*"

Vander sat at his vanity chair, facing the other three, enthralled by Cocteau's observations.

Cocteau continued to read, "*Imagine what a letdown it would be for some of us if at the end of that unforgettable lie Barbette were simply to remove his wig. You will tell me that after the fifth curtain call he does just that, and that the letdown down takes place. There is even a murmur from the audience, and some people are embarrassed and some blush. True. For, after having succeeded as an acrobat in causing some people almost to faint, he now has to have his success as an actor. But watch his last tour de force. Simply to re-become a man, to run the reel backward, is not enough. The truth itself must be translated, if it is to convince us as forcibly as did the lie. That is why Barbette, the moment he has snatched off his wig,* **plays the part of a man.** *He rolls his shoulders, stretches his hands, swells his muscles, parodies a golfer's sporty walk. And after the fifteenth or so curtain calls, he gives a mischievous wink, shifts from foot to foot, mimes a bit of apology, and does a shuffling little street-urchin dance—all of* *it to erase the fabulous, dying-swan impression left by the act. His affectations ought to be unbearable to us. The principle of his act embarrasses us. What is left then? That thing he has created—going through its contortions under the spotlight. An angel. A flower. A bird."*

Cocteau put down his writing and looked up, Vander could see the passion in his eyes. It was not artifice, but sincerity.

"I don't know what to say," Vander said quietly.

"You needn't say anything!" Violette interjected.

"We want to be your friends!" Radiguet said eagerly.

"You must see my new automobile! It is bright yellow!" Violette smiled.

"Please, we have champagne!" Radiguet pleaded.

Cocteau looked earnestly again into Vander's eyes, "Please?"

Vander looked at them all for a moment, like a litter of eager puppies.

"Of course!" he replied. "Let me get dressed."

"As Barbette?" the princess asked.

"Not tonight, darling!" Vander replied as he went behind his dressing screen.

"For shame! I was hoping for Barbette! She is quite a woman!" Violette laughed.

The three eagerly took Vander though a nocturnal forced march through the city in the shiny new, bright yellow Citroën automobile. Not minding the wintery cold evening, Radiguet and Cocteau put the top down at Violette's grand insistence. Cocteau seemed to produce an endless fountain of liquor—when the champagne ran dry, he offered a flask of whiskey and when that ran out, he revealed another from his boot. They all took turns taking swigs—getting sillier and sillier as their drive continued. Princess Violette sat in the back seat next to Vander, regally explaining her own noble Napoleonic lineage while pointing out the landmarks of the city. But with the streets nearly empty, Raymond Radiguet began to drive like a mad man, swerving wildly from lane to lane. That's when Violette protested in French to stop the car, lest she vomit.

Vander started laughing at it all: Laughing at the grandness of the princess's affectations and her dramatic upchucking into the gutter, laughing at Radiguet's insane driving, and laughing at Cocteau and Radiguet locked in a romantic embrace at the foot of the Arc de Triomphe awash in dazzling electric light. Vander Barbette loved Paris! He only desired more!

CHAPTER TWENTY-SEVEN

"We're so glad you could join us!" Cocteau said with his elegant French accent as Vander sat down at a table next to the front window of Harry's New York Bar, Sunday morning with Cocteau and his companion Raymond Radiguet. "We thought this place would remind you of home," Cocteau added. He and Radiguet were dressed comfortably for a midday Sunday meal in autumn, with open shirts, tweed jackets, and trousers.

"It was kind of the thought," Vander replied. He was dressed more formally than the other two in a neatly cut, double breasted suit and fashionable, striped silk tie.

"Let me tell you it was quite a sacrifice," Cocteau began, "this is the lair of that imbecile Ernest Hemmingway who is always sniping at Raymond. He was quite put out coming here knowing that the crass American might be in his presence. But today, the jackass appears to be elsewhere."

"I can handle my own," Radiguet said. "It was a good time last night, no? We called on Violette, but she is at her apartment with a hot water bottle on her head, recovering from the sins of last night." Radiguet's grin was warm and mischievous.

"I can't say that I blame her," Vander said.

Cocteau frowned for a moment and then he snapped his fingers in the air. A handsome waiter came up to the table.

Radiguet eyed him appreciatively. He then caught Vander's eyes urging him to also glance appreciatively back at the waiter. Vander tried not to laugh as he did so.

Cocteau ordered a Harry's invention, a double Bloody Mary, for Vander and another round for himself and Radiguet.

The waiter left and Cocteau looked at his two companions. "You see? Why is it your appreciation of the waiter must be done in secret? Why can we not simply tell him we think he is a lovely man? Why must my natural attractions be deemed any more debased than a man who prefers pussy?"

Vander nearly choked on the gulp of water he took from the glass before him.

"But in Paris, we are *tolerated*," Radiguet replied.

"I am not willing just to be tolerated. That wounds my love of love and of liberty."

Radiguet chose not to get into a deep conversation so early in the day. "The Casino de Paris is closed tonight? No?" he asked Vander trying to change the subject.

"Sunday and Monday," he replied.

"Then we must take you to a club where you can meet more people like us," Cocteau insisted.

Radiguet leaned in across the table to Vander and lowered his voice, "Paris is free when the sun goes down. Women can dance with women and men can dance with men."

"Yes, that is until the police arrive," Cocteau said his chin held high. "You see? This is what I mean. Why must a lookout be posted on the street in case the police arrive? We all scatter like mice—or even worse, pretend we are like everyone else, and start dancing with women. It is a farce. The police know it. We know it. Why must I be thrown in jail for loving a man?"

"In America, it's much worse," Vander replied.

Cocteau frowned. "Yes, this is what I've heard."

Vander looked at the two of them across the table. "I must tell you the queer thing that happened to me this morning while I lay in bed."

"Please do!" Radiguet replied with a devilish glint in his eye.

"You know the stories in the press—that I'm not really a man—or perhaps I'm even a hermaphrodite..."

"Yes, it seems the French believe you must be too good to be true," Cocteau remarked.

Vander nodded and continued, "This morning—a journalist walked unannounced into my hotel room! At least I think he was a journalist. He carried a notebook and a pen. No knock at the door. He simply forced himself in somehow."

"No!" Cocteau exclaimed.

"The gall!" Radiguet added.

"I was lying naked on my bed at the time. My face smeared with blackish skin-bleaching cream!"

Jean and Raymond burst out laughing.

"I can imagine the headline tomorrow," Cocteau quipped, "two sexed on the stage and two-colored at home!"

"His eyes darted around the room!" Vander continued. "He paid particular attention to seeing on my bedside table Joyce's *Ulysses* and your work, Jean, *Le Grand Écart*—he expressed amazement!"

"That you were literate or that Jean wasn't in bed reading it to you?" Radiguet laughed. The other two roared.

"We have a proposal for you," Radiguet said. "Next weekend, we are heading up to the mountains. It is barely the end of November, but we heard the snow is lovely this year. We will be taking Violette's auto. She will not go, but said we can borrow it. We can leave after your last show on Saturday and then return by Monday."

The waiter brought three double Bloody Marys to the table. Vander looked at his not taking a sip while he contemplated their proposal.

"I hope you don't take this the wrong way," Vander began, "but I already committed to Helen Gwynne, next Sunday. She is having me over to meet more of her friends."

"Boring Americans!" Cocteau scowled. "Present company excepted..."

"Suggest to her you are ill," Radiguet interjected enthusiastically. "No one wants to be ill this time of the year, so close to Christmas."

Vander shook his head, no.

"Very well," Cocteau replied, taking a liberal gulp from his drink. "Coco so wanted to meet you," he offered, hoping Vander would take the bait.

"Coco *Chanel*?" Vander gushed.

"The one and only. She is quite a skier, you know," Cocteau lied as he stared down at his drink.

"Of all the weekends!" Vander rued. "I simply can't make it! But tell her I love her work! Even in America, the fashion magazines speak well of her. I wonder what she would charge to clothe Barbette?"

Radiguet looked at Vander and then Cocteau. "We shall ask! I am sure she would be delighted!"

That's when out the front window of Harry's Bar, across the street, a young, black woman caught Vander's eye. She wore a three-quarter length black sable coat, unbuttoned, revealing beneath it a perfectly cut, bright crimson suit, with her tight skirt falling below her knees at the ideal length. In matching pumps with dramatically high heels, she strode down the avenue across from Harry's. Her hair was shiny, the color of midnight, lacquered onto her head and finished with swirls of curls framing her brown face. Crowning the side of her head was the smartest crimson hat Vander had ever seen. If her appearance wasn't striking enough, there was the matter of the fully grown cheetah walking alongside her. Lean and slinking on a sparkling chain attached to a jeweled collar—the cheetah most certainly put the woman over the top. Passersby cleared a path for the woman and her wild animal as she made way down the street, the woman's head held high and mischievously proud, pretending not to notice the commotion she was causing as she made way.

"Please! Stop looking at her!" Radiguet begged.

"Josephine!" Cocteau remarked with some excitement and knowing. "Your only true competitor—the great Josephine Baker! Look at how she walks down the street— African queen of the jungle! I don't know what they are putting into the water in America to grow such exotic flowers as you both."

Vander was well aware of Josephine Baker. Her scandalous dance, where she only wore a skirt of bananas tied low about her hips, was the talk of Paris. If Barbette's star shone bright, Josephine Baker was a super nova.

"She has a *cheetah*!" Vander exclaimed.

"Yes!" Radiguet said extremely agitated. He held his hand up to the side of his face to hide his visage from her so she would not recognize him if she turned her head toward the front window of Harry's. "The cheetah has an unpleasant disposition!" Radiguet warned. "Chiquita is her name. She terrifies me! How Josephine is not arrested on the spot for having such an animal roaming the streets!"

Vander could do nothing by gape.

"Don't look her way or she will come over!" Radiguet hastened.

"It is a good thing Princess Violette is at home, because you know she would have made a big fuss," Cocteau added. "It seems the princess fancies Josephine. She excites her. She finds her fascinating."

"In all my time in America, I've never seen a Negro looking like that!" Vander exclaimed. He watched Josephine move down the street, like an exotic cat herself—so strong and confident, yet her eyes were vivid and alert tingling with a hint of mirth. The woman owned the street, with or without her pet cheetah!

Then, almost directly across from Harry's Bar, a blonde driver in a black, gold-braided uniform emerged from a long, white Rolls Royce with sweeping lines and fancy running boards. The chauffer opened the rear door to the stunning automobile. Josephine was ten paces from the car. She released the cheetah's lead and the cat leapt inside of the auto in a single bound. Josephine smiled at her driver as she stepped into the auto.

"Unbelievable!" Vander remarked, eyes wide open. "I'm not in Round Rock, Texas anymore!"

"You most certainly are not!" Cocteau replied with a flourish.

"Thank *god* she is driving away," Radiguet said, quickly downing his Bloody Mary to settle his nerves.

"If there is one way to keep autograph hounds from running up, that is it!" Cocteau smiled. He too downed is midday cocktail and turned to Vander. He pushed back from the table. "Now, we must head onto our next great adventure. Vander, my dear, have you ever seen a pornographic film?"

...

"Monsieur Barbette!" Princess Violette said breathlessly as she burst into Vander's dressing room after his last Tuesday evening show. Vander was toweling himself off after having just been on stage. Her boisterous entrance startled Vander and put him off.

"My apologies for my vulgar manners," she began. "It is Raymond. He is very ill. They have returned from the Alps. Jean asked for you. Please, come at once!"

"I need to dress."

"There is no time."

Still in his stage makeup, but without a wig, Vander put on his winter coat and hat and fled the dressing room. The two ran into a startled Mimi back stage.

"I'll be back," was all Vander mustered.

Violette guided her yellow Citroën through the narrow streets of the Left Bank until she reached the Hotel Foyot. She took Vander inside up several flights of rickety wooden stairs. In her haste, sometimes dashing two stairs at a time, she looked like a frantic gorilla climbing up a hillside in her ample fur coat.

The two entered the simple apartment. A bed was along one wall and a small kitchen with heating stove and iron sink was positioned on the opposite side. The air in the room was stale and smelled of death.

A solitary lamp on a table by the bed was all that lit the room. Vander and Violette came up alongside of the bed next to a chair where Cocteau held vigil.

In the bed, Raymond Radiguet gasped for air, his lips murmured undiscernible, feverish French words. He looked wasted and old, not the robust young man with the gentle, easy smile Vander met only weeks before.

Cocteau put a rag into an icy bowl of water and then placed it on Radiguet's forehead. He gently brushed back his hair.

"Il doit être bien mon cher. Dors mon cher," Cocteau said softly. "Sleep my dear, sleep."

"Shouldn't he be at the hospital?" Vander asked not wanting to sound pushy.

"It is too late..." Cocteau replied. He too was lost— someplace far from Vander and Violette.

"Typhoid," Violette added quietly.

Vander gasped as he took a kerchief from his top coat and held it up to his mouth.

Then, Radiguet's body seized, as if he were a puppet being controlled by some unseen marionette. He shuddered and shook and then exhaled deeply until all that was left was silence.

"No!" Cocteau wept. "No! No! No!"

Violette tried to place her hand upon Cocteau's shoulder, but he pushed her away. "My love. Let me die with you!" Cocteau leaned down and kissed Raymond's lips. "Let me die with you!"

Violette protested, "No! Jean no!" She reached for his shoulders with all her force and pulled him off Radiguet.

Cocteau continued to sob deeply and he grabbed hold of Violette, burying his face in her coat. "No!"

...

Vander sat beside Princess Violette Murat in the packed, gothic church. Gentle voices from the choir chanting a mournful requiem washed through the space. Coco Chanel organized the service. Radiguet's coffin was draped in flowing, white silk and topped with a spray of unseasonable white roses.

Outside the church, in the mist of the overcast on the dreary rain-soaked street, awaited a horse drawn hearse pulled by four stallions and harnesses—all a brilliant white. The ancient monsignor from the pulpit on high presented his eulogy. He concluded with a quote from Radiguet's masterpiece, *Devil in the Flesh*: "*Facing death calmly is praiseworthy only if one faces it alone. Death together is no longer death, even for unbelievers. The source of sorrows lies not in leaving life, but in leaving that which gives it meaning. When love is our whole life, what difference is there between living together and dying together?"*

Cocteau, for his part, was not in attendance—too overcome by his own devastation. Violette daintily wiped tears from her eyes with her embroidered kerchief as sweet incense filled the cavernous space. Vander was still in shock—grieving the loss of his new-found friend.

...

Vander absentmindedly gazed out a window of his intimate suite at the Hotel Moderne. The chilled rain turned to gentle snowflakes, dusting the street scene before him. He watched passersby, a flight below, take careful steps on the pavement, not yet accustomed to the season's slick, sleet-covered sidewalks. It was not even much past three in the afternoon, and yet the sun shone little, the day darkening as it wore on. Vander rested on the settee next to the window, still dressed in his mourning suit.

Thoughts shifted from Radiguet to his own family. Once again, he constructed a letter in his mind to his mother. He felt he had to at last tell her about his life—that he was making a living—a good one at that—creating a fantasia of sorts as a woman. He tried over and over to get the wording right in his mind. In some versions, he even told her his preference for men, but that seemed to be altogether too much. Yet, with each version of the letter he constructed, he had to confront the question, *why?* As much as he wanted to tell his mother everything—somehow wanting his mother to experience the joy of his vocation—looking at it from her eyes, he thought she would think of him as some abhorrent creature, a biblical abomination. With the sun going down on the gloom out his Parisian window, Vander resigned himself to doing what he always did, sending a telegram indicating funds would be waiting for her at the Round Rock bank.

That was when he received a pounding on his door.

"*Monsieur Barbette?*" the muffled male voice called him out.

"A telegram has arrived."

Vander gathered himself and strode over to the door, unlatching the lock he made sure he now secured.

"*Oui?*" he said to the handsome young gentleman from the front desk.

"You have received a telegram," the man said again. He handed the neatly sealed envelope to Vander.

"*Merci.*" He hastily opened the letter still standing in the doorway. He read over the contents and grimaced.

"Bad news?" the front desk clerk inquired.

Vander was somewhat put out by his forthright question.

"No, no..." he replied distantly. "William Morris. I am to start a tour of Europe."

"You will be leaving Paris?" the man asked with a bit too much interest.

"Yes, in a fortnight."

"This is bad, very bad," the clerk replied. "I enjoy seeing you here," the young man offered. His soft blue eyes met Vander's. In a moment of understanding, Vander knew what he meant.

"I am finishing my shift," the man offered as he cleared his throat. "If you would like some company, I am free."

Vander swallowed hard, taking in the masculine beauty of the man before him.

"Yes, I would enjoy some company. Please, won't you come in?"

In his darkening room, Vander felt the force of the man about him. He groaned in pleasurable delight, taking in his power and sweated flesh. As the man engaged him, Vander looked out the window at his Parisian street scene—street lamps and store fronts coming alive with illumination amid the swirling flakes of snow. Passersby hurriedly moving about to reach their final destinations before the sun went down. The thrust of the man intensified. Vander called out. Then the two seized and shuddered—finally collapsing.

Yes, Vander pondered, in the morning he would send his mother more money.

CHAPTER TWENTY-EIGHT

"Princess Violette!" Vander called out as the yellow Citroën swerved at the last second to miss a pedestrian on the street. "Would you like me to drive?!" he asked exasperated. He knew he was a novice behind the wheel of an automobile, but at least he would dive in a sensible manner and not get them both killed.

"You are always too careful, Vander," Violette scoffed. "In Paris, this is how we drive!"

Thankfully, after they made a hair-raising turn, Vander could finally see the beaux arts façade of the Gare d'Orsay train station before them.

"I don't know what is more life-threatening, hanging from a trapeze on one foot or driving with you!" Vander called out as he clung onto the sides of brown leather upholstery of the front seats of the car.

Finally, Violette slammed on the brakes. The Citroën halted, perfectly astride the curb leading into the station entrance.

"Viola!" the princess smiled impressed by her driving. "See, that was not so bad!" She was bundled up in her abundant monkey fur coat, a dramatic purple scarf tied around her thick neck.

"Thank the good lord!"

"You worry too much, Vander. We have not taught you yet, how to live the Parisian life. You need to be free!"

Vander sighed. He looked at Violette and her preposterousness and laughed, "Perhaps you are right, your highness."

"Of course I am! When Jean returns from Monte Carlo and you come back from your tour—you will see. We shall all take a holiday together. We will give you lessons on how to be more French!"

Vander laughed. "I would very much enjoy that....." He then changed the subject. "Have you heard from him? Cocteau?"

"No, I am sorry I have not. Acquaintances have told me he is in Monte Carlo. I know Jean. When he is ready, he shall return."

"Yes, I'm sure," Vander said quietly. "Please, tell him I inquired after him. He and Raymond—you've all really been so wonderful to me. You've made me feel like Paris is my home."

"It is!" Violette smiled. "It is—*the home*—of Barbette!"

Vander smiled as a porter came up the car.

"*Voulez-vous assistance?*" the porter asked eyeing all of the bags and trunks stacked in the back of the automobile.

"*Oui! Merci!*" Vander said confidently.

Violette laughed. "You better be careful using those two French words. They can get you into a lot of trouble!"

"*Oui!*" Vander laughed as the porter opened his door. Vander reached for the princess's jeweled hand. "*Merci!*" he said and then kissed her rings.

Violette shook her head, "*Très bon, Barbette!* Very good. Have a wonderful trip!"

CHAPTER TWENTY-NINE

"I bet you're happy to be back home, Mimi," Vander said as he began to disrobe in his dressing room after his evening performance at London's Palladium. Touring Europe, Barbette became more of a sensation earning top billing in reviews. Lines for tickets grew longer. Theaters, night clubs, and music halls were packed with the curious, taking in his potent act of sensual mystification and aerial daring.

"Not so sure, me lord," Mimi replied as she fluffed out the ostrich feathers to Barbette's most majestic head piece. "Sometimes it's better to be away from the lot. You know what they say, distance breeds contentment."

Vander nodded as he sat at his vanity table.

"Have those papers arrived?"

"They're right here," Mimi responded as she put the headpiece on a mannequin's head and went to a small side table to retrieve the papers. Mimi handed the documents to Vander.

"If you don't mind me asking, me lord, what are all them papers?"

"Property deeds from Texas. I need to sign these and send them back to the states." Vander leaned back in his chair. He was shirtless with only the scantest of underthings covering his privates. He just washed body paint from his skin and was sitting at the table. With taught, strong muscles, it was hard to imagine his frame fooled anyone into thinking he was a woman.

"You buying land in Texas?" Mimi asked as she went about her chores while looking over his shoulder.

"Yes, I am. I figure one day, Austin is going to be a big town and when it does, I'll be rich!"

"You're a dreamer me lord, that's what you are, a real dreamer," Mimi shook her head. "I need to take these things to the wardrobe mistress, then I'll be heading home, me lord. Do you need me to take those to be posted?"

"No thanks, Mimi. I can do it myself. Have a good night."

"Indeed, me lord," Mimi replied.

After she left, Vander looked one last time at the documents before him. He never imagined he would have the ability to purchase some property in Austin. His mother always told him it was what separated the wealthy folks in Round Rock from those who were not—owning land. He was frugal with his tour earnings and was proud he could start purchasing parcels of property.

Vander heard a knocking at the door. He thought it must be one of the show girls again, trying to borrow something. Without putting on his robe, he opened his dressing room door.

Standing before him was *not* one of the chorus girls!

"Oh dear! Look what the cat dragged in—*Earl Winston Darby*," Vander sighed. He looked past him to see if others noticed his state of undress. "Please. Come inside. I'm not dressed for visitors."

Vander gestured for Winston Darby to enter.

Without any warning, Winston reached out and held onto Vander. He was dressed in black tie and tails, looking every bit as dashing as the night the two first met upon the high seas of the Atlantic.

"Winston!" Vander protested.

"I've missed you, Vander."

Vander could smell private label whiskey on Winston's breath and the aroma of Cuban cigars in the fabric of his tuxedo.

"Are we pretending we know each other tonight?" Vander said as he broke away from Darby's grasp. He recalled their last cold encounter so many months ago in the haberdasher's store.

"You must understand. You know my position. If I was to publically say I knew you, I would be ruined."

"Do you know how much I care?" Vander turned away from him. "Really, Winston."

"You have every right to be angry with me. You do. But you must remember, I didn't make this silly world and all of its rules. I only exist in it! We both do…Vander…Vander…" Winston murmured as he walked closer. "I've missed you, I have. If I have caused you any harm, any pain, for this I am truly sorry. If I should say anything, it's I have never felt anything for another as I do for you. Won't you forgive me? Please?"

Vander was silent as he looked into Winston's earnest, clear brown eyes.

He sighed, "Forgiven." He then leaned forward and kissed Winston on his full lips, tasting what he longed for so many nights ago. The two became locked in an embrace as Vander expertly moved to unfasten Winston's trousers. Vander reached down and grabbed hold of Winston's power. Winston exhaled in delight. Vander's lips were upon him, down there, thrilling Winston with erotic sensations. The gentleman's trousers fell to the ground and Vader continued to lustily ply him with affections.

"Get your mouth off his cock!" Mimi shouted. She was standing in the doorway to the dressing room. "A couple of Mary Ann's!" Mimi added in a venomous tone. Vander stood up while Winston hurriedly pulled up his trousers. "Call the cops! We've got buggers!" Mimi demanded.

Vander and Winston were stunned into silence.

"What's all the commotion?" they heard the stage manager grouse as he entered the dressing room to see the earl hurriedly fastening his pants and Vander wiping his mouth, desperately looking for his robe.

"Call the cops!" Mimi called out.

"You two Mary Ann's," the stage manager added, "don't you move a muscle or I'll crack both your skulls open!"

CHAPTER THIRTY

"The offenses against you, Mister Loving, are quite serious, quite serious indeed," Mister Brookings explained to Vander in a stone-walled cell in the basement of a London jail. Vander wore only some canvas blues which smelled as if another man had already worn them. He looked exhausted and totally angry. "As your solicitor, I must tell you the charge of gross indecency is punishable with penal servitude of at least two years."

Mister Brookings was a bald man of thirty or so, who wore a close-clipped Van Dyke beard and tidy suit. He cleared his throat and then removed his spectacles, cleaning them with his kerchief. He then continued, "Whilst a conviction of sodomy can lead to something even more severe. You would be imprisoned for the rest of your life."

Vander's eyes welled up, but he refused to cry. He swallowed hard. "What we were engaged in was private. It was no one's business."

Brookings grimaced. "I'm afraid it is no matter you were alone in your dressing room or the fact the dressing room door was closed. The magistrate will still view the activities as occurring in a theatre—a very public place. It shan't reveal itself well in the proceedings."

"And Earl Darby, has he given any indication to you about what he might report?"

Brookings looked intently at Vander.

"Winston Darby comes from an exceedingly prominent family. They have already succeeded in sealing the proceedings of this inquiry using an old military law. Divulging the contents of the proceedings would be a detriment to the safety of the nation."

"Good god!" Vander exclaimed, feeling as if he was in a legal bind completely out of his understanding. "What does it mean?"

"It means this—Darby has been your ally in this matter to some degree. For the proceedings will not be publicly recorded. It shall be sealed. Neither he nor yourself are even at liberty to speak of the arrest or the inquest."

"For how long?" Vander asked.

"Forever," Brookings replied. "You can see Darby's actions have worked in your favor. However, there is the matter of the action itself, the consent of the action, and the location of said intercourse…"

"I can tell you honestly, there was indeed mutual consent," Vander added.

Brookings frowned. "Already, I am hearing from Darby's defense they will be claiming it was not. They state you came upon Darby and forced yourself upon him. They will prove through witness testimony this was the case."

"That's just not true!" Vander protested.

"Mister Loving, the type of trial you are engaging in is one of inquiry. It is not like the American courts—where two sides argue against one another. Rather, the magistrate, the judge, will do the questioning and summons the witnesses. It is not our intention to impugn Earl Darby, but rather, to free your soul." Brookings took a deep sigh. He looked seriously into Vander's eyes. "I must tell you something. Earl Darby has engaged the services of a very prominent barrister. The charges against him have been dropped."

Vander felt lost and confused. He was revolted at the proceedings and angry with himself for not having more discipline.

"What then, do your propose be my defense, Mister Brookings?"

"I know this line of questioning will be unseemly. However, I do believe it shall be our only hope. Mister Loving, at the theatre that evening, did you engage in any sort, how shall I put it delicately, any sort of 'anal' penetration?"

"I did not," Vander replied in a forthright manner.

A slight smile of relief formed on Brookings's face. "Well, then, I believe we have our defense. For you see, sodomy entails such action occurred."

"You mean to tell me, because I was providing pleasure to Earl Darby by a different means, in British law it doesn't add up to sodomy?"

"Precisely!"

"So it can be thrown out?"

"That would be the intention. And, if this fact is proven, the notion of gross indecency in the mind of the magistrate may very well be lessened."

"And this is our only hope?"

"It is, I'm afraid, it truly is indeed."

. . .

"The court is now in session," the magistrate proclaimed in his proper, British accent as he pounded the gavel. He must have been a man nearing sixty, Vander surmised. His face was fleshy with folds and creases about his jowls and puffed bags beneath his spectacled-eyes. The white-powdered, horsehair wig perched upon his bald dome needed tending. His black robe was voluminous, made of a fabric which was more sensible than stylish.

"Please be seated," he continued. "The court has reviewed the state's charges against Mister Vander Clyde Loving and is prepared to make its inquest. Mister Brookings, is your client aware of the charges against him and prepared for this inquiry and the judgments of the court?"

Mister Brookings, also wearing a black robe and a white, horsehair wig of curls, replied, "He is, your honor."

"Very well," the magistrate continued in his tenor voice of fluid diction.

Vander was still dressed in his prison blues and had to sit behind fence of thick metal bars, like a caged animal. He scanned the room. There sat Winston Darby, encircled by his team of barristers. He was dressed in a finely cut suit. Vander felt a knot in his stomach for the free man, who refused to even gaze in his direction. It irked Vander no end to see him sitting there, chin up, the glint of indignity in his eyes. Behind him sat his sister, Gwyneth. She looked in Vander's direction, casting a disdainfully faint frown his way, and then she returned to looking at the magistrate who presided from a substantial wooden rostrum at the center of the room.

Astride from Gwyneth must have been the siblings' parents. Winston's father, whose titled name was Lord Fitch, was a stately man in his own right, fine white hair, a tidy, waxed, white mustache on a lean, elegant face. Lady Fitch was plump, but serious, dressed in black. She had an anxious look about herself, not at all sure she should be in attendance to witness this scandalous testimony, but wanting to be present for her son as he provided his account and cleared the family name.

The magistrate continued, "The court calls its first witness Mary Ann Stuart to the stand."

Mimi entered the courtroom and was guided to the witness stand and sworn in. Vander knew her outfit. It was her

Sunday dress—a neat floral pattern of whites and greys upon a rich navy blue. A belt with a simple, black buckle synched her thick waist. Her hair was freshly cut and styled. She looked plain and simple. Her face was serious, yet she fidgeted anxiously with her sensible cloth purse, which she placed on her lap.

The magistrate began his line of inquiry, "Missus Stuart, of whom are you employed?"

"Mister Vander Clyde Broadway Loving," she replied.

"Is Mister Loving in attendance today?"

"Yes, me lord," she nodded. "He's over there," she said pointing one of her white-gloved fingers Vander's direction. Vander tried to make eye contact with her, but she did not linger on his visage.

"How long have you been employed by Mister Loving?"

"A little over a year, me lord."

"What do you do for Mister Loving?"

"Well, Mister Loving is an entertainer. Goes by the name Barbette. He's a female impressionist who walks the wire and swings from the trapeze. I take care of his costumes and make sure everything is tidy for him."

"Can you tell the court what you witnessed the night in question?"

"Well, things were going just as good as always. Mister Loving finished his show. We were alone in the dressing room and then I went to go and work with the wardrobe mistress, putting all the costumes back in place for the next day. I was gone for about ten minutes, I would imagine. When I came back—that's when the two were grinding."

The magistrate winced a bit, but continue with his questioning.

"Tell me exactly what you witnessed."

"Well, there was the Earl standing up. His back was against the wall and his trousers were down on the ground. Mister Loving's mouth…." Mimi paused for a moment, upset by what she was about to reveal, "Mister Loving's mouth was about the Earl's wanker!"

Lady Fitch was overcome by the words. She produced a black, lace fan and began to frantically cool her flush cheeks.

"And then what occurred?"

"Well, I called out and that's when the stage manager come by and he saw what I did. Well, not exactly, because by that time, Mister Loving's mouth was not on the Earl's pecker."

"Missus Stuart, did you ever see Mister Loving attempt any such actions on other people whilst you were in his employ?"

"Me lord, if you mean did I ever see him doing it with another man, I most certainly did not! I would've reported what I saw if I did! Goes against God. Goes against the natural order of things!"

"Did you ever see Mister Loving have carnal relations with anyone?"

"I did not, me lord. As far as I knew he was chaste."

The magistrate's eyes narrowed a bit as he continued, "Missus Stuart, you mentioned the occupation of the defendant is that he impersonates a female whilst performing aerial acrobatics?"

"Yes, me lord," Mimi replied.

"Please forgive me for this line of questioning, but can you, in your capacity as his chambermaid attest to the fact Mister Loving is indeed a man?"

Lady Fitch and Gwyneth both gasped. Lady Fitch was now furiously fanning herself, much to her husband's distraction.

"If what you're asking, does he have a pecker, I can say yes he does, me lord."

"So he is a man?"

"Indeed, me lord."

"One final question, if you please…Was the dressing room door locked or unlocked?"

"Unlocked, me lord. Not sure if there is a lock on that door. If there is, I never seen a key."

"Very well, Missus Stuart," the magistrate replied. "You may leave the witness stand."

Not missing a moment, the magistrate called forth Earl Winston Darby.

Vander watched Winston enter the witness box. He looked young and nervous in Vander's eyes. No doubt, Vander surmised, what he was about to hear would be a coached pile of horse crap.

The magistrate began, "Were you in attendance at the performance of Barbette at the London Palladium the night in question?"

"Yes," Winston replied curtly.

"Why did you go backstage?"

"To greet Mister Loving."

"Prior to that evening, did you know Mister Loving?"

"Why yes," Winston replied. He gathered himself, becoming detached in a way from the words he uttered.

"How, did you know Mister Loving?"

"We met onboard the Majestic, the ocean liner. We dined together, with my sister Gwyneth and William Morris, the talent agent."

"Did you spend more time with him than one solitary dinner?"

"Yes. We were the only passengers aboard in our class remotely related by age and so we enjoyed each other's company."

"How did you *enjoy each other's company*, Earl Darby?" the magistrate questioned.

"Well you know, the usual things—we played shuffleboard, hands of cards—the usual things."

"And so your relationship aboard the Majestic was nothing but platonic?"

Winston looked at the magistrate somewhat startled.

"If your honor is asking if there was anything more, I can assure you there was not! I do not harbor particular friendships, your honor."

"Very well, Earl Darby... Why did you attend the show the night in question?"

"Whilst at dinner aboard the Majestic, Mister Loving introduced himself as Mister Barbette. My sister, Gwyneth, is a great fan of the stage. She recalled a female trapeze artist of that name. Mister Barbette told us this performer was his sister and he invited us to see her performance."

"And so the night in question was your first time to see Mister Loving perform as Barbette?"

Winston fidgeted a moment. He ran his hand atop his thick shock of combed and pomaded blond hair.

"Well no, your honor it wasn't. It was last year. When Mister Loving performed at the Palladium for the first time. My sister and I attended the performance then. We quite enjoyed Lady Barbette's aerial display, and when she removed her wig and we were shocked. Shocked and appalled! She was Mister Loving! We left the theatre immediately."

"Then, why did you return the night in question?"

"Well, I thought perhaps I was being rude. Other acquaintances had seen Mister Loving perform his stunts and were quite impressed. I thought perhaps if I looked upon his act with new eyes, I would find it more impressive. So I purchased a ticket for myself and attended the show yet again."

"Did you, Earl Darby, find Mister Loving's act more impressive the night in question?"

Winston looked again earnestly to the judge.

Vander was rapt by the testimony, how casually Winston wove together fact and fiction.

"Yes, I did, in a rather unsettling way. You see, the Mister Barbette I met on the Majestic was quite masculine, so it was certainly a surprise."

"Forgive me for asking such queer questions, Earl Darby, but please indulge my inquiry. Did you find the Barbette on stage attractive?"

Winston was silent for a moment. In all of his practicing mock interrogations with his barrister, the question never arose.

"As a woman or a man?" Winston asked.

"Either."

"Make no mistake when Mister Loving is Barbette he is quite beautiful, but only in a womanly way."

"Do you think his portrayal as a woman might have *confused* your senses?"

"Well, I'm not sure, your honor. Quite possibly. But I only went back stage to greet Mister Loving, as I often do with other entertainers, after seeing their performances."

"Of course, Earl Darby…So when you went back stage the evening in question, what occurred next?"

"Well, I asked a man back stage where I might find Mister Loving and he directed me to his dressing room door. I knocked and Mister Loving permitted me inside. We exchanged pleasantries."

"How did Mister Loving look? Was he dressed as a man or a woman at this point?"

"A man your honor."

"And what happened next?"

"Well, he attacked me! He was all over me like some rabid dog. I couldn't think. I was in shock. I tried to call out."

"You are a big, powerful man, Earl Darby, did you not try to push him off, punch him in the face?"

"You are right, I am a big man, but if you have seen Mister Loving's act, you will know he is incredibly strong. He overpowered me, your excellence."

The magistrate looked intently at Winston Darby.

"Did he, and again, please forgive the specificity of my questions, did Mister Loving ever enter you upon your posterior regions?"

Winston looked down for a while and then back up at the magistrate.

"No sir, he did not. Lest I save you and me both from further embarrassment and shame in your inquest, shall we agree the actions explained by Missus Stuart were quite accurate—for that *is* what he did."

"And what happened next?"

"Thankfully, Missus Stuart came in and stage manager followed. Then, we were arrested."

"Very well, Earl Darby, you may step down."

The magistrate wrote on a ledger before him, saying nothing for a long while. Then he removed his spectacles and cleaned them again with his kerchief.

"Very well, the court is now prepared to hear the testimony of the defendant. The court now calls Mister Vander Clyde Broadway Loving, alias, Barbette, to provide testimony."

Vander stood up and was sworn in from his caged cube within the court. It made him feel inhuman having to testify from behind bars, wearing his horrid jail blues.

"Very well, Mister Loving, the court shall now proceed. You may be seated...Mister Loving, you are an American, is that correct?

"Yes, your excellence. Born and raised in the state of Texas."

"The great frontier?"

"Yes, your excellence."

"Very well. What is the nature of your work?"

"I'm an acrobatic illusionist."

The magistrate's left eyebrow cocked.

"As an acrobatic illusionist, does your performance require you to appear as a woman?"

"Yes, your excellence," Vander replied.

"Yet, you are a man?"

"Yes."

"If you will forgive me, this line of questioning...Were you *born* a man Mister Loving?"

"Yes, of course," Vander replied somewhat indignantly. His solicitor Brookings grimaced slightly, not wanting his client to demonstrate contempt toward the magistrate.

"How long have your been performing this line of work?"

"As Barbette, you mean?"

"Indeed."

"A few years. Before Barbette, I performed aerial stunts as an Alfaretta sister and also with Erford's Whirling Sensations."

"Did you perform as a man or a woman in these shows?"

"As a woman, your excellence."

"But *why?*" the magistrate looked perplexed. "You are a perfectly masculine specimen."

"The only job I could find, it must be eight years ago, was as a female aerialist. Audrey Fuller, of the Alfaretta sisters—she and her husband made me dress as a woman in the act because they said the stunts looked better when a woman performed them."

"I see, so it was never your intention to impersonate a female—you only did so to survive."

"Perhaps at first, your excellence. But what I do, as Barbette, I have elevated to a degree of refinement. I believe the attraction of my act is that it is beauty—a strange beauty. I'm no mere man doing aerial stunts in a wig and a dress."

"I am sure you are not," the magistrate said earnestly. "How many shows do you think you have performed as a woman?"

"I'm not exactly sure, your honor. Thousands, I believe."

"And do you think being in such an unnatural state for such a long duration might cause some confusion to your senses?"

Vander sat quietly for a moment contemplating what the magistrate was implying.

"No, your honor, I do not. I know who I am. I have always known who I am."

Brookings wiped his brow with his kerchief, upset by Vander's reply.

"So you do *not* believe your impersonations of a woman might have affected your attractions to the sexes, male or female?"

"No, your excellence."

"*Indeed*, Mister Loving!" the magistrate responded, surprised by Vander's response. The magistrate gave Brookings a rueful glance and then continued. "Could you be so kind to describe when you first met the acquaintance of Earl Winston Darby?"

"It was aboard the Majestic. We dined together and became friends."

"Mister Loving, is that the entire nature of your relationship, simply *friends*?"

Vander considered the question. "There are different sorts of friendship, your honor."

"Indeed, Mister Loving. What sort of friendship was yours?"

Vander swallowed hard and cleared his throat.

188

"It was more than merely dining and playing cars, your honor."

"Was it intimate?"

The question rolled through the court. And then there was silence. Vander looked over at Winston, who for once was looking directly at him. Then, Vander returned his glance to the magistrate.

"Yes."

Winston Darby pounded his fist on the table before him. His mother, Lady Fitch swooned. Brookings again wiped his brow.

"This court will have order," the magistrate admonished. "In your opinion, Mister Loving, was this intimacy consensual?"

Vander thought of the love he shared with Winston aboard the Majestic. It all was so perfect back then, aboard the ship. They did not have to worry about convention or society's morals. Vander felt a flutter of excitement around Winston. He knew Winston felt the same. They both wanted to be with one another. If it wasn't love, Vander didn't know what it was.

"Of course."

Winston Darby thrust his body back in his chair in disgust. His mother grew more red-faced. Lord Fitch gathered her up and escorted her from the courtroom.

"Mister Loving, whilst onboard the Majestic, did you tell Earl Darby that Barbette was your sister?"

"Yes."

"Why? Do you make it a point to lie about your profession? Did you try to entrap Earl Darby in some sort of way?"

"I understand how the nature of my work might be distasteful to some people. I thought if I invited him to a show and he saw firsthand the performance, he would see how refined and beautiful it was and he would appreciate it."

"So that is how you planned to seduce him?"

"No, your excellence. That was how I planned to impress him."

"But the reason why you wanted to impress him was because you wanted to continue your particular friendship with him?"

Vander exhaled.

"I would agree with that statement."

"Mister Loving, did you have any encounters with Earl Darby after departing from the Majestic?"

"No, your honor. We met once in London, last year by chance, in a haberdasher's shop, but Earl Darby was quite distant to me at the time."

"So you did not know that he was in attendance last year whilst you were performing at the Palladium?"

"No."

"Let us turn to the present, shall we? Did you invite Earl Darby to your show the night in question?"

"No."

"Please, won't you tell the court, in your own words, what happened that night?"

"Well, I had completed my show. I took off my makeup and showered. I was nearly naked when Mimi left me to attend to my costumes. I heard a knocking on the door. I didn't see my robe immediately, but I was not expecting guests. I thought perhaps it was Mimi or the stage hand. You know back stage, your honor, it's quite normal for entertainers to wear little clothing. Well, I was surprised to see Earl Darby. He told me he was quite taken by my performance and wanted to reconcile. We were intimate in the moment, but I can assure you it was consensual. I would never force myself upon someone."

"So you admit to fornication with Earl Darby?"

"Is a kiss fornication? For I have seen many men exchange it."

"A kiss is not fornication," the magistrate answered.

"Well, that was all I engaged in—a kiss."

"*Indeed Mister Loving?*" the magistrate's eyebrows raises. "Well then are you *denying* the testimony of Earl Darby and Missus Stuart?"

"I never forced myself on Earl Darby. We kissed."

"Did you *kiss* Earl Darby's nether regions?"

"I did, your excellence," Vander replied with his chin up. "But it was not forced."

Brookings stared at Vander aghast at what he was revealing.

"Did you have intercourse of a sexual nature with Earl Darby? Did you enter his posterior region?"

"No, I did not."

"Very well, Mister Loving."

The magistrate's expression was deeply dour as if he had eaten rotten food. Earl Winston Darby sat seething in his chair unable to look at Vander. His sister, Gwyneth, finally stood up and exited the courtroom in disgust. Mister Brookings sat back—knowing Vander had been honest, but the honesty may have provided him with a sizable length of time in prison.

Vander, for his part, held his head high, no matter his jail cell attire. No matter the circumstances, he would retain his dignity.

"This court shall be adjourned until one in the afternoon. Then, I shall pronounce my verdict."

The magistrate pounded his gavel. All rose and exited the court. Vander and Brookings were escorted to a holding cell within the courthouse. For a long while the two sat at a table saying nothing to one another.

"I'm going to be found guilty," Vander said finally breaking their silence.

"Yes."

"And so I shall be imprisoned?"

"Yes."

Vander sighed deeply. He looked at Brookings and said, "I don't understand it. Why is my love is any different?"

"Because it isn't natural! It's against the laws of God!" Brookings said in a flash of rage.

"Do you *really* think so?" Vander opined. "If we go to the zoo this afternoon I'll take you to the monkey house where you'll see all sorts of unnatural activity done quite naturally."

"Your arrogance will get you years."

"That may be so, but I will have my integrity."

"So you feel no shame?"

"No. I don't. I don't know why I'm this way. I don't have any idea. I'm sure, if he could muster once ounce of truthfulness in his own mind and looked at himself honestly in the mirror, Earl Winston Darby would have to admit to the same."

"But even if you are this way—you needn't act on those inclinations!"

"You mean, I'm not to love? How does a man go through life without love? Can it be done?"

"You are so proud now, like a peacock, but two years for public indecency in a prison doing hard labor and what shall come of you? You will be ruined!"

"So you would rather have me lie? What sort of man are you? What sort of integrity do *you* have?"

"All I am saying is people's perceptions of what occurred can be quite different. Why you couldn't have said you were merely fixing a button on Earl Darby's trousers and Mimi must have been mistaken. How would it have hurt anyone?"

"It wouldn't have," Vander sighed. "It wouldn't have hurt anyone—but me. I have *my* dignity. I am a man, Mister Brookings."

"And you have the stubbornness of a woman!"

Just then, an officer of the court came into the holding cell. He told Brookings and Vander the magistrate was ready to provide his ruling. The two headed into the courtroom, behind the iron bars of the cage to witness his verdict. Once the magistrate entered the court, all were seated. The magistrate sat quietly at his rostrum for a while, scribbling notes on forms before him. Again, he took off his spectacles, cleaned them, and put them back on his fleshy nose.

"Mister Loving, please rise...You are a talented, although curious man. Though you might not agree with my saying, I do believe a man who must dress as a woman night after night in order to earn his keep, might indeed have some confusion about his attractions..."

Vander wanted to shake his head no, but he held still, taking in all the magistrate was saying.

"I cannot immediately dismiss Earl Darby's testimony nor that of Missus Stuart. In fact, you all were in agreement. Earl Darby was not sodomized. And so this inquest finds you not guilty of sodomy. Earl Darby states it was you who instigated this entanglement and there is some corroboration with Missus Stuart's testimony. However, it is not the duty of the court to rule on the legality of your relations with Earl Darby—but to rule specifically on the actions witnessed by Missus Stuart. Were the door to that dressing room locked, dare I say we would not be burdening the court this very day. However, as it is, Mister Loving, the court finds you guilty of public indecency."

Vander stood in stony silence.

"The laws of Great Britain guiding this inquest permit me some leniency in the sentencing. But before I pronounce this sentence, I shall caution all those present now or for any portion of this inquest—that this inquiry—its verdict and sentence are sealed and will remain so well beyond the lifetimes of all of those present. If elements of this inquest are made public, those perpetrating this disclosure will be dealt with severely. Is this understood by everyone in the court?" The magistrate looked at Vander and Earl Winston Darby, who was now only flanked by his father, Lord Fitch and his most senior barrister. They all nodded in agreement. "I will be very clear this seal also pertains to those who joined us in the court this morn. Do you understand, Lord Fitch?"

"Yes, your excellence," Lord Fitch answered. His diction was strong and powerful.

"Mister Loving, you are an American visiting this country for employment. Since you have violated the laws and covenants of this fair nation with a wanton disrespect, the punishment for your guilt of public indecency is you shall be forever banned from Great Britain. You are never again to step foot on British soil—for employment or for pleasure or any other reason. You are permanently forbidden to enter these isles. Do you understand this sentence?"

Mister Brookings smiled, but Vander was expressionless.

"I do your excellence."

The magistrate pounded this gavel. "Court dismissed!"

There was a flurry of activity in the court and those present made way for the exits.

Vander sat in his cage. Brookings came up to him.

"You see Mister Brookings, sometimes dignity triumphs over stupidity."

"Indeed, Mister Loving," Brookings sighed, "indeed."

CHAPTER THIRTY-ONE

JANUARY, 1925

"I do not like this bar!" Princess Violette protested as she looked about the cramped space of Claire de Lune. "I am encircled by men!" she argued. A deep frown sunk into her fat cheeks.

"I find it quite interesting," Barbette replied with a sly grin as he enjoyed the view. The two encamped at a table along one wall of the establishment. Although it was past two in the morning, the place grew more crowded, packed with young men in military uniform.

The princess produced a gold cigarette case from her glittering black handbag and lit a smoke. A young sailor sitting very close to her protested when she lazily held the fag too close to his head.

"Do not worry pretty boy!" she scoffed. "I shan't get ash on your pretty sailor costume."

Barbette took in Princess Violette's preposterousness and burst out laughing. A small jazz band played in the corner deep within the bar. The noise of their instruments further irritated the princess.

"Maybe if we look hard enough, we'll see one of the manly men is really a woman," Barbette joked.

"I doubt it, Barbette, I do," she exhaled wistfully into the direction of the offended sailor.

The slender figure of Jean Cocteau broke forth from the press of the boisterous crowd appearing before the table where the two were seated. In another instant, a very handsome young man sprung forth from the press of sailors to stand alongside of the artist. Cocteau grabbed the man's hand. Both were dressed elegantly in tuxedos, top hats, and overcoats.

Since Barbette returned to Paris and rejoined his friends, he noticed Cocteau looked different. There was a yellowness to the artist's complexion, a tightness to his expression. He seemed lost amidst an unspoken inner turmoil. But tonight, the charm of his old persona returned in the presence of the young, dashing man.

"Maurice, I present to you the magnificent Barbette!"

Cocteau turned to the aerialist and said above the din, "Barbette, I present to you the charming Maurice Sachs!"

Barbette and Maurice shook hands across the table.

"Ahem!" Violette protested.

"Ah yes, and this monstrous bear is the very wealthy Princess Violette Bonaparte Murat."

"So pleased to meet you, my darling," Violette said as she let Sachs kiss her extended hand. "Has Cocteau told you he has the clap?"

"Bitch!" Cocteau hissed. He then put his hand upon the young shoulder of Maurice. "Barbette, you both have so much in common. You escaped the clutches of the barbaric British magistrate while Mister Sachs escaped the sanctimonious grasp of a Catholic seminary. Shall I reveal, in both instances, the reason for such hasty departures was your unnatural inclinations?"

Maurice Sachs smiled broadly. He was no more than twenty years old, if that. Fresh-faced, thick, black hair parted on the side, he held a more robust, almost American frame, with eyes which were alive and curious.

"Mister Vander Clyde Broadway Loving, it is indeed a pleasure!" Sachs bowed.

"Please!" Cocteau admonished. "You must never speak of Barbette using that name. It is biblical really—just as Saul took the name Paul upon his conversion—so Barbette wishes to never be referred to by his old name having left it in Great Britain. Now in this thriving Gomorrah, he is only—*Barbette!*"

"Apologies," Maurice smiled. "Barbette, you are the sensation of Paris! You represent everything the surrealists are attempting to portray."

"Really?" Barbette drolly replied as he gazed at the man.

"Why, yes indeed!"

"So tell me Mister Sachs, how did you come to meet your paramour, Mister Cocteau?" Barbette asked appraising the handsome man before him.

"Our production of Romeo and Juliet!" Cocteau interjected and then he looked about the room, taking stock of the handsome young sailors around him.

"I'm sure you were a bewitching Juliet to Jean's Romeo," Barbette laughed.

"Coming from you, I take it as a compliment."

"You shouldn't," Barbette replied.

"This place bores me!" Violette protested. "If I flick any more ash onto the head of this fairy next to me, I fear I shall burn the whole place down!" The princess extinguished her cigarette, downed the remainder of her whiskey and gathered her enormous frame which was wrapped this season in an ample, black sable coat. "Come everyone! We must depart!"

...

The Princess Violette drove madcap about the city in her yellow Citroën until she rolled down a deserted side street on the Left Bank. Running over the side of the curb, she righted the automobile and attempted to park in a more civilized manner.

"Ssssshhh!" she hissed at Maurice Sachs as they all got out of the car. "You talk too much! Where we are going tonight, you must not speak!"

"Where *are* we going?" Barbette asked. By now it must have been three in the morning.

Princess Violette leered at him, "And you also ask too many questions!"

Cocteau came up beside Barbette.

"We are going to paradise tonight, my friend!"

Barbette cast a bemused glance at Cocteau as the four made way down the next block, Violette leading the way, a massive dark figure silhouetted in her sable coat by the street lamps.

She came up to a darkened doorway which looked no different from any of the others lining the little street.

"Ssssshhhh!" she scolded Cocteau and Sachs who were being entirely too chatty for her liking. Then, she steadied herself and knocked on the burgundy, lacquered door. There was no answer, and so she knocked again more forcefully.

A moment later, a small square window opened within the door at eye level. An older Asian woman, her face was round and filled the small, square opening. Princess Violette said something to the old woman in French that Barbette didn't quite understand. The old woman shook her head no, but Princess Violette continued pleading in a quiet, hushed voice as the other three stood silently by. Finally, Violette produced from her billfold a wad of francs and flashed them before the Asian woman's face. The small square opening closed and the three could hear the old lady maneuver the dead bolts of the door.

The four entered a tiny vestibule which was painted black and lit only by a solitary, gold, art nouveau sconce of a peacock set high one wall. In the darkness of the small space, Barbette saw the woman was dressed in a deep blue, kimono robe with long, draping sleeves and stitched with fanciful, golden designs. Her silver hair was pulled back in a tight bun. Barbette thought she must have been a beauty in her youth. Even now, in her old age, she held herself in a pleasing way.

In the dim lighting, there appeared to be two doorways to either side of the square vestibule. But when Violette and the old lady completed their transaction, the dowager pushed onto the shiny black wall before them and an opening appeared as if by magic.

The old lady led the four down a narrow hallway, also painted shiny black. The only light came from before them in the room ahead. It was flickering and dim.

Cocteau grew in excitement as the four were led, single file, toward the light. Cocteau was directly behind Sachs and kept on pinching his ass. The more Sachs protested, the more boisterous Cocteau became. Then, he turned around with a flourish and groped Barbette. Cocteau laughed in a manic manner. Barbette could already smell incense as he passed through a shower of tiny strands of red and gold glass beads.

The four then stepped into a room whose walls were draped in rows parchment paper and red silk. Upon the parchment were black painted slashes and dots, all vertically aligned. Barbette knew each figure represented a word, but he had no clue what they said. To him, they were only exotic wall decorations. Along two sides of the room about a foot off the ground were deep ledges, low beds, where tufts of cushions and pillows were strewn amongst crimson and gold silk throws of fabric. Round, paper lanterns, festooned with the black ink of the alien script and fringed with red, flickered overhead from the candles contained within.

The old woman gestured toward the low cushions and the ornately carved octagonal wooden tables in front them.

"Violette—let me have your coat!" Cocteau implored. "I want to fuck Maurice on sable."

"You may have it if you shut up!" she scowled.

Cocteau instructed them all to remove their coats, hats, and shoes—to get comfortable on the beds of cushions.

Princess Violette smiled as she and Barbette found satisfying spots amid the cushions. From their vantage, they watched the two on the other bed—Cocteau lustily kissing Sachs atop Violette's thick, fur coat.

A stooped China man entered the room carrying a tray. He too was old like the woman. From his upper lip and the tender spot below the lower, sprung a long, silvery mustache and beard—three strands of hair converging upon his red, silken chest and braided at the tip. A roundish cap of the same fabric and style as his robe perched on his head. The man set the tray with its ornate lamp and pipes on one of the octagonal tables before Cocteau and Sachs. When he did so, Barbette could see a another single, long, braid of hair—white at the top by the man's cap becoming black as it made its way down his back to just above his rear.

Although he had a considerable amount to drink before they arrived at their present encampment, Barbette was clear-minded enough to know he shouldn't partake in the unfolding ritual before him, but tonight, he felt reckless, as if his previous life was all shackles he wished to cast off. He gladly took the long, ornately enameled pipe of white on blue and watched with great interest the serene manner in which the oriental man prepared the opium.

"Would you like music?" the old woman asked as she returned to the room with a special bowl which she handed to the old man.

"Yes!" Violette insisted. "Tonight we listen to Mistinguett!"

"Oh please, no!" Sachs protested.

"Let her have her way!" Cocteau admonished him. "She is paying. They were once lovers. She can play with herself while she listens."

"That is not true!" the princess protested. "If Barbette listens to the way you are speaking, he will think I have slept with all of Paris!"

"Of course!" Cocteau laughed. "Including Gertrude Stein!"

The old woman produced a thick, black disk from a cupboard next to an elegantly carved Victrola. She lifted the lid to the machine and placed the disk on the turn table and then cranked the handle along the side of the cabinet. When she put the needle on the disk, from grooves of the record marred by scratches, came the unmistakable voice of Mistinguett.

"*Oh my man, I love him so! He'll never know...*" Mistinguett sang out in French. Violette took a long drag from her pipe absorbing the sweet ingredients into her lungs. She exhaled and softly sang along with the chanteuse...*"All my life is just despair, but I don't care...*"

Cocteau and Sachs also took long hits from their pipes. Cocteau then began to run his tongue into the curve of Sach's neck. Barbette took a deep breath of the dope. His lungs filled with the foreign smoke. He choked and coughed, but the little China man was there—offering him a cup of tea. The impact started gently, like a tide coming in at sunset, this gentle wave of euphoria. Then he felt as if he was up in the air floating on his trapeze, only now his muscles were relaxed and he needn't think or fear. He watched Jean and Maurice caress one another. Cocteau's hand reached within Sach's unbuttoned shirt savoring the feel of Maurice's warm, smooth flesh. They all leaned back and took more hits off their pipes as Mistinguett sang on.

Barbette's skin felt like honey. He was no longer in this little oriental den, but out in the sun—lying in a field—a gentle, warm, sun illuminating his skin—a soft breeze blowing through his hair. It was a place where all his anxieties and fears disappeared.

Just as the wave of euphoria landed upon his shores, a turbulent storm filled his gut. He felt a nausea like he never did before. Panicked, Barbette scanned the room for something in which to vomit. He saw a large, silver pot next to the Victrola. He did all he could to stumble and make it to the shiny urn. Falling onto his knees, Barbette wretched into the urn—all the tar, and liquor from the night coming forth in a shower of crud. The other three were too far gone to even respond, only looking on with bemused grins as Barbette heaved in agony.

The small China man came forth with an embroidered white kerchief. Barbette didn't know why, but the embroidery and its fine stitching made him think of his mother as he dried his lips. A sense of deep shame clouded his thoughts. Frightened, he looked for the door where they entered. Then, he stood up and stumbled toward the beads in the doorway. The old Asian woman gently smiled and gestured for Barbette to return to his spot on the beds, but he pushed her off. All he knew was that he had to leave the room, to get out of the den and into some fresh air.

Barbette made his way down the shiny, black hallway. The blackness growing with every step he took until he could see nothing before him—just an oily abyss. He pounded on the hard surface before him, begging to escape. The old lady came up to him from behind, carrying his coat, hat, and shoes. She pulled open the black door and the two were in the small entrance foyer once again. Barbette hastily dressed as the old lady looked on.

Barbette murmured a thank you in French as she opened the door for him. Her eyes narrowed and her face was expressionless as she closed the door behind Barbette. He could hear the dead bolts sliding closed again. The night air was brisk and overwhelmed his senses. His eyes darted around discerning which way to turn and then another wave of bile crippled him. He fell to the curb and let forth another wretch which seemed to spring from the center of the earth, the blackness of rot erupting with such fury. It took all of his energy to stand up. He then made way down the street steadying himself along the sides of buildings. He didn't know where he was or where he was going. He just knew he had to leave the street and never go down it again.

CHAPTER THIRTY-TWO

"I feel it is my fault that you had such a bad time," Cocteau told Barbette softly. It was eight in the evening and the two were recounting the events of the previous night in Barbette's dressing room at the Moulin Rouge.

"Would you like some of my egg?" Barbette asked as he stood up with the half-eaten, hardboiled egg in one hand. Cocteau looked tired with bags under his eyes. His skin was a sallow, yellowed color.

"Please," Cocteau said. Barbette handed the remaining egg to Cocteau as he sat in an armchair along one wall of the ten by ten foot space. Barbette was almost naked. He skillfully put on his leather girdle without any assistance.

"I knew what we were doing," Barbette added. "If I didn't want to be there, I would've begged off."

"It happens, you know, the first time you smoke opiates—a terrible nausea."

"Yes, I know."

"And how you are feeling tonight?"

"I'm feeling fine," Barbette replied as he sat down and opened a jar of whitish colored cream. He began to apply the cream to his legs and feet. "I've performed under much worse circumstances."

"Indeed," Cocteau surmised. He then silently watched Barbette prepare himself. Barbette went on stage hours later, at eleven, but already by eight o'clock, he was meticulously tending to every aspect of his appearance.

"You know," Cocteau began, "you have this conscientiousness about your preparations—a conscientiousness unknown to French actors. It is characteristic of clowns, Annamite mimes, and the Cambodian dancing girls who are sewn each night into their golden costumes."

Barbette smiled and continued to quietly prepare himself.

"Have you given it consideration, to ever have your preparations photographed?"

"Some things are best left a mystery," Barbette smiled as he applied a different luminous makeup to his face.

"But these photographs could be a part of the act...There is an American—Man Ray—his images are sensational. He would be able to tell your story both masculine and feminine. I could direct him. I could make the images a sensation!"

Barbette was silent for a while.

"Where's Maurice this evening?"

"He is with Coco...But don't change the subject. What you are now doing is pageantry. An overture. We must have Man Ray capture it! I shall cover the expense!"

Barbette sighed saying, "Okay, Jean, if you will just let me finish my preparations in silence."

"Very well, I shall see him in the morning and make all the arrangements."

Cocteau lit a fag and continued to study Barbette's transformation. He was already writing in his mind: *Although his persona was that of a funny young devil, his completed makeup was as precious as a brand-new box of new pastels— his chin enameled with something shiny—his body unreal—as if coated with plaster.*

Cocteau watched Dr. Jekyll become Mr. Hyde when Barbette put on his wig, fussing with hairpins, *imitating every last gesture of a woman arranging her hair! Jekyll is Hyde! Yes, Hyde! Because now I find myself frightened!*

An old French maid entered the room with a shimmering evening gown of silver and gold, with a matching cape embellished with layers of white ostrich feathers. Cocteau referred the woman to Barbette knowing she had an excellent reputation for discretion. The woman assisted Barbette in putting on the gown as well as ballet slippers. By now the clock grew closer to eleven. Barbette and the maid left the dressing room, the maid carrying the cape and a large ostrich feathered plumed headpiece. The dancing girls were about their dressing area as Barbette passed. They all stopped and gaped at the man/woman walking by. There was something so captivating about Barbette's appearance that forced the women to stop their preparations.

Barbette and the small retinue made it down a flight of stairs to the back stage. When the stage manager saw the arrival, he cleared the area as Barbette demanded. Only the maid and the stage manager were permitted back stage as Barbette prepared for a performance. Barbette would open the review. Cocteau could hear the murmur of the crowd from beyond the closed curtain—the lively chatter, the ring of champagne glasses joined in merry toasts. Cocteau took it all in, constructing in his mind: *He is still a man as he walks about the stage inspecting its equipment, does leg exercises, grimaces at the spotlights, hoists himself onto wires, clambers up ladders. The moment the question of danger is disposed of, he is a woman again—a society woman, giving her salon a last-minute inspection before the ball, patting cushions, moving vases and lamps.*

When everything was ready, Barbette turned to Cocteau. "You must go."

Cocteau worshipfully obliged and headed to the passageway guiding him back to the audience. There, he waited once again, to be captivated by the performance of Barbette.

...

Up high in the air, swinging from bent knees upon the trapeze—this was where Barbette felt alive. It was as if all the earthly weights of his existence were left on the ground down below—only to gape in awe at what she had become. Muscles strained at every seemingly effortless gesture, but they were not in pain. It was more of a hunger to be challenged again, to push limits of strenuous exertions, to feel more power. Uncompromising technique fused so seamlessly with artistry.

As her body cut through the smoky air, luminous from the spot lights upon her ivory-painted skin, Barbette was no longer there! She no longer needed the trapeze, because she was floating above it, like the woman she saw as a child at the circus—so high up in the big top—floating as if she had wings. Her mind pushed her body, every muscle used in economic perfection—a machine—a race horse galloping toward the finish—flexing then releasing.

It was all his creation. Barbette was his—his epiphany—his salvation!

She could hear nothing but her own breathing, not the sound of the orchestra playing Strauss, not the audience below, gasping at every daring move. It was all silence except for her breathing. She soared higher and higher, pushing herself for absolute perfection—then she released— confidently landing on ground. Then the noise came—all at once—the cheers, the applause—they were all there—all those she tried to escape.

CHAPTER THIRTY-THREE

"The poet doesn't invent. He listens," Jean Cocteau explained to Barbette as he assisted Man Ray in setting up his photographic gear backstage at the Moulin Rouge. "That is why Man Ray is a poet. He listens with his eyes."

It was Sunday afternoon, and whole of the Moulin Rouge was empty. They would have the theatre to themselves.

"I've wanted to photograph you for a long time," Man Ray said with his New York accent. He must have been in his mid-twenties, like Barbette and Cocteau. Dressed casually in high-wasted trousers and an open-collared shirt of a nondescript color, he looked more French than American. It was the little flourishes that made Barbette think so—how Man Ray wore his closely trimmed beard in a goatee fashion—the chapeau cap perched atop his full head of black hair—the manner with which he held his cigarette. Barbette found Man Ray's eyes the most interesting—deep brown, somewhat sad at the ends, yet their gaze was intense and probing, framed by thick, dark eyebrows which dramatically arched at their middle point.

"I like contradictions. We have never attained the infinite variety and contradictions that exist in nature," Man Ray said as he continued to assemble his gear.

"My art is a contradiction," Barbette smiled. He too was dressed casually in his usual Sunday attire. He was coming to the end of his Parisian contract at the Moulin Rouge. In another week, he would again be on the road, booked solid in Berlin, Brussels, and Amsterdam.

Needing more space for the cameras and lighting, Cocteau and Man Ray decided Barbette's dressing room was too small. They removed his vanity and carried it downstairs to one of the side wings of the stage. Cocteau fussed over objects for a while making sure it all looked as it did in the dressing room.

"What do you want me to do?" Barbette asked as he watched the two work.

"For this sitting, I want you to do exactly as you would starting at eight in the evening—as if you are preparing for your act," Cocteau said.

"That's all?"

"I will guide you at times, but for now, we shall photograph you as you prepare."

"Okay, then," Barbette sighed as he started to unbutton his shirt and then take off his trousers.

Cocteau pulled up a cabaret chair close to Barbette, but not so that he would be in Man Ray's field of vision. He swung the chair around and perched himself upon it, taking in the transformation as it began to unfold.

At first Barbette felt odd, with two men's eyes upon him as he dutifully set about his tasks, but then they started to fall away. Man Ray did not shout. He did not order. If he did suggest it was in a quiet and thoughtful manner. Even though he said he would direct, Cocteau was silent, permitting both photographer and subject their space to create. As if watching a great ballet, he reveled in what was unfolding before him.

Barbette and Man Ray worked throughout the day. Barbette knew what the photographer was after and would twist his body in a manner enhancing the feminine aspects of his physique. When he completed his makeup and hair and was in one of his elaborate stage costumes, Barbette took to the high wire, on ballerina point, ostrich plumes cascading from his waist, his hands delicately extended to steady himself.

While he was working, Barbette would occasionally glance over at Cocteau. The Frenchman looked on in his worshipful way. Barbette felt connected to him—the manner with which Cocteau understood what Barbette meant. Cocteau's eyes revealed an intensity that at once upset and tantalized the young aerialist from Round Rock. Cocteau was absorbing and appraising, peeling back the veneer of ivory powder and ostrich plumes seeking something deeper within.

At the end of it all, the three were exhausted. Cocteau and Man Ray disassembled the photographer's equipment and moved items back to Barbette's dressing room, while Barbette showered the paint from his body. As tired as he was, Barbette, felt satisfied. He was understood and appreciated as never before. He worked with Man Ray as a team, creating in a way that only elevated their work. All the while, Barbette felt Cocteau's worshipful eyes about him, his manic gaze.

When Man Ray finally departed, the two were alone. Cocteau looked pensive.

"We must go out to dinner! To celebrate this day!" Cocteau suggested.

"I have a better idea. Let's order in...Why not go to my hotel?"

"A marvelous thought!"

The air of the early spring evening was cool and moist, refreshing on Barbette's face. Cocteau lit a cigarette as the two casually strolled down the ancient, cobbled streets of the Latin Quarter. It was dark by now, a slight mist glazed the surfaces of the streets and walls, reflecting glints of golden light from the street lamps above.

"Sometimes, it's hard for me to believe I'm here, that this is my life," Barbette said wistfully.

"You have worked hard to get here," Cocteau replied as he took a drag from his smoke. "Art is not a pastime, but a priesthood."

Barbette stopped in the street and looked at Cocteau. He didn't care to see who witnessed it. He kissed Cocteau on the lips with tenderness and longing. He knew he shouldn't have done so, out in public, but tonight he felt free.

"I want you," he murmured into Cocteau's ear.

Cocteau smiled and laughed a bit. "I don't believe we shall dine tonight!"

Barbette smiled. "Not if I can help it!"

The two hurried their pace down the cobbled pathway, eagerly heading to Barbette's hotel.

. . .

Once safely in the Barbette's suite, the two silently undressed. Barbette savored Cocteau's appreciative gaze as he stood naked before him. Cocteau approached the muscular aerialist and then softly ran his index finger over Barbette's toned stomach, up to his chest, arousing one nipple. Barbette's body tingled at the gesture. Cocteau began to feast on Barbette's body—not aggressively, but passionately as if he was savoring every taut muscle, every bead of perspiration, and the sweet aroma each droplet emitted.

Barbette felt Cocteau's tongue about his lips and in his mouth, moving onto his chest. He exhaled and reveled in Cocteau's adulations, growing in excitement as the encounter became more intense. Barbette took in Cocteau, his thrusts of power filling him, driving him to a place between pleasure and pain. The force of Cocteau's affections overwhelmed Barbette, but instead of receding, he felt free to delight in his sumptuous advances. Their love was forceful and physical, yet filled with emotion. Together *they* created something—an explosion of sensuality which left them each emptied, but somehow deeply fulfilled.

...

Cocteau rolled out of the bed he shared with Barbette in the tidy hotel suite. The room was dark save for golden light from streetlamps gently streaming in from a window obscured by half-drawn drape. Still in bed, Barbette looked at Cocteau's thin, French frame slipping on his tweed pants, tucking in his rumpled shirt.

"I must get back...Maurice is expecting me," Cocteau said quietly with little emotion.

Barbette felt a flush of jealousy mixed with hurt. "Yes," he replied.

Cocteau continued to dress, synching his waist with a thin, leather belt.

"Will you tell him about us?" Barbette asked.

Cocteau sat on the side of the bed, putting on his shoes. "I do not think that would be helpful."

Barbette looked at the profile of the man, his pronounced nose, dark, brown hair swept off his noble forehead, eyes distant and unemotional.

"No?"

"It wouldn't be fair to him."

A flash of incredulity swept over Barbette, but he tried not to show it.

Barbette moved his naked torso up behind Cocteau so that his head was nearly touching the poet's.

"Goodnight," he whispered seductively into Cocteau's ear. Then he slipped his naked body out of the bed and headed to his bathroom. Once he entered the luxurious marble-sheathed space, his voice reverberated off the cold walls, "be sure to close the door when you go."

Cocteau saw the stream of light coming from the bathroom vanity grow narrower as the door closed shut. He exhaled as he stood in the shadows and darkness of the room. He was going to say something, but then decided not to. Then he left.

CHAPTER THIRTY-FOUR

"Double Bloody Mary," Princess Violette Murat ordered with regal authority to young male waiter at the Montparnasse café. It was Sunday, around noon. The café doors to the street were open this warm, spring day, but the temperature still felt too cool for Violette so she demanded to be seated farther inside the establishment. Barbette would have preferred seats outside and closer to the sidewalk where they could watch beautiful young people pass by, but it was too much of a fuss to argue with the princess.

"Black coffee for me," Barbette told the waiter as he appraised the help's looks.

Violette offered Barbette a cigarette from her gold case, which he declined. She took a robust drag from her smoke and exhaled.

"Your photographs by Man Ray—they are causing a sensation. All of Paris is saying so," she told Barbette. The princess was dressed in the latest spring fashions of Coco Chanel—layers of soft, flowing pink and blue chiffon fabric, and a multitude of strands of pearls sweeping dramatically down from her thick neck. Barbette thought Violette was too fat for Coco's couture, but he had to admit, the look did give her an aura of fashionable power. Violette may enjoy associating with artists, but she never let anyone forget her wealth and lineage.

"Yes," Barbette said as he gazed toward the open doors which led to the outside of the café. "Have you seen him?"

"Who? Man Ray?" Violette asked as their drinks arrived at table. "Of course, he is all over these day."

"No, Cocteau," Barbette replied.

Violette took a liberal gulp of the bloody, letting the vodka wash down her throat and steady her nerves.

"You think too much of him. Just because you fucked doesn't mean you will marry him," Violette said her blue eyes squinting.

"I know…I don't think of him," Barbette lied. "It's just…I haven't seen him in some weeks."

"I've heard he has left town."

"With Maurice?"

"No, not with that ass. I will tell you, but you must promise to keep it our little secret."

"Of course."

Violette leaned in across their small wood table.

"I've heard Jean has left to a sanitarium for his addiction to dope."

"To opium?"

"Yes! He never had any control."

"Pot meet kettle."

Violette frowned at him.

"*I* have control. I only enjoy dope when I want. I can stop any time—it is just that I think, why? Why stop?"

Violette started to laugh at herself.

"And Maurice?"

"That fucker ran off with Coco's money. I spoke to her yesterday. She said while he and Cocteau were staying with her, she went into a business deal with Maurice. You know his family are diamond merchants. The fucker stole her money! No one can find him!"

Barbette laughed at the news, feeling some sort of pleasure that Maurice's true character was being revealed. There was something to his effusive flattery Barbette always thought was a phony manipulation, and now his suspicions were vindicated! He sipped his rich, black brew with a smirk on his face. He then tried to change the subject.

"I received a cable from William Morris. It seems with Cocteau's essay about me published in *Nouvelle Revue Française* plus Man Ray's photos, I'm quite in demand across Europe this season. Everyone wants to see this French man/woman Barbette. I'll be leaving Paris for a tour. It'll last for some time."

Violette frowned.

"I do not like it, Barbette my dear! We have become such good friends. There is no one of your refinement for whom I can associate."

"You need to take a lover. What about Coco?"

"She only wants to fuck when she is high," Violette exhaled smoke from her fag. "Besides, she likes men too much."

"She is quite beautiful."

"Yes she is," Violette added in a tone that made it sound as if she did not want to continue this line of questioning.

"What about Josephine?"

"The woman is beautiful beyond belief!" Violette sighed. "As Cocteau lusts after you, I lust after the Negress, Josephine Baker! But I cannot fuck her and the cheetah at the same time. I just can't!"

Barbette let out a belly laugh. He looked happily at Violette.

"You are one insane princess!" he smiled.

Violette downed her double Bloody Mary and snapped her fingers at the waiter to bring her another.

"So true, Barbette! So true!"

CHAPTER THIRTY-FIVE

DECEMBER 24, 1929

"Barbette! Drive faster!" the Princess Violette admonished. "We told Charles and Marie we would arrive before noon and here it is almost four! The sun is going down!"

"I can't go any faster!" Barbette scowled as he twisted the wheel of Violette's new, bright blue Citroën violently to the left and then to the right as the auto hurled through the mountains of Hyeres in the south of France with great speed.

Violette rolled down the window, letting a rush of warm, sea air flood into the auto. "At last, we have left the winter of Paris behind! I love wintertime along the coast! The air is fresh and there are no ugly tourists ruining things!"

With this, Barbette would have to agree. The vistas were lovely—rolling green hills terraced with tidy rows of pruned grape vines. As they drove along the hilly coast, to their left, were the azure waters of the Mediterranean. The sky was broad and cloudless ultramarine as well. To their right, the setting sun cast long shadows into the lush canyons and ravines they travelled.

"Stop the car!" Violette demanded. "There it is! Villa Noailles!"

The princess and Barbette hopped out of the car and stood on the edge of the gravel road, looking off in the distance. Barbette took in the sweep of the villa.

"When I first set eyes upon it, it looks like some ancient ruin, an old castle forgotten..." Barbette studied the lines of the house further. "But now, it looks as if she's an ocean liner, thrust up into the land by some flood, lodged between two hills."

"Everything must always be new for Charles and Marie de Noailles," Violette shook her head, "their art, their homes, even their lovers!" Violette laughed. "Come on! They must be pouring cocktails by now!"

As Barbette wound around the twisting canyon road leading up to the villa, he continued to study the home trying not to drive off the narrow path. The setting sun cast mysterious shadows about the rambling structure. What at first looked like stone walls, Barbette could now see were really stucco walls, an ochre color, which matched the hillside. The villa's neatly squared walls pushed out from the mountainside. Piercing the walls were wide openings, like massive rectangular windows with no glass. There was no ornament, no reliefs or fancy detail. The lines were clean and radically modern.

"Do you think Cocteau will be there?" Barbette asked.

"Of course. All the surrealists suckle from the tit of deposed nobility—especially the Vicomte de Noailles!" Violette laughed as she held onto her sun hat which fluttered in the sea breeze coming from her open window.

Barbette smiled. "I've toured so much over these several years...It seemed every time I was in Paris, he was not."

"You are too sentimental—that is your problem!" Violette said as she turned her head from looking at the approaching villa to Barbette's profile. "You must move on—I know he has!"

Violette's words stung Barbette. He heard the rumors and gossip. Jean Cocteau had other lovers and young ones at that. Yes, Barbette too had taken men, but it was not like the connection he felt for the poet.

"Well, here we are!" Violette exclaimed as they pulled into a lot at one end of the villa's exterior wall. The two got out of the princess's now dusty, blue auto and stretched their muscles. Violette was dressed in a deep, red Chanel day dress which appeared one size too tight, her stomach budging atop the dropped waist of the bodice. A broad-brimmed white hat encircled by a matching red sash shielded her face. Barbette wore an expensive, lavender silk shirt, its collar open with sharply pointed tips. His grey, gabardine trousers were the perfect length and cut for his rakish physique. He went to open the trunk of the auto.

"Let's not worry about the trunks. Marie has the best staff. I am sure they will be out here momentarily to greet us."

"Where did they get their money?" Barbette asked turning his head to Violette.

"What a vulgar question!" Violette feigned protest. "If you must know, banking for Charles, and Marie—I do not know—land perhaps. Her line goes back to the Marquis de Sade. I believe he would be quite thrilled if he saw the way his progeny lived today—swapping beds like they change their underpants!"

Violette laughed to herself.

"Oh!" Violette stopped dead in her tracks, forcing Barbette to do the same. She turned her fleshy face to Barbette and stepped closer to him. "You must not mention it. You must not say a word...But Marie—and Cocteau—they were once lovers!"

Barbette's swallowed hard in disbelief.

"No one speaks of it, but it is well known!"

"But Jean likes *men*!"

"What can I say? I have had male lovers. Have you ever slept with a woman?"

"No…"

"Well, maybe you should try, but not this weekend," Violette continued, as they started walking toward the entrance space where the tall wall around the villa seemed to end and the house began. Beyond the portal, a lush, green, rectangular lawn flanked by topiary-like orange trees in massive indigo-glazed pots, stood in orderly attention along the inside of the thick, ochre colored walls with their massive picture window openings. "I've been told Charles is quite enamored by you. Who knows, perhaps this weekend your heart will forget all about Cocteau."

"Charles prefers men?"

"Oh you pretty little Texas flower—of course! He is French!"

Violette laughed so hard, her belly shook.

"Is that the voice of the princess I hear?" Marie de Noailles called out. Her face was beaming as she approached the two from the other end of the walk which led past the perfectly manicured green lawn. She was wearing only her bathing costume—a black and white horizontal striped tank stitched together with what looked like high-waisted black shorts—all made of wool. Her thick, brown hair was still damp. It was cut in a fashionable bob. Marie de Noailles wasn't a great beauty, Barbette already understood. Her chin was too weak, her cheekbones too soft, but as she spoke, in her elegant Parisian, upper class accent, there was a warm charm about her which was quite engaging, if not disarming.

"*Bon jour Violette*!" she said gaily, kissing both of the princess's round cheeks. Then, she turned to Barbette with a warm smile.

"This must be Barbette! We are so glad you could join us!"

The princess interjected in noble fashion, "Marie-Laure de Noailles, Vicomtesse de Noailles, I present Barbette of Round Rock, Texas."

Marie immediately took Barbette's hand and started to lead the two down the path from where she came.

"I am so glad you could visit!" she said enthusiastically. "Charles and I have adored your show! Cocteau is right—you are a beautiful creature!"

Barbette heard the name of the artist and felt his face flush.

Marie continued, "Oh, please, pardon my appearance. We were all just finishing a swim in the pool. We have it heated you know, but today, it is so fresh, one really doesn't need to. We've all agreed to meet at eight in the salon for drinks."

"So late?" Violette protested.

"Don't worry, my dear princess," Marie rubbed Violette's broad back with her free hand "I have champagne awaiting you in your suite!"

"That is *divine!* I shall have a bath and a glass of champagne at once!" Violette said with great relief.

A servant wearing a dark coat and starched, white shirt and black bowtie greeted the three at the broad entrance door to the modernist villa.

"Jacque," Marie smiled turning to the handsome young servant, "please show the princess to her chamber." Marie then clasped her hand more firmly around Barbette's. "My dear, I must take you to the pool at once! Do you know we have a trapeze hanging over it? We should be immensely flattered if you could perform for us—you know some time. It would be quite sensational!"

Marie led Barbette up another corridor and flight of stairs, her voice echoing off the solid, stucco walls until she could be heard no longer.

...

"*Monsieur Barbette*! At long last we meet!" Charles de Noailles exclaimed. He was dressed smartly in the finest tuxedo Barbette ever set eyes upon. The subtle fabric draped perfectly on his toned, well-proportioned frame. Charles was slightly taller than Barbette, possessing a full head of dark hair parted neatly down one side of his head, pomaded and swept back. The banker's hair color was a perfect match for the mustache over his kindly shaped lips. He mustn't be much older than his early thirties. Amid the splendors of his immense modernist villa, with its walls adorned with works of his friends Picasso, Miró, and Klee, Charles de Noailles possessed a comfortable, charming elegance. It was not a pretense, but something which he imbued. "I am so glad you can join us for this short holiday!"

"Thank you for having us," Barbette replied as he bowed slightly. He now was dressed in his own black tuxedo of a rakishly, fashionable cut. Adorning his pressed cuffs were stunning deco square-shaped emerald cuffs—a dash of holiday flair. "I've heard so many wonderful things about you," Barbette added with a smile.

Already, the spacious salon, with its soaring ceiling of abstract, illuminated glass squares, was filled with friends of the Noailleses.

"I can assure you they are all true!" Charles laughed. "I must say, I was pleased when I heard you could make it. I wasn't quite so sure."

"The night clubs are struggling. With the stock market crash in America, no one, it seems wants to travel Europe—especially this wintertime," Barbette said. "The Germans too. I haven't been to Berlin in months. I wonder if it's all coming to an end."

Charles smiled as he put his arm about the shoulder of Barbette. "I can assure you, the foolish mistakes the Americans made, will not wash upon our shores. France is well protected. Now, we must get you some champagne! I know you acrobats do not enjoy libations, but this evening, I insist!"

Charles gestured for a waiter who was moving about the guests with a tray full wide-lipped champagne glasses each filled to the brim with the bubbling elixir. The waiter arrived in front of the two. Again, Barbette was taken by this new servant's comely appearance and wondered if all the handsomest men of France worked for the Noailleses. Charles took two glasses off the tray and handed one to Barbette. He raised the other up in the air.

"To the great Barbette!" the banker's eyes twinkled as he made the remark.

Barbette smiled, "Cheers!"

The two took deep swallows of the champagne.

"Charles! Barbette!" came the familiar voice from behind them. Both turned. It was Jean Cocteau. He was also turned out in his own assemblage of a black evening suit, only around his open neck, he tied a flamboyant, burgundy, silk scarf. Though he aged since their last encounter—more lines and creases about the ends of his eyes—Cocteau effervesced more so than the champagne in their glasses.

"You both are looking well!" Cocteau smiled. "Barbette—my flower, it has been too long!"

"Yes!" Barbette smiled, unable to hide the feelings he felt toward the man before him.

"It has been a shame our paths have not crossed more frequently. It has been insane! When Marie told me you would be joining us, I was thrilled!"

Charles watched the two interact with a curious eye.

Cocteau turned to Charles and grinned.

223

"Vicomte de Noailles," Cocteau began regally, "I present to you the drawings you requested."

Cocteau held forth in his hands a leather-bound portfolio. Charles handed his drink to Barbette and took the one foot square portfolio into his hands. He opened the pages in a way for both Cocteau and Barbette to see as well.

Barbette watched the man pour all of his attentions into the renderings. His eye was critical and appraising. He made no remarks—no utterance—as he looked at the work. All that could be heard about them was the chatter of other guests and the jazz riffs of the African American pianist, in his white tux, rolling through happy sounding songs.

"Magnificent! Wonderful!" Charles enthused. "I know this night belongs to Man Ray and the debut of his film, but what I see here—Monsieur Cocteau—what would it take for you to produce an animation of such drawings? My friend, the composer, Georges Auric, he could like to write a score for an animated film. We could put you both together. You know, you would find an eager benefactor in me!"

Cocteau was silent, considering the proposal.

"But why animation?" he asked.

"The people in your renderings are so unique!"

"I could create a film using real people who would be much more interesting than the figures!"

"Really?" Charles inquired. "And I wonder, what might the subject of such a film be?"

Without a moment's hesitation, Cocteau outlined a surrealist fantasy. Did he just make it up on the spot or had he been thinking of it for some time knowing Charles would readily fund such a venture? Barbette was entirely unsure.

Charles listened intently while Cocteau outlined his plot.

"Would there be roles for Marie and myself? You know we had such a wonderful time acting in Man Ray's little project."

"It would be a pleasure!"

"The budget for Man Ray's film was a quarter million francs. Monsieur Cocteau, your vision is more elaborate. What would you propose for a budget?"

Cocteau looked seriously for a moment at Charles.

"I can deliver it to you for one million francs."

Barbette almost dropped both glasses of champagne in his hands.

"I will not pay a cent more," Charles said looking seriously at Cocteau. "We must be featured and it must be completed by March. Do we have an agreement?"

Cocteau smiled, "*Oui!*"

Barbette couldn't believe the transaction he just witnessed!

Charles grabbed another fresh glass of champagne from one of the handsome waiters and put it into Cocteau's hand and took his from Barbette. "To your film," he proclaimed as he raised his glass into the air. "What shall it be called?"

"*Le Sang d'un Poète*—The Blood of a Poet!"

"A marvelous title! To *Le Sang d'un Poète*—a surrealist masterpiece!"

The three drank liberally from their glasses.

"There you are!" said the fresh-faced Parisian man who came up to Cocteau. "You left the room before I was ready." He wasn't much older than a boy, really, maybe nineteen. He was tall and blond, with broad shoulders. Whereas Cocteau's appearance always bore a manic sort of quality, this man/boy had a confident poise about him. Standing next to the man/boy, Barbette felt positively ancient.

"Barbette," Charles interjected, "have you met Monsieur Jean Bourgoint? He is an acquaintance of Monsieur Cocteau's."

"A pleasure," Barbette smiled into Bourgoint's bright, blue eyes.

"I have heard so much about you!" the young man replied. "Cocteau—he speaks of you often, in almost sacred overtures."

"Thank you," Barbette replied. He wanted to say that he too read so much about Bourgoint. All of Paris, in fact, was talking about Cocteau's latest book, *Les Enfants Terribles*, and the real-life model for the hero and heroine of the story—Jean Bourgoint and his beautiful sister, Jeanne. Were they really involved in an incestural relationship or was it some sort of fantasy conjured up by the artist Cocteau?

Barbette was thankful when Marie de Noailles, sheathed in a silvery gown and a bucket full of diamonds about her neck, announced from the center of the salon, "My dears—my dears—dinner is served!"

Barbette felt Charles's arm reach around his own.

"Please, come with me. I insisted to Marie that you be my dinner companion!" Charles turned to Bourgoint and Cocteau, "Gentlemen, shall we?"

The guests began to file out of the expansive salon moving toward the dining room where tables were set and overflowing out onto the adjoining terrace and the enclosed green lawn.

"You know," Charles's voice could be heard as they left the salon, "the villa has its own pool—the first private pool in France! I installed a trapeze above it—just for you!"

. . .

After a lavish feast of foie gras, suckling duck, and chocolate crepe suzettes, the party returned to the salon where much of the furniture had been pushed along the walls of the room and a multitude of colorful cushioned pillows and chinchilla throws were piled onto the floor.

"Please, everyone, make yourselves comfortable!" Marie announced. "We have demitasse and once everyone has settled, we shall premier the most extraordinary film by Man Ray. We are so very pleased!"

Charles led Barbette to a central part of the oversized cushions on the floor where he insisted Barbette recline next to him. The brigade of handsome, smiling waiters marched into the salon with trays of tiny demitasse cups and saucers, which they served to guests. With white-gloved hands, the servants poured the rich café from shiny, streamlined, silver pots. Barbette took one and watched Charles throw back his café with a brisk nod. Barbette, never having demitasse before, chose to do the same. The effects of the caffeine mixed with the dinner wine were almost instantly felt.

Cocteau and Bourgoint were still standing alongside of Man Ray and his stunningly beautiful American protégé, Lee Miller. Cocteau was doing all the talking, Barbette could see, and after a bit, they all burst out into uproarious laughter.

Barbette wanted to join them in their merriment, but he knew Charles would be put off by such a gesture. Next, he witnessed a very tipsy Princess Violette come up to the group. Barbette could see she was unabashedly flirting with Lee, who seemed to take it all in stride. No doubt, Violette was swept up by Lee's pure beauty—her tall, long features, fresh, dewy face and just-washed blond hair.

Barbette met her before. He enjoyed speaking with the American. There was something to her spirit reminding him of his childhood friend, Rose.

Barbette thought of life back in Texas. What must his family be doing on Christmas Eve? He sent his mother more money, but again chose not to tell her his whereabouts or precisely what he was doing. What would she think of his menagerie of friends? He was now surrounded by a world of opulence he never dreamt of while picking cotton in the impossibly hot fields of Round Rock in the summertime. He had come so far. Tonight, he vowed, he would revel in his success.

Like a mother hen, Marie de Noailles had her servants collect the dollhouse-like demitasse cups and saucers and gestured for all to find a comfortable place to recline on the cushions. Man Ray and Lee Miller did not lie down, but moved to a sofa along the wall, while Cocteau led Bourgoint to a spot amongst the cushions and chinchilla throws right next to Barbette.

"I am so happy you reserved a spot for us!" he said cheerfully. "Reclining on a bed between such handsome men—no matter how shitty Man Ray's film—I am sure I will enjoy it!"

Marie shushed everyone as the abstract, illuminated glass panels overhead began to dim. Barbette took it all in— these wealthy people, sitting on the floor like school children awaiting their afternoon naps. When the room darkened, on one pristine wall, a square of brilliant white appeared and then the film started to roll. The title, *Les Mystères du Château de Dé* flashed onto the wall and everyone applauded.

"I funded the entire project," Charles whispered into Barbette's ear. Charles positioned himself so close to Barbette that Barbette could feel Charles's leg, covered in sumptuous fur, rubbing up along his own. Next, Barbette felt Cocteau's eyes upon him. Barbette turned to see Cocteau's warm smile next to him. The aerialist's face flushed. Then, he felt Cocteau reach for his hand under the throws. Barbette wondered if Cocteau's other hand was holding that of the young Bourgoint. The buzz from all the wine chased with the strong café brought on a lascivious air to the room. While Barbette's eyes were upon Man Ray's surrealist film flickering on the wall, he allowed the hands of the two men on each side of him probe his body.

When the film ended, the crowd applauded and called for Man Ray to take a bow. Once he did so, the Noailles's brigade of statuesque waiters came forth with trays filled with crystal jars each containing a small, lit candle.

"I know it is almost midnight, but I do wish you would join us at the pool, where Barbette has agreed to so graciously perform for us!" Marie said with a smile gesturing in Barbette's direction. The sleek waiters moved about the guests who started to stand, each taking one of the glowing candles emitting prismatic light from their crystal holders.

Barbette, for his part, was stunned by the announcement. Marie never asked him to perform this night. He felt as if he was in no shape to work a trapeze, but felt the obligation.

Soon, a flickering stream of lit candles snaked through the hallways and down a flight of stairs to the pool room. Merry chatter from the guests whose diamonds sparkled in the light, echoed off the villa's stucco walls.

"I don't have a bathing costume," Barbette said to Charles as the two made way with the crowd down to the natatorium.

"Do not worry—we have plenty swimming costumes in the changing rooms. I am sure we can find a suitable one!"

Charles led Barbette down another hallway from the pool to a dressing room.

"There you are," he said opening the door. "You will find a number of bathing costumes. Shall you need assistance?" Already Charles was trying to enter the dressing room, but Barbette shifted his weight to block him.

"I'm sure I can find everything myself, Charles. Darling, can you tell Marie, I won't be long?"

The banker's eyes revealed too much, Barbette thought. Clearly he desired his own special show.

Charles cleared his throat. "Of course," he stammered. He then abruptly turned around and headed back to the party.

...

Guests surrounded the perimeter of the rectangular pool, which was situated in an immense room nearly three stories high. Along one wall, ten foot tall, floor-length windows were slid back into their frames so that the guests were able to spill out into the adjoining terrace. The candles each guest held were the only illumination in the space. Marie asked that they all be placed about the edge of the pool. The lights reflected on the ripples of water, casting wavy shadows on the walls.

Marie cranked a Victrola on a table by one end of the pool. The record began to play, the scratchy voice of the popular American songstress Ruth Etting, playfully singing *Love Me or Leave Me,* echoed off the walls of the room.

Barbette entered the space on the opposite side of the pool from where everyone was watching. He dressed in a snug-fitting, one piece, black wool swimsuit. His muscular physique was only enhanced by the glow of the flickering candles. Barbette's hair was wet and slicked back over his head. He moved feline-like to a high platform on one side of the pool where the trapeze awaited him. Once he reached the top of the platform, his demeanor changed. He pantomimed that he was afraid to sit on the trapeze. The guests laughed as he blew them a kiss and then he mounted the apparatus. His movements were strong, yet exquisitely feminine—toes pointed, legs angled just so. He swung higher and higher. All the while, Ruth Etting continued to sing:

Love me or leave me and let me be lonely,
You won't believe me that I love you only,
I'd rather be lonely than happy with somebody else...

Barbette released his body, falling backwards and catching himself at the back of his knees. The crowd gasped.

You might find the night time the right time for kissing
But night time is my time for just reminiscing
Regretting instead of forgetting with somebody else
There'll be no one else, unless that someone is you, you, you…

Barbette smiled to the crowd and gestured elegantly as he swung back and forth, then he released again, catching himself on the bar by the backs of his ankles.

I intend to be independently blue,
I want your love but I don't want to borrow,
I have it today and give back tomorrow,
For my love is your love but there's no love for nobody else…

Grandly swinging back and forth over the pool, only secured by the backs of his ankles, Barbette spotted himself on the water below. Then he released, flipping his torso in the air in a tight tuck, diving into the water. The guests cheered as Barbette swam to the set of stairs at one end of the pool where he emerged from the water, his leg movements sensual and seductive, until he could take a bow. As the audience applauded, Barbette pointed to Charles and Marie who were smiling broadly at the aerialist. Barbette flexed his muscles and posed like a chiseled Greek statue, and then blew them a kiss. Then, he departed, into the hallway leading to the changing room, where his act began.

"You are welcome to spend all night by the pool if you wish!" Marie announced to everyone. "We will have breakfast in the morning and then head to the sea. Now please, everyone—enjoy!"

The handsome platoon of servants, this time carrying trays of aperitifs, passed one last time between the guests.

Someone put a Duke Ellington record on the Victrola. The room filled with laughter and chatter. Some guests returned to their chambers. Others remained by the pool.

"You were wonderful!" Charles said entering unannounced into the small dressing room. He quickly moved closer to Barbette, who was naked, drying his hair with a towel. The space was no larger than a small bedroom chamber, with a wall of showers and toilets down an adjacent corridor. The room was tiled in white, lit only by two small sconces flanking a vanity mirror mounted on another wall.

"Charles," Barbette gasped. He tried to regain his composure. "You surprised me."

Charles moved to within inches of Barbette's muscular body.

"You have the body of an Adonis," Charles murmured. He could no longer contain his passions and lunged at Barbette, grabbing hold of his shoulders and smothering his face with kisses.

Barbette was overcome. He felt the vicomte's lips about his neck.

The banker's hands reached down to Barbette's rear and pulled him closer. Charles's lusty breath filled Barbette's senses. The banker continued to shower Barbette with affections.

"Am I interrupting anything?" Jean Cocteau said stumbling into the room with an open bottle of champagne in his hand.

Charles looked startled and then pulled away from Barbette. He straightened his tuxedo tie and jacket while clearing his throat.

"No, nothing," he replied. He then quickly strode past Cocteau without bidding him or Barbette adieu.

Barbette reached for his towel, trying to wipe the aroma of Charles from his body. Still naked, he exhaled deeply.

"Well, darling," Barbette said looking at Cocteau, "it looks like you just lost a million francs."

Cocteau laughed. "Quite possibly," he replied, "but I could tell, the man did not know how to make love to you."

"Oh really?"

"*Oui.*"

"Well, why don't you show me how it's done?"

Cocteau put down his bottle of champagne on a nearby stool. He approached Barbette and gently kissed him on the lips. Then he stopped for a moment looking into Barbette's eyes.

"Better," Barbette responded with a sly smile.

Cocteau kissed Barbette again, this time even more softly, letting his lips gently linger on those of the beautiful aerialist.

"And the boy?" Barbette asked as he turned his head away for a moment.

"He is upstairs by the telephone trying to reach his sister."

"Do you love him?"

Cocteau's brown eyes looked sincere. "Of course. I love him. I love him and I love you."

Barbette wasn't sure why he said what he was about to say. Maybe it was the honesty of Cocteau's words. Maybe it was the intoxicating effects of the evening, surrounded by the sensuous pleasures of the Villa de Noailles. Maybe it was because he missed Cocteau. It didn't matter.

"Lock the door," Barbette whispered.

Cocteau smiled and obeyed.

. . .

Spent, the two rested on the cold tile of the dressing room floor. Their love making was passionate, but unlike their last encounter, it felt hollow and incomplete. It was as if each was satisfying themselves—trying to recapture what they once experienced—but it was lost, and they both knew it. They were different now. As the two reclined side by side on the cold, hard, white tile of the dressing room, sterilely lit by the electric sconces flanking the vanity mirror, they both regretted the encounter.

"I must get back to the boy," Cocteau said staring up at the white ceiling.

"Yes, Jean, you must," Barbette replied.

"Will you be okay?"

"Yes, of course," Barbette said as he slowly stood up.

In reality, Barbette longed for the connection they once had. In this white room, alone together with all the world shut out, it should have been wonderful—but it wasn't.

CHAPTER THIRTY-SIX

Barbette pulled back the drapes of his chamber at Villa de Noailles, taking in the dazzling beauty of the clear, blue sky. His gaze drifted out to the horizon of cascading green hills leading down to the misty blue of the Mediterranean Sea. He left the windows to his terrace open, but the air was still overnight. Now, with the drapes fully drawn, could he feel the sea breeze sweep into the room. Wearing only his underpants, Barbette walked out onto his terrace up to the simple modernist railing along its edge, which was so reminiscent of the rails on an ocean liner. Barbette savored the mid-day sun upon his body. For whatever reason, last night, he slept soundly and peacefully. He felt totally refreshed this Christmas morn. As he looked about the grounds of the villa, he could see no one—so he savored the peace of it all. Barbette would shower and wear a snappy resort ensemble he purchased especially for his little holiday and see if he could catch lunch. In his rush to leave Paris, he forgot to take his watch. Never mind. Time stopped this holiday.

...

"Where is everyone?" Barbette asked the Princess Violette as he entered the breakfast room of the villa. She looked dreadful—dark circles under her eyes, her body slumped in the wicker and chrome Bauhaus dinette chair. Even her red silk, oriental robe was stained with dribbles of coffee down its front.

"Gone," was all she said.

"Down to the sea? What time is it anyway? In all the rush to leave Paris, I completely forgot my watch."

"It is two in the afternoon. No one is down at the sea. I thought you would have heard all the commotion this morning."

"No…I didn't."

Barbette's mood changed as he looked seriously at Violette.

"The guests have all left. No one is here except us and Charles and Marie. They do not wish to be disturbed."

"What then? What the devil is going on?"

Violette looked up from her sugary cup of coffee.

"It is Jeanne Bourgoint—the sister to the boy who was with Cocteau. The one Cocteau wrote about in his latest book. You know how the character killed herself in the book? The little lamb, Jeanne Bourgoint, took her own life, in Paris, last night. Her landlady found her dead this morning."

Barbette fell into a chair next to Violette.

"Will you drive us back to Paris?" Violette asked. "I am already almost packed. We must leave. I have written our regards to Charles and Marie. Everyone else already departed ahead of us."

Barbette was gob smacked by the news.

"Of course," he muttered. "I'll prepare at once."

. . .

Barbette cast one final glance at the Villa de Noailles in his rearview mirror as he steered Violette's dusty, blue

Citroën around the twisting, gravel road away from the modernist residence. As it faded from view, he couldn't help but think of images from Man Ray's silly little film they all watched the night before—the masked gamblers in bathing costume merrily rolling their oversized dice on the pristine lawn of the villa's terrace. Was it all a farce? Were they all farcical fools, gambling, each in their own way, with their lives? Perhaps the film wasn't so silly after all.

CHAPTER THIRTY-SEVEN

MARCH, 1930

He thought he was dreaming, the ringing in his head—were they church bells or school bells? Then, Barbette came to his senses. In the darkness of his Belle Epoch suite decorated in royal red and gold leaf at the Hotel Metropole in Brussels, Barbette reached for the night stand and picked up the telephone.

On the other end, the operator informed him he had a call from Paris. Once Barbette responded, the female hotel operator made the connection.

"Barbette?" the voice on the other line asked. Barbette strained to hear the voice—it was barely above a whisper and the line crackled with static.

"Who's this? You'll have to speak up!"

"It is Cocteau!"

"Are you on dope? It must be three in the morning!"

"It is of no consequence…"

Barbette was still, lying flat on his bed. He was naked, red satin bedding draped about his waist.

"You've woken me up, Jean! What do you need?"

Cocteau responded but Barbette could not make it out.

"Please, you will have to speak up—I can't hear you!"

Cocteau tried again.

"I need you to come to Pairs at once!"

238

"Why?"

"It is my film—*The Blood of the Poet*—Charles and Marie refuse to permit its release."

"Why? What does this have to do with me?"

"They did not like the way I edited the film—their parts."

"Jean, what have you done?" Barbette asked ruefully.

"I simply filmed them in their theatre box at the opera applauding and then I filmed what they were applauding later."

Barbette sighed.

"And what were they applauding, might I ask?"

"A man's suicide."

"Good god! Jean! That's horrible!"

"It is only a symbol!"

"You're insane, Jean, truly insane."

"I need you to play Marie de Noailles. I have other actors for the other nobility at the opera, but can't you see how perfect it would be to have the great Barbette in the role of the vicomtesse? A drag queen playing one of the last descendants of the Marquis de Sade?"

"You're ridiculous!"

"I know you have told me you would not perform your act on film. I understand that it would be the ruin of your live act—but this—this, will be a chance for the great Barbette to become immortal! Coco Chanel has even agreed to provide you with a wonderful cape and gown. They are magnificent—gold that sparkles like diamonds. She will give them to you for free if you just come back to Paris and help me with this favor."

Barbette thought about it for a moment.

"This may ruin me..."

"It will not ruin you! It will only get more people talking about you. You can protest it even if there is outrage—tell people that you had no idea what was being intercut between your scenes. Your act is an outlaw act. This is the perfect outlaw part and it is just a cameo. Lee Miller is in it and she has a far more sterling reputation than you."

Barbette was silent, somewhat annoyed by the comparison. Then he responded, "Okay, I'll be there…I'll take the train to Paris. I can give you one day—Sunday, then I must return."

"Wonderful! But I have to tell you I cannot reimburse you for your train fare."

Barbette laughed.

"That's fine, you crazy artist."

"Times must be good for Barbette, staying at a suite at the Metropole."

"It's not as good as it seems. This depression is maddening. They offer me luxury suites, but pay half my rate. I had to let one of my staff go."

"A great tragedy!"

"Are you staying with Coco?"

"*Oui!* Come to her residence at eight Sunday morning and we will start from there. Bring your wigs and makeup of course."

"Of course. *Au revoir*, insane artist!"

"*Au revoir!*"

Barbette sat up in his bed for a while, wondering if he made a terrible mistake. There was something so irresistible to Jean Cocteau's charm, he had to admit, even when he was high at three in the morning. Barbette would cable the William Morris agency about it after the film was distributed. Mister Morris recently retired and was replaced by a more conservative team. He was sure they wouldn't approve.

CHAPTER THIRTY-EIGHT

"How come you do not go out at night dressed as Barbette?" Cocteau asked as he and the aerialist strolled the wide sidewalk along the Seine. The Sunday spring evening was cool and refreshing. A light mist coated the streets and buildings making them shiny and slick.

It was at night when Barbette thought Paris was its most beautiful. From their vantage, in the distance, they could see the searchlight atop the Eiffel Tower scanning the heavens above. Across the Seine, Notre Dame stood imposing and mysterious in the shadows. Motor cars and an occasional carriage passed by on the street.

They finished the day of filming. Barbette thought it was all quite amusing with Cocteau manically barking out orders—telling Barbette to look this way and that—to smile—to powder her face. Barbette thought it would might be a far more entertaining film if the camera was turned the other way on the director—chain smoking and swearing—laughing one moment—screaming the next. The two enjoying dinner together after the filming. Now, a stroll along the Seine seemed perfect.

Barbette considered Cocteau's question for a while as they walked.

"How can I explain it," he began, "would Picasso wear his painting? Because that is Barbette. Barbette is a painting I've created. She lives on the stage."

"And yet she is a part of you."

"Yes, she is. I am, I am Barbette, but on the stage she is female and on the street…"

"He is male."

"Yes."

Barbette looked back to Cocteau. "I'll leave it for you to contemplate. Sometimes I think you can see more to Barbette than even I do."

"You are an enigma, that is true," Cocteau said as he lit a fag. He offered one to Barbette who declined.

"Do you still see the boy, Jean Bourgoint?" Barbette asked.

"No. He has left Paris. He was too upset over the death of his sister. He went to pray at a monastery."

"When you told me there was a suicide in your film, I understood."

"No!" Cocteau stopped walking for a moment. "No one can understand!"

Barbette said nothing. Instead he watched the search light atop the Eiffel Tower for a moment and then they continued walking.

"It's hard being Cocteau," Barbette finally offered.

"*Oui*," the artist said pensively as he breathed in deeply on his cigarette. He exhaled, tossing the butt into the gutter.

…

The two made love that evening, back at Coco's apartment. If she was home, Barbette did not see her. *Why did they do it*, Barbette wondered. *Loneliness*, he replied to himself as he lay awake next to Cocteau who was turned away from him, sleeping heavily. It was more than just a physical connection. At times it seemed as if they were two blind men, groping in the night, not for the physical, but an emotional connection—searching for the lost key to unlock the chamber containing pieces of their hearts that seemed to be misplaced so long ago. Maybe this was their connection—a realization they each had something missing. Both so flawed and fragile. They disguised it in their own ways, but in the nakedness of their nocturnal encounters, it was there in the open for them both to touch. At once it was terrifying and yet they were drawn to it—this incredible emptiness within.

CHAPTER THIRTY-NINE

NEW YORK, 1935

"We have to give them girls and more girls!" the short man in the sharply cut, black double-breasted suit spouted. He was a constantly erupting volcano to Barbette—a never ending gush of words, manically switching from one idea to the next. Each thought went unchecked, uncensored—thoughts and passions erupting with unbridled enthusiasm wrapped in arresting crudity.

The inside of Manhattan's Hippodrome, a cavernous theater easily able to handle five thousand paying customers, was itself a molten explosion of activity. The back of the largest stage Barbette ever set foot on was ripped open as a flow of workers scrambled to bolster the floor and erect a substantial ramp from the lower level. Some ninety feet above, Barbette could see more stagehands constructing the draping lines of what was being made to look like the inside of a vast circus tent.

Having been so long in Europe, Barbette forgot the brash extravagance of the American way of doing things. Looking around, he knew he was in for an experience.

"Where do you think you're going?" asked a burly, man who towered over Barbette. Dressed in a slack-fitting pinstripe suit with a fedora pushed down over his forehead, he could have been a goon in a gangster picture. Even in the dim shadows of the performance hall, the man's face was a jumble of features, all misaligned, like an aged prize fighter.

"I'm here to see Mister Rose, Mister Billy Rose," Barbette replied, feeling slight next to the massive thug.

"What you need to see him for?"

Barbette reached into the pocket of his French suit. The thug powerfully grabbed Barbette's hand.

"Not so fast!" the man said darkly staring at Barbette.

Barbette could feel the strength of the man's massive grip around his wrist and didn't like it.

"If you would kindly unhand me, I'll show you my papers from the William Morris Agency. I'm Barbette. I'm in the show."

Then, the little man in the black suit, who was standing center-stage, some fifteen paces away from Barbette, turned toward the two.

"Barbette!" the squat man called out as he rapidly approached them. A small cadre of overdressed men followed behind, each looking uncomfortable in the sweltering summer heat of the Hippodrome.

As the little man came forward, Barbette was able to make out his features more clearly. He was young, probably younger than Barbette himself. His full head of black hair was freshly trimmed, greased and parted. There was a boyish quality in him for sure, like an impish prankster who probably gave the school master a hell of a lot of trouble.

"Moe, let him go," the little man demanded of the big man. Then he bounded toward Barbette. "Billy Rose!" he exclaimed eagerly exclaiming as he extended his hand in Barbette's direction.

"Barbette."

"Terrific you're here!" Rose replied, not wasting time to see if Barbette was going to add any more pleasantries.

"Sorry about Moe here. There's some cocksuckers who are causing me problems. Former business partners. I've got J. Edgar and the FBI so up their asses right now, I need to have my own protection."

Billy Rose looked Barbette over.

"Son of a bitch! I've gotta say, Fanny and I saw your act last year in Italy, and son of a bitch—I would never imagine you're the same girl, I mean guy!"

Barbette knew of Billy Rose, the impresario. He knew he was an acclaimed song writer, night club owner, and Broadway producer. He also knew the Fanny he was speaking about was his wife, the sensational comedienne, Fanny Brice.

Rose turned to his compatriots.

"Fellas, I want you to meet the legendary Barbette! This guy had me and Fanny fooled! He comes out dressed like a girl, like the most beautiful creature you ever set eyes on, and at the end of his trapeze act, I swear, I had a fucking hard on, and all of the sudden he takes off his wig. He's a fucking man! Son of a bitch! I've never seen anything like it."

Rose wrapped his arm around Barbette's shoulder as he looked at the other men around him. Instantly, Barbette recognized one of them.

"I want you to meet the star of the show, Mister Jimmy Durante."

Even in Europe, Durante was getting a name for himself. Barbette shook the young comedian's hand. He could see in Durante's eyes, the comic didn't quite know what to make of him.

"And this is the director of the show, he needs no introduction, but since I'm paying through my ass to have him, I have the right to say he is the best god-damned director in the business! Straight from the Ziegfeld Follies as well as a shit-load of other Broadway hits, Mister John Murray Anderson."

"Barbette!" Anderson said, extending his hand, smiling warmly. He was a foot taller than Rose and was at least ten years older. There was an elegance to Anderson's stature and manner that Barbette immediately appreciated. His longish face was warmly paternal. "Darling, I've heard so much about you!" the director said.

"As I have about you!" Barbette enthused. Even while in Europe, he admired the precision and attention to detail he saw in the news reels of Anderson's dancing women. They were stylish and feminine. Barbette felt an instant creative rapport.

"You ask me, I never thought I was going to get you," Rose added as he looked at Barbette.

"Well, Mister Rose, it seems Mussolini and Hitler are proving bad for business. Night clubs are shutting down and entertainers are being arrested, especially we of the, how shall I call it, *avant-garde* set. Let's say you caught me at the right time."

Rose frowned.

"Those fucking fascist cocksuckers! I swear, what is this world coming to?! You ask me, fuck the fascists! Fuck the Nazis! Fuck 'em all! It's their loss."

Rose still had his arm on Barbette's shoulder. He gestured with his other arm looking up at the hundreds of carpenters and electricians around them.

"*Jumbo* is going to be amazing. We'll give them a bolt—a ball of fire! We've got Rogers and Hart writing the score. Paul Whiteman and his orchestra. Two hundred animals, including an elephant. I'm going to put on a show the likes of which has never before been seen by the human eye!"

"Indeed, Mister Rose," Barbette replied.

Billy Rose turned and looked at Barbette seriously.

"I need you tomorrow to be ready for an audition. Jock Whitney's coming by. His family's worth a fortune. Loves to race horses. I need all of the specialty acts up on stage.

Jimmy's been going through some of his lines too. Whitney's coming over to see if he wants to underwrite the show."

Barbette looked at Rose seriously for a moment. Rose already outlaid a considerable sum to ship Barbette and his equipment and costumes to New York and put him up in a respectable hotel. He could see around him, thousands of dollars being expended on the production.

"You mean, *Jumbo* has no backing?"

"Have no fear, Barbette! Tomorrow afternoon, once Jock sees what we're putting together, he couldn't possibly say no."

Barbette looked at John Murray Anderson.

"Darling," Anderson chuckled, "and you thought you knew everything about high wire acts!"

CHAPTER FORTY

"That was marvelous, darling!" John Murray Anderson congratulated Barbette as he came off stage. Barbette was breathing hard. He had been at the Hippodrome since early morning, making sure all his preparations were in place. He performed in his most flamboyant ostrich-feathered cape and headdress along with his flashiest trapeze costume. When he removed his wig, revealing his male identity, he could hear Rose cackling up in the seats as he sat beside Jock Whitney.

"Okay, next up is Le Blanc," Anderson called out. The director gestured to the young aerialist several paces away. Tall, blonde and barely twenty years old, he cut a statuesque appearance. He was nearly naked, only wearing snug white trunks with a spangled sort of belt.

The young aerialist spoke to Barbette in French for a moment.

"He's concerned he hasn't had time to rehearse in the space," Barbette said to Anderson.

"Well, now is his time!" Anderson replied coolly. "Tell him he needs to get it right."

Barbette pursed his painted lips. He conveyed the information to Le Blanc. The young acrobat grimaced for a moment, but then turned around and trotted back to the stage. He leaped onto a springboard contraption Barbette had never seen before. It catapulted Le Blanc high into the air where he caught an awaiting trapeze.

If Barbette prided himself on his own acrobatic daring, watching Le Blanc was a revelation. He was bold, forceful, without a hesitation to his moves. Barbette's performance on the trapeze was that of an Amazonian woman, but Le Blanc's was all man!

Just when Barbette thought he couldn't be thrilled any more, Le Blanc leaped off the trapeze while it was at its highest point. It was a thrilling swan dive forward, up in the air and then downward to the stage, head first, into a leap of death. It looked as if he was going crash onto the stage floor. Everyone watching gasped at the sight.

Then, the safety line Le Blanc discretely affixed to his ankles took hold, catapulting him back up into the air, high enough so that he could swing freely above. The whole of the performance was thrilling and exciting. Barbette could hear Billy Rose and Jock Whitney hooting and hollering from their seats. That instant, Barbette knew Billy Rose had his backing.

CHAPTER FORTY-ONE

Scheduled weeks of rehearsals ran into months. There were so many technical aspects to the show and Anderson demanded perfection. The much-publicized Labor Day opening was fast approaching for *Jumbo*, yet the production still wasn't ready. Fusing a Broadway show with a circus spectacle proved nearly impossible. The whole of the production was only kept afloat by Rose's buoyant hyperbole and Whitney's exceedingly deep pockets.

Anderson was feeling the pressure as well…"If you can't get it right, I'll hire girls who can!" he admonished the bevy of dancing women who performed below Barbette while he was up in the air. "The elephant is easier to deal with than all of you!" he groused.

Over the course of the production, Anderson changed, growing in intensity, pushing everyone to work harder, losing his temper when the staging didn't come off. In the stifling heat of the Hippodrome, he refused to even change his suit, wearing the same clothing Barbette first greeted him several months before. His odor was ripe and as foul as his temperament.

But in Anderson's perfectionism, Barbette found a kindred spirit. Barbette could see what he was driving for. After completing his routine, he went up to Anderson as he brooded by the side of the circular ring that now was in place on the massive stage.

"Mister Anderson, if you'd like, let me work with the women. I'll show them what you're looking for, a little refinement. And I have a suggestion—Billy wants lots of girls—let's give him more girls! Why not put some up in the air around me as I perform? It will look spectacular. In large gold rings hoisted around me, nearly naked, striking poses. Billy will go mad for it!"

Anderson could see Barbette's serious intensity.

"How long will it take to let me see it?"

"Can you give me three days?"

Anderson looked at Barbette for a moment.

"Yeah, I can. Have at it."

...

Three days later, Barbette staged his own number, combining the spectacle of the circus with burlesque and Broadway as never attempted before. Anderson, and even more importantly, Billy Rose, loved it.

"Darling," as Anderson called Barbette, "I can see you were born to do this thing!"

Barbette smiled, glad his talents were appreciated.

"It was brilliant," the young Le Blanc said in French to Barbette as the two stood together off stage. "You have brought the Folies Bergère to Broadway!"

Barbette signed, "Oh, if only!" He looked at the handsome, blue-eyed man before him, searching his eyes for some knowing. He swallowed hard, feeling a little too old and too foolish for a proposition. Mustering his courage, he cleared his throat. "Would you like to join me for supper tonight—at my hotel? I was planning on dining in."

There was silence between them. In that instant Barbette thought he made a terrible mistake. Then, Le Blanc smiled, a gorgeous, youthful grin. "I have been waiting for you to ask me!"

Barbette laughed as the two started walking together toward the dressing rooms.

"Have you ever had an American hot dog?" Barbette asked.

Le Blanc looked quizzical.

"Hot dog?"

"Oui!" Barbette smiled.

"I do not think I have had the pleasure."

"Well, you will tonight my dear, with all the fixin's!"

…

Exaltation. Barbette thrilled at their encounter. All the while, before they supped, Barbette felt incredibly insecure. *What was a thirty-five year old man doing—enticing this young man, at least fifteen years his junior?* But after supper, as the two reveled in each other's flesh, Barbette could see and feel—Le Blanc was as beguiled by their entwined bodies as he.

There was something charmingly simple about Le Blanc's outlook on life. He didn't yet bear the responsibilities or the realities of an acrobat. With a wanton hunger, Le Blanc only needed to feel pleasure. He wanted to share it too, in such a free manner. Le Blanc was like some magic elixir who made Barbette feel young and foolish. Their passion leapt forth, culminating in frothy explosions of delight.

Consumed by each other's physicality, they clung to one another in the darkness of the night. Once they released, their naked bodies rested on the bed, illuminated only by street lamps and flashing neon signs through grimy, half-opened windows and yellowed shears gently swaying in the breeze of

Barbette's hotel room. In that moment, as Barbette playfully caressed Le Blanc's thick blond hair, the two savored their peace.

CHAPTER FORTY-TWO

"I cannot get it!" Le Blanc blurted out to Barbette in French.

"Yes you can!" Barbette encouraged. The two were in full costume, standing just outside the center ring of the mammoth stage. As much as Barbette insisted, a shadow of a doubt flashed into his own mind. What Anderson was asking of Le Blanc was really quite absurd, if he truly thought about it.

In a count of sixty-four musical beats, a chorus of fifty men sang a foreboding song while they assembled a lion's cage. Right before the last count of eight, they had to finish assembling the contraption because a half dozen lions would be released into the cage at that precise moment.

If it wasn't enough, Anderson cut out from the top center of the cage, a hole, no larger than eight feet across. On the very last count of music, Le Blanc was to release from his trapeze, where he was performing an acrobatic routine, and plummet through the air, diving head first into the opening of the cage—and as Le Blanc released from the trapeze, Anderson demanded the lights be killed—placing the whole cage of menacing tigers and the outcome of the dramatic leap of death in great doubt.

Everything worked well, except, Le Blanc couldn't get the timing right for the release.

"Listen!" Barbette hastened the harried acrobat as he turned toward him. Barbette began to hum the music to Le

Blanc. As he did so, he thumped the beat onto Le Blanc's bare, sweated chest. When he came to the end, Barbette hummed with greater emphasis and thumped harder on Le Blanc's muscular chest.

"Do you feel it?" Barbette asked seriously. "Bum, bum...*bum!*"

Le Blanc closed his eyes, visualizing as Barbette coached him again. He calmed down and opened his eyes.

"Okay, I am ready. I shall do it again," he said.

"Okay, Mister Anderson!" Barbette called out across the stage to where John Murray Anderson, still in his soiled suit, was looming. "He's ready!"

"From the top everyone!" Anderson called. The orchestra started again. The chorus of fifty men, in precise chorography moved about the stage handling large sections of metal cage they assembled it in place, singing as they worked. Up above the quickly forming cage, Le Blanc swung on his trapeze, performing his routine of stunts and tricks. On perfect beat, the last of the sections to the cage were put into place, the lions were released and eight counts later, with flawless ease, Le Blanc leapt from his trapeze. The lights were killed. Le Blanc hit his mark. His catch lines thrusting him back up out of the cage, so that a second later, he was swinging safely up above it. The lights came back up and the whole of the crew were on their feet applauding. Barbette beamed. *He did it!*

When Le Blanc came back down on the ground, Anderson came up to him and gave him a hug. "That's it my boy! That's it!"

Anderson then turned around and shouted, "Okay, let's do it again!"

Barbette turned to Anderson. "Give him a minute. Let him take a rest."

"Do you need a rest?" Anderson asked Le Blanc. Le Blanc's eager young eyes said no. And a short while later he was back in place on his trapeze, high above the stage performing his routine as the chorus of roustabouts below assembled the lion's cage.

Once again, the cues went off without a hitch. Le Blanc was perfect.

"Son of a bitch!" Billy Rose's body guard, Moe, muttered as he took in the whole of the production next to Barbette. "This is fucking nuts!"

Billy Rose was whistling loudly as he applauded along with everyone else as the lights to the cage were brought up, with Le Blanc swinging on his safety lines above the enclosure.

Barbette was relieved. He felt confident Le Blanc finally had it.

Before Le Blanc could get down from his line, Anderson called up. "Can you do it one more time? One more practice? Three *is* the charm!"

Barbette grimaced. He turned to Anderson. "He needs a rest."

Anderson didn't reply, only looking ahead at the action commencing before him.

From high above, Le Blanc swung his body back onto the trapeze. The orchestra struck up the music and the chorus belted out their full-throated Rogers and Hart lines:

> *Who will risk his life tonight to thrill the mob?*
> *Who has a date tonight with fate?*
> *Who will risk his life to make their pulses throb?*

On perfect beat, the cage was completed, the lions were released, and eight counts later, Le Blanc dove through the air. Only, this time, something went terribly wrong! The safety wires gave way! Untethered, Le Blank hurled though the hole into the cage headfirst. The thud of Le Blanc's body crashing into the stage floor was unmistakable and horrifying.

Without thinking, Moe leapt forward, revolver drawn, entering the cage, with Anderson in hot pursuit. Barbette called out. Before Moe could get a round off, somehow, the lion tamer was able to corral the beasts back into their pens.

"Get the medic!" Anderson shouted. "Dammit, get the medic!"

...

"He will live," the doctor said to the small cadre of cast members who gathered in the stiflingly hot waiting room of the midtown hospital. The menagerie of entertainers, some still in their performance costumes, caused quite a scene. Barbette, wrapped in a trench coat, but wearing his dramatic face paint, was beside himself.

"I need to see him!" he demanded to the doctor.

The doctor looked at Barbette in a detached way, ignoring his outlandish makeup.

"I'm sorry, that's impossible. Not for a while anyway. He needs rest."

Barbette gave the doctor a sharp look, but assented to his orders. He could have second-guessed Anderson and blamed him. Maybe he should have. But he knew this was a business of practice and risk. He knew it since he was a child. He too fell before. They all did.

"Will he perform again?" Barbette asked.

The doctor didn't say anything. He glanced at Barbette earnestly and then at his fellow performers. He shook his head, no.

Barbette quietly stood up. He looked at the others, their desperate eyes meeting his, and then he left the room.

...

The day was overcast and gray. A warm drizzle fell on the streets of Manhattan, making the red tail lights of taxi cabs and delivery trucks reflect on the pavement.

Barbette watched the liner, the *SS Normandie*, with the help of a small retinue of tugs, swing her raked bow out into the open water of the harbor. She blasted her horn, which echoed off the sky scrapers of the city—rolling and lingering, thunderous ghosts of sound. From his vantage, along the harborside, Barbette squinted at the open air promenade deck of the ship, trying to catch a glimpse of Le Blanc. The French acrobat was heading home. There was no other way. He could be cared for by his family.

Barbette's gaze darted about, from the bow to the stern, before the ship got too far away. He had to see him one last time. He searched the promenade deck through the mist in his eyes. He thought all was lost—until there he was! Le Blanc! Sitting in a wheelchair, rolled up to the railing, his body covered in a warm, *SS Normandie* woolen blanket. Through the dank weather and the growing distance, it was too difficult for Barbette to read the expression on his face.

His heart ached seeing Le Blanc slowly slip away. Barbette took off his fedora and vigorously waved, trying to catch his attention. But Le Blanc didn't see him, not through the misty gray.

It was the last time Barbette would ever see the young daredevil. The last time he would ever set eyes on Le Blanc.

...

On November 16, 1935, *Jumbo* opened at the Hippodrome to a packed, standing room only crowd. The reviews were sensational. Billy Rose had a sizable hit, performing 233 shows to a total audience of over a million people. However, the production was too grand and ultimately lost money for Jock Whitney.

Because of the perceived success, Rose was called pint-sized P.T. Barnum. Barbette and his production number also received rave notices. John Murray Anderson continued to direct Broadway shows and feature films, while Jimmy Durante, through a clever *Jumbo* radio program, became more popular than ever.

CHAPTER FORTY-THREE

NEW YORK, 1938
WINTER

Barbette stretched on the floor backstage at the Loew's State theatre, in the heart of Broadway in New York City. As he did so, he felt an uncommon chill. February in Manhattan was a sloshy mess of dirty snow and overcast days. He moved his body about, jumping up and down, trying to warm his muscles. His ivory makeup covered all of his body's aging flaws—the cracked skin, his blackened hands, the bruising his torso took at points where it met the trapeze. He stretched out again, trying to loosen the muscles of his legs. Then, he felt another draft of frigid air swirl into the backstage area.

That was enough! He didn't give a crap he was in full drag including his elaborate ostrich-feathered headdress and silvery, luminous gown. He was going to find where the draft was coming from. As he moved through the curtains and down darkened hallways, he saw it—the loading dock door wide open! Two beefy men were loading in trunks of equipment even as it neared eight in the evening.

Barbette was livid. He turned to the two workers.

"We've got a fucking show going on! Close that door!" he hissed.

"We need get this stuff in!" one of the stage hands protested.

"Do it some other time!"

"Fuck you, princess. We do it now!"

"You stop now, or I don't go on!"

"Oh, all right! Don't get your fancy girdle in a knot!" the worker said as he motioned to his buddy to stop unloading.

"Close the damn door!" Barbette demanded again. He stood there in his costume, plumes still billowing from the frigid air pouring into the space.

"Fucking fairy," the stagehand muttered.

Barbette heard the comment. He was furious.

"What the fuck did you say?" he asked as he approached the man. "You wanna say that to my face, because I'll rip your fucking throat out!"

"Hey—what's the shouting?" the stage manager asked as he approached the three.

Barbette turned to him is disgust. "I can't go on if they're going to work with this door wide open. It's too cold!"

"Fellas, wrap it up for now. We'll do the rest tomorrow," the stage manager said as he looked seriously at the men.

"Okay, boss…That's what we were doing."

"Thank you," Barbette said to the stage manager as he marched backstage where he would attempt again to warm his body.

From his vantage at one of the wings leading to the stage, Barbette could see the contorted image of Dorothy Lamour on the massive silver screen. The film was *Tropic Holiday*. Dorothy Lamour smoldered sensuality in the heat of a Mexican night as she sang the film's signature song:

> *So lovely is the moon on a tropic night*
> *No heart can be immune on a tropic night*
> *As a lonely guitar plays a serenade*

It was still too cold for him! Barbette's muscles were tight and tense. He felt every bit as old as his thirty-nine years while he stretched and jumped about. In the late 1930's, after *Jumbo* closed, he toured the United States, working for Marcus Loew's theater chains back on the vaudeville circuit. Loew's theaters were large and opulent. Barbette's act still helped draw a crowd. But all around him, he could see the world of vaudeville in a dramatic collapse. Feature films were now the entertainment Americans turned to. Like water holes in the African desert after monsoon season, vaudeville was quickly drying up. Old vaudeville houses were converting movie houses. It was cheaper to show a film and customers loved them. Barbette watched vaudeville stars like Bob Hope, George Burns and Gracie Allen make the transition seamlessly to radio and then film, but Barbette's act was different. It just wouldn't play on film.

Yes, there were offers from Hollywood—but he saw the other specialty acts destroy themselves by going for the easy money. Once their ten minutes were out there on film to be consumed, the public moved on.

Europe was becoming even more sinister and political. Hitler and his SS troops were swarming into countries, shuttering the clubs he used to play—hauling off the 'sexual deviants' who performed there. His friends, fellow performers and occasional lovers, either left Europe, went underground or even disappeared altogether never to be heard from again.

America was Barbette's safe haven for now. By 1938, he settled at Loew's State Theater in midtown, Manhattan. He played twice-a-day, matinees and evenings, between the feature films. Manhattan crowds still appreciated the live acts and the routines helped fill the seats of the massive, ornate Loew's State, which held almost four thousand customers. By the time Barbette was featured there, Loew's State was the last major theater in Manhattan where vaudeville acts performed.

Barbette's routine was now witnessed by shoe salesmen and teachers, firemen and nurses and even their popcorn-munching children. They never protested the scandalous nature of his performance. He was a jolting surprise kept at a safe distance up on the ornate stage.

By now, Barbette had to admit his body was different. At thirty-nine, he ate only the healthiest foods and never drank or smoked. It took him longer to warm up. Performing at his level twice-a-day was more exerting than when he did five-shows-a-day nearly twenty years before. At night, he slept ensconced in hot water bottles soothing his sore muscles.

His body felt especially weak that evening. There were extra aches in his joints, but as he heard his theme music begin, he felt everything right itself. Like he did thousands of times before, he would give the audience a wonderful performance!

Everything was going well. Barbette looked stunning, making her entrance—a statuesque woman, so feminine and seductively playful. She moved from the slackline, to the rings and finally, onto the trapeze. It all took great concentration and physicality—especially her trapeze.

Back stage, the frustrated stage hands saw Barbette was up performing the act and so they started their loading once again. At the end of Barbette's trapeze routine, when she was about to release into an Angel's fall onto the stage, a strong gust of frigid air billowed the stage curtain behind her. It caught her attention at the exact wrong time. The release was all wrong! There was no net below. Barbette came crashing down onto the stage with great force. The audience gasped. Some even screamed. The stage manager saw what happened from the wings and ordered the curtain be dropped immediately.

Barbette felt disoriented—searing pain—not able to breathe.

"Can you get up?" the stage manager asked in what seemed like slow motion to Barbette.

Barbette lost her wig on impact. One of the female dancers, who was about to go on stage, picked it up and gave it to Barbette. She took it as she tried to stand up with the stage manager's help. As she teetered in place, she instinctively, perfectly, placed the wig atop her crown.

"Let me go," she said. "I must take a bow."

The stage manager and the dancers all fell back as Barbette found the opening in the curtain. She pulled it open and stepped in front of it, smiling broadly and effortlessly, as if nothing happened at all. She blew the crowd a playful kiss and then disappeared behind the curtain. The stage manager tried to grab hold of her, but Barbette refused assistance.

"I'll be fine!"

Then, Barbette slowly and deliberately left the stage.

"All right ladies—places!" the stage manager called out in a loud whisper. He gave a signal to cue the music for the next act. The curtain pulled back to reveal a row of dancing girls tapping in time to happy music.

Backstage, Barbette refused to see anyone in his little dressing room. His body ached terribly. No longer able to afford a maid and a wardrobe mistress, he undressed himself and showered. Then he put everything neatly back in its place. His body was stiff and sore. Once everything was in order, he gathered his coat and hat and departed the dressing room.

The stage manager approached him.

"Are you okay?"

"You could have killed me!" Barbette snapped.

"The fellas are real sorry. Do you want me to call a doctor?"

"I expect those idiots to be sacked," Barbette replied as he put his fedora on his aching skull.

"I don't think I can do that," the stage manager replied.

"It's them or me. When I come in tomorrow—if they're still here, I won't go on."

Barbette turned and headed out the backstage door. As he did so, he could hear the lovely Dorothy Lamour, up on the silver screen, once again starting to sing her sultry song:

What lips can answer "No" when two lips invite
When there's wine in the air, lips are always careless
Lovers find their delight on a tropic night...

...

Barbette listened to the phone ring in his Astor Hotel room. He no longer could command a suite as he once did a decade before, but Barbette insisted on a fine address for his Loew's contract. Laying in his darkened room, with the heavy drapes drawn closed, Barbette knew it was his wake up call. It was seven in the morning. Then, the ringing stopped. The room was silent except for the sound of steam working its way through the building's venerable radiators.

Since the ringing awoke him, Barbette tried to move his body—to reach for the phone on his nightstand only inches from his head, but he couldn't. Desperately, he tried moving his legs and then his arms. It felt as if his body became a sack of sand overnight! As he came to a greater awareness of his condition, he panicked! *He could not move!*

The phone rang again. He tried with all his might to lift an arm to reach for it, but he was unable! Clammy beads of perspiration formed on his forehead. The phone stopped ringing. Barbette was now breathing hard. He felt totally, utterly helpless! The minutes seemed to wear on—all the while, he needed to take a piss. He tried one more time with all his might to reach his hand to the phone, but it was no use.

"Help me!" he called out as loud as he could. "Please, help me!"

He would try to listen for any people moving down the hallway outside of his door. When they approached, he tried again, "Help! Help me!" But no one stopped.

Unable to hold it any longer, Barbette could feel the warm urine soaking his torso. It smelled and he felt disgusting. Hours passed by with Barbette laying on his soaking bed, motionless.

The phone started ringing again. Was it the theater? In the darkened room, he listened to the ring continue. He tried one last time to move an inch, but he couldn't. He never missed a show. It wasn't like him. He knew this would give him a bad name with Loew's. They would say he walked out over a dispute. The William Morris Agency would be furious. He needed to get to the damned phone, but it was impossible.

Finally, a maid knocked on the door.

"Please! Come in!" Barbette shouted. "Please, help me!"

The maid unlocked the door and rushed over to him. At his insistence, she immediately called for the hotel's doctor.

CHAPTER FORTY-FOUR

Barbette opened his eyes. A nurse wearing a protective surgical mask hovered over him, covering the middle of his naked torso with a sheet. The biting aroma of bleach burned his nostrils. When he came to, he was more aware of his body—the aches in his muscles and the throbbing in his head. His arms were extended outward from his torso, tied to flat splints, which were attached by cables running up to pullies on metal stands flanking the sides of his white-painted iron bed. Barbette tried to move his legs, but couldn't.

When the nurse saw he was coming to, she departed abruptly without saying a word. Laying on his back, he looked up at the sterile, white, plaster ceiling. He could see the bed was surround by walls of white draping.

Barbette felt exhausted. An overwhelming sense of helplessness frightened him and caused him to panic. He felt a total loss of control—of his muscles, his body, his mind. He was trapped in that room. It was the last place in the world he wanted to be.

"Good morning, Mister Loving," the young man in the white coat said to him as he entered the curtained-off enclosure.

"What's good about it?" Barbette snapped. Catching himself, he was thrilled at least he could speak!

The young doctor chose to not reply, only making a notation on the clipboard he was carrying. He then put his fingers up to Barbette's neck with one hand and looked at his wristwatch on the other, measuring Barbette's pulse.

"Can you breathe in please?" the man asked.

Barbette complied.

"Exhale...Very good."

"Mister Loving, I'm Doctor Simmons, your physician while you are at Post-Graduate Hospital. You took quite a fall."

Barbette scanned his memory to understand what the doctor was speaking about—and then, the images of being up on the trapeze and the curtain billowing rushed back into his memory.

"I'm afraid you've broken both your legs. The folks down at the Loew's—they said you even walked on them after it happened. Mister Loving, you're one determined man!"

"If my legs are broken, why are my arms tied up? And why are you wearing that mask over your mouth?" Barbette asked. He studied the man before him. He was about thirty years old, tall and thin with receding, light brown hair. His demeanor was serious, almost pensive, but there was an earnestness in the man's eyes.

"It's a precaution. We performed a spinal tap while you were sleeping. The results will be in tomorrow."

"A precaution for what? How long have I been in here?" Barbette asked anxiously.

"This is your third day with us, Mister Loving. As for precaution—well, I'll be blunt. Our wards are filling up with patients suffering from infantile polio. It's unusual, in the winter months, for us to see so many. We performed the tap to see if you have polio."

Barbette looked into the doctor's eyes to see if there was any hint of jest, but there was none.

"That's impossible—I'm extremely clean."

"That may true, but polio can be transmitted many ways. Judging from your profession, working in the theater as

269

you do, your risk for exposure is quite high. Tell me, did your mother or father ever contract the disease?"

"My mother no. My father—I'm not sure. He died when I was a child. I didn't know him."

"I see," the doctor said looking down again at his clipboard and made another notation.

"I must use the telephone. I must call Loew's."

"You needn't worry, Mister Loving, we've already done so. And the hotel as well. All of your things have been put in storage and you have been signed out. A gentleman from William Morris came by yesterday to check on you."

Barbette's mind raced.

"What did you say to him?"

"We said you were resting. We aren't permitted to disclose more."

"Under no circumstances must you let them know I broke both my legs..." Barbette felt his face flush with rage. "Do you hear me? Under no circumstances must they know my condition! Because if they do—I'll be ruined!"

"We'll see to it." The doctor then leaned forward a little. "Do you have any next of kin we can contact? Any family?"

Barbette looked at the doctor. He was frightened. He didn't know what to say.

"No."

"You said your father passed. What about your mother?"

"She's alive, but I don't wish to trouble her."

"No brothers or sisters?"

"No."

"What about friends or acquaintances?"

Barbette was exasperated.

"No! I don't have any friends in this country! If I was in France, it would be a different story! There, I have princesses and counts and countesses—many people who would be at my side—but here in America—I have no none!"

The doctor gently touched Barbette's chest and said, "I'm sorry to upset you Mister Loving."

"Please, remove your hand. The name is Barbette. First and last name. Simply, Barbette. Please see to it all of my hospital records are changed. My name is Barbette! Do you understand?"

The doctor was quiet for a moment.

"We'll get you a sedative. It'll calm you down."

"I don't need to be calmed down, Doctor Simmons. I just need to walk!"

"Very well," he replied. Then, he turned and left the room.

...

"Any next of kin?" the nurse asked Doctor Simmons in the corridor of the hospital.

"No," Simmons replied as he removed his surgical mask.

"Did you tell him he has polio?"

"No, not yet. Just he broke both his legs. He was already too upset. We must monitor his breathing. If he is labored, you have my permission to move him to an iron lung."

"Yes, doctor," the nurse replied.

"From here on out, please call him only Barbette. He prefers it. I'll speak to admissions to have the records changed. You're going to have your hands full, I'm afraid," the doctor said shaking his head. "He's a spirited man."

"I can handle it," the nurse replied. "I've got one of those at home too!"

They both smiled.

The doctor continued, "Please, do not share his prognosis with anyone. We must give him that dignity."

"Yes, of course."

CHAPTER FORTY-FIVE

Barbette lay in his bed. He felt his own urine pass into the catheter affixed to the tip of his penis. *There was no way he could have polio.* A child's disease. He was too healthy—too clean to ever contract such a disease. No matter the state of his legs, he would leave this hospital, in a wheelchair if he must. He would board the first ocean liner for Europe and convalesce there. Perhaps even at Villa de Noailles. The natatorium, with all of its exercise equipment and refreshing salt water pool would be perfect. He would contact Marie de Noailles to make all the arrangements. He was sure the Vicomtesse would adore hosting him. But for now, all he felt he could do was sleep...

. . .

"You know, I'm a blunt man, Barbette," Doctor Simmons said the following day as he pulled up a metal chair next to Barbette's bedside. "We need to talk seriously about where we're at."

"Oh for shame! I was just about to head to the Rainbow Room for lunch. It'll have to wait."

The doctor, whose face was covered with a surgical mask, chose not to acknowledge Barbette's sarcasm and continued.

"You do have poliomyelitis."

"Oh god!"

Barbette heard the voice in his head, his mother—*"Big boys don't cry"*—but he couldn't contain himself. The tears flowed down his face and he was helpless to even bring a hand up to his cheek to dry them.

"No!"

The doctor took several Kleenexes from a newly opened box and got up, dabbing Barbette's cheeks. Then he sat down again.

"We can put you on a routine to restore your health," Simmons continued.

Barbette looked at him with devastated eyes.

"I'll never perform again?"

The doctor was silent. He could see the ache in Barbette's visage.

"No, I am afraid, never again."

Barbette erupted in tears. They flowed from a place deep within his soul.

"But with operations and years of therapy, you may be able to walk."

"Stop…Please stop what you're saying."

The doctor worked to wipe Barbette's face and helped him blow his nose. Barbette tried to calm down and regain his composure. He breathed hard—in and out.

"And if I choose not to have these operations?"

"You will never be able to walk again…In fact, you will most likely die."

Barbette continued to breathe hard—in and out— trying to control his emotions—fighting back his pain. He earnestly looked at the doctor.

"I wish to die, Doctor Simmons…For you see, without performing, I'm nothing."

The doctor abruptly got up and turned away from Barbette for a moment. Barbette watched the man's head slump as he took kerchiefs for himself and blew his nose. He reached into his white lab coat, then into his suit coat pocket and produced a billfold. He turned around.

"I want to show you something, Barbette," the doctor said as he sat down again in the chair next to Barbette's bed.

From his billfold, he produced a small, rectangular photograph of himself, his wife, and their young child who must have been about two years old.

"This is my son, William…He too contracted infantile polio."

Barbette looked at the boy, his robust cheeks and happy smile. He saw the joy in the faces of his parents as they happily sat for a family portrait.

"He's dead."

Barbette had no more resistance, tears streamed rivers down his face. Doctor Simmons wept as well.

"When?" Barbette asked. "When did he die?"

"Last year.…Barbette, I need you…You have a strong will. I don't know where it comes from, but I can see you're a fighter. You would be the perfect candidate for new, experimental treatments. They're seeing results in Australia. You'd have the possibility of regaining the use of your arms and legs—without bracing even—but I can't lie—the procedures are painful and costly. The rehabilitation will take years. I'm asking you to consider doing this Barbette, because we can work together to stop this deadly thing."

Barbette looked at the man before him, both their hearts were lay bare.

"And if the treatments don't work?"

The doctor sighed.

"If they don't work, you'll have the satisfaction in your heart you did everything you could to save yourself and the lives of children like William."

Barbette closed his eyes for a moment and exhaled.

"Can you leave me alone? I can't answer this request right now."

"Of course, I understand. I'll be back tomorrow in the morning. Perhaps if you have more questions then, I'll do my best to answer them."

"Yes," Barbette murmured. "Yes. Thank you, doctor."

"Thank you for considering this."

Simmons stood up and headed out of the enclosure.

CHAPTER FORTY-SIX

"We're here to see Mister Vander Clyde Loving," the woman said to the receptionist in the entrance lobby of New York University's Post-Graduate Hospital in Manhattan. People in small clusters, families mostly, moved in and out of the bustling room. The receptionist sat behind the counter along one wall, a stationary figure in the busy scene.

The receptionist adjusted her bifocal glasses on the tip of her nose as she looked at her roster.

"I don't see anyone under that name," she reported to the woman standing before her wearing trench coat that was too lightweight for the weather they were having outside.

"The people at Loew's told me y'all were keeping him here," the woman replied. The receptionist felt sympathy for the woman, because clearly from the sound of her accent, she was not from New York.

"Perhaps there is a different name?" the receptionist asked.

The woman in the trench coat with the southern accent thought for a moment.

"What about Barbette? Barbette Vander Clyde?"

"No, I'm sorry. I don't have any patients under that name..." The receptionist looked further. "Wait, I see just one name, Barbette. Could that be who you are looking for?"

"Yes! It must be him!"

The receptionist read further.

"I'm sorry, doctor's orders, no visitors."

The woman in the trench coat frowned.

"But we came all the way from Texas. We're family— practically anyway. Mary here is. But I'm an old-time friend—Rose is my name. Isn't there a doctor or a nurse or someone we can speak with? I'm sure Vander would be real happy to see us!"

"Let me see. If you could be seated. I'll check."

The two women stood along one wall of the lobby. There were no unfilled seats in the busy room. Cold drafts of wind whooshed into the space via the entrance vestibule doors, which always seemed to be opening and closing. The women from Texas watched the receptionist scribble out a note, put it in a canister, and then insert the canister into a metal tube running up into the ceiling. "It won't be long," the receptionist called out.

The two waited in silence for almost half an hour until the receptionist motioned for them to come to her.

"Please, directly behind me is a bank of elevators. Tell the operator you wish to go to the fifth floor. When you're there, Doctor Simmons will meet with you."

"Why thank you kindly," Rose replied. "Come on Mary, let's get a move on."

. . .

"I'm Rose and this here is Mary Loving—Vander's sister," Rose explained to Doctor Simmons. He took them to his office on the 5th floor where they could have privacy. The room was paneled in dark woods with built-in shelves behind the doctor's desk stacked with medical books and journals. The doctor chose not to sit behind his desk, but rather in one of the several wooden chairs in front of it, closer to the two women from Texas.

The doctor began to speak, "I'm sorry, but I don't understand. We have it only that Barbette has a mother. That isn't true?"

"No. It isn't," Mary spoke up. She was in her mid-twenties. She struck the doctor as a rather plain-looking woman with a strong farmer's jaw, but possessing Barbette's same, vibrant eyes. Her brunette hair was mostly covered by the large, protective brim of her coal-scuttle hat. "I came along after Vander left home."

Rose spoke up, "You see, Vander was on the road so much he wrote his family, but he never gave us any address to write back. He doesn't even know he's got a half-sister." Rose was well kept and tidy, her appearance more functional than fashionable. Work in the sun wrinkled her face more than northern women her age, but she had a proud visage and the fiery hazel eyes of a woman who meant business.

"We came to town as a surprise. When we heard Vander was performing in New York—why we said it was better now or never—because we never have seen Vander do his act. I mean, I did as a little girl, when he was out walking on his mammy's clothes line. I was even his assistant! He was such a wonderful, dear friend." Rose's face lit up as her heart filled with reminisces.

Mary interjected, "Then we heard he was taken ill and he was staying with y'all. We came all this way. Now we thought it might cheer his spirits, you know, meeting me, and seeing his old running partner, Rose."

The doctor looked at them seriously for a moment.

"Did the theater say what happened to him?"

"Just that he had a real bad fall," Rose added.

The doctor studied the two. He knew if Barbette was going to have a shot at recovery, he could use all the allies he could find. Simmons decided to gamble.

"I'm afraid it's true, Barbette had a fall. A very bad one. Both of his legs are broken."

"What?!" Rose exclaimed as Mary's mouth gaped open.

"How bad is it?" Rose asked.

"Well, if it was just his legs, why with his determination, he may be able to walk and perhaps perform again."

"I see," Rose said seriously.

"But unfortunately, there's more...." The doctor turned to Mary. "Is there any history of polio infection in your family?"

"I'm not sure. I know our mammy lost one child, but I never asked."

"Sometimes certain families are more susceptible," the doctor said explaining his curiosity.

Rose's mouth dropped. "Are you saying he has polio?"

The doctor looked down at the oriental carpet covering the darkly stained wood floor of his office.

"Yes, I'm afraid."

Rose was shocked. She reached for Mary's hand.

"Is he going to make it?" Rose asked forthrightly.

Doctor Simmons exhaled.

"That's entirely up to him, I suppose. The infection hasn't spread to his lungs and with his fever receding, hopefully it won't. There are new treatments for his limbs. From Sister Kenny from Australia. They're proving promise. But he'll also have to endure orthopedic surgery. You see, the tendons in the body, the legs and arms primarily, recede and tighten, so they must be lengthened. It's extremely painful."

"And if he doesn't do the treatments?" Mary asked.

"Well, the treatments themselves are very controversial. There're no guarantees they'll work. But if he doesn't do them, at best he'll be very weak. He may not be able to regain basic motor skills like walking...and he won't have long to live...."

Rose heard enough.

"Doctor, I don't mean to tell you your business, but let me tell you about Vander Clyde Loving. He was one tough runt of a kid. He may not've been as big as the other boys, but he was a fighter. And he could make his body do just about anything he wanted it to. He's smart too. You give him this treatment and you'll see, he'll come out fighting."

Doctor Simmons smiled slightly.

"That's what I was hoping. He's the perfect subject to undertake this type of therapy. He's in excellent shape and he's disciplined."

"Well, Doctor, can we see him? I'll get him to work for you. You'll see," Rose responded.

"If I tell him he has guests, he'll refuse to see you," the doctor replied.

"Well hells bells, doctor, take us to his room and we'll just have to pay him a surprise visit."

...

Barbette lay in his bed looking up at the white plaster ceiling of the hospital room. He could tell the room was slightly larger, containing one or two more beds, but he could see no one, only the white ceiling and white drapes of a curtain wall surrounding his bed. His arms were still extended out from his sides, resting on the wooden paddles supported by the pulley contraptions. He felt like a prisoner, held captive in a body which had once been so complaint.

His body was an instrument he learned to play over the years. He could manipulate its form to make himself appear female. When he called upon his muscles to support him upon the trapeze or slack rope, they were always there, ready to withstand the exertions. Now, he could scarcely move his head. He hated every moment of this imprisonment.

"Good morning, Barbette," Doctor Simmons said as he entered the curtained enclosure. He went about his usual inspections, taking Barbette's pulse, noting his general condition.

"Good *morning*, Doctor Simmons," Barbette said grandly. He let the doctor run through his usual routine. He had to admit, he was starting to enjoy the young doctor's company.

Without warning, Rose and Mary entered the curtained enclosure. They had taken off their trench coats and were both wearing surgical masks. The doctor warned them of what Barbette looked like, his physical state, limbs fastened to pulleys stretching tendons.

Before Barbette could say anything, Rose's eyes sparkled. She was thrilled to see her long-lost friend!

"Hey wildflower!" she said enthusiastically.

"Oh god!...Rose!" Barbette exclaimed. No matter it had been over twenty years—the voice, the eyes—he could recognize her anywhere. He was overcome.

"Now, is that anyway to greet your best friend?" she asked. She was truly excited to see her beloved Vander no matter what condition he was in.

"I'd give you an embrace, but you can see I'm all tied up!" Barbette quipped with a grin.

Mary burst out laughing.

"Doctor Simmons," Barbette scowled, "Please! You are being a terrible host! This is my dear friend, Rose, and I'm sorry darling, what is your name?"

"Mary."

"Please, let's get Mary and Rose some chairs."

Doctor Simmons smiled.

"Coming right up!"

He left the room and came back a moment later with two metal chairs he placed near the bed.

"How on earth did you get here?" Barbette asked in wonderment.

"We came up to see your show!" Rose replied. "We heard you were playing back in the states so we decided to take a little vacation and head on up to New York."

"And Mary, is she your friend? No offense darling, but I can't possibly believe you're Rose's daughter."

"Well, no…" Rose began, "actually, it's you two who're related. After you left Round Rock, a whole heck of a lot of stuff went down. Vander, this here is your sister, Mary! She was born about a year after you left town."

Barbette felt a flush of emotion come over him. He couldn't believe what he was hearing!

"*Mary*," he said again out loud. "You're a beautiful young lady!"

Then another wave of emotion hit him. His eyes began to tear.

"I'm so sorry I truly am…" he said.

"It's okay Vander," Rose consoled taking tissues by the bed, drying Barbette's eyes. "It's okay."

"I've been a big fan of yours," Mary spoke up. "Momma is so proud of you too. She reads all the letters you send her again and again. And the money has kept us on our feet in the hard times. You know, we made a scrap book even. Momma started it, when I was a baby. Any notice, any picture we could find in the papers, we collected right here." Mary held up the scrap book which she had in her hands to show Vander. She stood up over the bed. She opened the book for Barbette to see the contents as she gently turned the pages.

Barbette was overwhelmed.

"Momma?" he asked. He was silent for a while as Mary turned the pages. Next to some of the articles, he could see dates written in white pencil on the black paper in his mother's hand. "Is she well?"

"Strong as an ox!" Rose interjected. "Still doing her needle work and making her hats."

"And Sam Loving?"

"Sam is Sam. I suppose it feels good to know you once gave him a whoopin'!" Rose laughed.

Barbette smiled. He looked at more pictures in the scrap book. Each one recalled a memory. He was never one for nostalgia. He was always propelling himself forward, but in this one moment, he took in the journey he travelled. He turned to Rose.

"It was magnificent Rose. It was. All of it. Hard work—but magnificent!"

"Did you ever wanna just do your act straight?" Rose asked boldly. "I mean a man dressing up to look like a woman! Hells bells, Vander, I know how much it takes! And you look prettier than me!"

Barbette laughed.

"No," he replied. He was quiet for a moment. "Remember how Miss Nelson taught us some of the men dressed as women to play the female parts in Shakespeare's time? Well, somehow I knew I was born to play the female parts."

"Pa...um, Sam doesn't like it. He gets mad when momma and I talk about your beautiful gowns!" Mary added.

Barbette didn't say anything. He was lost deep inside himself.

Rose finally spoke up.

"Penny for your thoughts, wildflower," she said gently.

"Do you have children, either of you?"

"I've got a couple of young boys, strong as bulls!" Rose smiled. "I'm sure they're raising hell while momma's out East."

"I'm not yet married," Mary added.

"Why you wondering?" Rose asked.

"Either of them come down with Polio?"

"Thankfully, no," Rose replied.

"The doctor wanted me to do some new treatments. They're radical. He said if I do them, maybe I can get back on my feet. And if I don't, I…"

Rose stood up and walked over right next to the bed.

"Listen here, Vander. I've known you since we were little kids. I've seen people try to beat you down. I've seen them try to trample you. But just like that wildflower I picked for you that day—growing up through the sidewalk—you proved them all wrong! You bloomed! Bolder and better than all the rest of 'em! And I watched from afar saying to myself—That Vander Clyde! He did it! My wildflower bloomed! And let me tell you, right now, I'm not gonna see you die! Yes, it's gonna be painful. And yes, it's going to take time. But Vander, you never backed down from a challenge. Never."

Barbette let Rose's words wash over him. He was silent for a long while. Then, he looked at Doctor Simmons who was standing beside the white-curtained partition.

"Okay," he said as he regained his resolve, "let's beat this thing."

"Amen!" Rose exclaimed. "That's my wildflower!"

CHAPTER FORTY-SEVEN

Up there. Up in the air—high in the sky of the big top. She floated so softly, on a line no thicker than a spider's web. She danced her ballet, up there in the sky...She was beautiful. An angel, sent from above...

"You're doing great!" the nurse said as Barbette steadied himself. Barbette dragged his left foot forward a scant seven inches. He took the step alone. He was not relying on any crutches or leg braces as he slid his foot ahead. With great determination, he put his weight on the foot and started to drag the right ahead, this time even farther than the last. Beads of sweat formed on his forehead. It took all of his concentration. All the mental strength he acquired learning how to balance his body on the high wire now was being used to learn how to walk again.

The days he worked up to this one moment stretched into months. First, he rebuilt some of his range of motion with his arms. They had shriveled like his legs from lack of use, but in time, with an enormous force of will, through excruciating operations, he was able to bend his arms at their elbows and even raise them over his head.

Walking was even more difficult and painful. He mastered his wheel chair, then moved to leg braces and crutches, but he was determined to walk with his own legs under his own power.

The journey to this moment took him from Post-Graduate to other hospitals and recovery sanitariums across the country. All Barbette earned, all of the property he so judiciously purchased for his retirement had to be sold.

The best clinics were on the east coast and so once again, he did not see Rose or Mary or his mother. Barbette was cheered by the letters they sent him, but he was still as yet unable to maneuver his hands to write them back. He knew one day he would. And he knew one day he would walk under his own power. Rose was right, when Barbette put his mind into it and battled for something, he would prevail.

With each tentative step, Barbette was learning something about his body. Like a technician, he studied how much weight he could put on each leg, how to control his balance. With each move forward, he tried to smooth out his gate, to push his foot just a bit farther than the last time.

At night, when he rested, he listened to the radio, no matter where he was, to broadcasts of the war raging in Europe.

When the barbarian rolled into France, strutting like a peacock on Paris's Champs-Élysées, he knew his dear friends in his beloved city were in grave danger. From the newspapers, occasionally he would read how some of his friends fled France while others stayed. Barbette wondered if they thought of him, or did they take him for dead? He wondered, would they still want to make his acquaintance now that he was crippled?

Barbette's time on the stage may have passed, but not his creativity. This, he felt assured. His mind couldn't rest. It had to create. Aerial ballets under the circus big top. He would think of it all—the costumes, the routines, the lighting, the music. He planned it all in his head. He knew when he was ready, where his future lie.

"You walked twenty steps today! Barbette! That is wonderful!" the nurse congratulated him. Barbette was exhausted.

"Twenty steps today—thirty tomorrow," he replied.

"Yes!" the nurse exclaimed. "Thirty tomorrow!"

CHAPTER FORTY-EIGHT

AUGUST, 1941

The three women stood on the Round Rock train platform. There was no letup in the sweltering heat on the clear, August evening. Being just past eight, the sun cast a blaze of pink light into the indigo sky. They were all proud women, strong. Rose brought her two boys with her. Mary peered round the bend, trying to spot the train's arrival.

When the whistle blasted and black smoke could be seen over the treetops, Harriet Loving, clutched her purse a little bit tighter. The ravages of time played their cruel tricks upon her. They lined her face and stooped her figure, but she was still a handsome woman with bright eyes and stately appearance. All the ladies wore light cotton, print dresses, belted smartly at the waist. Rose and Mary didn't bother with wearing hats—why go to the trouble in the heat? But not Harriet. She would always be properly dressed, in a hat of her own design, looking like the rich folks she washed and sewed for all those years ago.

With the train's bell clanging, the black behemoth shook the ground when it rolled slowly past them. It let forth a pelt of steam as it came to a halt.

"Round Rock!" the ladies heard the conductor call out as he stepped from one of the passenger cars ten paces from where they stood. Harriet felt her pulse quicken, a lump forming in her throat.

Then, with careful movement, Barbette stepped down from the train. Dressed in a sleek, grey, double-breasted summer suit, looking as fresh as when he boarded the train three days before in Manhattan, Barbette tipped his fedora to the fat-faced conductor, who was flush from the heat. Barbette carried his lone, brown, leather suitcase with his free hand.

The ladies were struck in their places as he walked toward them. His gate was smooth and practiced, more like an actor moving across a stage. The showman in him made it all seem so effortless, no matter the pain he felt with each step.

"Hells bells, Vander Clyde!" Rose blurted out. She stepped forward and gave him a big hug, and then Mary too. Once they had done so they cleared, revealing Harriet.

"Good evening, momma," Barbette smiled.

Harriet stepped forward to greet her son. She hugged him and held onto him, kissing his cheek.

"I've missed you son," she said with tears in her eyes. "I've missed you!" She held onto Barbette for a long while. Then she released, stepping away from him, still holding his hand.

Barbette grabbed the kerchief from his suit coat pocket and gave it to her.

"Here you go momma. Don't cry," he smiled. "Big girls don't cry."

"The hell they don't!" Rose said happily.

"Kids, why don't you help your uncle Vander with his bags? Is this all you got?" Rose asked.

"Yes," Barbette replied.

"These here are my boys," Rose gestured, "Darrell and right behind him is Donovan."

Both the boys were dressed neatly in their Sunday best—plaid, short-sleeved shirts and lightweight gabardine trousers. They were tall and broad shouldered—good looking farm boys close to twenty years old.

"*Well!*" Barbette exclaimed taking in the handsomeness of them both. "I'm glad they still grow them big in Texas!"

"Come on Vander," Mary said eagerly. "We've got a whole dinner waiting for you back home—ham, fresh sweetcorn, homemade bread, and all the fixin's. Momma even baked some of her rhubarb pie, just for you."

They all piled into Rose's old black Packard. As they drove away from the depot, Barbette absorbed the sights. Trees lined the streets of Round Rock where open fields used to be. They passed down Main Street, its buildings now brick and mortar, no longer wood frame. The Packard made a couple of turns rolling on newly paved road that was once rutted dirt. The Packard drove down the once familiar side street.

Rose stopped the car. They all looked out the window. The lot where his mother's limestone house once stood was empty. Barbette's heart filled with reminisces. The house that held so many memories was demolished.

"You remember those shows you put on out in the back of the old house?"

"Sure do," Barbette smiled.

"Boys, Vander used to put on the most spectacular shows."

The boys heard their mother's stories a hundred times, but didn't complain, hearing her talk about them again in the presence of Barbette.

"You know, I still don't know how you did it, getting up on your momma's clothes line like you did."

"I'm not so sure either."

Barbette's mind continued to fill with memories of the olden days.

"How's old Sam?" he asked.

"Getting on," Harriet replied. She was sitting in the front row bench seat—in the middle—alongside her son. "You know, he became county sheriff. He's retired now, but he's busy in town, still."

Barbette didn't say anything. Maybe it was a good thing the old house was torn down. Because as many good memories there were in the old place, there were bad ones too.

The Packard moved farther down the block and then turned right. They pulled up to an ample, white-painted, wood-framed farm house with deep porches crowded with sage-green wicker furniture. The window frames of the home were painted the same dark green color as were the planks of the front and side porches. Large oak and pecan trees surrounded the home providing comforting shade. The black Packard rolled up the gravel drive next to the front lawn, which still managed to stay green even in the punishing heat of August.

Everyone headed out of the car. Barbette stood for a moment, looking at the handsome, clean lines of the home. With the sun almost set, the glow of electric lights filled the windows on the first floor.

"You've got a good looking house, momma," Barbette said approvingly.

Mary stepped alongside of him.

"It's your house, really," she added. "Isn't it so, momma? All that money Vander sent you and Sam. We could never be living in something so nice."

"Now, don't get Sam all riled up," Harriett cautioned. "The windows are open."

No matter it was his first time at the farmhouse, from the moment he stepped inside and smelled the cooking, Barbette knew he was home. As he entered the front door, Sam got up out of his easy chair—with its rounded arms and white doily set atop the headrest. His mustache was white and cut more closely about his lip than Barbette remembered. His frame seemed shorter, and he was considerably stouter. Sam wore only an undershirt with trousers held up by suspenders. The retired sheriff took out his kerchief and wiped the sweat from his bald dome.

"Boy," he said in his manly way, as he reached his hand out.

"Sam," Barbette replied.

The two shook hands. Barbette expected it would be another test of the wills, but this time, the hand shake was firm, but not challenging.

"Where's your nice shirt?" Harriet scolded her husband. "I laid it out just for you. I told you I wanted you to wear it."

"The boy don't mind. Do you son?"

"No, I don't mind."

"Come and have a seat. Take your coat and hat off," Sam gestured to the other easy chair in the parlor which sporting the same doily, draped atop its back. "Let's let the ladies get the grub."

Rose's two sons sat in the floral print sofa next to the window. A large, black, oscillating fan futility attempted to blow in cooler air from the outside.

Barbette removed his hat and suit coat, draping them on the sofa.

"I'd say you're about as bald as me!" Sam laughed looking at Barbette's smooth dome.

Without the flattering padding of the jacket, the nature of Barbette's shriveled limbs and awkward frame were revealed.

"Come on boy, let's listen to the war report. It's almost on. You lived in those parts? England and France?"

The half-moon dial of the radio, coved in wood veneer sitting atop a side table, glowed.

"France, yes," Barbette replied.

"What the hell has gotten into these Huns? Damned Nazis! If I was young again, I'd be out there taking them all on!"

"With that sir, I'd have to agree."

"Ha!" Loving slapped his knee. "That's all we need! A crippled, pansy fighting for us!"

Barbette gave Sam an incredulous stare. He quietly stood up.

"Rose," he called out.

"Yeah?" she said from the kitchen.

"I need you to take me to a hotel."

Rose stepped out of the kitchen, wiping her hands on an apron.

"What're you talking about?" she asked and then she saw the sheepish expression on Sam's face.

Barbette turned to Loving.

"A pleasure, Sam, as usual. A pleasure."

"Samuel Loving!" Rose scolded. "What on earth have you been sayin'?"

Harriett now came out of the kitchen. Mary followed behind her. Barbette's mother looked concerned and angry.

"Aw calm down everyone!" Sam groused. "Look here, Vander. I didn't mean nothing by it. Hell, I'm sorry. Will you accept my apology?"

Barbette looked at him and then looked at his mother. He said nothing.

"I will not have this starting all over again!" Harriett said stepping forward. "Sam, you mind your manners or I'll kick your butt out of this house!"

Barbette picked up his coat from the sofa and put on his hat.

"Rose, have one of your boys get my bag. I'll be waiting out by the car."

Barbette went up to his mother and gave her a kiss on her stunned cheek.

"It was good seeing you momma."

Barbette turned to Samuel Loving and looked at him coldly.

"Good day."

He then turned and walked across the room with his smoothed gait. He left the farmhouse. The screen door slammed behind him. They all could hear Barbette's footsteps move across the front porch and down the stairs.

"I'll go talk to him," Rose said as she took off her apron.

She made it out to the car, where Barbette was already sitting in the passenger seat.

"Come on, Vander," Rose said as she walked up to him. "With how far you've come, are you going to let that old man get under your skin?"

Barbette wouldn't look at her. Instead he looked straight ahead.

"Please Rose, get my bag. Certainly, Round Rock is big enough now to have a hotel."

"Come on, Vander..." she tried to cajole him.

"Please, Rose! If you don't get my bag now, I'll walk into town and find the damned hotel myself."

"You'll be upsetting your momma," Rose tried one last time.

"No. I won't. Let's make it clear. *Samuel Loving* will upset my mother."

By now Darrell was on the porch holding Barbette's leather bag. Rose motioned for him to bring it to the auto and put it in the back seat.

She walked around to the driver's side, got in, and turned the key, which she had left in the ignition. The Packard rumbled to life.

As the car backed out of the drive, Barbette looked at the house one more time. The boys, Darrell and Donovan, stood out on the porch. Donovan waved his hand goodbye.

Barbette sat motionless in the front seat. He wouldn't be insulted by his family, never again.

...

"Where're you taking me? This isn't the way into town," Barbette said as Rose steered her worn Packard down a gravel road. Dry, dusty air swirled into the open windows.

"I can't have you coming all this way out to Round Rock without you looking up at the stars. They're beautiful this time of year, Vander."

Barbette looked at Rose, her hands clasping the wheel as she squinted past the dashboard looking straight ahead. In a few minutes, they reached their destination. Rose put the old Packard in park and turned off the engine.

"Come on! Get out!" she gestured as she opened her own front door. Barbette obliged. "Careful for the cow patties," Rose added.

She guided the two out into the pasture which was on a gentle rise of earth. From a distance, the two could see the twinkling lights of the little town of Round Rock. The air was still hot, even with the sun down.

"I swear, with that southern wind coming up, it's like the devil himself is exhaling his scalding breath right through Texas," Rose said as she pulled her brown hair off her neck. Barbette stood alongside of her.

"I haven't been up on this rise since we were kids," he said. He took in a deep breath. "It still smells the same. Texas earth has a smell all its own, doesn't it?"

"Especially in the summer. Kind of unbelievable. We used to pick cotton out here. Hell, that was miserable," Rose laughed.

Rose looked at the multitudes of stars above them in the moonless night.

"After you left, when I got a little older, I used to come up here in Daddy's old jalopy and think of you, Vander."

"You did?"

"Yes, I did! I used to imagine you in all sorts of exotic places, seeing the world. Every time a circus rolled into Austin, I had to go. I'd look for you, one of the performers, but I could never pick you out. There were times I was so mad at you! *Why* didn't you take me with you, I'd wonder. Why didn't you write? When things got bad at home, or I was frustrated over something, I would come right up here and give you a piece of my mind."

Barbette looked into Rose's hazel eyes. They were still filled with the same vitality of her youth, only now rimmed with fine lines and creases.

"I pictured you up there, in the stars. I'd shake my fist at you and let you have it. But over time, I started to understand. When postmaster Johnson brought the first item about you from the papers that mentioned your name and had this little picture of you dressed like a woman—holy crap! Vander, you should have seen the look on old Sam's face!" Rose cackled. "But I thought to myself, that's my wildflower. He bloomed! Not in a way that anybody'd expect. But there he was, beautiful as I always knew he'd be."

"Thanks, Rose."

"I pictured all of the kings and queens of England and France you must have met. All of the fancy dinners and elegant balls you must have attended."

"It wasn't quite like that, but it was wonderful. It was."

Rose looked at Barbette seriously.

"Where are you gonna go, Vander? I mean, now that it's over? Where you gonna go?"

"I want to see about a job staging some of the circus acts. I'll head down to Sarasota. It's where most of the acts go when they finish their runs for the year. In November, they head down there."

Rose's gaze intensified. "It's a long way to November. Your momma said you had to sell all of your holdings to cover your medical expenses. If you go now, you won't have anything to do and you won't have a dime to live on."

Barbette was quite for a while. He knew she was right.

"I won't have you living on the streets, Vander. I won't have it! Now, I know Samuel Loving is one son of a bitch, if you'll excuse my French. But hells bells, you deserve to live in that house just as much as he does! I know how much money you gave your momma over the years. I can't tell you how excited she was to know you were coming home. She just beamed with pride. She is so darned proud of you! Vander, can you stay on for a while, just for her? She's getting on in years. She needs her son too."

Barbette looked at the limitless array of stars above them on the cloudless night. He shook his head and laughed to himself.

"You know, I think you had it about right, Rose. I was up there, in the stars, and the view from there was…was, amazing! What I wouldn't give to be back up there again…but…it'll never happen. Not in the way it once did. I've reconciled myself to that."

"Stay in Round Rock, Vander! Just for a while. I know it hurts your pride. We all want you here. Hell, even Sam does, if he doesn't know how to quite say it."

Barbette stared out at the stars. Then he turned to Rose. "Momma made her rhubarb pie, didn't she?"

"Hell yes! And I made an apple one too."

"You know, I'm going to need you to keep my sanity."

"That's me, Doctor Rose, at your service!"

"I love you, Rose," Barbette smiled.

"Oh dear, how long I've waited to hear those words!" she chuckled. "Now give me a hug, but don't tell my husband Darrell senior 'cause he'll whoop both our asses!"

The two clung onto each other for a while under the blanket of stars.

"Come on," Rose said breaking away and smiling as she took Barbette's hand. "Let's get some grub!"

CHAPTER FORTY-NINE

DECEMBER 8, 1941

"Yesterday, Dec. 7, 1941—a date which will live in infamy—the United States of America was suddenly and deliberately attacked by naval and air forces of the Empire of Japan..."

Barbette sat in one of the floral easy chairs with rolled arms next to the identical one where his mother sat. Samuel Loving anxiously paced the parlor as all three listened to the crackling voice of President Roosevelt. Loving went up to the wooden radio, and fidgeted with its glowing dial, trying to get better reception. The voice stopped for a while, causing Harriett great consternation.

"Sam! Stop fooling with it!" she admonished.

Roosevelt's voice returned, strong and confident as he delivered his plea to congress. Loving stopped pacing for a while standing rod still as they took in the news.

All three were too preoccupied by the broadcast to have noticed the bicycle rider make way up the gravel drive to the house. They didn't hear the footsteps climb up the stairs and move onto the ample front porch of the home.

But there was a knocking on the screen door. The three turned toward the door. Sam grimaced.

"What the?" he muttered as he went to the front door. "If it's those Gypsies again, I'll run the whole batch of them out of town!"

"Western Union telegram sir," the teenaged boy in the spotless uniform said. "For Mister Vander Barbette."

Samuel Loving frowned. He looked over to Barbette who pushed himself up out of his chair. Loving signed for the sealed telegram and fished in his trousers for a couple of nickels. "There you go, son," he said closing the door and handing the envelope to Barbette.

Barbette opened the envelope with Sam looking over his shoulder.

DECEMBER 8, 1942

NEEDED IN NEW YORK AT ONCE. (STOP) RINGLING MEETING. (STOP) SERVICES REQUESTED. (STOP)

JOHN MURRAY ANDERSON

Barbette stared at the message trying to glean from it unwritten details.

Loving looked at Barbette. "Don't those fellas know you're a cripple?" he asked. The days since Barbette's August homecoming had turned to weeks and then months. Everyone seemed to manage, even if they did get testy with one another every now and then.

"Shhh!" Harriett scolded her husband for talking as she continued to listen to Roosevelt's address.

"Looks like I'll be heading to Manhattan," Barbette said quietly.

Harriett was about to shush him, but then stopped herself. She looked at her son, trying to comprehend what he just said.

Barbette handed her the telegram which she read to herself. Frowning, but not saying a word, so as not to speak over Roosevelt, she looked up at her son.

"I shall leave tomorrow."

CHAPTER FIFTY

"The business is changing, that's for sure," Ringling said as he affixed another cigarette to his ivory holder and lit it. He leaned back in his ample, blue leather chair and put his freshly polished black and white, wing-tipped shoes on top of his massive hand-carved, inlay desk.

The whole of Ringling's office suite was magnificent. It was more the décor of a robber baron than circus producer. In reality, John Ringling North was an average looking man— average height and weight. He had the face that could easily be lost in a crowd, but his perfectly tailored wardrobe of the finest materials gave him away, revealing he was a man of considerable importance.

"The circus is bigger than ever," Ringling continued, "we've got over fifteen hundred Joe's on the payroll. We're putting out four thousand six hundred meals a day for the cast and crew. Ninety double-length rail cars to move the show. This season alone, we'll put on over twenty thousand miles!"

Each grand statistic made Ringling's eyes twinkle. "Looks like we're gonna top four million tickets sold and that's not counting the fifty thousand comps for our troops."

John Murray Anderson looked as stately as usual standing next to one of the office's windows. He calmly glanced out the large portal to the multitudes of people on the Manhattan sidewalk below.

Barbette knew John Ringling North loved the hyperbole of his circus. His was the biggest, the best there ever was. No one could do a circus like John Ringling North—not even P.T. Barnum himself.

"Do you know, I've got the war department haranguing me—telling me we're too big? They say we're on the rails too much. They need to keep them open for their freight trains. So for next season, we've got to replan the whole thing. Longer engagements in bigger cities. We're going to have to be even more spectacular to draw them in from the outlying towns."

"That's why you're here, Barbette," Anderson interjected. "John hired me on as his director. I told him I must have you."

"The 1942 circus is going to be like nothing anyone has seen before," Ringling continued. "Do you know right now, we've got the choreographer Balanchine working up a ballet for the elephants? They're dancing to a polka by Stravinsky! Fifty elephants in pink tutus! My family thinks I'm nuts!"

Anderson sat down in the leather club chair next to Barbette's and leaned in toward him.

"When we worked together on *Jumbo*, I saw something I need. You had ideas! Wonderful, creative ideas. And you worked so well with the ladies. Now, we know about your fall and your serious illness, but I wanted you here to personally offer you this opportunity—to direct the aerialists—something completely new!"

Barbette looked at Anderson. He was stunned. All the while, he wondered why he had been summoned to New York. He fretted Anderson would want him to reprise his old routine, which he knew was forever impossible. What he was hearing was a revelation! All his time in recuperation, his mind was creating. Now was his time to unleash his very best ideas and he was certainly ready!

Barbette looked at the two men. His eyes glowed with excitement.

"I'll need lots of girls—over sixty at least. And the rigging. We'll need all new rigging. Not just for one ring either. The whole tent, streamers of silk from the rafters. Women wrapped into the lines, all performing in unison, in identical costume. It'll be spectacular. More magnificent than anything ever attempted or seen before!"

A small grin appeared over Ringling's lips as he took in Barbette's vision. He liked what he was hearing.

"Consider it done!" he said definitively. Then, his face turned more sober. He took his shoes off his desk and removed the long cigarette holder from his lips. He leaned into Barbette. "How's your health? You look good. You up to what this'll take?"

Barbette looked at the two men with a broad smile.

"Of course! When do I start?"

Anderson slapped his knee in satisfaction.

"Immediately!"

CHAPTER FIFTY-ONE

"Listen up, darlings! Barbette called out in a booming voice to his team of female aerialists who encircled him. Scattered around the big top were support cables and silk hanging ropes of Barbette's design. The performers wore bold, bright costumes in a rainbow of colors. "One week and we'll open in New York. Without good reviews in Manhattan, we'll be nothing! Do you understand?"

A tired-looking young woman entered the big top wearing a black leotard. As she came nearer, Barbette disdainfully looked her over. "Miss Hanneford, we all know your ass is dead but *MUST* you drape it in black?"

The other ladies burst out laughing while the young woman scurried to her mark.

Once Miss Hanneford and the other performers were set and in place, Barbette called out, "Okay, from the top! I want you to sell it!"

The women readied themselves.

"Cue music!" Barbette shouted.

Loud speakers placed throughout the big top began to play the festive entrance theme, as the team of women moved about their stunts in the heights of the big top. Some hung by their teeth from leather straps swinging on cables attached to metal rigging up above, just like Barbette did with Erford's Whirling Sensation—only now the women were sheathed in far more spectacular luminescent butterfly costumes. Their full, fanciful wings unfurled as they spun high, overhead. Other women hung from the special rigging, with legs and torsos wrapped around long, silk ropes. Handlers down below swung the ropes, like one end of a jump rope. The women twirled in the air, performing their aerial ballets with dizzy perfection. There was movement and color everywhere throughout the big top. Barbette's keen eyes took it in, noting the imperfections and corrections that needed to occur.

Other acts stopped their own rehearsals to witness the spectacle. John Murray Anderson was immensely pleased! It was bold and dramatic—a completely captivating performance. When the routine was complete, the other performers gave the aerialists a round of appreciative applause.

Then, out of the shadows, not minding the heat of the big top in the humid Sarasota spring, came the handsomely attired John Ringling North, in a navy double-breasted suit. With his customary cigarette holder set in his mouth, he too applauded as he came over to Barbette and Anderson.

"Things look like they are well in hand, Barbette," he said encouragingly.

Barbette was glad Ringling was pleased.

"There's more work to do," he replied. "They're not there yet."

"I like what I see."

"Thank you. We'll be ready to take Manhattan."

Barbette knew this was his one shot and he would not let it go to waste.

"Very good. See you both in New York," Ringling said as he turned and left just as quickly as he arrived.

...

APRIL, 1942

Barbette fussed over each aerialist's costume, making sure every last detail was perfect.

"All right ladies—this is when we steal the show away from the elephants," he said, like a colonel before a cavalry charge. There was electricity in the air—opening night in Manhattan at the legendary Madison Square Garden. The show was bigger and more daring than ever. Ringling wanted spectacle and he was getting it. With good reviews, Ringling's goal to bring in more crowds from the outlying parts of the metropolis could work. Every act was up against it opening night, especially Barbette and his aerialists. They were clustered together at the entrance to the arena.

Their music began to play. "Sell it ladies!" Barbette barked as the women stepped into the spotlights and began their performance.

Barbette watched his aerialists take off from the ground and fly throughout the immense space, unfurling their dazzling costumes in a rainbow of colors as the audience gasped and then cheered. The sight was breath-taking, ethereal, like a fantastic dream.

Barbette studied the aerialists, watching from the shadows. His mind raced back in time to his desperate conversations with his doctor, the torturous recoveries from operations he had to endure—those first, painful steps to learn how to walk again. It all came back to him as he watched his aerial fantasia unfold.

When the women finally landed back on the ground, some with daring angel's leaps, swinging out over the crowd, only several feet over the customer's heads, the audience applauded wildly.

The women scurried back to the performers' entrance, returning to a beaming Barbette.

"That was wonderful!" one remarked.

Barbette beamed, "More fun than a sex party!"

CHAPTER FIFTY-TWO

APRIL 28, 1946

Fiasco. It was the only word Barbette could use to describe back stage at the Boston Opera House. Barbette stood in the wing helplessly looking on: rushes of actors and choristers surging onto stage and then being sent back, realizing the wrong cue had been called—so many props and set pieces piled up, the wings looked like a museum warehouse—backdrops crashing to the floor only to be hoisted up again. This wasn't your average bad night in the theater. This was a full-out assault—a blitzkrieg of incompetence.

Barbette did his best to steady his circus performers before their act hit the stage. They were experienced artists used to the chaos of the big top. Tonight, Barbette worried about them, the line walkers and aerialists he so carefully prepared. They didn't have enough time to rehearse in their costumes, having received them at the last minute when the director was able to get them out of hock. The acrobats and trapeze artists needed quiet for mental preparation and it was impossible.

Forty-eight tons of sets, fifty four stage hands, seventy cast members, over forty scene changes, plus a sixteen hundred pound mechanical elephant and no dress rehearsal! The look in the stage manager's eyes—one minute sheer terror, the next complete, utter rage, said it all.

"Is this London?" the actress onstage asked as stagehands around her fumbled to put set pieces in place while a backdrop of the Rocky Mountains hastily lowered behind her.

"Yes, this is London all right," replied another actor.

The audience roared.

And there was the master of it all—amid the wreckage of his production—producer, director, and actor—Charles Foster Caine himself—Orson Welles—ironically costumed as Fu San, an oriental magician. He looked utterly bewildered, completely overwhelmed by the chaos around him.

Barbette wondered—*How did it all come to this? How did he let himself get involved in such a fiasco?*

...

AUGUST 7, 1945

Barbette read the *New York Times* headline:

First Atomic Bomb Dropped on Japan; Missile is Equal to 20,000 Tons of TNT; Truman Warns Foe of Rain of Ruin.

Barbette had been in New York for several days, undergoing tests with Doctor Simmons from Post-Graduate Hospital. It was an annual appointment they agreed to make. Barbette travelled by train the evening before, leaving the

Ringling circus in Ohio, where he continued to direct the lavish spectacle of his female aerialists. He would only be in Manhattan a short time, and then would rejoin the troupe seeing to it his ladies maintained the elegant refinement he demanded.

Standing on Park Avenue at a newsstand Tuesday morning packed tight with curious New Yorkers, Barbette scanned the headlines of the morning newspapers. All anyone could talk about was the atomic bomb.

Barbette paid for his paper and turned away from the kiosk and started to make way down the avenue when he heard the voice.

"Barbette!"

He thought he was imagining it at first.

"Barbette, darling—it *is* you!"

Barbette looked up from his paper, allowing his eyes to adjust to his surroundings.

"Cole!" he happily called out as Cole Porter, using a cane, jauntily joined Barbette. Porter was always dressed the way a man should present himself—double-breasted summer suit cut in a fashionable manner, topped by a new fedora. In fact, the two were nearly identically dressed this day. Barbette could never think of wearing casual attire on a Manhattan street. It was just not the proper thing to do.

"What the devil? It has been too long, Barbette!" Porter smiled.

"Yes! Before the war, in Paris."

"I heard about your accident," Porter gestured to Barbette's legs with his cane. "Linda and I so wanted to send an encouraging word, but we were traveling at the time."

Porter looked Barbette over for a moment.

"Well, you look *marvelous*! Are you in town for a while?"

"A couple of days. I'm seeing my doctor, actually. Annual checkup."

"Oh yes, I know those well. We are so alike, Barbette. I think we have one good leg between us!" Porter joked looking down at his own two limbs.

Barbette laughed. He well knew of the terrible fall Porter took on horseback in 1937. Like Barbette, doctors said Porter would never walk again. "They should have shot the horse," Barbette said.

"Yes, when will we ever learn to be more like the French? They eat their horses instead of riding them! Say, why don't you come up tonight for a cocktail, say ten? Linda is in the Berkshires—you know the air in Manhattan this time of year is just too much for her. Vincente and Judy are in town— I'm sure you've read all about it. Their honeymoon in New York."

"Sounds delightful!"

"I may even be able to rustle up some young sailors to join us. Anything to support our men in uniform," Porter winked.

"Cole, you haven't changed!"

"Ten o'clock then?"

"Are you still at the Waldorf?"

"Of course."

"I'll be round at ten."

"Excellent!"

· · ·

Barbette listened outside the door of Cole Porter's high rise apartment at the Waldorf Hotel. Porter and his wife, Linda Lee, purchased adjoining apartments on the top floor. The press spun the notion they didn't share the same apartment because Cole preferred his accommodations to be quite cold, while Linda wanted her apartment soothingly warm. Not to mention, Cole preferred composing well into the night. Separate quarters meant Linda could get her rest while Cole worked. Society knew of other reasons, of course, for the two apartments—the Porter's open marital arrangement. Cole and Linda had a unique bond. Cole adored Linda and theirs was the deepest friendship, but no more—dalliances were permitted, no questions asked.

From outside the door, Barbette could clearly hear the ebullient lungs of Judy Garland belting out Porter's *Begin the Beguine* and he didn't want to ring the bell until she finished.

Barbette finally heard applause and so he rang. After a moment, the door swung open.

"Barbette, darling!" Porter said as he opened the door.

"It's okay, Judy!" he called out. "It's only Barbette!"

Porter turned to Barbette and said in a stage whisper, "She thought you were *Orson Welles* and now she's hiding in my bedroom. Did you have any idea she shtooped Citizen Caine before she married Vincente? *I* didn't."

Porter, with onyx-headed cane in one hand, cocktail in the other, led Barbette through the stylish apartment furnished with pricey art deco decor carefully grouped atop slick, black marble flooring. The apartment had the aroma of expensive cigars and liquor. As they entered the main salon, Barbette heard the husky laughter of young men.

The lights were dimmed in the living room, while the drapes were pulled back on the oversized windows, revealing the enormity of the nighttime Manhattan skyline. Young sailors in their white uniforms mixed with handsome collegiate types in the dramatic space. Some of the men huddled around Porter's grandly ornamented piano, one of them even dared to thump out a tune.

"Vincente, *dear!*" Porter called out Vincente Minnelli, Judy's husband and MGM movie director, who was seated alone on a black and gold striped sofa next to one of the windows, casually smoking a cigarette. Between Minnelli,

Porter, and Barbette, it was hard to tell which gentleman was better dressed for the evening. *"This is Barbette!"*

Minnelli forced a shy smile and stood up. The two greeted one another and then sat down, while Porter went to the bar to make Barbette a cocktail.

Judy Garland entered the sumptuous salon wearing a deep, emerald-colored, off the shoulder evening gown. Her auburn hair was styled up in a sophisticated way. She was thin and radiant, if not a bit tipsy.

Judy turned to the young men around the piano. "I don't want to hear any more about the bomb!" she proclaimed. "Tonight is about joy and laughter!"

Barbette and Vincente stood up again as Judy stepped next to Porter.

"Barbette!" Judy smiled as she grandly extended her hand toward him, which Barbette promptly kissed. "Vincente was just saying he saw you perform before the war. He said you were marvelous!"

"Thank you," Barbette smiled. He took the cocktail Porter offered him.

"Come on Judy!" Porter announced. "I can't hear another note of that *dreadful music* coming from my piano."

The two hustled over to the piano and soon the room was filled with delightful music.

You're the top!
You're the Coliseum.
You're the top!
You're the Louvre Museum.
You're a melody from a symphony by Strauss
You're a Bendel bonnet,
A Shakespeare's sonnet,
You're Mickey Mouse.

"You were sensational on stage," Vincente said to Barbette. He was a quiet, elegant man, an introvert to Judy's extroversion. "Cole told us about your accident. If you don't mind my asking, what are you doing now?"

"I direct the aerial ballet for Ringling."

Vincente's eyes lit up.

"Did you do last year's show? I adore circuses and I have to say, the aerialists were spectacular."

"Yes. For the past several years. They're my girls."

"Wonderful!" Minnelli took another drag from his smoke. "Would you ever direct a circus scene for a picture?"

Barbette looked into Minnelli's kind eyes.

"Yes, of course. I would be quite eager, actually."

You're sublime,
You're turkey dinner,
You're the time, the time of a Derby winner
I'm a toy balloon that's fated soon to pop
But if, baby, I'm the bottom,
You're the top!

Minnelli was silent for a while. Then he leaned in. "Judy's due back at Metro for a picture, about Jerome Kern— *'Till the Clouds Roll By*. It's a showcase piece, really. She just has a couple of numbers. One of them is staged at a circus."

Minnelli's voice dropped so low Barbette had a difficult time hearing him over Judy even though they were seated so closely together.

"We think Judy's pregnant. If she is, we'll have to start filming immediately. I'm going to ask Sam Goldwin to permit me to direct her portion. It'll be easier for everyone concerned. Are you booked for the next several months? I would like to work with you on this."

Barbette looked into Minnelli's eyes and could see he was serious.

"I've a contract with Ringling. The show finishes first week of November. I could leave the show in October, I'm sure."

"That would be excellent."

"But we'll need the performers. If you want the best, you'd have to wait 'til November."

Judy finished her number and Porter ended with a piano flourish.

"Please, keep Judy entertained," Porter said to the sailors huddled by the piano as he got up with his cane and headed over to Minnelli and Barbette. "It is her *honeymoon* after all."

Porter looked at the two on the sofa. "*Darlings,* I do hate to break up your tete-a-tete, but I must have Barbette's assistance in the kitchen.

"That's alright," Minnelli said. "I hope I haven't monopolized your time, Barbette."

"No, of course not."

Barbette got up from the sofa and headed with Porter to his kitchen. Porter made sure the doors were closed behind them.

"My staff made a cake for the two—before I sent them home for the evening. Here it is, delicious looking, really." Porter nodded toward the round, white cake perched atop a crystal stand, covered by a dazzling glass dome. "I need you to help me take it inside, but before we do, I wanted to speak to you about something."

Porter looked over his shoulder at the door to the kitchen to make sure it was secure, then he moved closer to Barbette. He looked seriously at him as he spoke in hushed tones.

"I am planning to associate myself with the crazy and unusual production of the theater—the kind of thing one dreams about but never quite dares to attempt."

Barbette wasn't quite sure what he was talking about, but Porter continued.

"I shall never follow a pattern again—which means I shan't write the kind of musical show I have been doing for so long. Frankly, it's because I am bored. I want to do something different. This is a drama with music."

Barbette wasn't sure why Porter was confiding in him. They were merely acquaintances, really.

"Orson Welles *is* coming up tonight. He is finishing up a script for a radio program for tomorrow. He broadcasts from the Waldorf, you know. We've been working in secret on an idea of his. A Broadway show. An adaptation of Jules Verne's *Around the World in Eighty Days*. It's going to be a *mammoth* production, really."

Barbette listened as Porter looked him in the eye.

"There is a circus number in the show. He wants to do an oriental circus, but doesn't have a clue how to pull it off. I told him you would be here tonight and he was *entirely* thrilled. When he comes up, I'm sure Judy and Vincente will clear out. Are you up for it? Consult with Mister Welles?"

Barbette was flattered beyond belief! First Minnelli and now Welles.

"Of course," Barbette said.

Porter's face cast a sly grin.

"Dare I say, if you want to sample some of the candy, you should do so before Orson arrives. He's not that sort, you know."

"I think I'll just settle for the cake tonight," Barbette smiled.

Porter took the crystal glass lid off the top of the cake stand revealing a savory, white frosted confection.

"Suit yourself," Porter grinned as he put a sparkler into the cake and lit it, "but the big one by the piano with the *adorable* blue eyes is all mine!"

...

"I can think of nothing that an audience won't understand. The only problem is to interest them—once they are interested, they understand anything in the world," Orson Welles said while puffing on one of Porter's Havana cigars, sipping a large snifter of cognac.

By now it was two in the morning. Hours ago, Judy and Vincente headed to their apartment at a lower floor of the Waldorf. Barbette, Porter, and Welles sat in gilded, empire-styled club chairs surrounded by the burgundy lacquered walls of Porter's study. Before them, scattered about a sleek deco writing desk was a myriad of sketches, some by Welles's own hand, and others by paid artists.

Welles laid out his vision for Barbette of the entire show. Porter suggested musical numbers here and there as Welles progressed.

Immediately, Barbette could see there was too much show. Surely Porter knew the same thing. There were too many scenes. Too many set changes. It would take a small army just to dress and clear the stages quickly. The story also was rough and not cohesive. The whole of the presentation went against all of Barbette's better instincts. He had seen Cocteau pull off such lunacy to great effect. Billy Rose hired John Murray Anderson to make his fantasies coherent. Was he witnessing a mad genius or just madness?

"Who's writing the check for all of this?" Barbette finally asked.

Welles smiled slightly as he sat back in the golden chair.

"Michael Todd and his investors."

"And he has seen your vision? Don't get me wrong Mister Welles, but this is quite a show."

"I expect limitations. The absence of limitations is the enemy of art."

Welles puffed on his cigar.

Barbette picked up a notebook-sized rendering of an oriental circus Welles worked up.

"We can create something quite wonderful, here. The thing of it is to make it happen all at once—acrobats performing flips and jugglers with flaming batons down on the stage floor. Up in the air women aerialists on silk lines, spinning. We could have a tightrope walker stage left and a couple on the trapeze, stage right. They would all be costumed in brilliant colors of red and blue. Paint the backdrop with golden dragons. The whole thing would have movement and color."

Welles's eyes twinkled with childlike excitement as Barbette presented his suggestions.

"And an elephant. Could we have elephants on stage?"

Barbette looked at Porter to get any indication if Welles's question was sincere or a joke.

"They're too heavy. They did it at the Hippodrome for *Jumbo*, but Billy Rose spent a fortune reinforcing the sage. Otherwise, the floors wouldn't hold."

Welles pondered the pachyderm predicament.

"A mechanical one?" Welles eyes glistened. "We could have a mechanical one. Do you think it would work?"

"I...I guess..." Barbette rubbed his forehead. "We could use a prop elephant. We could have the aerialists even start their performance by coming out from a hatch on top of it."

Welles was clearly delighted by the possibilities, no matter how outlandish. He puffed more on his cigar. "We'll be on the road next spring. I want to open on Broadway in May. "

"The acts we need, they'll be on winter holiday in Sarasota in January. We can begin rehearsals then. But you know as well as I do, they'll have to return to Ringling in April. That's when their season begins."

Welles frowned for a moment, then his face lit up again. "We'll have to buy them out for the year, won't we? Can you get me a list of what we need by tomorrow and I'll present it to Mister Todd."

Orson turned to Porter.

"Mister Porter, I believe we are going to have a magnificent show!"

. . .

Barbette thought about Welles's expression that evening. How contented and confident he looked. Now, dressed as an Oriental magician in a red silk robe with long, flowing sleeves and a fake fu manchu mustache hastily glued to his face, Welles's eyes looked completely different.

Months before, the work with Vincente Minnelli was quite different. Everything was rehearsed, camera angles and shots were blocked to perfection. Minnelli was a fabulous colorist, personally seeing to every detail of costume and fit. His sets were quiet and calm, no matter the elephants, horses, marching band, and aerialists assembled for the spectacle.

Minnelli was nurturing to Judy and she relied on him to assuage her insecurities. When she wasn't filming, Barbette even taught Judy how to walk more like a lady while wearing heels, crossing one foot in front of the other to make her narrow hips sway, which Judy adored.

With the scenes completed for *Till the Clouds Roll By*, Barbette turned his attentions to Welles's *Around the World*, and as winter turned to spring, Barbette could see they were in trouble. Porter was too rushed in writing his musical numbers. The songwriter begged Welles to postpone the show's

Broadway debut until fall so they could all have more time to make it work.

Then, Michael Todd backed out when Welles insisted on having an oil gusher explode on stage every performance, dousing the expensive sets and costumes. Welles had to borrow money from RKO movie studio boss Harry Cohn to get the production off the ground. As things went from bad to worse, the situation wasn't helped by Rita Hayworth, Welles's wife, frantically calling from Hollywood in tears, demanding some of the director's attention.

That April night in 1946, the first tryout in Boston, Barbette had to work fast to bring his performers back into focus. With their general state of shock, Barbette jumped into the fray. He hastily gathered the performers for the circus number around him. With fiery intensity, he demanded their attention.

"Listen up!" he said in a loud whisper to the performers huddled around him. The curtain was closed and stage hands furiously moved set pieces and props into place. As a precaution before the show, Barbette made sure all of his circus troupe tested their lines before the performance began. If he could just get them to only do what they rehearsed, and not get caught up in the chaos around them, they would be okay.

"Forget the rest! Do you hear me? Forget the rest and focus on your performance! That's all you need. Focus!"

The performers broke and scrambled to their marks. The orchestra began the number. Barbette's team was ready. On cue, they became a flurry of color and motion—coming from all parts of the stage—like a flower bud bursting open in the springtime. From the wing, Barbette could catch glimpses of the enthralled audience. They oohed and ahhed and applauded as the performers' tricks became more spectacular and daring. It all ended on a grand crescendo of music. The audience cheered as the curtain closed. The houselights came up and intermission commenced.

Welles hustled backstage to change into his next costumed disguise. As he passed Barbette, he stopped. "Thank you," he muttered and then he disappeared.

After the show, Barbette and his aerialists and acrobats decided to stay up late, awaiting the reviews from the Boston papers. Orson Welles was nowhere to be seen. Some gossiped he left town while others surmised he went on a bender. Porter came by the restaurant where Barbette's team encamped. He looked quite glum, but was gracious enough to thank everyone.

"Can it be saved?" Barbette asked pulling him aside. Both looked positively exhausted.

"I don't think so. We needed more time."

. . .

Around the World opened on Broadway, May 31st, 1946 to pallid reviews, excepting Barbette's Oriental circus number, which was highly praised. The show closed after seventy-five performances. Welles was broke and his career shattered. He returned to Hollywood to fulfill his obligations to Harry Cohn and try to patch up his marriage to Hayworth. The result of his efforts for both was the film noir classic, *Lady from Shanghai.* Cole Porter was also thought to be washed up after the show, having suffered his third Broadway flop in a row. But he came back the following season to write some of his best music for the smash hit, *Kiss Me Kate.*

Michael Todd, to Welles's great furor, went on to make a movie, *Around the World in 80 Days,* and it became a massive international sensation.

Barbette watched it all unfold from a distance, on the road, directing stunning aerial ballets for the Ringling and Shrine circuses.

CHAPTER FIFTY-THREE

NOVEMBER 2, 1949

WESTERN UNION TELEGRAM

ROUND ROCK, TX

COME HOME ASAP (STOP)
YOUR MOTHER VERY ILL (STOP)

ROSE

Barbette held the telegram in his hands outside of the big top pitched in an open lot next to the Pittsburgh train station. The circus was in its last days of its season.

He knew he needed to head home.

...

The scenery of Midwestern farms reached to the horizon as he gazed out the window of the train. The midmorning sun was already bright, but the leaves on the trees surrounding white farmhouses were bare; the fields plowed under for the winter. Barbette cracked open the window slightly. A rush of crisp, fall air flushed his cheeks.

His thoughts turned to his mother. Barbette knew he had his mother's drive. She imparted that in him. When he was younger and grew tired of rehearsals, he would think of his momma out in the fields, on those long, hot summer days picking cotton until her back ached and her fingers bled. He knew if she could do that to keep them alive, he could train harder, practice longer. Barbette was well aware of the reputation he was acquiring in the circus—too particular, too perfectionistic. He chalked it up to the laziness of the troupes. He would never understand why anyone would want to settle for anything less than their absolute best. The audience deserved as much. When his mother worked for clients, even the ones she detested, she made sure her hats and needle work were the very best.

As an adult, Barbette kept things from his mother out of respect—or was it fear of rejection? It was as if they lived on different planets, different galaxies of life. He didn't think she could ever know who he really was and accept it. So he kept it from her, allowing her to think what she wanted, but never broaching the subject in his letters to her.

Barbette wondered if their relationship would have been different, if Sam Loving never entered the picture. Maybe. Barbette would have visited more for sure, without the condescending shadow of Loving hovering over them. Would Barbette have revealed his deepest secrets, his innermost longings? Probably not—they were too queer, too foreign for her to understand.

...

Rose picked Barbette up from the Round Rock train depot in the late afternoon on November 7th. The wind from the north seemed to follow the train. The Texas air was cold and dry. As they drove through the town, the two said nothing. Rose worked the gears of her weathered, column-shifting, Ford pickup as Barbette looked out the window at the buildings along Main Street in Round Rock. Streets were paved in smooth, black asphalt. The giant live oaks, defied the season, looking green and full.

Finally, Rose pulled up the gravel drive to the house. There were more cars outside, but the place looked the same as the last time he was there.

Barbette was about to get out of the pickup when Rose reached across his lap to stop him.

"No, Vander. We've gotta talk," she said. She took a deep sigh. "I know you and Sam sometimes don't see eye to eye. I get that. I understand it. But you've gotta remember, your momma married him. She loved him. And he loved her. You've gotta respect that."

Barbette looked quietly into her eyes.

"I will."

Rose saw the seriousness of Barbette's expression and knew he was telling the truth.

The two hopped out of the pickup and headed into the white-painted farm house with its steep, pitched roof and ample, wrap around front porch.

"Hey Vander," Mary said. She was standing on the porch while holding a girl in her arms who looked to be about two years old.

"Hey Mary," he said as he carefully made way up the stairs to the porch. Each step up still gave him pain. He kissed her cheek and then looked at the girl in her arms, her eyes moist from crying.

"This here's Uncle Vander," Mary said to the child. "He works in the circus. Vander, this is Beverly, your niece. I'm so glad you're here."

Barbette reached out to touch the little girl's cheek, but she turned away, having nothing of the affection.

"Well, she's got momma's sprit, that's for sure," Mary said.

"Yes. She sure does."

The front screen door opened and a man came out leading two other children, a boy who must have been seven or eight and a girl who looked a couple of years younger.

The middle-aged man was dressed in a grey tweed suit. His neck tie was loosened having just come in from work.

"This here's my husband, Jasper, who I wrote you about," Mary said. "These two are Richard and Sharon. Kids, this is your uncle Vander."

Jasper was tall and thin with a receding hairline. He was at least a decade older than Mary.

Barbette shook his hand. He then turned to Mary.

"I've missed a lot."

She headed to one of the rocking chairs on the porch. "Yeah, Vander. You sure have." Mary sat down in the chair making sure Beverly was comfortable. Then she looked back toward Barbette.

"But I understand, Vander. You've got a Gypsy spirit. We're all glad you're here. Sam's glad too. Momma's inside. She's been waiting for you."

A special hospital bed was set up in the front parlor of the house, all the other furnishings were pushed to the side. Sam sat in one of the chairs, his face flush with grief. He struggled to get out of the chair, trying to stand when Barbette entered the room.

Sam looked disheveled—his shirt haphazardly tucked into his pants, stains of food dibbled down his front. His face was unshaven and his silver mustache grew over his lip.

Their eyes met. Barbette saw it. A glint of deep distress. Sam joined Barbette as he stood alongside of his mother's bed while she struggled to capture air in her lungs. Her cheeks were hollow and grey. Her lips parched—hair was thin and white. Yet, even in her emaciated appearance, Barbette could see the beauty of her features. He watched his mother mumble in her delirium, eyelids fluttering.

Barbette found his mother's hand under a quilt she sewed so many years ago. It was cold and bony to his touch, with none of the muscled strength he recalled it having when he was a child.

He bent over and whispered in her ear.

"Hi momma. It's me. Vander. I'm home momma."

Hattie exhaled deeply, letting out a loud groan of air.

"It's okay, momma. Everything's gonna be okay," Barbette said as he let his free hand brush a few errant stands of hair from her forehead.

He didn't like to see his mother struggle, fighting for every breath.

"It's okay momma. It's okay."

As the sun went down, Hattie's complexion turned sallow and her fight to breathe became more intense. Barbette sat in a chair next to his mother's bed, putting wet compresses on her head, just like she did for him when he was a child when he was sick so many years ago.

Sam stayed in the parlor, pensively resting in his chair along one side of the room. Neighbors seemed to come and go bringing food and paying respects. Mary and Rose greeted folks, making room for the covered dishes already filling the dining room table.

After midnight, both Sam and Barbette were finally alone with Hattie. Mary and Jasper left earlier, having to get back to their home in Austin to get the kids to bed. Rose also departed to her nearby farm, promising to be back in the morning.

Barbette and Sam started to doze when they were awakened by Hattie struggling for air, exhaling deeply. Her eyes opened looking upward to the ceiling. She exhaled again and then went still.

Sam stood up and came over to the bedside. His face was red and clouded with tears. He pulled out a soiled kerchief from his pocket to wipe his eyes and blow his nose.

Barbette looked at his mother's lifeless body. So still. He sighed deeply, wanting to cry, but he couldn't. "*Big boys don't cry,*" he remembered his mother telling him so long ago. "*Big boys don't cry.*"

CHAPTER FIFTY-FOUR

"Sam, you're not even dressed," Barbette said as he entered the second floor bedroom of the Round Rock farm house. Sam sat on the end of a neatly made bed which was covered with a patch quilt by Harriett's hand. It was a simple room with wooden floors meeting white, plastered walls. An art deco-styled bureau of blond wood to one side of the room matched the nightstands and headboard of the twin bed. They looked as new as the photos of them in the Sears catalogue they were purchased from many years before. His mother's hand-carved rocker was in another corner. A wicker basket filled with her kitting things sat silently next to the chair. With Sam moving downstairs in his study, the bedroom Hattie and Sam shared was free from clutter, a tidy reminder of the way Hattie liked it.

Sam only wore his boxer shorts, stockings, and undershirt. He forced his thick body to stand and then he walked several paces to the large, lace-sheared window to one side of the room. Sam drew back one of the shears and looked out onto the view, past the live oaks to the plowed-under fields. He said nothing.

Barbette joined Sam at the window also silently staring out to the horizon, watching the sun rise over the dull, brown earth. The morning light breaking through the oaks illuminated Sam's wrinkled, fleshy face and white mustache.

"I've got to tell you something, son," Sam finally said.

"Not now, Sam. Not the morning of momma's funeral."

"Yes, son. Now."

Sam cleared his throat. He kept looking out the window. "I've never had a chance to say I'm sorry. I promised your momma—before she took a turn—I would tell you what was in my heart. You know, sometimes I speak before I think. Stupid things come out. I've gotta tell you son, your mother was real proud of you, real proud. I know you didn't come round much on account of me and I know that hurt your momma..."

Sam cleared his throat again. "And it hurt me too...But I know I've got no one to blame but my thick-headed self. You see, son, this world doesn't give a damn. You've gotta be tough or you'll get run out of town. I was just afraid your momma spoiled you, sissified you. I told your momma I didn't look at that scrap book she and Mary made up of your act, but I did. When she was asleep. I snuck glances. Sure, I didn't quite understand it, but I know one thing. Son, you've got to be one tough son of a bitch to do what you've done. Balls of steel if you ask me. I'd like to think it was me who done that. But when I look in the mirror, in all honesty, I know it was your momma. She did that. There's a spot, in the cemetery son, right below where we're laying your momma to rest. I want you to know, it's for you. I've seen to it." Sam turned and looked into Barbette's eyes. "Son, I'm truly sorry for any pain I've caused you."

Barbette felt overwhelmed. He took a deep breath. "I never expected to hear those words. I forgive you, Sam. I do. I know it's what momma would want. But more than that, it's what I want too."

Sam extended his hand. Barbette looked at it for a moment and then reached his own out to shake it. When they did so, Sam began to cry.

"Come on Sam," Barbette said as he released his grip. "You know momma wouldn't want you crying." Barbette stood back from Sam. "Now, we've got to get you dressed. Momma always enjoyed you looking your best."

Sam wiped his eyes with his hand and sighed deeply. "Yes, she did, son. That's for sure."

CHAPTER FIFTY-FIVE

"This concludes our gravesite ceremony," the minister said to all of those gathered at the Loving plot at the Round Rock cemetery. "Y'all are welcome to go on back to the house for supper."

Barbette and Jasper did their best to help Sam get up out of the chair he had been sitting in during the solemn ceremony, while Mary tried to corral her children who were fidgety and uncomfortable in their Sunday clothing.

Sam stood before the open hole in the ground which was now filled with his wife's casket. When Barbette helped him dress that morning, he stuck a white rose in the button hole of Sam's lapel. Through his tears, Sam Loving now took the rose in his hands and held it for a moment. He mumbled something and then tossed the rose onto the casket.

He stood there for a long while, not wanting to leave. Finally, Barbette and Jasper steadied him as they all headed to the cars to go home.

Barbette allowed the busyness of tending to Sam protect him from his own feelings of grief. He fought his mind as it so desperately wanted to transport him back to his boyhood. If he thought too much about that time, the solitary space when he was her one and only, it would overwhelm him, so he tried to block it out.

After the service, Hattie's hospital bed was cleared from the parlor and it seemed all of Round Rock came over to pay their respects, and also gossip about the famous Barbette.

He heard the whispers around him, folks noting his appearance, stylish, yet bearing the scars of his performing days and the ravages of polio. Some townsfolk were even surprised he wasn't dressed like a woman. But now, nearing fifty, having been through all he had, he didn't feel like he had anything to prove to these people. He was graceful and gallant to everyone who had the courage to look him in the eye, just the way his mother would want.

CHAPTER FIFTY-SIX

"He doesn't want any help. He's told me a thousand times. He's one stubborn man," Mary said of Sam while rocking in her chair on the porch. It was late in the evening.

All of the guests from the funeral reception finally cleared out of the house. Mary already put her kids to bed in a spare bedroom upstairs, while Sam turned in as well. A while ago, he had another smaller bed put his study on the first floor, so he could be closer to Hattie as she slept in the parlor. With his arthritis, Sam decided to keep his bed on the first floor. No sense in climbing up the tall flight of stairs each day.

Jasper sat next to Mary in another rocker on the porch, while Barbette chose one of the faded sage-green, wicker armchairs opposite them.

"I don't know how long he's gonna last without her. I can bring Beverly and Sharon up to be with him during the daytime while Richard's in school," Mary said. She was still wearing her black mourning dress. She looked tired from the long day.

"Mary, I'm sorry I wasn't here to be with you," Barbette offered.

"It's okay, Vander. We're just glad you're here, right now with us."

Barbette looked at his half-sister. He was gob smacked by her sincerity.

"Thank you, Mary. I don't know what to say."

"Mary's still got that old scrap book she made for you," Jasper added. "You had one hell of an act."

Barbette chuckled and took a sip from an ice-cold bottle of Coke leftover from the noontime meal.

Jasper continued, "Mary and I, we've been talking about it. We'd like you to stay on this winter while the circus is on hiatus."

"With Sam?" Barbette asked.

"No, not with Sam. Down in Austin with us. We've got a spare bedroom," Jasper replied.

"Yeah, Vander," Mary began, "we know you like to be on the road, but our door is open. It would be wonderful spending Christmas with you. You could even help decorate the tree."

Barbette took another sip of his Coke. He smiled. "Just please tell me you buy real and not one of those *horrid* aluminum things!"

Mary and Jasper both sheepishly looked at one another and then burst out laughing.

"Well, I guess we'll have to drag that box out to the trash!" Mary smiled.

"Sounds like you're in need of my services."

"That's about right," Jasper added.

"Well, I guess I could..."

"Wonderful!" Mary exclaimed. "This will be wonderful!"

CHAPTER FIFTY-SEVEN

"Terrible!" Barbette frowned as he took in Mary's appearance. It was Christmas day and the suburban ranch home in north Austin was bustling with activity. The three children were in family room, playing with their new toys. Jasper was there as well, trying to get a clear image on the tiny screen of the family's first television set. Barbette stood over the stove in the kitchen, stirring the gravy, while Mary came to join him, wearing a deep green velvet dress. In a short while, Rose and her family along with Sam would be arriving for the traditional holiday meal.

"Santa headed back to the North Pole for the winter, but looks like your girls decided to go south," Barbette said appraising his half-sister. "Please, tell me you have a better brassiere."

"Vander! Your language!" Mary protested. "This's all I've got."

"Oh dear," Barbette shook his head as he turned down the heat on the stove.

"Mary, you will *never* be a natural beauty. You must do everything in your power to overcome this."

Mary put her hands on her hips in protest.

"Back to the bedroom!" Barbette pointed grandly.

"But they'll be over any minute."

"Darling, you'll be amazed what the right shade of lipstick can do for a woman. Come on, it'll only take five minutes."

...

"Well, how do I look?" Mary smiled as she entered the family room glancing at her husband and three children. She knew she was a knockout. She hadn't felt this special since her wedding day to Jasper eight years before. Barbette completely reworked her makeup, adjusted her brassier. He swapped out a different belt for her dress and restyled her brown hair, putting up one side behind her ear with a rhinestone pin.

Jasper stood up from crouching down in front of the television, its tiny screen still filled with snowy, white dots. He smiled. "You look like Rita Hayworth!"

"Well, let's not go too far," Barbette quipped as he came up alongside Mary at the entrance to the living room from the back hallway. "Susan Hayward, *maybe*."

Everyone laughed.

"I've a surprise for you both," Barbette then said to them. "Come on, let's head to the dining room."

Barbette slid open the pocket doors leading to the dining room revealing a magnificently set table. A spray of white and red roses on a bed of lush holly flanked by ornate silver candelabras with long white tapers adorned the table that was perfectly set with fine china, silver, and cut crystal glasses.

Mary silently walked up to the table taking in the beauty of what was before her. She ran her finger on one of the gleaming plates with blush floral trim.

"Momma's china," she murmured softly, her eyes welling up with tears.

"Rose brought them down last week. Sam said he didn't want them. Rose and I grabbed the silver pieces and goblets from an estate sale."

"They must've cost a fortune," Mary said.

"Let's just say we got extremely lucky. Did you notice the table cloth? Some of momma's lace."

"It's just beautiful!"

"Really fine, Vander," Jasper added.

Barbette pulled out a kerchief from his lapel pocket and gave it to his sister.

"Blot your eyes, darling. You're ruining my makeup."

Mary laughed.

"Come here, Vander," she said as she gave him a warm embrace. "Thank you."

The doorbell rang.

"Oh dear! They're here. Jasper, can you get the door?" Mary asked. "Vander, come on with me. Let's do a touch up. I want everyone to see how pretty I look."

...

"You ask me, it's a mistake shuttin' down the Mexican school," Sam said while he puffed on a cigar, his belly full of Mary's delicious Christmas feast. Everyone was now enjoying delicious homemade pies and coffee.

"I don't see what's the big deal," Rose said. She sat next to her husband, Darrell Senior, who was also smoking a Dutch Master. Darrell Junior couldn't make it because he was overseas with the Army, while Barbette made sure Rose's younger son Donovan, who was now in his early twenties and quite handsome, was seated next to him. Mary's children already left the table except for the youngest, who sat on her lap, sound asleep.

"First it's the Mexicans and then what? The Negros'll be getting all uppity and be demanding integration too."

"Perish the thought!" Barbette said.

"Just because you've done a lot of traveling doesn't make you none the wiser, Vander," Sam said. "There's a way we do things in the south. It's called tradition."

"It's called racism," Barbette replied.

"You can use all those fancy words, but what's right is right. Nothing's gonna change it."

"Now, Donovan," Barbette said as he patted the top of the young man's hand and then reached for a bottle of sweet wine, refilling his and Donovan's glass to the brim, "someday you'll leave Texas, and you'll come into a world that's called *civilization*. In civilization, it doesn't matter the color of your skin or where you're from."

Sam harrumphed. "After this war, this whole country's changing and none for the better."

"None too soon, Sam," Barbette said. "None too soon."

CHAPTER FIFTY-EIGHT

MARCH 9, 1953

Barbette held his sister's hand as the two listened to the uniformed soldier play *Taps* on his rain-soaked bugle. The wet grounds of the Round Rock cemetery were covered with blue bonnet wildflowers bursting forth in pale springtime sprays. In a choreographed flourish, two more soldiers lifted up the ends of the American flag draped on the coffin and folded it into a tight triangle, putting it into Mary's hands. Samuel Loving, Spanish American War hero, was dead. The sergeant at arms shouted out the order and riflemen commenced firing their salute into the air. Barbette sat next to his sister, taking it all in. It was the end of an era, he realized. The world was changing and changing fast.

CHAPTER FIFTY-NINE

JULY, 1958

"Elbows off the table," Barbette instructed his two nieces. "And sit up straight. You're young ladies of culture and grace, you must comport yourselves as such."

"Vander, enough with the charm school!" Mary protested.

The kitchen of the north Austin home was sweltering in the heat of the summer day. Mary, who was an elementary school teacher, was off for the summer as were her children. Richard was away at camp while the two girls stayed home with their mother. Mary put down plates of hot dogs and French fries before the girls. Barbette ignored his sister's protestations.

"*Thank you*, mother," Barbette reminded the two girls. Sharon, who was in her early teens and Beverly who was eleven, parroted their uncle. "*Thank you*, mother," they said in unison.

Barbette turned to Mary, "You're not going to wear that dress all day are you?"

"Vander, I've had just about enough! It's hot. I'm irritable, and I don't want to hear it coming from you today."

"You're having a hot flash, aren't you?"

"I'm not having a hot flash! Listen Vander, I know work has been slow, but you've gotta get out of the house more often. You're driving me crazy."

Barbette was about to respond, when the phone rang. Mary went over to the wall where the avocado-colored phone was affixed. She answered. "Hello?...Why yes...Who shall I say is calling? Yes, very well."

Mary put her hand over the mouthpiece of the phone. "You majesty, a funny sounding man with a German accent, a Mister Wilder, wishes to speak with you. Shall I say you're in or are you out riding horseback in the meadows of your estate?"

Barbette silently gestured for the phone to be brought over to him. Mary did so, the long, avocado phone cord stretching across the kitchen.

"This is he," Barbette answered. "Mister Wilder, of course. I'm a great fan. What can I do for you?...Yes?...I believe I may be of some assistance...Yes, have your assistant make the arrangements. I'll make preparations at once. Very good. Have a good day, Mister Wilder." Barbette regally handed the phone back to his sister. He turned to the girls.

"Did you listen to the formality? The clarity of diction? Did you notice I didn't speak with my mouth full? *That* is refinement ladies."

"What did he want?" Mary asked.

"He needs me to head to Hollywood at once. He has two actors for a new picture. A comedy. They're impersonating women and he saw my act in Berlin many years ago. He wants me to give them lessons on how to be proper ladies."

Barbette looked at the girls at the table. "Do you see? Your uncle gives you free lessons on how to be a lady. You don't even have to pay."

"That's wonderful! What's the name of the movie?" Mary asked.

"Oh, what was it?" Barbette scanned his memory. "Oh, yes, now I remember—*Some Like It Hot.*"

. . .

"No, no, *no!*" Barbette scolded. "That's all wrong!"

Tony Curtis and Jack Lemmon stood uncomfortably in their specially made, high-heeled shoes. Barbette clipped large towels about their waists and over their trousers, emulating the shape of pencil skirts.

"You've got to tighten up your asses, and stand up straight!"

Jack Lemmon rolled his eyes at Tony Curtis.

"Mister *Lemmon*," Barbette said with one hand on his hip, "I wasn't personally flown out by Mister Wilder to have you *waste* my time. Remember—ass tight...And when you walk, cross one leg over the next. You see?"

Barbette, who was wearing his customary French-cut suit, demonstrated what he was looking for. "When you cross one leg over the other, it gives you the illusion of womanly hips."

"It sure does!" Lemmon said sarcastically. Curtis elbowed him in the stomach.

"Enough! Just do it."

The two actors practiced their walks back and forth in the Hollywood rehearsal studio.

"Very good, Mister Curtis...Mister Lemmon, that was *dreadful*."

Barbette walked over to the two. "Mister, Lemmon, why don't we take your trousers off. You're not feeling like a woman."

"Ohhh nooo, Barbette!" Lemmon cautioned. "I remember that move from back in the service. I know what's next,"

Tony Curtis burst out laughing.

Barbette sighed deeply.

"How about this, Mister Lemmon. Let's work from the waist up."

"Now, you're talking."

Barbette went to get his fedora from a nearby chair and returned to the two men.

"Mister Curtis, place the hat on your head."

As Tony Curtis did so, Barbette squeezed his right bicep.

"Fresh!" Curtis said in a high falsetto.

Lemmon cracked up.

Barbette chose to ignore the quip.

"Do you feel how your bicep is flexed when you put the hat on? Far too masculine. It will never play"

"Yes," Curtis acknowledged.

"Now, take the hat off and you are going to put it on again. Only this time, roll your wrist so that the bottom faces outwards. There. That's it. Now put it on."

Curtis did as Barbette instructed while Barbette held onto his arm muscle again.

"You see? When you turn your wrist out, your bicep doesn't flex. It gives your arm a more womanly appearance."

"Well, I'll be!" Curtis responded.

"Now, Mister Lemmon, you give it a try."

Barbette handed the hat to Lemmon, who wasn't having any of it.

"Listen, Barbette, I know you mean well, but this is a comedy picture. If we do stuff wrong, that's the gag. We're not supposed to really be women."

Barbette looked at Jack Lemmon intently. "But in order for it to be funny, it has to be plausible. Darling, you're not plausible. Now let's try it again. Take the hat, turn your wrist out while you put the hat on your head. There. See? Your bicep is no longer flexed. That wasn't so hard now was it?"

...

Early Morning. The Following Day.

"Billy, you've gotta help us. This guy's running us into the ground," Jack Lemmon said as he and Tony Curtis sat in the director's office bungalow on the Hollywood backlot.

Billy Wilder looked at his two actors with a bemused smirk. "Save your breath, Jack. Barbette already came by this morning. He said Tony had potential, but you're hopeless. I booked him on the *Il de France*. He's off the show."

CHAPTER SIXTY

Barbette stood on the topmost deck of the *Il de France*. The ocean liner gained speed as it departed New York Harbor. The late day sun cast a golden glow on Lady Liberty when the ship rounded her, heading into open water. With first class passage, and wallet full of cash, Barbette was thrilled to be heading back to Paris. He held up his champagne glass and silently toasted the great Billy Wilder. *"Salud! Paris, ici je viens!* Paris, here I come!"

...

"I'm so glad you came to visit," Jean Cocteau said to Barbette as they slowly strolled the lush summer gardens of his villa in the charming town of Milly-la-Forêt, about an hour's train ride from Paris. Cocteau dressed casually, in an open collared shirt and trousers, while Barbette wore his travelling suit. Cocteau had aged in an elegant sort of way, his thick hair now a lovely shade of gray, his body still lean with a now elegant carriage men of a certain age possess.

"Of course," Barbette replied. "I only wish I could've seen Jean Marais."

"He is making another pirate film. When you are in love with a matinee idol, you must endure these realities, but he is here, around us in spirit. We purchased the masion after the war. We had to get out of Paris. I couldn't stand it. It is peaceful here."

Amid the hum of circling dragon flies, Barbette took in the unkempt, overgrown garden. They walked among its beds of wild flowers—sprays of orange, red, and yellow mixed with dabbles of white and blue. The colors looked vibrant in the late-day sun. The gardens were framed by thick, limestone walls about ten feet tall. Ancient moats carved through the garden. In the distance, a forest could be seen as well as the robust turrets of a nearby chateau.

"Your garden is quite lovely," Barbette said.

"It gives me an example of the absurd stubbornness beautiful plants."

Cocteau led them to a secluded spot in the garden, along one of the tall limestone walls, which happened to be under siege from some sort of ivy vine. There, under the canopy of a towering elm, was a clearing containing a suite of aging white, wicker furniture. A black cat lazily rested on one of the faded blue cushions of a chair. With a flourish, Cocteau roused the creature, who quickly hopped off.

"She will be back, I can assure you," Cocteau smiled as he gestured for Barbette to sit. "I love cats because I enjoy my home—and little by little, they become its visible soul."

"This is lovely," Barbette said as he sat in one of the chairs closest to Cocteau. From his vantage, he could take in the whole of the garden, which was now ablaze with light from the setting sun. "I believe if Princess Violette Murat was here, she would try to take your poppies and smoke them."

"Violette," Cocteau laughed, "she was always more of truffle than a violet."

"What came of her?"

"It is sad, really. She retired to Toulon, along the Mediterranean coast. Not far from Villa Noailles—before the war. She purchased an old boat, a submarine hunter. She made it her home. It is said she corrupted all the sailors stationed there. Sadly, she succumbed to her addictions."

The two were quiet for a moment.

"Do you think about it often, death?" Barbette asked.

"Yes, every day. Here I am trying to live, or rather, I am trying to teach the death within me how to live. We are born and what is life, but some grand march into what will be an inevitability, our own demise."

Barbette was quiet for a moment and then he spoke up.

"After my fall, when I was told I would never walk again, I begged the doctor to let me die."

"Because perhaps you already did?"

"Yes, Jean. Because I was already dead."

"Yet, you chose to live. Why? Was it a fear of death?"

Barbette thought for a while.

"No. I wasn't afraid of death. When you are up in the air, walking a line with no net, or you are holding onto a trapeze only with the backs of your heels, you have no one to rely on other than yourself. I'd grown quite comfortable with that arrangement. Every day, I faced death, only surviving because I willed it. It was my preparation, my strength, my determination keeping me alive."

"Is that why you are alone?"

"Orson Welles used to say we're born alone. We live alone. We die alone. Only through our love and friendship can we create the illusion for the moment that we're not alone...I detest giving up control and yet, I'm finding as I get old, it's all I'm doing."

"And so after your illness, do you regret living?"

"Yes...sometimes."

"Is that why when I greeted you at the train station and offered to take your coat, you chose to keep it on?"

"Yes. It was. I didn't want you to see what my body had become."

Cocteau said nothing for a while.   Then he stood up before Barbette.

"Get up," Cocteau ordered.

"What?"

"Get up, I demand it."

Barbette stood up. The two were only several feet apart.

"Take off your jacket."

"No!"

"Take it off Barbette!"

Barbette slowly unbuttoned his coat, taking it off and handing it to Cocteau, who tossed it onto one of the wicker chairs.

Cocteau's appraising eye looked over Barbette's frame.

"Is this what you fear?"

"Yes."

"Take off your shirt and tie, Barbette. You must."

Barbette stared into the artist's intense eyes. His hands shook. He slowly removed his tie and shirt, casting them to the ground.

Cocteau studied Barbette's scars, his misalignments, his withered limbs.

"Your trousers."

"No."

"Your trousers!"

Tears started to form in Barbette's eyes.

"Your trousers!"

Barbette kicked off his shoes. He loosened his belt, letting his trousers and underpants fall to his feet.

Cocteau's intense gaze appraised Barbette's figure, standing naked, with glints of the setting sun shining on his body. He smiled broadly.

"Beautiful."

Cocteau reached for Barbette and held him, taking in his aroma. He kissed Barbette's salted tears while he ran his hands about the scars and ravages of the aerialist's body. "You're now more beautiful than you ever were," Cocteau murmured into his ear.

Barbette let go, falling into the protective arms of Cocteau.

Dragon flies swept about them, while the sweet fragrance of summer jasmine filled the air.

. . .

Barbette listened to the locomotive make way to the station at Milly-la-Forêt.

They spent a week together at Cocteau's masion. Sometimes they walked into the village, exploring the shops, or buying fresh produce for dinner. Cocteau's neighbor and dear friend, Edith Piaf, joined them in the evenings, drinking wine and talking about the war, until the early light of dawn.

Every night, the two shared Cocteau's bed. Both knew it was for just this moment in time. Something captured for an instant. They held onto it, cherishing the bond between them. And then, just as soon as they thought they possessed it, it floated away. They each felt it and understood.

The locomotive stopped and the conductor called out.

"Goodbye, Barbette," Cocteau said intensely looking into his eyes.

Barbette kissed the poet's cheek.

"Goodbye."

Barbette's coat was packed in his bag. He greeted the conductor in an open-collared shirt and casual trousers. When he carefully, with concentrated effort climbed the stairs, he turned around. The train began to move forward. Barbette looked at Cocteau standing alone, staring at him. Barbette waved and then watched Cocteau. A grin formed on the artist's lips, as he grew smaller and smaller in Barbette's eye, until the train rounded the bend and he could see no more.

It was the last time they would meet. Cocteau died four years later at Milly-la-Forêt, overtaken, hearing the news the day before that his dear friend, Edith Piaf had passed.

CHAPTER SIXTY-ONE

JULY 30, 1973

"Do you like them?" Mary asked Barbette as she held up the panel of gold and brown mod draperies.

"I would if I lost my sight," Barbette replied. He reclined in the comfortable La-Z-Boy arm chair in the family room of Mary's ranch-style Austin home. The television, ensconced in a large, simulated wood box, was turned up too loud. The Watergate hearings were broadcasting all day on the big three networks.

"I think they'll look nice in the kitchen," Mary said not minding Barbette's sarcasm.

He didn't reply as he continued watching the proceedings.

"Don't you think they will look good in the kitchen?" Mary tried again.

"Yes. Yes, they'll look as if Rhoda Morgenstern personally did your decorating."

Mary sighed and then shook her head. Then, in a flash, she remembered something.

"The pillows! I forgot the pillows at the store! Oh, shoot!"

"Call it divine providence."

Mary went over to the kitchen to get her sunglasses and purse.

"I'll be back in a few!"

Barbette heard the garage door open and close as the hearings continued to drone on.

He looked at the curtains unfolded over the back of the sofa. In a moment of inspiration, he wanted to surprise his sister. Barbette sat upright in the La-Z-Boy. The past several years, the pain in his legs increased considerably. Ever the actor, he chose not to disclose how frail he was becoming.

For the past three years, Disney hired him to stage the aerial ballets of their traveling road show, *Disney on Parade*. In just two weeks, he would be back in rehearsals collaborating with the talented Disney staff and aerialists. He was personally amused an old drag queen such as himself would be hired by the company a mouse built to stage their family-friendly routines—but such as it was. The world was racing, changing around him.

Barbette pushed himself out of the recliner and walked over to the draperies. His legs felt heavy and sluggish. He allowed himself to wince in pain as he moved across the family room, knowing no one else was home to see him struggle.

Grabbing the panels, he shuffled over to the kitchen. He looked at the drapes. Mary actually made a pretty good choice, he thought. The curtain rod was already in place, but Barbette couldn't quite reach it well enough to attach the new fabric.

He thought of getting the ladder in the garage, but it seemed like too much effort. Instead, he pulled out one of the Windsor chairs from the kitchen table. Barbette strained to raise his first foot high enough to step onto the seat of the chair, so he braced himself, holding onto its back with one hand while holding the drapes in the other.

Once he mounted the chair, he realized he didn't place it at the best angle. He strained to reach the end of the rod. It happened in an instant. The chair slipped out from below him. Barbette fell, his head colliding with one end of the kitchen table with a loud whack. His body lay on the newly laid linoleum floor, motionless.

...

"I got here as soon as I could," Rose said in a rush as she entered the waiting room of Brackenridge Hospital in downtown, Austin. She sat down next to Mary who was by herself. "How is he?"

"It was terrible. I thought he was dead. I came home from the store and he was out cold on the kitchen floor. He fell trying to hang the new curtains I got."

"He thinks he's still twenty-one and up on that trapeze," Rose said shaking her head.

"Since Jasper left, and the kids are all doing their own thing, I think Vander likes to do projects around the house. It makes him feel useful, you know."

"We're just getting old, Mary," Rose said seriously. "Me and Vander. We're not able to do what we once could…What the hell was he thinking? Good lord!"

A middle-aged man in a white coat came into the waiting room.

"You're Vander Barbette's next of kin?"

"We are," Mary said as she grabbed hold of Rose's arm.

"Please, come with me. We need to talk."

…

"Mister Barbette has quite a medical history," the doctor said, glancing through the pages of records on his clipboard. He glanced up at Rose and then Mary. They all sat in a small, windowless sitting room decorated in bland colors and institutional furnishings.

"He's a fighter, that one," Rose said.

"Have you ever heard of post-polio syndrome?" the doctor asked.

Mary and Rose shook their heads, no.

"You see, when a patient overcomes polio like Mister Barbette did, it takes an incredible toll on the body. In order to walk or raise his hands, his body had to literally be retaught to use secondary nerve terminals in the brain and spine. After about twenty years, those parts start to wear out, like a car engine that's run too many miles. The pistons are shot. Has he complained of joint pain?"

"My brother doesn't like to complain about his discomfort. He doesn't want to upset us."

"Have you noticed a heaviness of breathing or difficulty sleeping?"

"Yes…That's why he was taking his sleeping pills."

"What's happening is that the muscles of his respiratory system are weakening."

"Doctor, is Vander going to die?" Rose asked.

"Frankly, I'm not sure how he's made it this long. A man in his mid-seventies. He must be in a great deal of pain."

"Will he be able to walk again?" Mary asked.

The doctor was silent, looking at the women.

"No, I don't think so."

Mary's face flushed.

"He's supposed to go out with Disney," she said. "He directs their aerial routines, you know. In two weeks."

The doctor looked at them both.

"I'm sorry."

"What am I going to do? He won't want to go to a nursing home."

"I can take care of him, when you have to go to work," Rose replied. "It'll give us a chance to talk old times."

"He's awake if you want to visit," the doctor added. "Feisty too."

"Yes, we would like that," Mary said, knowing their lives would now be so very different.

. . .

"Hells bells Vander, the way they've got your head all bandaged up, you look like Cruella Deville!" Rose said as she and Mary entered his hospital room.

Barbette laughed. "Why is it every time I fall ill, you two come to harass me? Besides, I thought I look much more like Gloria Swanson in Sunset Boulevard!"

Rose and Mary stood alongside of Barbette's hospital bed.

"Has the doctor spoken to you?" Rose asked.

"Yes. He has. He said he doesn't think I'll be able to walk again, but he doesn't know Barbette, does he?"

"No, no he doesn't," Rose replied. Both she and Mary noticed his labored breathing, but said nothing.

Rose spoke up, "I've volunteered to take care of you, when Mary's out. We've got you covered, Vander."

"Thank you. You're always so kind. Can you both stay with me a while?"

"Of course," Mary replied.

"I just feel like talking tonight, you know Rose? Like when we were children and you wanted me to tell you a story."

"Oh, Vander, I love your stories! I think that's when I first fell in love with you, when you were telling me one of your stories."

"Very good. Then pull up chairs and make yourselves comfortable."

The two ladies took the two chairs in the room and pulled them close to Barbette's bed.

"You'll remember this one, Rose, because in the first scene you were with me...We were walking home from school, one windswept, fall day, in our little Texas town, called Round Rock. Some notices blew off the front seat of Postmaster Johnson's brand new Model T. We scooped them up, excited beyond belief—because the flyer said the circus was coming to town! A *circus* was coming to town!..."

357

CHAPTER SIXTY-TWO

AUGUST, 5, 1973

"Now are you sure you're going to be okay?" Mary asked. In the several days home, she was now managing to get Barbette into his wheelchair and to the restroom all by herself, but she knew as he grew weaker, there would be no other choice than to get him into a nursing home, something they both refused to discuss.

Barbette was back in bed again, his head propped up on a pillow.

"I'm just going to be at church. I'll be staying a little later for bible study. Rose'll come by in a bit. She's got a key to let herself in. Do you need anything?"

"No. I'm okay."

"Fine," she said as she turned to leave the room.

"Mary," Barbette called after her.

"Yes?"

"Thank you. Thank you, dear."

Mary smiled. "Get some rest."

Barbette listened to the garage door open and then close. The only noise in the house was the central air conditioner turning on and off, cooling the residence on the hot, August day.

Barbette took in the simple bedroom, its furnishings, its smell, the light coming in from the window with the drapes pulled back. Using what little strength he had, he reached for the bottle of pills and a glass of water on his nightstand. He asked for his sleeping pill prescription to be refilled while at the hospital. After the doctor told him his prognosis, he had commenced planning.

Once he consumed all the pills, he set the empty bottle and glass back down on the nightstand. He reached under his covers for the letter he wrote. It was sealed in a crisp, white envelope. He placed it on his chest.

The effects of the pills were almost immediate, for he felt himself floating high, in the air, reaching for the heavens above. He saw the woman, ahead, on the wire, up in the big top, walking on her pointed toes, so elegant and beautiful. Then she started doing her little jig—on the line no thicker than a spider's web. She stopped her routine and turned toward Barbette—looking directly toward him, into his soul— she motioned for him to join her. Barbette floated toward her until they both met. They touched and then became one—up high in the air—free. She was an angel, a flower, a bird.

The End.

Barbette's cremated remains were buried in the Round Rock Cemetery below his mother's in the Loving plot where the name on the tombstone simply reads, 'Barbette'.

Author's Photo

NOTES

Much information of Barbette's childhood has been lost to time. Complicating research is the fact Barbette was an entertainer who furnished backstory of his life that at times was inaccurate. For example, he would publically claim his birthdate was in 1904, when it was either five or possibly even eight years before. Research at the Round Rock Library provided me with Barbette's own recollections of his life in a 1969 *New Yorker* article, *An Angel, A Flower, A Bird* by Francis Steegmuller. I chose not to interview any surviving family members of the Loving family for this fictional story, relying solely on published accounts of his life to provide factual basis for events.

Barbette listed his biological father alternately as Henry or Jeff Broadway on various documents. His Travis County death certificate lists his father as Jeff. Hattie Wilson Broadway was listed as a widow in the census when she was twenty-one. The circumstances of her first husband's death remain unknown to the author. Hattie did marry Samuel Loving in 1906. They had five more offspring including Mary who was the youngest, born in 1915. I chose to only feature Mary in order to streamline the story.

The character Rose was inspired by an account in documents at the Round Rock Library, where a longtime Round Rock resident remembered Barbette walking her to school and his performing magic shows and stunts in the family's backyard. She spoke affectionately about his kindness and good nature.

Barbette's mother, according to Barbette himself, was a popular milliner. Barbette claimed to have used his mother's clotheslines to perform in his backyard and I could find corroborating evidence this was the case. In the summer months, he said he picked cotton in the fields of Round Rock. Research indicates all of Round Rock's population was engaged in the harvest as it was the lifeblood of the town at the time. Railroad tracks were laid to pass through the town especially to haul away the harvest. The train service also carried passengers into Austin and beyond.

Samuel Loving was an enlisted soldier in the First Calvary and was one of the Rough Riders who fought with Teddy Roosevelt during the Spanish American War. He was a longtime Round Rock resident, volunteer fireman, and Williamson County Sheriff who was also a witness to the shooting of legendary outlaw Sam Bass. There is a wonderful photograph of Samuel Loving online with his bushy mustache, standing next to his horse proudly holding a gun and outfitted for battle. It was taken before he shipped off to Cuba and reveals his cavalier spirit.

There is no public record of what sort of relationship Loving had with Barbette. Loving was a true man's man in every sense of the word. Barbette was a bright child, who it seems had a way with words and even sass. I felt it wouldn't be out of the realm of possibility the two would come into conflict. However, Barbette is buried in the Loving plot at Round Rock cemetery. In my imagination this meant there must have been some ultimate peace between the two.

Barbette recalled in the 1969 interview, he traveled to San Antonio to reply to a job posting in *Billboard* magazine by one of the Alfaretta sisters. Barbette noted the sisters were a trapeze and swinging ring act. They may have been a vaudeville-only act, but I chose to place the act in the circus after seeing some scant information this may have been factual. No name is given to the two sisters, but Barbette does say he replaced one sister who died.

The intimation the death may have been from nefarious circumstances is my creation only. The names Audrey and Bobby Fuller are fictitious as well. (I found a list of family names from *Alpharetta*, Georgia and I chose Fuller from the list.) Barbette does note that the Alfaretta sister he worked with was married to a black-faced comedian billed as "Happy Doc Holland." I could not produce more information about Holland's career, other than the fact black-faced comedians were quite popular on the vaudeville circuit during this time. Again, because of the circus setting, I chose to make his character more like a circus clown. I wanted to also show Barbette got his sense of craft and attention to detail partially from clowns, something Jean Cocteau later notes in his writing.

Barbette remembered the remaining Alfaretta sister wanted him to dress in drag because women's clothes always made the act more impressive. "The plunging and gyrating are more dramatic in a woman," he recalled. There are no records as to when or why he left the act. Next, he said he moved on to Erford's Whirling Sensation.

Erford's Whirling Sensation were a popular act on the vaudeville circuit. One component of their act was they swung from lines secured only by clenching their teeth onto a leather straps. Steegmuller reported Barbette had a mouth of crooked teeth and I wondered if this was a consequence of the act. I chose to use this idea as a catalyst for Barbette leaving this act.

Barbette said he chose his stage name when he went solo because it sounded French and exotic. Indeed, Barbette is a French word for a military defensive structure, which I don't believe Vander Clyde even knew about when he created the name. When I researched the Erford family, I found there was a preponderance other Erfords at the time who had names starting with the letter 'b'. Since the surviving photos of Barbette with the other two Erford sisters show all three sisters together in identical costume, I decided to give the two Erford sisters names beginning in 'b' which forced Vander to create one that followed suit so he would fit in. I'm not exactly sure of the Erford family's historic European origination. I did see indications they were of German or English heritage. I chose to make them German—symbols of immigrants who would do just about anything to make a better world for themselves— even becoming daredevils, hanging from their mouths only from leather straps. Photos of the Erfords' costumes at the time are so outlandish, I wanted Barbette to have some hand in their creation.

The character of Monty Pearson is a complete fabrication. I wanted to depict the clandestine way gay men met up in the early 20th century in America. It is a mystery how Barbette came into sexual maturity. What were his first sexual experiences? Colleagues recalled toward the latter half of his life he certainly did not hide his orientation in the right circles.

By 1919, E.F. Albee owned a massive network of vaudeville theaters. He controlled the talent union and management of vaudeville. The Harlem Opera House in 1919 was owned and operated by Albee. Albee was notorious for black-listing artists who did not follow his rules, including a very famous tiff with the Marx Brothers about the time when Barbette signed with him. (The Marx Brothers went on tour to Europe in vaudeville's off season and were subsequently banned from Albee's monopoly. Thankfully, they went to radio, Broadway, and films instead.) The review of Barbette's opening night performance at the Harlem Opera House is authentic.

I found it curious Barbette, like the Marx Brothers before him, moved from Albee to William Morris, a major competitor of Albee's. Morris was known for cultivating his talent rather operating theaters. Performers preferred him because he treated them with greater respect and could develop acts beyond vaudeville, which started to die off with the advent of movies and radio.

For the personal accounts of Paris, I used Barbette's own descriptions from his interview with Steegmuller. Barbette explained how he loved Paris from the instant he arrived there. He felt respected because Parisians took his performance for what he intended it to be—a work of art. Barbette arrived on the scene at the ideal time, with France rebounding from a terrible, oppressive war, and the young, avant-garde surrealist movement flourishing. Barbette's act was supported by this radical wave of artistry, and it could be argued he never would have attained such success if the artistic climate in Paris was not what it was in the 1920's.

Jean Cocteau's review of Barbette's performance in this book comes from an amalgamation of letters he wrote to friends about Barbette as well as his own famous 1926 essay, *Le Numéro Barbette*. By their own individual admissions, Barbette and Cocteau were close friends and associates. Several accounts report the two had an affair, but it was short-lived.

Cocteau was fascinated by Barbette for a number of years—effusively writing friends to welcome him into their circle, raving about his feminine portrayal in his famous essay. He personally hired Man Ray to produce the iconic images of Barbette and his transformation from man to woman. Cocteau also turned to Barbette in desperation when the Noailleses demanded to be cut from his surrealist film, *The Blood of the Poet*. Cocteau's descriptions of Barbette come from a man who intimately observed the aerialist.

Barbette told Steegmuller he was introduced to the Princess Violette Murat via an American society patron, Helen Gwynne. The princess in turn introduced Barbette to Raymond Radiguet and Jean Cocteau. As I looked into the lives of

Radiguet and Cocteau, I discovered Radiguet became terminally ill with typhoid fever about the time Barbette came to France. He died quickly. There are different accounts as to how Cocteau coped with his lover's death. His recorded actions speak loudly even from almost one hundred years after the fact. He did not attend Radiguet's funeral, which was planned by their friend, Coco Chanel. Instead, he headed to Monte Carlo. In Monte Carlo, Cocteau legendarily binged on opium, leading to his infamous addiction.

In the Harry's Bar scene, the account of Josephine Baker and her pet cheetah came from fashion maven Diana Vreeland. There was more to her story. She claimed she actually witnessed Baker and her cat sitting together in a movie theater and then after the show, the scene with the cheetah leaping into the Rolls Royce took place.

The account of Barbette's hotel suite being broken into by a reporter comes from Barbette in his interview with Steegmuller. I attempted to make as few edits as possible to Barbette's own account of the incident.

The character of Lord Winston Darby is fiction. Barbette was arrested in London while on tour. Some research indicated he was on tour with Ringling Circus in 1924 when the arrest happened. The Ringling Circus archival material I reviewed did not indicate the circus toured Europe during this time. The Ringling brothers themselves did travel to Europe in the winter months scouring local circuses for new acts as well as attending auctions to add to the vast Ringling art holdings in Sarasota, but I could not find the circus toured Europe at this point. That the arrest seems to have happened at the Palladium may give further indication, Barbette was performing as an independent act at the time.

Accounts of Barbette's life indicate there was an arrest in London for homosexual activity backstage. The sentence for the crime appears to be he was forbidden to return to Great Britain for the rest of his life. I noticed scandalous trials of this period were put under seal to protect aristocracy, so I added that bit.

Was Barbette heterosexual or homosexual? Accounts in books from various Round Rock historians dodge the question—even to this day. Old circus hand Bill Strong recalled an anecdote revealing Barbette's own self-identification:

Parley Baer told this story to Mac and Peggy MacDonald and I on his show, in Temple, Texas, in 1974. Parley and Ernestine threw one of their big parties and Barbette casually asked what they were having. Parley said, "Tossed salad, roast beef with all the trimmings, hot rolls, and all kinds of fruits." Barbette smiled and said, "You needn't be rude."

Couple this account with the fact of the arrest in Great Britain, as well as reminisces of people who worked with Barbette and the picture becomes clear. What relations Barbette had with men is lost to time.

The Villa de Noailles Act: So many pieces of this portion of the story echo elements of what actually occurred. I conflated the activities of 1929 into these scenes. Barbette is quoted as saying he met Charles and Marie de Noailles in 1923. Both were independently wealthy. Marie de Noailles was once the lover of Cocteau, before he turned to men exclusively. She was proud to trace her familial lineage the Marquis de Sade. Charles and Marie had an open relationship. Marie was aware of Charles's homosexual trysts. She also took a host of lovers.

The two lived amicably together and ensconced themselves as the grand patrons of the surrealist art world, which is ironic to me because the whole image of surrealism was an abandonment of the past—a throwing off of old shackles, which one would expect the Noailleses to represent. In reality, many surrealists were underwritten by this couple, who were voracious collectors.

Their villa in the south France is considered to be a modernist masterpiece. Charles and Marie had a stupendous residence in Paris, yet they enjoyed entertaining at the villa in the winter months. The couple continued to expand the home so it became quite sprawling with a large number of bedrooms. The villa does have an indoor swimming pool opening to a terrace. There was a trapeze over the pool—but no word if Barbette ever swung from it. I remember old films of Charlie Chaplin fooling around at San Simeon, the Californian castle of William Randolph Hearst, and imagined Barbette would find the apparatus and its location quite irresistible. One account claimed the Noailles swimming pool was the first in modern times constructed in a French residence.

Villa De Noailles was featured in Man Ray's film, *Les Mystères du Château de Dé*. Man Ray said it was the Noailleses who approached him with a commission to make a film featuring the villa. The offer of a quarter million francs was too good to refuse, so Ray shot the film. You can watch it on YouTube today. At the time, Man Ray was dating the very beautiful Lee Miller who first sought Ray out to be her photographic mentor. Miller was featured in Cocteau's *The Blood of the Poet*, the same film Barbette provided a cameo.

It seems Cocteau moved from Maurice Sachs to another handsome, yet complicated young man, Jean Bourgoint. Bourgoint and his sister, Jeanne, were the inspirations for Cocteau's 1928 novel, *Les Enfants Terrible*. The two became caught up in Cocteau's opium binges and detoxifications. Shockingly, Jeanne took her life on Christmas Eve of 1929. Jean was so devastated by his sister's death, it led him to follow a vocation and he became a Trappist monk. Both Jean and Jeanne were immortalized in portraits painted by Christopher Wood—Jeanne's on again off again lover.

I came across two known pieces of film featuring Barbette—*The Blood of the Poet*, where Barbette, wearing a luminous Chanel cape, gives his take on preoccupied French nobility. The other is an old trailer from 1935 featuring Barbette in the Broadway show *Jumbo*, starring Jimmy Durante. In the clip (which I created a link to on my web page, www.billiondollardreamer.com) you will see a very dynamic Barbette mount the trapeze amid a bevy of other female acrobats. Even though the film is in black and white and quite old, one can still see the dynamism and performing polish of Barbette—he even doffs his wig in a spoof to Durante's claim he loves women. (In my mind, producer Billy Rose must have schemed how to put Barbette's signature ending of removing his wig into *Jumbo*. The final product is shown in the newsreel.)

We can piece together basic information about the relationship of Barbette, Billy Rose, and John Murray Anderson. Billy Rose and is wife, Fanny Brice, went on an extended holiday to Europe around 1934. There, Rose hatched his idea to try to combine a Broadway show with a circus sort of revue. It seems quite plausible he encountered Barbette's act while travelling and brought him back to the United States. Coincidentally, there were many other specialty acts hired for *Jumbo* besides Barbette. Some look to have been hand-picked by Rose while in Europe, while others auditioned in June of 1935, in Manhattan.

Before Rose began his *Jumbo* odyssey, he was in trouble with former unsavory backers of his night club ventures. He did report them to J. Edgar Hoover and the FBI. Because of threats to his life, he rarely left the Hippodrome while in rehearsal. He took dinners privately with Brice and he hired a body guard for protection.

The best account I came across of the *Jumbo* production came from director John Murray Anderson's autobiography. It is his account of the trapeze artist who fell while rehearsing his 'leap of death' after Anderson insisted he try it one last time. The real artist's name was Vabanque, not

Le Blanc as I write. Old publicity materials reveal he worked with the Ringling circus in 1933. Anderson said he was from Holland. Billy Rose's press release in June, 1935, claimed he was from Algiers. (The same press release also claimed Barbette was from Naples!)

The affair between Le Blanc and Barbette is my imagination only.

There was another act that also suffered a horrific fall during rehearsals. It is the one also featured in the Paramount newsreel. The act featured one acrobat seated in a mock airplane suspended from a central mast, while on the opposite side of the mast was an aerialist hanging from a pole upside-down spinning at a very fast rotation. The acrobat swinging from the pole also had a career-ending fall. Certainly, *Jumbo* was an expensive, complicated, and dangerous production.

Anderson speaks highly of Barbette during their collaboration in *Jumbo*. One could see their desire for perfection coupled with their highly creative minds must have been quite stimulating for each of them. A few years later, when Anderson was hired by John Ringling North to direct the next season's circus, Anderson claimed it was he who brought Barbette to Ringling. Anderson also said it was Barbette who staged the spectacular aerial ballet for the ground-breaking 1942 circus. The ballet featured over fifty women, positioned throughout the arena, simultaneously performing aerial stunts on silk ropes and lines. There are photos of the later 1949 Monte Carlo aerialists Barbette also directed for Ringling (you can find them online) that reveal just how fantastic the spectacle of this large a number of aerialists performing in unison must have been.

There seem to be a couple of different stories about when and how Barbette's performing career came to an end. Photographs of a very healthy, and glamorous Barbette from the mid 1930's including the *Jumbo* Broadway trailer for Paramount exist, lending one to think whatever ended his career must have happened after those fascinating images were produced.

A good estimate of when he finally stopped performing was the year 1938. Europe was getting more dangerous. Fascism's tyranny spread. In Berlin, night clubs were closing down and gay people were being arrested. Many entertainers from Germany and France fled their respective countries. It makes sense amid the unrest Barbette found himself back in New York performing on the vaudeville circuit once again.

Vaudeville peaked by now and was on a speedy decline. It was cheaper to show a movie than to hire vaudeville players. However, Loew's maintained a vaudeville circuit during the late 1930's in the New York region providing solid work for vanguard entertainers in big houses. The Loew's State on Broadway in Manhattan, with nearly four thousand seats, was a massive, opulent theater featuring two-a-day vaudeville shows, matinées and evenings, between major motion pictures. In vaudeville history, the Loew's State is known as the last great house to continue vaudeville. It ceased offering live performances in 1947. It was the site of Barbette's last performances.

There are two occurrences that seem have impacted Barbette's performing. One was a terrible fall he had, when a curtain billowed behind him, distracting him. The date of this fall is unclear. I chose to conflate that fall with the onset of his polio which happened while he was performing at the Loew's State. There is some evidence these two events did happen together as I presented them. Barbette said it was drafty at the Loew's State when he was performing and he became ill. He went to bed, and then next day he felt as if his body turned to sand. He was unable to move.

Accounts I came across indicate Barbette most likely had infantile polio. The story I came across said Barbette's prognosis was so bad he wanted to be left to die, but his doctor, who just lost his own child to polio, convinced Barbette into trying more radical operations and therapy.

Barbette's intense discipline and remarkable athleticism, which were chronicled by all those who encountered him, could explain why he would have been a good candidate to test new therapies. Accounts from Barbette and those who knew him report he went through a series of operations and treatments lasting over sixteen months. His medical care was orchestrated through Post-Graduate Hospital in Manhattan.

I noticed Barbette was listed in the 1940 census living with his mother and Samuel Loving and their various other children in Round Rock. I chose to make Barbette's return to Round Rock happen a little later than the actual date for streamlining purposes. I also chose to make Barbette more or less on the rebound from his therapy when he returned to his family's home. He probably convalesced in Round Rock for a period of time until hired on to work with Ringling for the 1942 circus.

Barbette most likely had more contact with his family than what I provide here. His sister, Mary, was born in 1915— when Barbette already left home and was on the road. Barbette lived with Mary off and on during the latter portion of his life after acquiring polio. According to the records I reviewed, her husband's name was Jasper. He was about ten years older than she. They may have divorced. Mary died in 1997. She is not buried alongside her husband. Instead, she was laid to rest in the Loving plot in Round Rock below her mother and next to Barbette.

We can track Barbette's involvement with the Ringling circus starting in 1942 when he was hired to be the director of the female aerialists at the request of John Murray Anderson. He seems to have had at least a year and a half of recuperations from polio. The statistics about the circus John Ringling tells Barbette are factual.

There are reports from some historians Barbette travelled as a performer with Ringling in the 20's or 30's. This could be the case, but I could not find actual verification in the Ringling route books. Starting in 1942, he is listed in the Ringling circus reports, 'Vander Barbette', usually as the director of the aerialists.

By 1945, John Ringling North was ousted as the head of the Ringling circus. One of the bones of contention with other family members was the circus lost its traditional feel, which Barbette no doubt played a role in. Interestingly, when North later regained control of the circus, he again hired Anderson and Barbette. Barbette's 1949 Monte Carlo aerial ballet for Ringling is a thing of legend, even to this day.

During his time away from Ringling, Barbette was quite busy. In 1946, he was credited with working with Vincente Minnelli, staging Minnelli's wonderful circus scenes in '*Till the Clouds Roll By* starring Minnelli's pregnant wife, Judy Garland. Minnelli and Garland were married in June of 1945 and took a two month honeymoon in New York. (During the time, the first atomic bomb indeed was dropped on Hiroshima.) When Garland returned to Hollywood, post honeymoon, the studio announced she was pregnant and they would try to film her performances for *Clouds* in November.

November, 1945, is significant because on the 3rd of that month, the Ringling circus concluded its tour. This would have allowed Barbette and a select number of performers to work with Minnelli and Garland, which production logs indicate they did. You can view the sequence Barbette staged for Minnelli on YouTube. It concludes with a heart-stopping leap of death by one of the aerialists.

Also in the summer of 1945, Orson Welles and Cole Porter did the book and the blocking for the colossal Broadway flop, *Around the World*.

Seeing that Cole Porter lived in Paris during the time Barbette was at his peak, one could assume their social circles had to overlap to some degree.

The scene in Porter's apartment is fictional, but the dialogue where he describes beginning *Around the World* is authentic. Both Barbette and Porter were dapper gay dandies from America. Each entertainer struggled with health problems twith their legs. I couldn't find any quotes where one talks about the other, but with their wits and vivacious personalities, I imagined the two would be quite comfortable around each other.

It is well documented Garland had an affair with Orson Welles before she fell for Minnelli. For my scene, I imagined Judy might not have been emotionally capable to deal with confronting Welles right after her wedding to Minnelli, but that is only my imagination.

Orson Welles loved circuses and magic shows. He wanted *Around the World* to be Broadway's biggest blockbuster. However, the production was too elaborate. Porter was too rushed in writing the songs, even asking Welles to delay the opening of the production so they could rework it. Welles was the writer, director, producer, and one of the stars of the show. It was too much for one person.

Michael Todd, the original producer of the show, backed out, when Welles insisted one of the stage props be an oil gusher that doused the performers' expensive costumes each performance. It was the last straw in a series of budget-busting requests on the director's account and the last straw for Todd. With Todd out, Welles invested thousands of dollars of his own money, and borrowed heavily from film studio honcho Harry Cohn promising him future free directorial services. The show's costumes were in hock for nonpayment until right before out of town openings. The show had no dress rehearsal. The first tryout in Boston was a disaster.

Interestingly, Barbette's oriental circus number, which closed the first half of the show, was well received by critics. After only seventy-five performances in Manhattan, *Around the World* closed in the summer of 1946. Orson Welles never directed another Broadway musical. Cole Porter bounced back with the smashing score to *Kiss Me Kate*.

'Till the Clouds Roll By was a huge hit for MGM. Judy Garland gave birth in March, 1946 to Liza. Porter, Minnelli, and Garland teamed up in 1947 on *The Pirate*, an MGM musical, while Barbette returned to directing circus aerial acts.

Barbette was involved in other film productions in Hollywood, many with circus themes, including the film version of *Jumbo*. But none of the films had more lasting appeal than the famous comedy classic, *Some Like It Hot*. The scenes I wrote about Barbette's involvement are based on two separate accounts by Billy Wilder and Tony Curtis. Wilder recalled he saw Barbette's performance in Berlin before World War II. He wanted Barbette to help Tony Curtis and Jack Lemmon with their female impersonations. He remembered cautioning Barbette to be careful not to make the impersonations too perfect.

Tony Curtis also wrote about his and Lemmon's encounter with Barbette. He remembered from the moment they heard the name of the man coaching them was 'Barbette', they didn't quite know what to expect. Curtis said Barbette taught the actors how to walk like women—one leg crossing over the other—to make male hips more feminine. (Watch Ru Paul walk a runway and you will see the Barbette walk perfected.) Curtis also remembered how Barbette taught the two actors to raise their arms with wrists out so their biceps wouldn't flex.

Jack Lemmon protested Barbette's lessons because he believed Barbette was taking the drag too seriously. Curtis remembered the two had a difficult time as Barbette pressed Lemmon.

Wilder recalled Barbette came to him in the morning after the rehearsals began, reporting Tony Curtis had potential, but Lemmon was hopeless. Wilder said he bought out Barbette by offering a trip to Europe on the *Il de France*.

Some Like It Hot seems campy and quaint today, but back in the late 1950's it was considered notorious for its drag. Wilder chose to not even have it coded by the Hays Office. The film wound up being a smash hit. Jack Lemmon was nominated for an Academy Award.

Barbette spent the 1960's working with a series of circuses including the famous Shriner Circus as well as assisting in choreographing routines for film. He always worked with the aerial acts and his routines were well received. He was hired by Disney at the end of the decade, staging the aerial routines of their travelling shows.

Accounts of Barbette's suicide say the impetus for the attempt was his failing health. It could have been due to post-polio syndrome which typically has an onset fifteen to thirty years after the patient recovers from the first bout. Post-polio syndrome happens when motor neurons controlling skeletal muscles begin to wear out causing muscle atrophy, fatigue, and extreme pain. It is testament to Barbette's intense force of will he was able to work as long as he did.

I came across an account of the end of Barbette's life saying he fell in his sister's home hanging curtains. His polio-riddled body entrapped him. No longer able to travel for Disney directing their aerial performances, Barbette took his own life on August 5th, 1973, by overdose. His remains were cremated and buried in the Loving plot in Round Rock, with the simple moniker on his tombstone, *Barbette*.

Charles Gesmar designed the wonderful cabaret poster of Barbette used on the front cover. Barbette used the image when he toured Europe. Gesmar was a sought after costume and production designer for all of the top cabaret talent in Paris in the 1920's. It is quite possible some of Barbette's more outlandish costumes were designed by Gesmar, who was a fan of abundant feathers and over-the-top headdresses. Gesmar was gay and travelled in the same circles as Barbette.

Throughout the book, I attempted to slip in actual quotes from Barbette, Cocteau, Porter, and even Orson Welles.

I especially wanted to thank librarians at the Round Rock public library for assisting me in pulling the research for this book!

Please check out my web page for more information about Barbette as well as my other books: www.billiondollardreamer.com. I've loaded it up with pictures, videos and blogs from people who knew Barbette!

Finally, thank you for reading *Wildflower*. Throughout its writing, my admiration for Barbette grew. I felt a distinct obligation to tell this fantasia in a way that honored this enigmatic entertainer. *Wildflower* was a labor of love and I sincerely hope you enjoyed it!

Be sure not to miss:

Now Available in Paperback!

An Exciting Story of Adventure and Romance!

Your gay billionaire uncle dies and you find out in the middle of the night you have inherited his fortune. What do you do? For patriotic high school history teacher, John Driskil, the choice was obvious: Save the SS United States, the world's last great ocean liner from the scrap heap and sail her into New York Harbor on the Fourth of July.

Accompanied by his small potatoes lawyer and best friend Humberto Cabral, John Driskil sets out on a journey to rescue the fabled ocean liner, pulling out all stops in a no expenses spared renovation of the Big U.

Along the way, he dreams up other projects from rebuilding the first giant Ferris Wheel to recreating lost Frank Lloyd Wright masterpieces.

On a much needed vacation from the pressures of being a billionaire, John falls head over heels in love with Caleb, a British cabin steward aboard the rented luxury yacht, Esperanza.

John is having the time of his life until a mysterious will appears in the mailbox of his back woods brother, Jeb. This will gives Jeb, his sister Tissa and their mother Jo Ellen dibs on the entire fortune.

Will John lose control of his uncle's estate? Will the SS United States sail again? Will John and Caleb's love endure? There is only one way to find out!

Made in the USA
Middletown, DE
13 March 2017